THE BELIAL WAR
A BELIAL SERIES NOVEL

R.D. BRADY

SCOTTISH SEOUL PUBLISHING, LLC

BOOKS BY R.D. BRADY

The Belial Series (in order)
The Belial Stone
The Belial Library
The Belial Ring
Recruit: A Belial Series Novella
The Belial Children
The Belial Origins
The Belial Search
The Belial Guard
The Belial Warrior
The Belial Plan
The Belial Witches

Stand-Alone Books
Runs Deep
Hominid

The A.L.I.V.E. Series
B.E.G.I.N.

[A.L.I.V.E.](#)
[D.E.A.D.](#)

Be sure to [sign up](#) for R.D.'s mailing list to be the first to hear when she has a new release and receive a free short story!

** A list of characters can be found at the end of *The Belial War*.**

"The greatest test of courage on earth is to bear defeat without losing heart."

Robert Green Ingersoll

"When the will defies fear, when duty throws the gauntlet down to fate,
when honor scorns to compromise with death - that is heroism."

Robert Green Ingersoll

PROLOGUE

9,789 BCE

DWARKA, INDIA

The torchlights flickered, throwing moving shadows along the Hall of Knowledge. Tall, thick pillars lined the middle of the room, holding up the forty-foot-tall ceiling. During the day, Yamini loved this room, but in the darkness of night, the shadows seemed to reach for her as she rushed past, her pale student's shift rustling loudly in the quiet of the room.

He comes. Yamini tried not to let the terror overwhelm her. The vision had been the most frightening one she'd ever had. But she needed to keep her wits about her.

"Young Yamini, where are you off to in such a hurry?"

With a cry, Yamini stumbled to a stop, taking a step back as Jagrav stepped from behind a column. The high priest was a member of the Council of the Children, but Yamini did not trust him. She did not like how he looked at the young pages that were being initiated. He said all the right words, but he did not feel them.

She inclined her head. "Learned Jagrav, I did not see you there."

His dark eyes pierced into hers. "Perhaps because you were in such a rush. Is something the matter?"

She forced herself to not look away. "No, Brother. It is just the shadows. I do not like being in here at night."

He paused a beat before responding. "Come now, child, you know there is nothing to hurt you in the Temple of the Children. Unless you have *seen* something that has caused you worry?"

Lying was never Yamini's way. She did not believe when people said that at times there was a reason to lie. That was a reasoning the Sons of Belial used. But right now she could not tell him the truth. "Are you never afraid in the dark?"

He puffed out his chest. "Not since I was a child."

"Perhaps one day I, too, will outgrow these fears." She stepped to the side. "Good evening, Brother."

"Good evening to you as well, Yamini," he said as she passed.

She felt his eyes on her, and she had to restrain herself from sprinting down the hall. She pushed through the tall wrought-iron doors at the end of the room, pausing to glance back. Jagrav stood in the same spot. She gave him a nod before slipping through the doors. Then she sprinted to the stairwell, taking the stone steps two at a time. She flew around the corner. Sister Maya's door was open, a light glowing from inside.

She's still up. Yamini had worried she would have to wake her mentor. This news could not wait. She hurried into the room, and her mentor and friend looked up. In the candlelight, some of the wear and tear of her fifty years was washed away. The wrinkles around her eyes and mouth were less pronounced, and her dark hair streaked with gray looked almost brown.

A smile crossed Maya's face, the lines around her eyes and

chin reappearing as she caught sight of Yamini. "My dear, it is late. Why are you still here?"

"Oh, Sister, I have had a vision."

Maya hurried around the desk, ushering Yamini into a chair. "It will be all right. Whatever you have seen—"

Yamini gripped her hand. "No. They are coming."

∞

THE COUNCIL MET as dawn broke. The thirteen elders sat along the long polished stone table at the front of the room. As the group's leader, Maya had the place of honor in the middle.

Yamini had been to meetings before, all of the Children had. But she'd never been to a closed-door meeting. Today it was only the council and their aides, who sat behind the council members, ready for their orders. The only one sitting in front of them was Yamini. Maya stood, addressing the council.

"Yamini has had a vision. Samyaza comes for us." She nodded at Yamini, who stood and recounted the arrival of Samyaza and his followers as well as the destruction that would follow.

"Are you saying Dwarka will not survive?" Ellghad asked.

Images flew through her mind—the bodies of the people she knew and loved floating in water, their faces frozen in horror. Her voice broke. "No, Brother. It will not."

She retook her seat as the council began to debate. Yamini only half listened, her mind replaying what she had seen. Samyaza striding down the Hall of Knowledge, his minions flaring out behind him, cutting down everyone in their path even though they offered no resistance, the giant wall of water washing over Dwarka and pulling it to the bottom of the ocean. Her hands trembled. She clasped them together tightly in her lap.

"But the knowledge must be saved," Jagrav said. "It cannot die with us."

"We should have destroyed the instructions long ago. No one

who wants the power it yields should ever have it," one of the other sisters added.

Yamini started. She knew there was knowledge forbidden from all but the council. She had heard rumors of what it might be, but no one knew for sure. But, of course, that would be why Samyaza was headed their way.

One of the other brothers shook his head. "We don't know that. Perhaps there will be a time when—"

Maya raised an eyebrow but not her voice. "When humans are no longer human? When we do not want more than what fate has provided us? To allow people to awaken the power of a god within others? No good can come of that. The knowledge must be destroyed before Samyaza and his forces arrive."

Jagrav's mouth narrowed to a slit. "And what of Samyaza? How will we protect against him?"

Maya looked at him, shaking her head. "We cannot. If Yamini's vision is correct—and they always are—Samyaza will destroy us all."

"And we will just sit back and allow that?"

"We chose these paths before we ever breathed a single breath. You know that. We are put on this plane of existence to learn, to love, to embrace the beauty of humanity. If this is our destiny, then so be it."

Yamini understood their teachings. She believed them. But when faced with imminent death, it was hard not to wish for some other action.

"We will make sure we evacuate our children and their caretakers. But the rest of us must stay so as to not let Samyaza know they have gone. Not until it is too late."

Maya nodded to her aide, Keshini. Keshini reached down, pulling a box from underneath her stool. Yamini knew the box. It had always been in Maya's room, but she had never seen inside it. Keshini placed the box in front of Maya. With a nod of thanks,

Maya stood and opened it, a faint white glow highlighting her hands.

Maya reached in and pulled out a glowing sphere. At first glance it appeared perfectly round, but then the angles on its face became clear. A murmur rose amongst the table. Yamini couldn't even seem to think for a moment. *It's a belial stone. Maya has had a belial stone all this time.*

The stone was the ancient power source of their brothers and sisters in Atlantis—and also the method of their destruction.

"When Samyaza arrives, we will unleash the power of the stone," said Maya. "We cannot allow him or his followers access to our knowledge. When they are in the center of the city, we will bury them."

"And what of us?" Jagrav demanded.

For the first time that Yamini could remember, Maya sounded tired. "We will be buried with them as well."

No one moved for a moment, but then one by one the priests at the table nodded their agreement. All save Jagrav.

"This is madness," he said. "We should take the knowledge and go before they arrive."

"They will run us down. Now that Samyaza knows where the Omni is, he will stop at nothing. No, this is the only way to protect the world from his power."

"But all our knowledge will be lost."

"Is that truly a bad thing?" Maya asked. "We have the knowledge that would allow someone to gain godlike powers, to become immortal. Tell me, which of the Fallen have demonstrated any kindness or morality with their power? Which of them is a beacon we can point to and tell our children to emulate? This knowledge is not meant for our world. The Belial are not meant for our world. Better we take this knowledge with us than allow it to fall into the wrong hands."

Jagrav's words lashed out. "You condemn all of us to die."

"I condemn all of us to protect this world. That is our mission;

it has been from the start. You do still believe that, do you not, Jagrav?"

Jagrav seemed to finally notice the looks the other members of the council were giving him. The anger slipped from his face, hidden behind a mask of neutrality. But Yamini could still see it lurking behind his eyes. "Yes, of course. I was merely surprised by all this news."

"It is not easy for anyone to face their mortality. Let us all take some time to meditate on what we have discussed here." Maya stood, signaling the end of the meeting. Yamini dropped her quill. Reaching down to pick it up, she saw a pair of sandals stop next to her chair.

She straightened. Jagrav glared down at her. "Afraid of the dark, were you?"

"I . . . I . . ."

"Yamini, I need you," Maya called.

Jagrav whisked past her. Yamini got to her feet, hurrying to Maya's side, a new fear rising in her chest.

∽

THE NEXT EVENING, Yamini stood on the bridge of the ship along with the other refugees as Dwarka disappeared from view. Four ships had set out, loaded with four hundred people. Four hundred of five thousand. She took a trembling breath, picturing Maya the last time she had seen her. She would never see her again.

No, I will. Just not in this lifetime.

One by one, everyone else drifted away from the railing, but Yamini stayed. She stayed long after the island was out of view. Finally, as darkness fell and a cool wind began to blow, she turned to go inside. Lights shone along the cabins, and hushed voices and the occasional laugh could be heard as she made her way to her room. She would share it with three other initiates. Yamini picked up her pace, suddenly wanting their company. She did not want to be alone.

She climbed down to the second level. Her cabin was halfway down the hall. She pushed the door open, the light spilling out into the hall.

"Did any of you—" A hand slid over her mouth and a strong arm wrapped around her waist, yanking her inside. She struggled for only a minute before she went still. A small cry erupted from her as she took in the sight of her friends, lying on the ground, staring at nothing, long red jagged cuts across their throats. Men she knew stood near them, pulling sheets over them.

"Finish up," Jagrav ordered from behind her. The other men finished rolling her friends up in the sheets, removing them from Yamini's view.

Jagrav leaned down, his lips touching her ear and making her shiver. His voice was a hiss. "If you yell, if you make a sound that draws any attention to this cabin, I will kill you and whoever comes to help you. Nod if you understand."

Yamini nodded.

Slowly, Jagrav released his hand then his arm. Yamini whirled around. "Why?"

"Why? How can you ask that? Your *mentor* dooms us to death while you escape? I don't think so. Besides, we are on a greater mission."

"Wh-what mission?"

"To protect the knowledge of Dwarka."

"But we have brought the books with us already." She paused as the truth hit her. "But that's not the knowledge you want to save. We can't, Jagrav. It's too dangerous."

"What do you know? You are a child."

"But the Great Mother, she chose mortality to save us."

"Perhaps she wasn't as wise as we were taught to believe."

Yamini stared at him in the dim light. His hair was unkempt, sweat dotting his forehead and blood-splashed tunic even though the cabin was cool. His gaze kept darting around the cabin, his lips moving but no words coming out. That's when she noticed the serrated blade in his hand, blood dripping from it in a pool at his side. "What are you planning?"

He smiled, his gaze focusing on her. "To protect that which needs protecting. To bring it back to the beginning."

She frowned. "I don't understand."

"You don't need to."

He sliced the blade across her neck.

CHAPTER 1

PRESENT DAY

GALETON, PENNSYLVANIA

Hand flying to her neck, Delaney McPhearson sat straight up in bed, her breaths coming out in pants. She ran a hand over her face and through her red hair before grabbing a bottle of water on the side table and taking a long drink. Wiping her mouth, she sat up against the backboard. *What was that?*

But even as the question flew through her mind, she knew what it was. When she was coming into her powers, she had dreams of her past life as a ring bearer. But this time she hadn't been a ring bearer. She'd been an initiate in the Children of the Law of One. And she'd lived on Dwarka, the island civilization off the coast of India that had been written off as myth by Western scholars until pieces of it began to be found.

But why show her this? What was she supposed to learn? The dream had shown her Dwarka before it was destroyed. Like Atlantis, they had known the end was coming. They had planned to end it. The man who'd killed Yamini had spoken of protecting knowledge. Was it the Omni? But Elisabeta already had powers. Was she looking to create an army of Fallen?

The priests of Dwarka had wanted the knowledge to die with them. It should have. The Omni was too powerful for anyone to wield it. Governments would pay billions of dollars to get their hands on such a weapon.

But that wasn't what truly worried Laney. It was the sense that there was something even more dangerous than the Omni that the council was speaking of. And that was terrifying. The Omni could grant someone the powers of the Fallen or take them away. What could be more powerful than that?

The Great Mother chose our fates. A chill rolled over Laney's skin. She pulled her knees to her chest. The Great Mother was now sleeping in a playpen down the hall—a harmless child. Victoria had done many things throughout her lifetimes, but there could only be one thing that phrase referred to: when she had chosen to end humanity's immortality.

Was it possible the priests of Dwarka had found a way to grant it again?

She would like to think that was impossible. And that if it was possible, that Jagrav, as unwound as he appeared, had been unsuccessful in his attempt to protect it for the future of mankind. But too much had happened over the past several years for her to believe that. She could hope, sure, but believe? No, that she could not do.

She had to prepare for the unthinkable. She ran a hand through her hair. *But how exactly am I supposed to do that?*

CHAPTER 2

CASABLANCA, MOROCCO

The blood glistened as Elisabeta Roccorio held it up to the sunlight streaming through the window. She watched the changes in the blood as it shifted.

She placed it back in the tray on her desk with the other two tubes and grimaced at the lab report next to it. The report detailed the blood's composition, including a CBC test, along with a bunch of more advanced tests. But no matter how much science they threw into the explanation, the conclusion was still infuriating: normal.

After all her work and the destruction of an entire precious tube to testing, all the labs could determine was that it was normal human blood. She pictured the violet-eyed bitch it had come from, not as the toddler she'd last seen her as but as a full-grown woman, who held the knowledge of the ages in her frail, vulnerable body.

As well as the key to immortality.

I was so close. A different woman now took center stage in her mind. Delaney McPhearson, the woman who had snatched Elisabeta's victory from her hands. *But I snatched something from you too, didn't I?*

She ran a hand over the cover of the book. It was a simple leather cover, which no doubt had been replaced many times over the years. But underneath the unassuming cover, lifetimes of knowledge existed. Pages were made of different materials. The early pages were a material that Elisabeta could not identify, but later pages were obviously animal skin, papyrus, linen, rice paper, and every other form of paper used by mankind. The book was a living testimony to the rich variety of textiles used to maintain human history.

But Elisabeta cared about none of that. No, she was more interested in the knowledge garnered from its pages. She ran a hand carefully over the book. The ring bearer thought it was merely a recounting of the lives Victoria had led.

The ring bearer has no idea what power you truly hold.

It had been two weeks since Elisabeta had been forced from her Chicago penthouse. But she had planned for just such an occurrence with accounts and property hidden under other names across the globe. The news stories that detailed her life and her wealth hadn't even touched the tip of her financial iceberg. Nor did they have any inkling of the plans she'd first started developing soon after her powers had manifested.

Because Elisabeta Roccorio, heir to the Roccorio fortune, didn't simply want everything that money could buy. No, she wanted *everything*—power, immortality, and control. She ran her fingers over the test tubes—all that was left of Victoria's blood. *And soon, I will have it.*

She opened the book, looking at the first few pages, written in a forgotten language that had once been the language of all of the world. In the Bible, the shift was recounted in the tale of the Tower of Babel, where God smote down the humans and the tower they built to be His equal. But Elisabeta knew that the true reason was because of greed and selfishness.

She smiled. *And power. Always power.*

Each page seemed to have a sketch of Victoria at a different age in a different lifetime. Elisabeta had lived just as many lifetimes, but unlike Victoria, she did not remember those lifetimes. Only Victoria had been allowed to keep her memories as she shifted from one life to the next.

Elisabeta's computer pinged, interrupting her thoughts. It was a Google alert. She quickly clicked on the accompanying link, then scanned it briefly before stopping on a picture of a group of archaeologists and their latest find. She read the description under the picture. A tingle ran through her, and she nearly laughed out loud. This was simply too easy. But then, she found fate often played a role in making the things that were meant to be happen. *And my ascension is very much meant to be.*

She picked up her phone and dialed. Troy Healey picked up quickly. "Yes, Samyaza?"

"I need a progress report."

"The dive continues. We've found some artifacts."

"Any carvings?"

"No, Samyaza."

"I need you and your team on a plane as quickly as possible."

"We can be on one within three hours." He paused. "Should I leave some men at this site?"

"No. What we are looking for is not there." When Elisabeta had sent her team out, it had been a long shot that they would discover anything worthwhile. But fate had allowed what she needed to be uncovered at just the right time. Divine intervention at work.

"Where are we heading?"

Elisabeta smiled, excitement coursing through her. "Göbekli Tepe. Call me when you are on site." She disconnected the call, pulling the book back toward her.

So many incarnations Victoria had. Most thought of her first identity as that of Lilith, the evil villainess hidden at the outskirts of Genesis. But before she was Lilith, she was known as Gaia, the mother goddess, the Mother of All.

Elisabeta could not read the first few pages, but she had no doubt they spoke of Victoria's time as Lilith, maybe even mentioned her Gaia incarnation. She just hoped that the information she needed was not on those pages, for there was no one alive who could translate it for her.

Although perhaps there is one, she thought, picturing Cain, the dark-haired immortal with black eyes.

Nevertheless, she'd had her translator working around the clock ever since she'd acquired the tome. A knock sounded at her door, causing her to look. That should be him now. "Come in."

Dr. Isaac Chen, the premiere global scholar on ancient languages, strode across the room. Age fifty-four, he had spent his life translating esoteric texts. It had cost a pretty penny to pull him away from his work with the Chinese government, but hopefully that investment was about to pay off.

Chen took a seat without waiting for Elisabeta's invitation. He nodded. "I have completed my latest round of translations. I believe I may have found what you are looking for."

She held out her hand.

He ignored it, settling back into his chair. "It was quite involved. I do not think there is anyone else on the planet who would have been able to translate it. You are truly lucky that I agreed to work with you."

Elisabeta curled her hand into a fist, imagining how good it would feel to punch through the arrogant academic's chest. "*For* me, Dr. Chen. You work *for* me, not with me."

"I'm not sure why a woman such as yourself would even be interested in such a topic. It does not seem to coincide with your philanthropic endeavors."

Elisabeta had to keep herself from snorting. Chen had been sequestered since he'd begun

his work, at Elisabeta's command. He did not know what the world now knew of Elisabeta's abilities.

She swallowed down her growl of impatience. She was so sick of this man and his ego. Not to mention his not-so-veiled sexism. "The translation, professor. Now."

He harrumphed, taking his time to leaf through his folder before pulling out three sheets of handwritten notes. Elisabeta snatched them from his hand before settling in to read. Chen stood up.

"*Sit*," she ordered without looking up.

He grumbled something under his breath as he sat, but this time she ignored him. She read through the first page, her anticipation growing. Halfway down the second page, she found it. She read through to the last page before returning to the section. A smile spread across her face.

"I take it you have found what you are looking for."

"I have indeed." She finally looked up. "And you have made no notes, no copies, electronic or otherwise?"

Chen glared at her. "I'm not sure how I could. I have not had any access to my computer or even my phone since I began working for you."

"Well, it looks like our work is coming to an end, so that will no longer be a problem."

Chen stood. "Good. I expect my payment will be placed in my account within the hour."

Elisabeta smiled. "Oh, you will be taken care of long before then."

"Fine. Now I'll—"

Elisabeta moved quickly around the desk, slamming her fist into the professor's face while holding on to his shirt. Blood and two teeth sprayed across the room before she plunged her hand through his chest and yanked it back out.

The professor didn't even have a chance to scream. His eyes simply went wide before the light in them disappeared. She dropped him to the ground with a nod. She was right. That did feel good.

CHAPTER 3

BALTIMORE, MARYLAND

Noriko smiled as she walked along the preserve. The preserve was a ninety-acre estate halfway between the Chandler School and headquarters that had been out of use for years. Near the middle of the property was a tall research hide, thirty feet off the ground, for the researchers and vets. The whole area was enclosed with a fifteen-foot electrical fence, and a secondary fence had also been erected to keep any would-be neighbors from getting too near the electrified one. At the front gate was a guard hut that was staffed 24-7.

The old house on the estate was modified to serve as the shelter for the animals. There were two dozen Javan leopards in residence, whose genomes had been manipulated in a lab. The result was they were all much larger and stronger than standard leopards, most standing at four feet at the shoulders, all of them highly intelligent.

As Noriko walked, Tiger, one of the youngest, a yellow-and-black leopard, rubbed against her side.

Noriko ran a hand through his fur. An image of Cleo appeared in her mind. She looked down at Tiger. *She's with Laney. I don't know when she'll be back.*

Happy.

Yes, I'm sure she is.

Lou Thomas jogged up with Snow, the white leopard with the bright blue eyes, at her side. Rolly Escabi joined them, his dachshund, Princess, in his arms. "I am hungry," he announced, "and so is Princess. Aren't you, baby?"

Princess licked him in response.

Apparently I'm not the only one who can communicate with animals, Noriko thought as she watched them.

Since she'd come to the mainland, her abilities had been evolving. She'd always been able to understand animals, but the two-way conversations were new. But that ability was not the one that had everyone worried. It was her psychic skills—they had grown much stronger than she ever thought possible. She could now almost choose what her visions were about by focusing on a particular topic. But sometimes those directed visions were tough to come out of.

Really tough.

Lou, Rolly, Zach Grayston, and Danny Wartowski seemed to have set themselves up as her personal babysitters. One was with her at all times, ever since the last vision—the one that had knocked her out for hours. But she hadn't had any visions since then, directed or otherwise, so she thought she might be in the clear.

Lou shrugged. "I could eat. How about the Afghan place?"

"Ooh, I love that place," Rolly said.

"Noriko?"

"I'm okay. Why don't you two go? Maybe bring me back something?"

Lou and Rolly exchanged a glance. "Yeah," Rolly drawled. "We'll just go grab some food and bring it all back. We'll eat here."

"You don't need to babysit me."

"We're not babysitting," Lou said quickly. "Just making sure you're okay while your abilities develop."

Noriko wanted to be mad, but she kind of liked that they were keeping an eye on her. "Okay."

"We'll be back in twenty, thirty minutes." Lou paused. "No trying to have visions while we're gone."

Noriko put up both her hands. "No problem. I am just going to hang with the cats."

Rolly raised an eyebrow. "Promise?"

"Promise."

"Okay." He grabbed Lou's arm, pulling her down the path. "Let's go, toots."

"Toots?" Lou asked.

Rolly grinned at her. "I thought I'd try it out."

"Consider it an abject failure."

Rolly shrugged. "I don't know. I kind of like it."

Noriko listened to them banter back and forth until they faded from view. She turned to Tiger and Snow. "Come on, guys." She headed for the center of the preserve. There was a large hill with a landing that offered a great view. It was Cleo's favorite spot in the preserve and had become Noriko's as well. A sense of loss fluttered through her as she thought of the black leopard, the matriarch of this group of cats. She missed Cleo, but she was glad she was reunited with Laney.

She took a seat on the ground, leaning her back against the rock outcropping. Tiger curled up on one side, Snow on the other. Together the three of them looked out over the preserve. Noriko felt content for the first time in ages. The children were back where they belonged. Elisabeta had disappeared, and the government was now trying to find her, and the cracks were getting wider in the fake narrative Samyaza had concocted around Laney. Cleo was back with Laney. And Laney, well, she was sort of back. All in all, life was looking up.

With a sigh, she leaned back. Snow snuggled in closer with a purr. Noriko smiled. "I know, girl. I'm pretty—"

Pain lanced through her head. She gripped both sides of her skull as her sight dimmed.

The visions never hurt like this, she thought just before she crashed to the side.

CHAPTER 4

As the head of the Chandler Group, Henry Chandler had overseen multimillion-dollar deals and maneuvered through impossibly complex international relations. His reputation tended to intimidate people before he stepped in a room. His seven-foot-two stature furthered that intimidation once he was in the room.

The man sitting across from Henry now, however, was not even slightly intimidated. And for good reason. They were evenly matched physically. Henry was a Nephilim and Gerard a Fallen, but their powers were the same—enhanced speed, strength, and healing ability. On a personal level, though, Gerard Thompson was a man adrift. All he knew had been ripped aside when he'd turned his back on Elisabeta. Yet the man looked as polished as usual in a crisp lavender-colored shirt and gray slacks, his blond hair perfectly in place.

Henry didn't know what to do with him. He had helped the children Elisabeta had kidnapped. There was no doubt about that. He had shared with Henry and his people everything he seemed to know about Elisabeta's vast network. Everything he had shared so far had checked out—the bank accounts, business, real estate, etc. All had been traced back to Elisabeta.

"So, where do we go from here?" Gerard asked.

"I'm not sure," Henry said. "This is rather new territory."

Gerard had been in Elisabeta's employ for years. In actuality, though, their relationship had been much closer and much more complex than a simple employee-employer relationship. Truth was, Henry just wasn't sure if he could trust the man. But Laney had vouched for him. Henry had no idea what to make of that. After all, Laney had been in hiding for the last year. When exactly had she gotten to know Gerard?

"Look, I understand your hesitation given my track record. But my allegiance to her has been severed—permanently." Gerard's usually expressionless face flashed with pain so quickly that Henry thought he might have imagined it.

Henry had pulled Noriko aside to get more details about what she knew of Gerard's break with Samyaza. She had explained about his wife and children. Although it had happened thousands of years ago, for Gerard it was as if it had happened yesterday. Or at least, that was what Noriko believed. But she was very trusting, always seeing the good. With her upbringing, it was hard for her to see the duplicity in others. But if what she said was true, Gerard had more reason than most to be against Samyaza.

Plus, Laney had asked him to make a place for Gerard, and he was so damn happy she was back that he'd do anything for her, even this. Henry stood, offering his hand. "Thank you for speaking with us. You are welcome to stay while we figure everything out."

"Thank you. I'll take you up on that."

"Good. Let's meet again tomorrow, and we can discuss—"

Gerard jolted, taking a step back, his eyes unfocused.

"Gerard?"

Gerard looked at Henry, and in a blur, he was gone.

Henry stared after him, the door swinging with the force of Gerard's exit. *What the . . .*

He grabbed the phone and called security. "Mark, Gerard just—"

"Blew through the front gate and down the road," Mark Fricano, the front gate guard, finished for him. "Dylan grabbed a Jeep and took off after him, but at the speed he was going, I doubt he'll catch him."

"Let me know when Dylan reports in." Henry disconnected the call. *What the hell just happened?*

CHAPTER 5

Flames dancing in the distance along the tree line were the first thing Noriko noticed as she opened her eyes. She was in a clearing about thirty feet wide. She could feel the heat of the flames even from where she lay. A sweat broke out across her body.

This isn't right. The visions aren't supposed to be this real. She got to her feet and stumbled in the opposite direction.

The wind shifted. A wave of smoke blew over her, causing her to cough. She stumbled forward, pulling her shirt above her mouth while squinting her eyes. She stumbled into the trees, moving quickly forward. Eventually, the air cleared. She gulped in a mouthful of pure air, her hands on her knees.

She stood looking around with a frown. *This is strange.* Everything felt so real, not like a vision at all. Her visions usually had an almost dreamlike quality to them. Even though she experienced everything, a part of her brain always knew it wasn't real. She reached out and touched a branch, feeling the smoothness of the leaves attached, the roughness of the branch. Nothing here felt like a dream.

Ahead, she could hear a low murmuring. Voices. She made her

way toward them. Then the trees disappeared. The shift was disorientating. But now she knew where she was—in the mist again. She felt relief. At least this was familiar territory. The voices grew louder. She hurried toward them, wanting this vision to end.

I'll just learn what I need to know and get out of here.

She came to an abrupt halt once again as the scenery changed. The mist disappeared. She was in a courtyard. She hurried behind a pillar, not wanting to be seen. Even as she shifted from view, she knew how idiotic her actions were. No one could see her here. A door banged loudly. A woman strode out, three large men following in her wake.

"Make sure everything is ready," the woman said. "I won't have anything ruin my plans." She paused, tilting her head to the side. "What is—"

Noriko's gaze snapped up as a cylindrical object screamed in from the sky, landing right where the woman stood. The blast wave spiraled out, slamming into Noriko and throwing her into the wall behind her.

She crumbled to the ground, her whole body radiating with pain. She reached for the back of her head. Her hand came away wet.

I'm bleeding? How is that possible? Fear charged through her. *I need to get out of this.* She stumbled to her feet, pushing away concrete that had been part of the ceiling above her.

And that's when she heard the laugher. It sent shivers of fear racing through her. It was inhuman. Her whole body shaking, she stumbled forward over the debris and looked out into the destroyed courtyard. The woman she had seen stood there, her clothes seared, her arm hanging on by tendons.

Noriko's jaw dropped. How was she still alive? Noriko scanned the ground. Parts of the men who had been with woman were strewn across the ground. Her stomach heaved.

The woman pushed her arm up toward her shoulder. Noriko's

eyes widened as the skin began to knit. She gasped, and the woman's head turned toward her.

Noriko stumbled back, scrambling away from the woman's gaze.

She can't see me. She can't see me, Noriko repeated over and over as her heart pounded. She turned, getting to her feet. A gust of wind blew, flinging Noriko's hair into her face.

Then the woman was in front of her. She grabbed Noriko by the neck, pulling her up. "And who are you?"

Terror clawed at Noriko's throat. *This is not possible.* Noriko's hands tried to pry the woman's hand from her throat, but she couldn't even budge her. Blood was splattered across the woman's face.

"Tell them they'll have to do better than that." She flung Noriko away.

Noriko soared through the air with such force that she knew that when she hit the ground, she would be dead. She pictured Aaliyah, her adoptive mother, who'd raised her since she was an infant and who'd warned her how dangerous her visions could be.

I'm sorry. I should have listened. Pain lanced through her as her back slammed into—

"Wake up!"

Noriko's eyes flew open.

Gerard looked down at her, his blue eyes intense. His shirt was lined with sweat, his chest heaving. Her head was in his lap. The cats encircled them. She stared up at him in confusion. "What—"

Lou and Rolly sprinted up to them, stopping short at the sight of Noriko on the ground.

"Get away from her!" Lou yelled.

"Wait." Noriko swallowed. "Wait." She struggled to sit up. "He didn't hurt me."

Rolly strode over, his face mutinous. "Are you sure?"

Noriko nodded, still feeling dizzy. "It was a vision. He pulled me out."

Lou's anger immediately shifted to concern. "A vision? Are you all right?"

"What did you see?" Rolly asked.

"Let's just give her a minute to collect her thoughts," Gerard said, although it was more of an order.

Lou glared at him, but Rolly grabbed her arm, holding her back. "You okay, Noriko?"

"No. Just give me a minute." A minute turned into five as Noriko tried to calm her breathing and sort through what she had seen. She reached up to the back of her head, surprised when her hand came back dry.

I was bleeding.

Rolly looked between Gerard and Noriko before tugging on Lou's sleeve. "Come on. Let's go get Henry and Jen."

Noriko frowned, trying to figure out how he knew that and then realized he must have sensed them.

Lou crossed her arms over her chest. "Are you kidding? I'm not—"

"Lou, she's fine. Let's give her a minute." He tugged her harder.

Lou slapped at his hand. "Quit pulling. We will be right back." She gave Gerard a long glare before she followed Rolly.

Gerard rubbed Noriko's arm. "Are you all right?"

"Yes. It was just strange. It was like I was really there, as if I was a participant."

Gerard frowned. "What did you see?"

Noriko recounted the vision, her voice dwindling off after she described the missile attack.

"So she was killed," Gerard said.

"No. She was hit. But she survived. She . . ." Noriko swallowed. She struggled to find some other interpretation for the next part of the vision. *It can't be. It can't.* But there was no other explanation. "She was immortal. Which I don't understand because the kids—they were saved. She doesn't have access to the blood."

Gerard's voice was without emotion, but Noriko felt him

tense. "Then she found another way. Do you know when this is going to happen? Has it happened yet?"

"I don't think so."

"So there's still time," he said softly, and Noriko had the impression he was talking more to himself than her. She sat up, and he moved so he was now crouched in front of her, taking her hand. "Noriko, you can't tell anyone what you saw. It needs to stay between us for now."

"What? Why?"

Gerard glanced over her shoulder, then back at Noriko. She could just make out the sound of voices. "I can't explain it right now. But I need you to trust me. Can you do that?"

She looked at him, but it wasn't Gerard in this moment she saw. It was Gerard the father, on his knees, grieving for his two young children. Noriko looked up as Henry and Jen Witt, her sister, blurred into view. The sisters had the same dark hair and dark eyes, a gift from their Polynesian mother, but their different fathers could be seen in the lighter brown of Noriko's eyes and the sharper planes of Jen's cheeks.

Henry frowned hard at Gerard. "What's going on? I got a call that Gerard blew into the preserve, leaping over the gates."

Noriko looked up at Gerard. He shrugged in response. "I knew I needed to get to you."

Jen stepped forward, her gaze inspecting Noriko, looking for any injuries. "What happened?"

"She had a vision—a bad one," Lou said. "Gerard apparently pulled her from it."

Jen and Henry exchanged a look before Jen spoke. "What was the vision?"

Noriko didn't look at Gerard. "I don't remember."

CHAPTER 6

GALETON, PENNSYLVANIA

The cabin was quiet as Laney walked up the steps. She'd finished her run, Cleo distracting the guards so she could slip through their ranks and really stretch her legs. It had been intended to help her clear her mind. The dream had happened yesterday, and she hadn't been able to shake it, even after a grueling run.

She wanted to do a little research, but stuck here in the woods of Pennsylvania with the governments of the world not exactly sure if she was a good guy or a bad one didn't leave her a lot of options. She'd already used up the internet sources she could find. But hopefully her exile would be ending soon. The world seemed to finally be coming around to the idea that she wasn't the devil Elisabeta had made her out to be. That instead, Elisabeta was the one law enforcement should be focused on.

Thank God I made that recording.

It had been a fluke that she'd even thought of it. But getting Elisabeta to tell the world in her own words what she'd planned to do with those children and the rest of the world, well, there was really no context where her words looked good. Laney had hoped that would spur the governments of the world into action.

The governments' wheels, though, were working slowly. But it wasn't just the vision that was spurring Laney on. She wanted to get back to her regular life. She needed to be back on the estate with everybody, and she wanted to see the cats. She knew Noriko was doing a good job with them, but it had been too long.

And now that the danger may be ratcheting up again . . .

Cleo stepped from the trees. Laney carefully pulled back her thoughts. Sometimes sharing a mental bond with Cleo was not the easiest thing.

Cleo paused, tilting her head to the side. *What's wrong?*

Nothing.

Cleo walked slowly toward her, her nose twitching.

An image flashed across Laney's mind—Gerard. Laney winced. *Just leave it alone. Please.*

Cleo watched her for a long moment before heading back into the trees. *For now.*

Her phone rang just as she was climbing the steps. She glanced at the screen. "Hey, Matt." Matt was Matthew Clark, reinstated director of the Special Investigative Agency (SIA), underneath the Department of Defense. The agency had been shattered after the warrants for Laney's arrest had been ordered, but the events of the last few weeks had convinced the powers that be that having a government agency specializing in tracking down the Fallen was probably in the U.S. government's best interests. Of course, they now had a lot less autonomy than in the old days, but it was a step in the right direction.

"Delaney?"

Laney covered her other ear, trying to hear Matt better. "Matt? Where are you?"

"In a chopper on the way to the airfield. I'm heading to India."

Laney frowned. "India? Why?"

"I just got a hit on some of Elisabeta's known associates.

They're in India, on the western coast. Satellite imagery reveals they've been there for three days." Matt paused. "They're diving in the Bay of Cambay."

Warning bells went off as a picture of Yamini flashed through her mind.

"I have a team assembled, and we should be on site in about seven hours. I just wanted to give you a heads-up. I'll let you know what I find." Matt disconnected the call without waiting for a reply.

Laney put the phone down slowly, not bothered by Matt's abrupt phone manners. But she was bothered by his words. Elisabeta's people were in India, and they just so happened to be diving around the area where Dwarka was believed to have sunk.

She started to climb the steps, then stopped. No. Her head was too full right now. She couldn't face her uncle, Drake, Victoria, Cain. She needed a little more time. She turned back toward the woods.

Maybe just another few more miles.

CHAPTER 7

BALTIMORE, MARYLAND

The morning light had broken the sky a little while ago. Luckily, no one was about. Ever since everything had happened with Laney, the school had lost a lot of students. Noriko hitched her backpack higher on her shoulder, her heart racing as she leaned against the wall in the foyer.

She peered around the corner, but there was still no one about. Only the nightlights were on, casting a dim glow through the hall. She glanced nervously at the window a few feet away, but she could see nothing through it. She took a shaky breath. She was not a fan of the dark.

She glanced at her watch. 7:17 a.m.

Did I miss him? She had been so sure he would come this way. Gerard had stayed at the school last night. He'd said he just wanted to see the school, but Noriko knew he was worried about her. But she'd known he'd be gone first thing in the morning.

What if I misunderstood? What if he's already gone? What if—

"And what are you doing skulking about this early?"

Noriko jumped, her heart in danger of leaping out of her chest.

Hand on her chest, she turned to face Gerard, who had somehow snuck up behind her.

He raised an eyebrow. She struggled to get a little moisture in her mouth so she could speak. "I, um, I was waiting for you."

"And you thought I'd be wandering the halls before dawn?"

"I know you're leaving."

He paused for only a second. "And why would you think that?"

"I saw it."

"Even so, I'm not sure how that involves you."

She ignored the little stab of hurt at his words. "I'm going with you."

He laughed. "No, you're not."

She straightened her shoulders. "Yes, I am."

He looked over her head down the hall. "Noriko, you are a child. You will only be in the way."

The little hurt in her chest grew larger. "I'm supposed to go with you."

"Supposed to? According to whom?"

"I don't know. Fate, destiny, take your pick. I had a vision."

Alarm flashed across his face.

She spoke quickly. "It was just a small one, no harm done. But I'm supposed to go with you."

"No."

"I know you're going after the Omni."

He tensed, his eyes scanning the hall before they returned to Noriko. "Have you told anyone that?"

"No, no, of course not."

"Then you need to keep it to yourself while you stay here." He turned and began to stride down the hall.

"You won't find it without me. I've seen it."

He stopped, staring up at the ceiling before heading back to her. He kept walking, backing her up against the wall, towering over her. "Are you lying to me?"

"No, no. Why would I lie?"

He looked down at her, running a hand along her cheek. "Because everyone else does."

She slid along the wall, out of his grasp. "Well, I don't."

"If I go without you—"

"You won't find it. We're supposed to find it together."

"And why might that be?"

"I guess whatever is responsible for my visions thinks we make a good team."

He studied her face. "Is that why you think they are sending us together?"

Noriko wasn't sure why his words made her breathless. "Yes. What other reason could there be?"

"You really are young, aren't you?"

She knew she should be offended, but honestly, right then and there, she felt young. As if he was having a whole different conversation than she was. "I don't know what you're talking about."

"No, I suppose you don't. Did you tell anyone where you were going?"

She shook her head. She'd wanted to say something, but she was worried Jen or Lou would try and stop her. "I left a note."

She held her breath as Gerard went silent, his gaze roaming the hallway. Part of her was hoping he'd say she couldn't go. The idea of this trip terrified her. But at the same time, everything inside her told her she needed to go. She needed to be there, or Gerard would not succeed. But Elisabeta would.

He sighed, then held out his hand. "I'll take your pack."

Relief and a tingle of fear rolled through her as she grasped the shoulder strap. "It's okay. I've got it."

He leaned over and slipped it off her shoulder. "I know you've got it. But I would like to carry it for you."

She let him take it. "Um, thank you."

"You're welcome. Now let's go." He hurried back down the hall.

Noriko had to practically run to keep up with his long-legged stride. He didn't look back to make sure she was there. Of course, since she was already panting, she was pretty sure he knew exactly where she was.

He held open the door for her. She slipped through. A few minutes later, they were driving off of the grounds, no one the wiser.

His face looked harsh in the dim light. A little sliver of fear rippled through her. What was she doing? She didn't know Gerard. All she knew of him was from a handful of interactions and what her visions had shown her. This was crazy.

"Having second thoughts?"

She shook her head, but her voice shook. "No, of course not."

"Sure."

They drove for a few minutes in silence before he spoke again. "So, I need you to find the Omni."

Certain of this answer at least, she nodded. "Yes."

"And do you know where we are going to find it?"

"Egypt."

CHAPTER 8

WASHINGTON, D.C.

The hall leading to the Oval Office was narrower than most people expected. But when the building of the White House first began in 1792, on a site chosen by George Washington, homes were smaller. Sometimes whole families lived in one-room buildings. The first White House was burned down by the British in the War of 1812 and was not reoccupied until 1817. It had been added on to over the years and rearranged but still maintained the smaller hallways and rooms of the bygone era. Now, however, the rooms off the hall were filled with computers, modems, and electronic equipment the founding fathers never could have imagined.

As Nancy Harrigan walked down the hall, people scurried out of her way with a nod. In these halls, Nancy was one of the big sharks. *She* did not step aside. As secretary of state, her job was relegated to the foreign affairs of the United States. The Elisabeta Roccorio situation wasn't officially within her purview. But Elisabeta had so blurred the lines between domestic and foreign actions, no one was technically in charge of everything she was accused of—attempting to instigate World War III, domestic attacks, political takeovers, and generalized authoritarian tactics. No one in the United States government had a position that covered all of those. Nancy wasn't even sure what the title of such a position would be. Director of Apocalyptic Activities? Secretary of World Security? Chief of Last Chance Tactics? Tsar of Biblical Carnage?

So Nancy had stepped in to fill the void. Besides, she had the time. Right now no one cared about trade agreements or boundary disputes. Nope, everyone was focused on finding Elisabeta.

Nancy turned into the outer office of the Oval. Neil Jakub, the President's aide, caught sight of her. He headed for the door to the Oval. The Oval Office itself didn't come into existence until after the Taft Administration—Lincoln's bedroom used to be the President's office. The spot where the Oval Office now stood used to be a secretary's office. But it was later determined the President should be at the center of the action. Before the President took over the space, it was modified to a complete Oval and had remained relatively unchanged since 1934.

Hand on the knob, Neil nodded at Nancy. "She's ready for you."

Nancy took a deep breath as the door opened. It didn't matter how many times she stepped through this doorway, she was always filled with awe at the history that this room had borne witness to. Visiting always reinforced the responsibility she felt for the role in history that she was currently playing.

President Margaret Rigley looked up from the Resolute desk, perhaps made most famous by JFK in the whimsical picture with his son John peeking out from the kneehole panel underneath. There was no whimsy in this President's appearance as she looked up at Nancy, though. She pushed back from the desk, waving Nancy toward the two couches facing each other. As usual, the President took the large club chair between the couches.

Nancy took a seat, waiting for the President to speak first.

The President placed the folder she'd been reading on the table next to her chair. "Your file is detailed, but I have a feeling there is a lot left out."

Nancy nodded. "I believe a lifetime of information, or if everything Matthew Clark says is true, lifetimes of information. I tried to scale it down to the most relevant."

"You trust this Clark?"

Nancy did not hesitate. "Absolutely. He is a straight shooter. As straight as they come."

"And also a Fallen."

Nancy nodded. "So it seems."

"I have to confess, I'm not sure what to make of all this—Fallen angels, a ring bearer, Samyaza. It sounds insane."

"Agreed. And yet . . ."

The President nodded with a sigh. "And yet."

Both lapsed into silence. Nancy struggled with what to say. The President was one of the most intelligent people Nancy had ever met. Nancy knew she was looking at this issue from a myriad of angles Nancy hadn't even contemplated yet. But she also knew the President was well aware of the political fallout that could result from picking the wrong approach.

"Are you sure Delaney McPhearson is not a terrorist?"

Nancy paused, weighing her words carefully. "From my read, Delaney McPhearson was thrust into a position she had no inkling of just three years ago. Her actions have always involved protecting the lives of others, often to the detriment of herself. In Israel, she could have let the bomb go off to avoid her abilities being uncovered, but she chose to sacrifice her anonymity in order to save thousands, if not more, from the war that would have resulted. I do not think she is the bad guy in this drama."

"You believe that role is played by Elisabeta."

Nancy nodded.

"What of all her charitable works? Her philanthropy?"

"A cover. We've seen it before. And if what I am reading is accurate, the threat she poses is well beyond anything this world has seen before."

"Samyaza, leader of the Fallen angels . . . do we actually believe that is who she is? And that even if she is, that it is somehow relevant in the modern world?"

"I've sent you the clips of the Fallen incidents we are aware of. And the history of Samyaza's attempts to dominate this world. I believe she is the single biggest threat to the world at large."

"And what of the threat of Delaney McPhearson? She can control the weather, electricity, animals, and she can control these Fallen. Isn't that power a greater threat?"

"Potentially, yes, I think her power may be a greater threat. Someday. But today, I think she is our greatest hope in stopping Elisabeta."

Silence descended, stretching between them. Nancy did not know which way the President would fall on the issue. She was glad at that moment that the decision was not hers.

"Has there been any sign of Elisabeta?"

"No. All our intelligence agencies have made finding her a priority, as have most of the governments of the Western world. But so far, she has not been sighted."

"That alone is damning." She paused. "I've spoken with the attorney general. He does not support dropping the charges against Delaney McPhearson."

Nancy wasn't surprised. Dick Chenwick was a staunch law-and-order guy.

"He believes McPhearson is guilty, as does forty percent of the country," said the President.

"True. But another forty percent believes she is not. And testimonies from the people she's saved that keep cropping up are increasing that percentage every day."

The President nodded before turning to look out the window. Clouds dotted an otherwise beautiful blue sky. "The Fallen have powers that no human should have. It tips the scales too much in their favor."

"It does."

"And Delaney McPhearson's power outweighs even theirs. If she should choose to utilize that power for her own gain . . ." The President left the thought unfinished.

"Delaney McPhearson is a risk. But the immediate problem is not Delaney. She is a problem for the future. The disappearance of Elisabeta is the current problem. The woman is not hiding quietly in the shadows. She is plotting. She is planning."

"Are you sure she isn't just holed up somewhere, licking her wounds? Her movements are restricted due to her notoriety. She is pinned, cornered."

Nancy remembered her conversation with Matt yesterday. "And when an animal is cornered is when it is the most dangerous. I think that when Elisabeta's mask was ripped from her, it did cause her to stumble. But now that she's regrouped, she's planning. She no longer has to hide who she is, what she can do. I think when Elisabeta reemerges, well, we'll need to pray that Delaney McPhearson is available to take her on."

"And if she isn't?"

"Then God help us all."

CHAPTER 9

GALETON, PENNSYLVANIA

The extra miles had helped tire Laney out, but her mind had continued to churn as she climbed the porch steps. Why India? It had to be related to the Omni, but whatever was there had been hidden for over ten thousand years. What did Elisabeta think she would find after all this time? She crossed the last few feet to the door and let herself into the cabin, shutting down her thoughts.

Her uncle turned from his spot at the stove with a smile. The early morning light highlighted the gray that had begun to appear in Patrick Delaney's red hair. But his blue eyes twinkled, and his Scottish brogue sounded a little stronger in the quiet. "How was your run?"

"Good." She sat down at the table.

He placed a mug of tea in front of her before taking a seat opposite her. "How far?"

"Um . . ." She glanced at her watch. "Not sure. Somewhere between ten and twelve miles."

"Ah, to be young again."

Laney gave him a distracted smile, her hands wrapped around the warm mug of tea. It was unseasonably cool this morning. Even with the run, the tea was a nice little spot of warmth.

"What has you so lost in thought?" her uncle asked, his blue eyes focused on her above his own mug of tea.

Laney shook her head, clearing her thoughts. "A little bit of everything." She paused, studying her uncle. He'd raised her since she was eight, and there was no man she trusted or respected more. And she realized she wanted his opinion to help her sort through the noise in her mind.

"Actually," she began slowly, "I've been thinking about immortality."

His eyebrows rose. "I see."

"Victoria and I spoke about it once. She told me that humans at our earliest incarnations were almost immortal and that it was not good for humanity."

"I would think that was probably true. Humans do not do well with excess, be it wealth, power, or even just social standing. The potential to abuse seems to be hardwired into our DNA."

"Do you think immortality will always bring out the worst in people?"

"Is this about Drake?"

Laney jolted. "Drake? No, no, I hadn't been thinking about him at all. Where is he, anyway?"

"Sleeping." Patrick studied her. "So if this isn't about Drake, it's about Elisabeta. You don't think she's given up her quest for immortality."

"No. I don't think that is something she'll give up, and I don't know how we'll fight her if she's unkillable."

"Nothing's truly immortal. After all, Victoria found a way to stop humanity's immortality. There's always a way."

Laney nodded, hearing Cain somewhere outside singing with Victoria. *But that knowledge is locked away in the mind of a toddler.*

"Rulers have tried for centuries to find the key to everlasting life."

Laney nodded, her mind rolling through the points in history. Gilgamesh, after losing his best friend, hunted down an alleged immortal named Utnapishtim trying to become immortal. After uniting China in 200 BCE, the first emperor of China was desperate to find the key to immortality. During his bid, he ingested mercury pills, which hastened his own death. Other emperors took on the quest, eventually resulting in the creation of a substance, which, rather than creating immortality, hastened mortality: gunpowder. In the Western world, legends abounded about the Kingdom of Prester John, which allegedly held the Fountain of Youth. Searchers all came up empty.

But the search for immortality was not only an interest of those in the past. Modern-day efforts to unlock the key to immortality continued. Russian Internet mogul Dmitry Itskov believed he would be able to make humans immortal by 2045. The Methuselah Foundation was dedicated to findings cures to seven types of age-related damage such as loss of cells, excessive cell division, and inadequate cell death. In fact, there were a slew of Silicon Valley initiatives directed at either slowing down, reversing, or even stopping aging.

Patrick paused. "But it's not an academic conversation you wish to have."

She shook her head.

"Would you ever want to be immortal?"

"No," Laney said without hesitation.

"That was pretty definitive." Patrick frowned, studying her. "It's not just her search that worries you. It's what you might have to do if she achieves it. That you might have to become immortal yourself to defeat her. What exactly worries you?"

She considered not answering or giving him a shallow response. But she needed someone to talk to. "I worry that I would change. That I wouldn't be me. That if I took that step, I wouldn't be able to take it back."

He reached out, grasping her hand. "Mortal or immortal, you'd still be you."

"I don't think that's true. That power has to change how you view the world. Victoria, when she spoke of immortality, about how we humans used to be, she told how we got greedy, that we got spoiled by it. What if that happens to me? In fact, it *will* happen to me. Who will I be if I never have to fear death?"

"But you will always fear the death of those you love. You love, Laney, that's how you keep it from happening. You love the people in your life and you recognize that other people feel the same way by others in their lives. That's how you stay the path."

Laney stared at him, feeling all the love she had for him. Tears crested in her eyes. "I still wouldn't want to live this life without you."

Patrick leaned in, placing a kiss on her forehead, his voice shaky. "I love you, Laney. But I was always going to go ahead of you. But even when I am gone, I will still be with you."

"But what about a normal life? A family? Do I get that?"

He frowned. "Who says you can't have that?"

"Who says I can?"

The back door slammed. Laney turned her attention to the hall, happy for the distraction. Her uncle's gaze was a little too knowing, his questions too close to a truth she couldn't yet reveal.

She smiled as little Victoria sprinted into the kitchen with a giggle, Cain right behind her. "Gotcha," he cried, swooping her up into his arms. She squealed, wrapping her arms around his neck. He nuzzled her cheek before dropping her gently back to the ground. She toddled into the living room, plopping on the floor in front of her basket of toys.

Laney hadn't been surprised at how good Patrick was with Victoria. But she had been surprised at how good Cain was with her. She studied Cain, whose face was soft as he watched the little girl who had lived lifetime after lifetime. She was good for him. He had stepped into the role of father with no prodding. He was the first one by her side when she cried at night, the first to feed her in the morning, the last to hug her before she went to sleep. Victoria had given him a chance to love, and he had blossomed in that role.

Cain made his way to the kitchen and poured himself a cup of tea, looking over at Laney and her uncle. "Why do you two look so serious?"

"Not me," Patrick said. "The seriousness is all her."

Cain turned his black eyes to Laney and raised an eyebrow, waiting.

"There's a lot going on. Not the least of which is what to do with Victoria, where to hide her. We can't stay here forever."

"Are we in any immediate danger?" Cain asked.

"No, but I just feel like we are on the edge. Like something's about to happen."

Patrick and Cain exchanged a glance.

"You two feel it, too," she said. It wasn't a question.

"Yes. But until we know what is heading for us, there is little for us to do," Cain said.

She sighed. On the floor, Victoria pulled two stuffed animals from the basket and placed them on the couch before tucking the blanket on the couch over them. Kissing each of them, she plopped down on the floor with a book, which she opened and began to read upside-down.

"When I look at her," said Laney, "it's difficult to see her as just a child. I mean, she is the Mother of All wrapped in a toddler's body. I *wish* I could look at her as just a child."

"Patrick and I have been speaking about that," Cain said slowly. "And we think that there might be a way to help with that."

"What's that?"

"Her name," Patrick said. "We've been calling her Victoria, but she's not Victoria. Not yet. She's an innocent. I thought perhaps we could change her name. Help her have a childhood."

Laney glanced at her again. "Huh. I think you're right. A new name would be a good way to help remind us all who she is, and most importantly, who she is not." Laney paused, glancing at her uncle, who nodded back at her with a smile. She turned to Cain. "You should name her."

Cain's mouth fell open. "No, I think—"

"Cain, you've known her longer than the rest of us," said Patrick. "You've loved her longer than the rest of us. One day, when she does remember, she will approve of you having been the one to give her her name. Do you have any in mind?"

Cain nodded slowly, his voice unusually hesitant. "I . . . I have always liked Nyssa. It's a Greek name. It means new beginning."

"Nyssa," Laney said, trying it out. She smiled. "It's beautiful."

"And appropriate," Patrick said. "This is her new beginning. So I guess Nyssa it is."

Cain smiled. "Now, what are your thoughts on a puppy? Every little girl should have a puppy."

Laney laughed. "How about we find our permanent hiding spot before we add any more members to this ragtag crew?"

"Fair enough."

Laney squeezed his hand. "You are one good daddy."

Cain jolted but then smiled, squeezing her hand back before heading toward the living room. Laney watched him swing Victoria—*No, Nyssa*—into his arms.

"Well, little one, what do *you* think of Nyssa?" She started babbling away again. Cain hugged her before settling her back on the ground.

Laney never would have imagined when she'd first met Cain that they would reach a point where his joy became her joy. But they had. Somewhere in all this craziness, he'd become family.

Patrick leaned over and kissed her on the forehead. "And you are one good daughter." Patrick took her empty mug, heading to the kitchen.

Pushing open the screen door, Cleo wandered in, and after rubbing against Laney, she headed for Nyssa and lay down right next to her. Nyssa turned, leaning her back against Cleo with a smile. She pushed her book toward Cain with a look of expectation.

Cain picked it up and began to read aloud. "Piddle puddle was a little duckling."

Laney looked from her uncle at the sink to Cleo stretching as she lay next to Cain and Nyssa. All of them had been through the fire. Yet somehow they'd all found one another and made something incredibly special.

An image of Elisabeta slipped into her mind. Laney shuddered while promising herself she'd protect them from whatever storm was on the horizon.

Her cell on the table rang. Her uncle glanced at the screen before handing it to her. "It's Henry."

Laney frowned. She's just spoken with him this morning. "Henry? Is everything okay?"

"Yes. In fact, I would say things are better than they've been for a while. I just spoke with Brett."

Laney pictured the tall, distinguished lawyer whom she'd met just before she'd gone on the run. "And?"

She could hear Henry's smile through the phone. "And the charges against you have been dropped. You can come home."

Laney's mouth fell open. "You're sure?"

"I'm sure. It's over, Laney."

CHAPTER 10

OVER THE ATLANTIC OCEAN

The plane had lifted off from the runway with barely a bump. Noriko ran her hand over the smooth leather of her chair. Gerard had a plane already at the small airport, but for some reason he had chartered a different jet to take him to Egypt. When she'd asked why, he merely shrugged and said convenience.

Noriko had drifted off shortly after takeoff. She woke up with a start, not knowing where she was at first. She was lying in a bed. She lifted the shade on the window. Clouds were outside, looking close enough to touch. She wiped her eyes, then walked a little unsteadily toward the door and peeked out.

Gerard looked up from where he sat working on a laptop. "Ah, Sleeping Beauty awakes."

Tugging self-consciously at her wrinkled shirt, she nodded back to the bedroom. "Thank you for letting me use the bed."

"Not a problem. There was plenty of room for both of us."

Noriko's jaw dropped open. Heat flared across her face. "Both of us?"

He nodded, then smiled. "Just kidding. I slept for a little bit out here. Your virtue is quite safe."

She didn't know what to say to that, so she looked around the cabin, inspecting everything to avoid his gaze.

"There are some drinks and food in that little galley to your right."

Happy for an excuse to step away for a minute, she ducked inside and took a breath, not sure why he always made her so nervous. Okay, well, everybody made her a little nervous. But with Gerard, that nervousness was a little different.

She found a glass, poured herself some orange juice, and then managed to make herself a ham and cheese sandwich on a croissant. A little fruit on the side, and she had a meal. She peeked back into the cabin. "Um, would you like anything to eat?"

He kept his gaze on the laptop. "I'm good."

Grabbing her plate and glass, she headed back out to the cabin, taking a seat two rows away from Gerard, where she could see him between the seats, but could easily shift so she couldn't be seen. She raised the shade on the window near her, watching the clouds go by as she ate, lulled into an almost trancelike state by the engines of the plane.

She wasn't entirely sure why she was here. She *did* think she was supposed to be here, but she wasn't sure what she was supposed to do. She hadn't had a vision of where they were going or where the Omni was hidden. She just felt this certainty that she was supposed to be here and that the answers they sought would be in Egypt.

She felt a little thrill at the idea of actually going to Giza. To see the Sphinx, to touch the Great Pyramid. She'd never really wanted to have visions, especially since that one with Elisabeta. But what if she had one that showed her how the pyramids had been built? Or who had created the Sphinx? That would be amazing.

"Any answers in clouds?"

She looked up, surprised to see Gerard sitting next to her. She hadn't heard him move.

"Um, no. No answers, just a little daydreaming."

"So you said you are supposed to be here, that we're supposed to find the Omni together. Do you know where it is?"

When she shook her head, his jaw tightened. Realization hit her. "You don't know where it is, either."

He sighed as he leaned back. "Not entirely true. Like you, I have a very strong feeling that it is in Egypt. And being I once lived in Egypt, I think I'll start there."

Noriko knew Gerard had once been Barnabus, the adopted son of the King Proteus, who had ruled Northern Africa in the time of Helen of Troy. Proteus was known as the ruler of the seas. Even though he had a sumptuous place on the mainland, he preferred to spend his time on the small island of Pharos off the northern coast of Africa. Pharos, of course, was famous the world over for housing one of the Seven Wonders of the Ancient World —the Lighthouse of Alexandria.

The 350-foot-tall lighthouse had been covered in mirrors that were allegedly used to set ships that illegally entered Alexandria Bay on fire. The Lighthouse was reported to have been visible from as far away as thirty-five miles. At the time, the only taller structure in the world was the Great Pyramid at Giza.

Until 1994, it had only been a legend. Then divers found remnants of the Lighthouse. Now it was known that the Lighthouse had survived up until the fourteenth century. It was damaged by an earthquake in 1303 and completely destroyed by a second earthquake in 1323.

"You think it's at the Lighthouse?" Noriko asked.

"No. The Lighthouse wasn't built until the third century BCE, a thousand years after Barnabus lived."

"After you lived," she corrected.

He nodded.

"So it must have been hidden somewhere that existed at the time of Barnabus."

"And hopefully it still exists today."

And that was the problem. Of the Seven Wonders of the Ancient World, the Great Pyramid of Giza was all that was left. The Hanging Gardens of Babylon, the Statue of Zeus at Olympus, the Temple of Artemis at Ephesus, the Mausoleum at Halicarnassus, the Colossus of Rhodes, and the Lighthouse were all gone. They had all disappeared into the mists or sands of time. Some people even doubted they had ever existed. But if those amazing structures failed to survive, what hope did they have to find the Omni buried in some less important location thousands of years ago?

"Do you think it's still there?" she asked. "Do you think we'll be able to find it?"

Gerard smiled. "You're the one who said fate thinks we're a great team. So who are we to question fate? So yes, it's there. And we'll find it."

CHAPTER 11

GALETON, PENNSYLVANIA

After grabbing a shower, Laney was just finishing up drying her hair when her cell phone rang. Matt again. *Probably with another short but sweet report.* "Hey, Matt. How's the flight to India?"

"We had a change of plans. I was on my way to India when I got a call telling me that one of Elisabeta's men was seen in Turkey."

"Turkey? What would—" Laney went still. "Göbekli Tepe."

"That's what we think, although we don't know why. I was hoping you might have an idea."

"I don't. Have you gotten any more details about what's happening in India?"

"Well, I told you about that report about diving activity in the Bay of Cambay. Whoever it was wasn't authorized to be there. When officials moved in, there was a firefight. Most of the law enforcement officials were killed. One managed to get back to shore. He said the assailants had incredible strength and speed."

"Fallen." The Bay of Cambay was off the western coast of

India. For years, people along the coast had spoken of an advanced civilization that had disappeared below the waters in the distant past. Mainstream scholars had blown off the talk as the imaginings of a primitive people.

Then the ruins had been found. "I think they were trying to find Dwarka."

"That was what I was thinking as well, although I can't figure out why."

A chill ran over Laney as she recalled her dream. "The Omni. She's going after the Omni. The priests of Dwarka created it."

"Do you think they were able to find it?"

"No. Samyaza attacked Dwarka, and the priests submerged the city to destroy him. He died there."

"Is there any chance the Omni or clues to its location could be found at Göbekli Tepe?"

A chill ran over Laney as she remembered the crazed look in Jagrav's eyes from her vision. "I don't know. I mean, the site dates to 12,000 BCE, so the timing is right. But Göbekli Tepe has been only monoliths. They haven't even found a belial stone yet."

"Do you think that might be what she's looking for?"

"She likes power, but unless one has been discovered I can't see why she'd go in now. Only a small percentage of the site is uncovered. And it's been buried for thousands of years. Unless she knew exactly where to look, I don't know how she'd find it."

"Okay. Well, I'm on my way there. Mustafa is already on his way with a team. He was in Egypt visiting his parents."

"Wait, isn't his sister working at the site?"

"Fadil has been there for a year."

"Has Mustafa spoken with her?"

"He's been unable to get through. The cell reception in that part of the country is dicey."

A sense of foreboding fell over Laney. "Oh."

"Hey, none of that," Matt said quickly.

"None of what?"

"You are finally going back to the land of the living. This could all be a wild goose chase. Enjoy your freedom, Laney. Only worry when you need to. And right now you don't need to."

She smiled. "You're right. Just be careful."

"I will. And you—have some fun. You've earned it."

After they hung up, Laney held the phone for a few moments. *Göbekli Tepe. That couldn't be. What did Elisabeta—*

"Everything all right?" Drake asked from the hallway.

"Um, yeah."

"Well, that was completely unconvincing." He was leaning against the doorway, his blue eyes watching her. His lean frame was accentuated by the washed jeans and perfectly fitted T-shirt. She wasn't sure how he did it. He literally rolled out of bed looking drop-dead sexy. *He's not human, he's—*

She paused in mid-thought, realizing she was right. He was an archangel, one who'd been in love with her for thousands of years.

And the sight of him made her feel light-headed and muddled her thoughts. Yet despite feeling in her bones that he was hers and she his, she couldn't quite take that next step.

Nyssa started to cry from down the hall. *Maybe because we are currently living with a toddler, a priest, an immortal, and a psychic leopard.*

"Laney?"

"Um, sorry. What did you ask?"

"Are you all right?"

Laney smiled. "Yeah, sorry. Elisabeta's making some moves, but I can't quite see what her endgame is."

Drake frowned. "Do we need to do something?"

"I don't think so. Besides I don't know what *to do*. Matt is on it."

He reached down and pulled her up. "Good. Then let's get you on that chopper."

Tingles ran up her arms from his touch which she ignored as usual. "You sure you've got everything here? I can stay."

"Go see your brother. I can babysit for an afternoon."

"I'm sure Cain and my uncle will keep an eye on Nyssa. I'd ask you to go, but I'd feel better knowing you were here with them."

"And I will keep on eye on them."

Cleo roared from the hallway.

Drake rolled his eyes. "Along with your pushy pet. But it will cost you."

"And what is that?"

"Just some of your undivided attention for at least an hour, as soon as circumstances allow it."

"Deal." She wrapped her arms around him.

He returned the embrace, leaning his chin on her head. "It will be all right Laney. Whatever Elisabeta is planning, we'll handle it."

Laney just hugged him tighter, visions of violence floating through her mind. *I hope so.*

CHAPTER 12

CASABLANCA, MOROCCO

The CNN anchor stared straight at the camera, her expression serious. "The search for Elisabeta Roccorio, the wealthy famed philanthropist and now alleged terrorist continues."

Elisabeta snorted. *Alleged. Please.*

"Roccorio is believed to be behind an attempt to start a conflict in the Middle East by an attempted bombing of the Temple Mount. Experts vary in their opinion about the impact such a move would have had, but all agree the effects would have ranged from violent to catastrophic. Roccorio has not been seen since FBI agents attempted to apprehend her at one of her Chicago homes. She escaped in a helicopter and has not been seen since.

"Roccorio is also believed to be the mastermind behind the attempt to paint Dr. Delaney McPhearson as an enemy of numerous states. McPhearson is perhaps best known for her flight over Jerusalem, when she removed the bomb from the Temple Mount, allowing it to explode in the Mediterranean Sea without any injuries or casualties. McPhearson is now being hailed as a hero for her work as more and more people step forward to defend her."

With an angry punch of the remote, the screen went blank, and Elisabeta tossed it on the couch. *Hero of the people. The scared, pathetic people.*

Walking over to her desk, she rifled through the paperwork there. The incident in Chicago had been expected, and Elisabeta did not regret it. Although she had to admit losing Hilda, who was in the FBI's custody, was a blow. Hilda had been loyal, tried and true. From the reports she'd received, Hilda had remained loyal while inside. Elisabeta was considering rewarding that loyalty with an extraordinary gift once her plans were realized. *Perhaps I still will*, she mused.

Hilda was a concern for another day, though. There was much to do before her aide could be made a priority. Right now, Elisabeta was on the cusp of greatness. She had spent too much time in the shadows, hiding who she was. She was done with that. Now she could be exactly who she was. *And who I am meant to be.*

She frowned, not seeing the report she wanted. She punched the intercom button on the phone.

"Yes, madam?"

"Where is the report from the retrieval team?"

"Um, it is . . . Ah, yes, it was just emailed to you. Would you like me to print off a copy for you?"

"Yes." She released the button. A minute later, a knock sounded at her door. "Enter."

Artem crossed the room quickly, his face its usual mask. During her search for the Tome of the Great Mother, Artem had overseen Elisabeta's overseas interests. He had made contacts across the globe and infiltrated the governments she would need in the upcoming weeks. He had laid the groundwork for the days to come. Now that Elisabeta had arrived, he had been shifted back down to executive assistant. But if the demotion bothered him, he did not show it.

Elisabeta took the paper from him. "Have you read it?"

"No, ma'am. That is not my place."

She nodded, her eyes scanning the report. A smile crossed her face as its contents revealed their success. *They found it.*

"Good news?"

"The best." She placed the report in the table. "Now, what of our other projects?"

"The teams are almost all in place for the U.S. situation. And the plane is ready."

Elisabeta raised her eyebrows. "What about General Vasiliev?"

"An unfortunate car accident last night has taken the general's life, along with his family's."

"How unfortunate indeed. Be sure to send flowers."

"Yes, ma'am." Artem gave a small bow before exiting the room. Elisabeta watched him go. He had been with her for ten years. Always reliable, always willing to do whatever was necessary. Sometimes having a psychopath on the payroll was quite useful.

She turned back to the report, reading the final lines. *Box was uncovered this morning. Pictures attached.*

Elisabeta moved to the computer and quickly pulled up the first image. A dusty box made of ivory appeared on the screen. She zoomed in and could just make out the carving of a woman, her hands thrown to the sky, her hair streaming behind her. For the first time, she smiled at an image of Victoria.

But it was the other image that truly brought her joy.

Ah, the Dwarka priests were not so bright after all, were they?

She immediately sent a note to her team, who had been waiting patiently to be called in for duty.

Target acquired. Details attached.

SHE FORWARDED the note along with the contact information for her source.

Eliminate source once target is acquired.

ELISABETA SMILED, pulling her cloak from behind her chair and wrapping it around herself before heading out the door. Yes, her unmasking was just the beginning. The beginning of her finally realizing her destiny.

"Any sightings of the child?" she asked Artem as he fell in step with her.

"Not yet. It is still believed Delaney McPhearson is in hiding with her, and once she steps out of hiding, the child's location will be known, although we have received intel that Delaney McPhearson may arrive at the estate today to meet with government lawyers."

Elisabeta nodded. She knew the U.S. government was planning on dropping all charges against Delaney. It was strongly believed that the other countries of the world who'd sworn out warrants would follow suit.

"They'll drop the charges. I am now their focus. If McPhearson shows up, be ready for the trifecta plan. I assume everything is in place for it."

"Yes, ma'am." Artem paused, opening the car door for Elisabeta. "If she does show, should she be the first target?"

"No. Delaney is last on my list. She is not to be harmed, not yet." Elisabeta smiled, picturing Delaney's face as Elisabeta removed, one by one, those closest to her. That would be a pain much worse than any death. *That* was what she deserved.

"Let me know when the government makes their move."

"Yes, ma'am."

"How long until we reach the airport?"

"Ten minutes."

"Wonderful. Have some champagne chilled for when our business in Sudan is concluded. I have a feeling this is going to be a fulfilling day."

CHAPTER 13

BALTIMORE, MARYLAND

The Chandler estate was 500 acres of rolling hills that sat about twenty minutes outside Baltimore. It had been part of the Chandler family for around 200 years. Laney felt a pang of longing as the chopper flew along its boundary, heading for the helipad on the east lawn. God, she had missed this place.

But even as much as she was looking forward to stepping onto the grounds again, she couldn't deny that she had a small twinge of fear racing through her. She had been elated at Henry's call, but that elation had diminished when he said that government officials wanted to meet with her. She'd thought she was free and clear, but she had a feeling some tight strings were going to come with her freedom.

Drake and Patrick had offered to come with her, but she'd told them both to stay behind with Victoria. *No, not Victoria,* she had to remind herself again. *Nyssa.*

That was going to take some getting used to. But in the long run, it would be better for her. They needed to think of her as just a child, because right now that's what she was. And she deserved a childhood free from the baggage of Lilith for as long as they could manage it.

Three figures came into view as she spied the helipad—Henry, Jen, and Jake Rogan. Tears welled up in Laney's eyes as she soaked them in. The chopper had barely touched down before Laney was opening the door, ducking low, and running for them. Henry wrapped her in his arms, twirling her around with a laugh. She held him tight, her laugh mingling with her tears. He gently placed her on the ground. His eyes were bright with tears as well. Hands on her shoulder, he turned her, and then she was engulfed in Jen's hug.

"I have missed you," Jen said.

"Not nearly as much as I have missed all of you."

"All right, all right. My turn," Jake said.

Laney felt herself being turned around again and pulled into Jake's embrace. Emotion wafted over her at the thought that somehow, even with their breakup, they had managed to stay such good friends. "Oh, Jake."

"You're home, Laney."

She nodded into his shoulder and felt the truth in his words. *Home.*

∼

LANEY SAT at the kitchen table in the main house, a mug of tea wrapped in her hands. The staff had loaded a buffet on the giant island. Now she was happily—bordering on uncomfortably—stuffed. She'd been on the estate for almost two hours. There had been a parade of people through the kitchen. From the security team to the administrative assistants, it seemed like everyone had stopped in to welcome Laney back.

Laney had managed to carve out a quick trip down to see Dom to thank him for helping her disappear. Now Dom's face was on the iPad that sat on the table, listening and joining the conversation every once in a while, usually to correct a factual inaccuracy.

Lou, Rolly, and Zach had stopped by along with Danny. Snow, the all-white Javan leopard had been with them. Laney was happy to see how bonded she was with Lou.

Henry's watch beeped, and he looked at it with a grimace. "The government people have arrived. They're being shown to a conference room now."

A sliver of apprehension fluttered through her stomach. "So we're sure this isn't just some ruse to arrest me, right?"

Jake patted the gun at his side as he stood. "We are prepared for that possibility."

Brett Hanover, head of the Chandler legal department walked in at just that moment. Normally Brett was unflappable, always in a stylish suit and tie, never letting stress show. But at Jake's statement, his mouth fell open. "You cannot bring a weapon to an FBI interview!"

Jake shrugged. "I have a permit."

"You still cannot bring it with you.

"It's joining the meeting, Brett. But if it makes you feel better, I'll tell the snipers on the roof to stand down."

Brett's eyes went larger than Laney had thought physically possible. "*Snipers on the roof?* Are you insane?"

Laney took Brett's arm. "It's fine. And I'm sure Jake's joking about the snipers." She glanced at Jake.

"Sure I'm joking." He gave her an exaggerated wink.

Laney groaned.

Henry quickly took Brett's other arm and led them out of the room before Brett had a heart attack. Jake followed behind them.

Laney turned to Brett. "Any last-minute advice?"

Brett glared at Jake over his shoulder before turning to Laney. "Yes. Remember, Dr. McPhearson, you say nothing unless I give you permission, all right? And offer as short and succinct a reply as you can, all right?"

"Yes, no, I don't recall?"

He patted her arm. "Exactly."

No one spoke as they headed to the conference room on the first floor of the building. Normally conferences were held on the third floor, but Henry and Jake did not want to let the government people any farther into the building than they needed to. If it had been up to them, they probably would have told the officials they could speak through the front gate, with the officials on one side and Laney on the other. Luckily—or unluckily, depending on how this went—Brett had prevailed by arguing that showing the government courtesy could help ease tensions.

Laney couldn't speak for the government, but she wasn't exactly feeling a reduction of tension as she spied the door up ahead. She glanced back at Henry and Jake as she caught sight of the scaffolding outside the door. "Is the room under construction?"

"Huh, so it is," Jake drawled.

Laney chuckled, but Brett glared at the three of them. "Really? You three do realize we're trying to get the government to *drop* the charges and not add new ones, right?"

Henry just shrugged. There was no time to change anything; the government people were already inside.

Shaking his head, Brett adjusted his tie, wiping the annoyance from his face. "Here we go."

Brett stepped in with Laney only a step or two behind him. Laney tried to keep her face as neutral as the lawyer, but the state of the room made it a little difficult. A giant scaffold had been pushed against the back wall, and dozens of paint cans were stacked up underneath it. Drop cloths covered mysterious objects on either side of the conference table. The table itself had been wiped clean, as had the chairs around it. Coffee and bagels had been set up at one end, but the attempts of the staff to tidy up the spot were sorely outclassed by the disrepair of the walls, which were unpainted sheetrock with only half the spackle completed.

Even the light fixture above the table had been removed. Now instead of one the Chandler Group's signature chandeliers, a bare bulb on the end of a long wire dangled from the ceiling.

Laney put her hand to her mouth to hide her smile, then coughed at Brett's glare. Straightening his shoulders and no doubt cursing Laney, Jake, and Henry silently, Brett just headed for the chair across from the three suited individuals, two men and a woman, none of them smiling. They stood up as Brett pulled out his chair. Laney recognized the man in the middle, Attorney General Dick Chenwick. To his right was the deputy director of the FBI, Andre Revken. The woman on the right, however, she did not know.

Brett made introductions. The woman was Danielle Patine from Homeland Security. Laney pictured Moses Seward, the psychopath who'd had Cain beaten within an inch of his life, who'd also been from Homeland Security.

Danielle met her gaze with a cool one of her own but said nothing.

None of the government offered to shake hands. Laney didn't either. Apparently this was not going to be a friendly meeting. Once everyone was seated, Brett folded his hands on the table. "Now, what can the Chandler Group do for the United States government today?"

CHAPTER 14

GÖBEKLI TEPE, TURKEY

Two men in white with a stretcher between them hustled down the path toward the waiting ambulance. Mustafa Massari stepped aside, blanching at the arm that fell from under the sheet, blood sliding along the fingers to the ground.

The news of the attack had reached Mustafa as he was on the way to the Göbekli Tepe site. Matt hadn't heard anything about it until he *reached* the site. The Turkish officials were trying to keep a lid on it.

He'd been a bundle of nerves the whole ride from the airfield. He'd been unable to reach his sister or Matt. He knew it was the spotty cell service. Matt had managed to get a voicemail through, telling him Fadil was alive, but still, it had been one of the most nerve-racking hours of his life.

She's fine. Matt saw her. She's fine. Mustafa reached the end of the path and collared a man in a long blue tunic splattered with mud and a spray of blood. "Where are the people who survived?"

The man's eyes were large, seemingly unable to focus.

On a hunch, Mustafa asked the same question in Arabic, even

though he knew it was only spoken by a minority of the Turkish population. "Please," he added.

The man finally met Mustafa's gaze. He pointed down the path to the right. "At the main dig site. Those that lived, you'll find them there."

"Thank you." Mustafa patted the man on the shoulder and walked on, but he couldn't help turning around and watching the man. He hadn't moved. He stood now with his hand on his chest, tears streaming down his cheeks as another stretcher with a body too small to be anything but a child's passed him by.

Mustafa turned away, picking up his pace, trying to staunch the horror that was slowly crawling over him. This was not his first mass murder site, but this was the first one that was personal.

From the reports he and Matt had received on the way over, no one on the dig had suspected anything when they began their work early that morning. The gunfire bursts were the first sign, and those had been aimed at the site's security.

But from the eyewitness reports, they knew that most of the attackers didn't need guns. The guns were a cover, used to confuse law enforcement into thinking it had been an ISIS-inspired attack by people angry at the uncovering of a historical pagan site.

The fact that there had been survivors was a miracle. The gunmen had taken down everyone that moved. No one was spared. But one woman had the quick thinking to grab as many people as she could and hide them within a small cavern. Fadil's actions had saved a dozen people.

But Mustafa knew that no matter how many she'd saved, it would be those she hadn't been able to save that would haunt her. Forty-two people had been killed, the youngest six years old. No mercy or hesitation had been shown. Another seven were injured, but it did not look good.

The signs of violence became more apparent the farther into the site he went. Ancient obelisks that had been protected by the earth for thousands of years now bore witness to the violence of the modern age with the bullet holes that had permanently altered their appearance.

Pools of blood were scattered across the site. Some bodies still lay where they'd fallen, the sheer scope of the wounded overwhelming the responders. The dead would have to wait their turn.

Mustafa wound past all of it, heading for the easternmost part of the dig. Ahead, a ring of law enforcement officers stood with weapons at the ready. Matt was already ensconced with them. He had paved the way for Mustafa.

Mustafa could hear the cries of men and women. As he drew closer, he saw the lucky twelve huddled in small groups, comforting one another. A quick glance showed they were all uninjured, although the blood staining their clothes and hands testified to their attempts to save their colleagues and friends. The group was a mixture of races and ethnicities, from blonde Scandinavians to dark-haired Chinese and Pakistanis to brown-haired individuals who could have been from just about anywhere. Mustafa only gave them a passing glance, his gaze focusing in on one dark-haired girl who had grown up outside Cairo and who used to bug him for a bedtime story every night from the time she was four until she was seven.

"Fadil."

Fadil Massari looked up from where she sat her arm around an older woman with graying hair. Her eyes went wide, and she quickly spoke with a blond man next to her, who took her spot. Mustafa searched her for any injury. There were scratches on her arms and she limped, but otherwise she seemed uninjured.

Mustafa hurried forward and wrapped her in his arms. She clung to him as a shudder ran through her. "Mustafa. You're here."

"Of course I'm here." He held her until her shaking subsided. Then he pulled back to allow himself to look into her eyes. "Are you all right?"

Fadil nodded. "We hid. We opened up a small cavern earlier today. The dirt was packed so hard it protected everything inside. We weren't sure it was stable because of the hole we made, but I pushed everyone inside. I thought it was our only chance."

A simple statement, but he knew how terrified she must have been. But according to Matt's message, she had kept her head and hurried everyone into the hiding spot when the gunshots rang out. And she had been one of the first to leave the spot to check for survivors.

His voice was thick as he thought of how close he came to losing her. "You did well, little sister."

Tears filled her eyes. "I hid like a coward. Robin, she was out there. And she . . ."

Mustafa closed his own eyes, feeling the loss. Robin and Fadil had met on the dig last year, and Mustafa knew that his sister had never been happier. Just these last few months, their parents had finally consented to meet Robin.

"I should have found her. I should have—"

"Shh, shh. There is nothing you could have done. The people who attacked the site, you would not have been able to stop them. You would have been killed, too." Mustafa kissed her on the forehead. "You did well. No one could have done any better."

"But so many people died."

"Look at me, Fadil." He waited until his sister's dark brown eyes looked up at him. "In these types of situations, you can constantly question what you have done, what you should have done. The truth is you saved people's lives today, and yes, lives were lost. But that responsibility is not on your shoulders. It is on the shoulders of the cowards who targeted a defenseless group of people. Don't take that on."

She nodded, but Mustafa knew she had a long road ahead of her filled with even longer nights. He pulled her close, promising to be there for her when he could and to make sure he found whoever had forced this fear into his sister's eyes.

"I saw one of them. He smiled as he shot my friend Asir. Smiled. And then he ran so fast he became a blur." She paused. "He was one of them, wasn't he? One of the Fallen."

"Yes."

"But why? Why attack? What did they want?"

Mustafa looked around. "I don't know. That's what we are here to find out. Is there anything that you can think of that they would have been interested in?"

Fadil shook her head as she wiped her eyes. "This site is thousands of years old. What could possibly be of importance for them to do this?" She gestured to an obelisk. "I mean, this is history captured in stone. It makes no sense."

"Mustafa."

Mustafa turned. Matt stood a few feet away. "I'd like you to take a look at something."

Mustafa looked down at Fadil, who nodded. "Go ahead. I'll just—"

"Actually, I'd like you to come look as well," Matt said.

Mustafa shook his head. "No. She's not—"

"I'm fine, Mustafa. And if it will help, I want to."

Mustafa glared at Matt before looking down at Fadil and giving her a tight nod. Matt headed down the path, winding his way through the site. Following, Mustafa took Fadil's hand and clasped it tightly in his.

Matt led them to the other side of the site, stopping above a dig. Mustafa stopped on the edge, looking down. As Fadil came abreast of him, she gasped.

"I take it this destruction is new?" Matt asked.

Fadil nodded, seeming unable to tear her gaze from the piles of rocks littering the ground. "There were ten obelisks in here. Yann's team just finished excavating them two days ago. Why would they destroy them?"

"I believe it is what was on them that they were trying to destroy. Were photographs taken?"

"Yes, of course. They were linked up to the main site." Fadil's voice dwindled away as she watched Matt. "What?"

"Your server has been hacked. All the information has been removed. And the computers and all cameras on site have been removed as well."

Fadil's face fell.

"Is there any other record of the site?" Mustafa. "Anyone who might have taken some pictures?"

"No, it was—" She paused. "Actually, Yann, he was old school. He had a throwaway camera. He always started a new camera with each new excavation. He probably still has it. I can ask him."

Mustafa glanced at Matt, who shook his head. Yann hadn't survived either.

"I'll take care of it," Matt said, not unkindly.

"But—" Fadil's face fell. "Oh."

"Is there anything else about this site that makes it different?"

She shrugged. "Just the skulls."

Mustafa started. "The skulls?"

Fadil nodded. "Four skulls were found buried at the base of one of the obelisks in a stone box. We had them carbon dated. They're 11,000 years old. But that wasn't the strangest part. There were carvings on the skulls themselves, done postmortem." She stared off into the distance, a shudder running through her.

Mustafa gently touched her shoulder. "Fadil?"

"Sorry, um, and there was one last thing that I found odd, although not everyone agreed with me. The skulls all had holes in them."

"As in surgery?" Mustafa knew that surgery, even brain surgery, had been conducted in Ancient Egypt, but he not heard of anything like that in Turkey. There was no advanced civilization believed capable of that here. Of course, it had to be a highly advanced civilization that created Göbekli Tepe, so he supposed it was possible.

But Fadil shook her head. "I don't think so. I had the chance to look at them, and I believe the holes were made postmortem, or at least, were worn down postmortem."

"Worn down?" Matt asked.

"It's strange because the edges are smooth, like a drill was used and then a rope placed through them to carry them."

"Why do you find that strange?" Mustafa asked.

"Because there's only one other place in the ancient world that we know of that drilled holes in skulls and carried them on ropes."

"Where?" Matt asked.

"India."

CHAPTER 15

BALTIMORE, MARYLAND

Attorney General Dick Chenwick leaned forward in his chair. "The case against Delaney McPhearson is very complicated. There are warrants sworn out against her in four separate countries in addition to the United States. There's also her direct involvement in the death of SIA agents in Australia, and then there's the incident on the Francis Scott Key Bridge, also currently under investigation."

Laney did not like the attorney general's tone.

Apparently neither did Henry. He crossed his arms over his large chest and leaned forward. "I was under the impression that the United States government was going to be dropping the charges."

Danielle narrowed her eyes, her voice cold. "We are leaning in that direction, but there are still some unanswered questions."

"Such as?" Brett asked in his unflappable lawyer mode.

"For one, it is not clear how exactly Dr. McPhearson stopped the bus on the bridge—if that's what she did—from going over the side. From the recording, it seems more likely she just stood back and did nothing."

Brett shrugged. "Well, even if that were the case, that would not be a crime."

"But if she tampered with the bus—"

Brett cut in. "That has already been disproven. As has the duplicity of the woman known as the Priestess and Elisabeta Roccorio's roles in both the Australian incident and the Temple Mount incident."

Dick scowled. "Yes, but there is still the—"

Brett stood up. "We took this meeting in good faith. If the government is not fulfilling the agreement we reached on the phone, then we will be leaving."

"And if we decide *not* to allow a wanted criminal to go?" Dick asked.

Jake stood. "Then we will have a problem." Henry stood as well.

Laney, however, felt like banging her head on the table. Everyone's ego was out of sorts. The government wanted to save face for starting a manhunt for the person who'd actually saved thousands. The Homeland agent wanted to save face for their personal psychopath. The attorney general no doubt wanted to save face for pushing so hard behind the scenes to take the Chandler resources in response to Laney going on the run.

Laney put up her hands. "Okay, enough. How about we all take a seat?"

No one did.

Laney sighed. *Great.* "Okay, we are all missing the bigger picture. I get it. The government has egg on its face for how it handled this by believing Elisabeta's trail of breadcrumbs. If it makes you feel better, she is really good at what she does. But that is irrelevant. The important task at hand is figuring out what she is up to and where she's gone. That is where all of our energies need to be focused right now." She looked up at Jake and Henry. "You know I'm right."

With a huff, Jake sat, and Henry followed. The feds across the table also resumed their seats. FBI Deputy Director Andre Revken nodded. He'd been silent so far. "I agree with Dr. McPhearson. We need to move forward. If Roccorio is planning something, we need to know what. And due to the extent of the plan in both Australia and the Temple Mount, that is our priority." He looked to the attorney general. The man had not taken his eyes off Laney.

Time seemed to inch by before he dropped his gaze. Finally, he opened the folder in front of him, pulled out a sheet, and slid it across the table to Brett. "This is the agreement we discussed over the phone."

No one spoke while Brett read through it. Laney was afraid to even breathe too deeply. She was so close to getting her life back.

Finally, Brett nodded. "It's good." He slid it toward Laney along with a pen.

The attorney general's gaze returned to Laney. "Just to be clear, this is *not* a get-out-of-jail-free card. If you violate the law, you will be held accountable. I will personally see to it."

"*Asshole*," Jake coughed.

Dick narrowed his eyes. "What did you say?"

Jake just smiled.

Laney signed the paper quickly before the man could rescind the offer. She slid it across the table. The attorney general inspected it, and with a nod, placed it back in his folder.

Brett stood. "I believe this concludes our business."

The feds stood as well. "I'll see you out," Brett said, heading for the door. Without another word, they filed out of the room.

"Well, they're lovely," Laney said as she stood.

Jake grinned. "Who cares? You're free. It's over, Laney."

Henry laughed.

"What?" Laney asked, wondering what she had just missed.

"Jake called the attorney general of the United States an asshole."

The tension from the last few months drained away as laughter bubbled up inside of her. Soon the three of them were laughing hysterically. And it wasn't just Jake's comment. It was the fact that a weight had been lifted. Laney leaned into Henry, who wrapped his arms around her. "Welcome back."

She hugged him, smiling at Jake. "Thanks, guys."

CHAPTER 16

TOKAR, SUDAN

The Mercedes kicked up dust as it drove through the dirt-packed streets of Tokar. Elisabeta watched the scenery pass by with distaste. Crumbling houses, poverty as far as the eye could see. Women with colorful burkas walked by, their heads ducked against wind that tossed more dirt in the air. The driver slammed on the brakes. Elisabeta threw out a hand to keep from being flung into the seat in front of her. She opened her mouth to yell at Artem but then caught sight of the reason for the braking.

A goat. Slowly crossing the road.

She curled her lip as it passed, and then they were on their way again. Her current location was a far cry from the jet-set life she had lived previously. But it was only temporary. And necessary. The warehouse was near completion. Now she was just awaiting the shipment. She had similar stashes across the globe and similar arrangements with other pseudo-government types. But she had had to come personally to deal with the general.

The "general"—it was a self-proclaimed title. He'd been a pastor at one point before deciding that the job of overlord paid better. He controlled the port at Tokar and access to the Red Sea. He was known for his penchant for kidnapping for ransom, murder, bribery, and even setting up an underage brothel by the docks, not to mention his child soldiers.

This upstart of a general had put a kink in her carefully laid plans. Normally she would have one of her subordinates handle this type of problem. But Elisabeta wanted it to be known what she was capable of and that anyone who crossed her would pay the consequences.

Plus, she was angry. Delaney McPhearson had forced her hand, putting Elisabeta's plan into place before she had intended. But while Elisabeta had made it work, the rush had only fanned the flames of anger that had been slowly building since Chicago.

Now she was looking for an outlet to release that anger. And General Mansur, who had forced her into this throwback to the Stone Age, was going to be the lucky recipient of her wrath.

Artem pulled to a stop in front of a three-story building with balconies on the second and third floors. Six men in fatigues with large machine guns stood guarding the building, two on each floor facing the street. All glared at the car.

Artem walked around and opened Elisabeta's door. She got out and strode toward the entrance. One of the men stepped in front of her.

"Halt. State your—"

Elisabeta grabbed him by the throat and squeezed. "Get out of my way." With a flick of her wrist, she sent the man flying into the dust.

She didn't even bother looking at the other man as she strode up the steps. Artem quickly opened the door for her.

Loud voices and laughter greeted her as she stepped in. It took a moment for her eyes to adjust to the darker lighting. Sheet rock, hastily and poorly patched, dotted the walls. Unvarnished floors with an occasional missing piece further accentuated the rundown nature of the place. The sitting room to her right held two threadbare blue couches facing one another and a few mismatched chairs. Hanging between the couches on the far wall was a single piece of "art": a portrait of General NaNomi Mansur.

The general was portrayed with a chest full of ribbons and a strong, penetrating glare. The artist had taken some creative license with his height, build, and complexion. The halo of light surrounding him gave him an ethereal impression. She snorted at the sight before continuing toward the voices. Cigar smoke drifted down the hall, making her wrinkle her nose.

Idiot humans. Their lives were short enough.

Without hesitation, she stepped into the kitchen. The general sat at the table in a white T-shirt stained with what she thought might be the remnants of the breakfast on the table before him. The four men sitting with him all had the same fatigues as the men outside, although none had theirs buttoned.

Catching sight of Elisabeta, surprise flashed across the general's face, and he smiled. "Ah, our benefactor. What a pleasant surprise. Can I offer you some breakfast?"

Elisabeta curled her lip. "No. But you can put out those disgusting cigars."

The general took a long inhale of his cigar before blowing the smoke out. "If you are not here for breakfast, what can I help you with?"

"We had a deal, and you are not upholding your part of the bargain."

"The deal has changed. It will now cost double. After all, I am now dealing with an internationally known criminal."

The men around the table laughed. He smiled in response. "Besides, you are wealthy. You can afford it."

"My wealth is not relevant. Your mortality is."

It was the general who laughed this time. "Dear Elisabeta, you are playing at terrorist. I don't know why these other fools believe you to be dangerous. You do not know the first thing about living in this world. Your fancy schools and fancy parties are hardly preparation for the world you are trying to navigate. Now run along and send me my money and we will consider how many of my weapons it will buy you."

The men around the table laughed again. One of the men closest to her leaned back in his chair, blowing cigar smoke directly at her.

Elisabeta narrowed her eyes. "Is that so?"

The general smiled even broader. "I have heard the inflated tales of what you can do. But you are no fighter. You are a spoiled aristocrat. Now you are interrupting my time with my men."

Elisabeta didn't bother getting angry. Why be angry at an ant? In a blur, she grabbed the man who had blown smoke at her by the back of the neck while pulling the cigar from his grasp. She plunged the cigar into his cheek. He screamed as the smell of burning flesh mixed with the cigar smoke. Tossing the cigar to the side, she shoved him away from the table.

The general stood. "How dare you come into my home and—"

"How dare I?" Elisabeta asked, quietly stalking around the table toward him.

"No, no," the general said, backing away. "We ran into some shipping problems, that is all."

"According to my satellite information, my weapons were received last week, and yet you have not contacted me. You weren't thinking of trying to sell them to someone else were you, NaNomi?"

The general looked at his men. They jumped to their feet. Two placed themselves in front of Elisabeta. Without breaking her stride, she slammed her shin into the groin of one and broke the neck of the other, flinging him against the back wall.

One of the men across the table pulled his gun and fired. The shot caught Elisabeta in the ribs. With a grunt, she looked down at the wound, then over at the man. His eyes went wide. He aimed the gun again, his hand shaking. She grabbed the table with one hand and flipped it onto him, pinning him to the ground.

The last of the general's men tripped past her. She grabbed him, plunging her fist through his chest. Letting him drop, she turned back to the general. "Now, where are my weapons?" she asked softly.

"I-I have them. I will have them loaded onto a ship—"

"No. I have a cargo plane waiting for them. Get them in trucks. You have one hour."

"An hour? But I cannot possibly—"

She reached out and took his face in her hand. "You have tested my patience enough, NaNomi. Do not test it any further."

He swallowed, bobbing his head. "Yes, yes, Elis—Ms. Roccorio. Of course."

"Good boy." She patted his cheek before turning and stepping around the man still curled in the fetal position on the floor. Behind her, the general gasped, falling back against the wall.

Artem stood in the hallway and handed her a wet wipe as she reached him. He glanced at the blood on her side but said nothing.

Elisabeta wiped her hands as she headed down the hall, throwing the wipe on the floor. "Our people are at the warehouse?"

"Yes. They arrived just as we arrived here."

Elisabeta nodded, saying nothing until they were pulling away in the car. "Once we have all the weapons secured, dispose of the general and all of his people. We'll consider it a public service."

Artem said nothing and handed the whole box of wipes over the seat.

Elisabeta took them and wiped the remaining blood from her hands, sighing at the stains on her sleeves and by her ribs. "Ugh, this will never come out."

She turned to Artem just as his phone rang. He answered it and nodded. "Yes. Send it immediately."

He met Elisabeta's gaze. "They've completed it. It is being sent to you as we speak."

Elisabeta turned on her phone. She quickly made her way

through the layers of security to her encrypted email account. It took a minute, but finally the message appeared.

She ignored the entreaties from the sender, skipping down to the translation itself. It was broken up into four separate sections, one for each skull. She read carefully, making sure she understood every word. But in many ways it was very simple—it was a recipe. One for everlasting life. One that required a unique ingredient that she had acquired without even realizing how important it would be—Victoria's blood.

She sat back with a small laugh. *After all this time, I will be immortal.* She'd have different people create different aspects of the formula so no one person would have the complete formula. And then once they'd made the dose she needed, she would kill them. Speaking of which . . .

"Artem."

"Yes?"

"Have the translators killed."

"Yes, ma'am." He typed something quickly into his phone. "Done."

"Good. What is going on with the deal with Delaney?"

"They've agreed to the terms, and both sides have signed. She is a free woman. She is scheduled to leave the estate shortly."

Elisabeta glanced out the window at a group of children in their bare feet, running down the road. "Perfect. As soon as she is far enough away, tell the teams to move in."

A little girl with her hair in braids waved at Elisabeta. Elisabeta smiled as she waved a bloodstained sleeve in response picturing the pain Delaney McPhearson was about to experience.

Let it begin.

CHAPTER 17

BALTIMORE, MARYLAND

Laney stayed on the estate for another two hours after her meeting with the feds, but she knew she needed to get back. Now Laney stood with Henry and Jen on the back lawn. Henry hugged Laney tightly. "Are you sure you need to head back?"

Laney nodded into his chest before pulling back with a sigh. "We need to figure out a place for Nyssa. And this place is too public, too well known. And until then, I'd feel better being with her to make sure Samyaza doesn't come after her."

"You really think she will?" Jen asked.

"She has not given up her bid for immortality. And Nyssa is still the only way to achieve that. So for now, I stay where she is."

"I don't like it, but I understand it," said Henry. "But we will see you soon?"

"Yes. I promise."

"I'm holding you to that. And I will have a place for Victoria, I mean Nyssa, within twenty-four hours." Henry shook his head. "That's going to take a little getting used to."

"It will be better for her, though."

"I suppose you're right."

Jake drove up in a golf cart. "Your chariot awaits."

Laney smiled, giving Jen one last hug before climbing in. She waved at Henry and Jen as Jake pulled away, then turned to face forward. She watched Jake from the corner of his eye. He seemed happier, more relaxed than she had seen him in a while. "So, how's Mary Jane?"

Jake growled. "Who told you?"

Laney chuckled. "Jen. She said you seem pretty happy."

"It's not like that. I mean, Mary Jane's been through a lot and—"

Laney put her hand on Jake's arm. "Hey. Cut that out. If you have found something good, hold on to it with both hands. Life is short, Jake. We know that better than most."

"Are you following that advice with Drake?"

Laney felt her cheeks flame. "Uh, well, that's a little more complicated."

"Oh, sure, it's *your* love life, so it's complicated. Mine is straightforward."

Laney nodded. "Exactly." Ahead, the chopper sat waiting on the helipad. Laney frowned as it started up. "I thought you were flying me back."

Jake brought the cart to a stop. "Actually, there was another volunteer for that job."

Laney frowned, spying two legs underneath the chopper, walking toward the front, before the person they belonged to appeared. Only five-foot-two, he was bald with a muscular build that professional body builders would envy. She grinned. "Yoni."

Laney gave a Jake a quick hug. "Go see Mary Jane," she whispered.

Jake swatted at her. "Get out of here."

Laney laughed, climbing from the cart and heading for Yoni Benjamin. He met her halfway, twirling her off the ground. "I have missed you," he said. "Don't ever do that again."

She didn't think she had hugged or been hugged over the course of her life as much as she had been in the last few hours. She grinned down at him as he put her down. "How's Sascha? How's Dov?"

"They are great. And Sascha made me promise to get *you* to promise to come see them as soon as we get all this Elisabeta mess sorted out."

"I will. I miss them. Dov must be getting so big now."

"He is, and he's talking up a storm." Yoni's smile was full of pride. "And in a few months, he's going to be joined by a little brother or sister."

Laney's face broke out in a smile. "What? Oh, Yoni, that's great. I'm so happy for you."

"Thanks. And just so you know, both Sascha and I expect you around for when the little one shows up. None of this 'the whole world is gunning for me' excuse. Sascha said you need to have this all wrapped up before she goes into labor."

"I will get it done because I would not like to cross Sascha."

"Smart girl." Yoni held the chopper door open. Climbing into the copilot seat, Laney buckled her seatbelt as Yoni did his final preflight run-through. A few short minutes later, they were flying over the estate.

Laney looked down, once again smiling. She really did love this place. And hopefully, once everything settled down, she could once again call it home.

CHAPTER 18

Two of the large cats slipped through the trees, crossing the path twenty yards ahead of Danny. Both cats were yellow, one darker than the other. He thought it might be Jerry and Cinnamon, but he still hadn't figured out how to tell all the cats apart.

"Pretty cool Laney's coming back, huh?" Rolly asked from next to him.

"Yeah. They think the governments are going to drop all the warrants." Danny smiled. Seeing Laney had been so good. He'd hated that she'd been forced to hide away for so long.

But that wasn't the only thing making him smile. Henry had told him this morning that today was finally the day he was going to propose to Jen. It was funny. Henry always seemed so confident. Yet he'd been a bundle of nerves ever since he'd bought that ring. Danny had been the one assuring him it would be fine. Talk about role reversals.

He glanced at his phone. Nothing. *Come on, Henry.*

"I still can't believe Samyaza turned all of them on her like that. I mean, it's Laney, a real-world superhero. How could anyone think she was the bad guy?"

"Well, Samyaza has had a lot of practice at being the *actual* bad guy. But I'm hoping those days are numbered, too."

"Any luck tracking her down?"

"No."

And that fact was eating at him. He had tried every way he knew to track her down, but he had come up empty-handed. He'd been the one who'd linked up the activity in the Bay of Cambay and contacted Matt. He had a few dozen areas around the globe flagged for any sort of activity. Göbekli Tepe had been a surprise, though. That attack had seemed to come out of nowhere. And that was the problem. His approach was entirely reactive. He could let Matt know when something happened, but he couldn't do anything to *prevent* something from happening.

He'd also put tracers on Elisabeta's bank accounts, her holdings, her associates, but there'd been no movement on any of them. He hoped that meant she was laying low, but he couldn't help but feel they were all in the eye of the storm, and whatever was coming was going to devastate them all.

A horn sounded from the front of the preserve, pulling Danny from his thoughts. He exchanged a grin with Rolly before they started to jog back down the path. A minute later, they stepped out of the path. Lou and Zach were already there, moving toward the silver SUV as the driver's door opened.

A tall blonde woman stepped out with a smile. Sascha Benjamin turned, hugging Lou, only the slightest hint of a belly to show for her pregnancy. Zach disappeared around the side of the car before reappearing only a moment later with a small boy with light brown hair rubbing his eyes sleepily. Dov Benjamin, Yoni and Sascha's two-year-old son, looked like he'd just woken up from a nap.

"Are you ready to see the cats?" Zach asked.

Dov nodded, looking around. His eyes went wide as Tiger slunk out from the trees, followed by Snow. Letting out a squeal, he squirmed in Zach's arms, scrambling to get down.

Zach lowered him with a laugh. "Okay, okay. I can see when I'm not wanted."

But Danny knew that wasn't true. Dov adored Zach. And the feeling was mutual. Dov was a big reason why Zach had started to come out of his shell after all the damage his parents had inflicted on him.

Dov tottered over to Snow. "White," he said, flinging his arms around Snow's neck. Not to be left out, Tiger walked over and licked Dov's cheek. Dov wrapped a little fist in his fur as well.

Sascha watched the little group in amazement. "I still can't believe how good they are with him. He's going to really miss them."

The cats weren't going anywhere, but Sascha and Dov were. With everything going on, she and Yoni decided it was probably best if she and Dov headed out to Arizona to stay with her parents until Samyaza was found. It was only a precaution, but no one was interested in placing either of them in harm's way. Although, it was going to be awfully strange at the school without Sascha there as the mother hen.

Of course, it was *already* strange at the school. Once Laney had been made public enemy number one, a lot of families had pulled their kids from the school. Only the kids of those families that truly knew Laney—or the kids who had no family to speak of—were left. Just this morning they found Noriko gone. She'd left a note saying she was going away with Gerard. That had not eased anyone's concerns.

Lou smiled at Sascha. "We got the rest of the cats together. I thought Dov might like to take a walk with the full pack of leopards."

"It's a leap, not a pack," Danny said.

Lou rolled her eyes. "No one cares, Danny."

Sascha smiled. "I care, Danny, and he would love that."

"All right, little buddy. How about a ride on Snow?" Zach

picked Dov up and deposited him on Snow's back, careful to stay right next to him, his hands still on Don's waist.

A sharp intake of breath gave away Sascha's nervousness. Zach met her gaze. "I won't let anything happen to him."

"I know. Well, let's get this party started. We have a plane to catch." Sascha followed alongside Tiger, running a hand through his fur as Snow led the way down the path.

Danny watched them go, the sight of Dov on Snow's back reminding him of a scene from *The Jungle Book*, when Mowgli rode on the of the big bear Baloo. The rest of the teens at the school might have all had somewhat of a rocky childhood, but Dov was getting one that was downright magical.

"We lead an unusual life," Rolly said.

"True, but the stranger it gets, the more I realize I wouldn't trade it for anything in the world."

Rolly grinned at him. "Me, either."

CHAPTER 19

GALETON, PENNSYLVANIA

The little cabin was quiet as Drake approached. This type of rustic living was not what he was used to. Before he'd revealed himself to Laney, he'd lived in a three-bedroom luxury suite in the Bellagio. Room service, maid service, concierge—anything he'd wanted was only a phone call away. Now he was residing in a three-bedroom cabin that had creaky wooden floors, no insulation, and one bathroom that had not been renovated since the eighties. Yay for pink tile.

And yet despite the material losses, he wouldn't change a thing. Well, maybe a few less chaperones and one more bathroom. But he'd found a feeling of contentment since he'd linked up with Laney again that he could not remember having before. And although he would deny it to his dying breath, he had to admit there was a feeling he got seeing Patrick making tea, Cain singing to Victoria/Nyssa, even Cleo slinking in and out that was not . . . unpleasant.

He'd just finished his patrol of the perimeter. Henry had sent a dozen men, half Fallen or Nephilim to guard the place, but Drake still performed a perimeter sweep every ninety minutes. Laney had left three people incredibly important to her in his care. He had no intention of letting anything slip through his fingers.

A rustle of the leaves to his right caused him to whip around, the hair on the back of his neck rising. Cleo slipped into view with a huff that sounded suspiciously like a laugh.

"Very funny, furball."

Cleo huffed again. Laney's giant cat seemed to take great joy in sneaking up on him and showing Drake just how close she could get without his notice. Truth be told, he was a little unnerved by it himself. At the same time, he knew if she could sneak up on him, she could do the same to anyone else who attempted to breach their defenses. He did not mind *that* one little bit.

"Any problems?" he asked.

Cleo just looked at him before slinking back into the trees. He shook his head.

I'm asking a cat for a security report. Oh yeah, I've fallen down the rabbit hole.

Entering the cabin, he walked into a very domestic scene. Cain was putting the last of the morning's dishes in the dishwasher. Patrick was wiping Nyssa's face. Drake frowned, looking at her. She was cute, there was no doubt, but she was one messy eater.

"Oh, good job." Patrick wiped the last remnants of applesauce from her hands and undid the straps from the high chair, pulling her into his arms. "Oh, someone's getting so big."

Patrick's cell rang. He walked over to where it laid on the counter, jiggling Nyssa on his hip, and she giggled in response. Patrick's face fell. "It's the Church."

Cain turned from the sink. "You should talk to them. Avoiding them's not going to work forever."

"I suppose." Patrick caught sight of Drake and smiled. "Drake." He held Nyssa out to him.

"Um, shouldn't Cain—"

Cain held up his hands. "Up to my elbows in dirty dishes. Your turn."

"Uh, okay." He took Nyssa under the arms, holding her out awkwardly.

"She doesn't bite." Patrick swiped his phone from the counter. "Why don't you walk her around outside for just a little bit? She's about ready for a nap."

"Um, okay." Drake awkwardly pulled her into his side and stepped outside, pretending he did not see the amused glance between Cain and Patrick. Drake took a seat on one of the rocking chairs, placing Nyssa on his lap. "Okay. Now what?"

Nyssa looked up at him with those big blue eyes of hers. She blinked a few times, then let out a large yawn. Drake tucked her into his chest and began to rock. She snuggled into him, one hand wrapped in his shirt, the thumb from her other hand in her mouth. She yawned again, her eyelids starting to close. She flung them open a few times, trying to fight sleep.

"It's okay, little one. Go to sleep." Drake gently rubbed her back.

Her eyes closed. Her breathing evened out. He sat there contentedly rocking, just listening to the quiet and enjoying the light breeze. Even though, right at this moment, without Laney here, he felt like he was in a bad remake of *Three Men and a Baby*, he had to admit there was something enjoyable about sitting and rocking with Nyssa. He'd never really considered kids before. To be honest, he wasn't sure he *could* have any, at least biological ones. But right now, he couldn't help but think about him and Laney with a little girl with Laney's red hair and Drake's sense of style.

He chuckled. Laney seemed terrified of the idea of them having been lovers in a past life. He didn't think him sharing his visions of them in suburban family bliss would calm those fears any. Besides, to say they were nowhere near ready for that was an understatement. With the chaos of Laney's life, the conversation of "where do you think this is heading" was going to have to wait a long, long time. Drake ran a hand through Nyssa's hair. She let out a little sigh.

He leaned down, whispering in her ear. "But if it's all right with you, I think I might just let myself pretend for a little bit that you are mine and Laney's. And I promise, I will protect you like you are."

He smiled as she snuggled even closer. Before he knew it, his eyelids were trying to close. *Maybe just a quick nap,* he thought, letting his eyelids close as he held Nyssa securely.

Then his eyes flew open. *Oh no, I am not doing this.* As tempting as it was, he needed to do another perimeter sweep. "You'll just have to nap for the two of us," he whispered as he stood, careful not to wake her as he carried her back into the cabin, nodding at Cain.

Cain was sitting at the table with a crossword. He started to stand when Drake stepped in with Nyssa. Drake waved him back down, mouthing, *already asleep.*

Cain nodded, retaking his seat. Patrick's raised voice came from his bedroom as Drake passed it. *Sounds like Patrick's phone call is not going well.*

He pushed open the door to Nyssa's room with his foot and made his way to the playpen they were using as a crib. He carefully laid her down. He frowned as her brow furrowed. Grabbing the stuffed chicken from the corner of the playpen, he placed the toy in her arms and then pulled the blanket over her. He watched for a moment to make sure she was actually going to stay asleep. He'd been fooled before. Convinced she was well and truly out, he let himself out the back door.

He rolled his shoulders, relieving some of the tension in them. He was tempted to continue the nap he'd begun on the front porch. The sun was warm.

But instead, he headed for the trees. *One more patrol and then maybe a little nap.* He paused as he neared the security perimeter.

The woods had gone quiet. He couldn't hear any of the security guys. A tingle ran over his skin just as Cleo roared.

And even without Laney's ability, he knew exactly what message Cleo was conveying.

Danger.

CHAPTER 20

BALTIMORE, MARYLAND

Henry stood on the lawn watching the chopper carrying Laney and Yoni fly off. He smiled, feeling that at least at this moment in time, all was right with the world. Having Laney back here made the place feel like home again. It was strange. He hadn't known she existed five years ago, and now, having his sister by his side helped complete his world.

A tingle ran over his skin. *And there's one of the other giant pieces.* He turned as Jen walked toward him. She'd stepped inside to call about Noriko again. "Any luck?"

"Maybe. It seems Gerard chartered a plane."

"Out of where?"

"Martin State. It was recorded heading over the Atlantic. The flight plan says London."

He studied her, noting the furrow between her brow. "But you're not buying that, are you?"

Jen scowled. "No. When I get my hands on Gerard . . ."

Like Henry, Jen's acquisition of a little sister was new to her as well. She and Noriko had been spending more time together, but they still weren't highly bonded. Probably because their lives had been so different. Jen had been in and out of foster care since she was seven. Even before that, her mother wasn't exactly the warm and cuddly type. Noriko, in contrast, had been completely and totally loved by Aaliyah, the woman who'd raised her.

Henry knew Jen didn't entirely understand her incredibly trusting, naive sister. Jen had been skeptical of humans since she could talk. Noriko only seemed to see the good in people, and that included Gerard. And Jen had not exactly embraced the Fallen. But Henry couldn't quite shake the picture of Gerard's concern about Noriko after her last vision in the animal preserve.

"What?" Jen demanded.

He winced, knowing Jen was not in an "I'm open to alternative opinions" kind of mood. "It's just, I don't think Gerard will hurt her. He seems to care for her."

Jen looked like she was going to yell at him, but then her shoulders dropped. "I don't think he'll hurt her, at least not intentionally. But Noriko's been so sheltered her whole life. She is *not* ready to deal with someone like Gerard."

Henry had to admit that was true. Even unintentionally, Gerard could really hurt an innocent girl like Noriko. "It's going to be okay."

"I hope you're right."

"She's not a little kid, even if she seem like it sometimes."

"I know, I know. It's just weird having a sister I never really knew and jumping right into worrying about her."

"Another thing we have in common."

He smiled as Jen slid her hand into his, nodding in the direction the chopper had disappeared. "She'll be all right, too."

He smiled down at her. "Walk with me?"

"Happy to."

The two of them walked hand in hand. Henry breathed in deeply, the ring box in his pocket practically burning a hole through his trousers. He'd been walking around with it for two weeks, waiting for the perfect moment. But the moment had never appeared. He'd come to the realization that there was no such thing as the perfect moment, especially with the chaos that was their lives. Truth was, life wasn't perfect, but there were little moments, just brief interludes, where you could take a breather.

This was one of them. That gnawing worry that had been a constant in his stomach had lessened now that Laney was back with them and Elisabeta was in hiding.

Noriko was a concern, but he really did believe that Gerard would not hurt her. It would be dishonorable, old-fashioned as that might sound. But he had a feeling that being honorable was important to Gerard.

They walked around the perimeter of the estate without talking, but it was an easy silence, the silence of two people who just enjoyed being with one another. He glanced over at Jen. She looked happy, peaceful, which, with Noriko AWOL, was odd. "What's going on with you?"

She opened her eyes wide. "What? Nothing."

"No, something's up. You look . . . happy."

"Well, gee, I didn't realize I was walking around with such a sourpuss face all the time."

Henry laughed. "It's not that. It's just, I don't know, there's something's different about you."

"Actually, I wanted to talk to you about that." Jen wrung her hands as she fell silent.

Henry frowned, not sure where she was going with this. But even with the hand wringing, she still looked happy.

She took a breath, then laughed. "I never thought I'd be saying these words." She looked up at him, her dark brown eyes shining. "I'm pregnant."

Henry's world tilted left, and it took a moment for her words to register. "You're . . . you're . . . Are you sure?"

"As sure as five home pregnancy tests and one visit to a doctor can make someone."

Henry just stared down at her, shock rolling through him.

Jen grasped his arm, her smile fading. "Henry?"

He smiled, then laughed, grabbing Jen and twirling her around. "We're pregnant!"

Jen threw her arms around his shoulders, laughing as well.

Then Henry stopped, quickly putting her down. "Oh, I'm so sorry. Is the baby okay?"

Jen laughed. "The baby's about the size of a pea. I don't think a hug could do much to him or her."

Henry just smiled down at her.

"You're happy?" Jen asked.

Henry couldn't seem to bring himself to stop smiling. "Oh, Jen. You have no idea." He knelt down, pulling the ring box from his pocket, opening it. "I've been carrying this around, waiting for the right moment."

Jen's mouth fell open.

Henry took a breath. "Jennifer Witt, ever since you appeared in my life, it has gotten better. You've filled a piece of my soul I didn't know was missing, and now I can't imagine my life without you. Without us." He took a breath. "Jen, will you do me the honor of becoming my wife?"

Tears shone in Jen's eyes as she nodded. "Yes."

Henry took the ring from the box and slid it onto Jen's finger. Jen placed her hands on either side of Henry's face and kissed him deeply. In that moment, Henry wondered if someone could truly die of happiness. She loved him. She was pregnant with their child.

"I love you, Jennifer Witt."

"And I love you, Henry Chandler." Jen tugged him to his feet. "We need to tell Danny."

"He knows. I didn't feel it was right unless he was part of it. He helped me pick out the ring."

Jen looked at the ring in her finger. "I've never been much for jewelry. But this thing is so big, I don't think it can be called jewelry. I think it technically counts as a weapon."

Henry laughed. "That's what Danny said. We should call your parents and your brothers."

Ahead, the main house of the estate came into view. "Does Jake know?"

"Not yet."

"Well, let's go find him, and then we need to call Laney."

Henry kissed her hand. "Your wish is my command."

Jen leaned into his side, squeezing his arm. Henry pressed a kiss against the top of her head.

They stepped onto the path when Jen pulled him to a stop, her head jolting up. "What's—"

The main house exploded, the power of it throwing Jen and Henry into the air.

CHAPTER 21

GALETON, PENNSYLVANIA

Patrick rubbed his temple as the dull ache signaling the beginning of a headache began to form. He walked from his bedroom to the living room, hoping the change in environment might help his frustration level, which seemed to be rising every minute the conversation continued.

"Sean, I just don't see how that is possible at this moment."

On the other side of the line, Father Sean Kirkpatrick sighed. "Patrick, I realize you have a lot going on, but you *are* still a member of the priesthood. And that comes with responsibilities. You cannot turn down a summons from the Vatican."

Cain rolled his eyes from across the room. "Tell them to stuff it. You're busy."

Patrick covered the mouthpiece. "You're not helping."

Cain shrugged as he took a seat on the couch. "I'm not trying to."

Rolling his eyes, Patrick turned his back on the immortal to focus on the conversation. "Sean, surely the Church can understand that while I appreciate the need they have for information, my calling lies here at the moment."

"Your calling lies where ever the Holy See says it lies, Patrick. You seem to have forgotten that."

Patrick blew out a breath. No, he hadn't forgotten that. He was just all too aware of the human failings that often got in the way of an individual's true calling. Right now, though, taking care of Nyssa and helping Laney however he could was where he was supposed to be.

"Let me see what I can arrange. Perhaps in another few weeks, I could—"

"Another few weeks? Patrick, I am trying to help you here. You are making it very—"

The line went quiet. "Sean?"

No response.

Patrick pulled his cellphone from his ear to look at the display. *Call lost.* He frowned.

"What's wrong?" Cain asked.

"The call was lost. And I no longer have a signal." While the cabin was remote, the signal strength had always been excellent.

"That's odd."

Patrick shrugged, sliding his phone into his back pocket. "Well, at least that's a small reprieve."

"You don't need to follow their dictates, Patrick."

Patrick sighed, knowing Cain would never understand. He had been on his own for eons. He had come into being long before organized religion was even a thought. The idea of sacrificing your personal desires and wants for the greater good, to be determined by a separate body, was not something he could easily grasp.

Truth be told, Patrick was having a bit of a hard time accepting it these days as well. The more he learned about history through Victoria, through Laney, through Drake, through Cain, through his own research, the more he had come to question the Church's role and their mission. It had been more than a little world shattering. Since he was a boy, the Church had been the one constant in his life. His mother had raised him and his sister with a strict Catholic upbringing: no meat on Fridays, confession once a week, church on Sunday in your best clothes. There was consistency there, a comfort in its reliability. Jesus himself had always been a point of solace for him. Long before it become a trite cliché, whenever faced with a moral dilemma, he had found himself asking: What would Jesus do?

He still asked himself that. And protecting the innocent, doing what was right, even when it was difficult, was exactly that. The Church, however, seemed to disagree with him.

"I know it is not easy for you, Patrick. But you are one of the most moral men I have ever met. You will make the right decision. It is who you are."

Patrick looked across the room at the man who was now his closest friend and the world's first murderer. He respected Cain. He came at the world from a decidedly unique perspective. "Thanks. Now how about we go grab the little princess for a walk? Perhaps—"

Cleo's roar tore through the house, setting Patrick's pulse racing. He glanced at Cain for only a second before the two of them were sprinting down the hall for Nyssa's room.

CHAPTER 22

BALTIMORE, MARYLAND

The cellphone lay on Henry's desk, taunting Jake. He'd come in here to review the security reports, but he was having trouble concentrating. He glanced at his phone again before shoving aside the reports and picking it up. He held it for a second, then put it down. Mary Jane McAdams's number was displayed on its face. He'd been debating for the last hour whether or not to call her. He'd spoken with her yesterday, but Laney had gotten him thinking.

He picked it up. *Okay. I'll just ask how Molly's doing.* That was a good reason to call. She was still figuring out her powers. It was reasonable he'd be concerned about her. *You big chicken,* a mocking Laney taunted him from inside his mind.

Oh, shut up. He used his thumbprint to open the phone.

The building shuddered. His head jolted up as the windows exploded, sending glass shards into the room. With a yell, Jake dove behind Henry's desk. Part of the ceiling crashed over the desk, but Jake, pressed up against it, was spared.

Three more blasts sounded, but they were all farther away.

Jake crawled out from the debris, his ears ringing. His mouth dropped. The picture windows at the back of Henry's office were gone. Parts of the ceiling had caved in. He picked his way through the debris to the windows and leaned out.

"Jesus."

The wings on either side of the main house were a complete wreck. Fires burned what was left standing, but the middle of each was rubble. He pulled out his radio, wiping at blood that dripped onto his nose from a cut on his forehead. Wincing, he pressed his hand against the cut.

"This is Jake. I need a report."

"Fricano here. The front gate was hit, along with two explosions on Sharecroppers Lane."

"I'm at the main house. Looks like there was a double explosion here as well. Fire crews and ambulances on the way?"

"As we speak."

"Good. Call in all off-duty security. We need all hands. Evacuate all buildings, and anyone who can help, put them to work, but no one is allowed off the estate."

"Jake?"

Jake took a breath. Six simultaneous explosions. No incoming missiles, no warning. "Someone bombed the estate, Mark. We need to make sure this wasn't an inside job."

Mark paused before responding. "Roger. I'll make sure no one gets out."

"Good. And everybody needs to start looking for survivors."

"Roger."

"I'll oversee rescue efforts at the main house. Send Dylan to Sharecroppers."

"Got it."

"Any word from Henry?"

"Not yet."

"Okay. Jake out." Jake pocketed the radio and headed to the hall to see what damage had been done. He said a quick thank-you that the teenagers were safe at the animal preserve and had escaped all of this. He paused, looking over Henry's destroyed office. Where was Henry? And Jen, for that matter? With their speed, they both should have been here already. They were probably down on Sharecroppers Lane helping out.

After all, they were practically indestructible.

CHAPTER 23

GALETON, PENNSYLVANIA

Cain reached Nyssa first and swooped her out from the playpen where she'd been sleeping. Gunfire rang out somewhere in the distance. Patrick opened the closet door and unlocked the gun safe, pulling out the Remington 870 shotgun. He loaded the tube with four shells, chambered one, then loaded one more shell. He reached for an AK-47, shoved a magazine in, and looped it over his shoulder.

"What do we do?" Cain asked, Nyssa carefully clasped in his arms. She rubbed her eyes tiredly.

"We stay in the cabin for now until we can tell what is going on. Drake should be here any moment. But let's get into the hall. There's no windows. It'll be safer for her."

"I'll take one of those as well." Cain nodded toward Patrick's shotgun. Patrick grabbed another one and loaded it before holding it out to him. Cain ignored it, grabbing Patrick's arm. "If they make it into the house, you and Nyssa need to get behind me. Hitting me will hurt them."

Patrick wrenched his arm free. "I'm not using you as a shield."

Cain took the shotgun. "Yes, if it comes to it, *you are*. Because our priority is keeping this little girl safe."

Patrick met his gaze but refused to agree. Cain needed to stop trying to make up for past mistakes. And Patrick would never intentionally harm him.

"We'll see." Patrick strode for the door.

"You are one stubborn Irish man."

"I'm Scottish," Patrick tossed back over his shoulder.

"Even worse," Cain mumbled, making Patrick smile.

But the smile disappeared as the woods outside went silent. He crept out into the hall, waving Cain down toward the floor. Crouching low, Cain moved to the middle of the hall with Nyssa pulled to his chest while Patrick moved to the front of the house. The hair on the back of his neck stood straight up. His every breath felt like a shout in his heightened state.

Drake should have been back by now. Cleo, too. The fact that they weren't and that the woods had gone silent . . . Patrick swallowed hard.

He peered into the living room. Two windows lined each side of the front door across from him. There was also a window above the sink to his left. Too many openings. He couldn't cover them all at once.

A board creaked on the front porch. Patrick tensed. A shadow crossed the window, heading for the door. They stopped out side the door, waiting. Patrick didn't. He blew a hole through the door.

A scream sounded. Gunfire ripped through the door from the other side. Patrick dove for the kitchen table and flipped it over to provide cover.

The remnants of the door were kicked open, and two men burst in. Patrick caught the one nearest him in the thigh. The other one turned, but Patrick managed to catch the man in the ribs before he could bring his weapons around. He vaulted from his spot, kicking both men in the face before kicking their weapons away. He frowned, staring down at the men.

They're human.

Glass broke toward the back of the house. Smoke began to fill up the hallway. *Damn it.*

Nyssa cried out as Cain stumbled from the smoke, part of his shirt trying to cover Nyssa's face. Tears rolled down her cheeks, her face red.

"We need to get her out," Cain choked out before pushing Nyssa toward him. "Take her."

Patrick grabbed her. "What are you—"

"Stay behind me," Cain ordered, not waiting for Patrick to respond before moving to the door.

"No!" Patrick grabbed for him, but he had already stepped outside. A bullet tore through Cain's arm. Cain grunted, but somewhere ahead of them, a man screamed.

"Cain, no!" Patrick hurried after him.

But Cain just moved forward. A second shot rang out. Cain crashed to his knees, blood spraying from a wound in his thigh.

Patrick dropped next to him, shoving Nyssa at him and scanning the woods around them with his rifle.

"You are not expendable," Patrick said through gritted teeth. "Can you walk?"

Cain nodded.

"Now *you* follow me. And stay low."

Patrick headed toward the woods, scanning the area around them. A glint of metal on his left caused him to let off a volley of fire from the AK. A shot rang out, cutting into the tree next to them. Patrick grabbed Cain and shoved him to the ground while pulling the trigger. Cain scrambled behind the large oak, Nyssa screaming in his arms.

Patrick dove in after them. "You guys okay?"

Cain nodded, looking pale and unfocused.

Patrick gripped his shoulder. "Cain, stay with me."

"I'm with you, Patrick." Cain blinked hard, then slid to the ground.

"Cain!"

Nyssa scrambled out of Cain's arms, rolling forward.

"No!" Patrick leapt for her just as a gunshot rang out.

CHAPTER 24

BALTIMORE, MARYLAND

The sun was playing peekaboo through the clouds, and there was a light wind, making the weather perfect as far as Danny was concerned. Ahead on the path, Dov was happily riding on Snow's back, gripping her coat with Zach on one side and Sascha on the other. The rest of the cats all had appeared as they'd made their way through the preserve to the hill in the middle. Its apex provided a great view of the preserve and the land beyond it.

Rolly stepped closer to him, keeping his voice low. "What do you think about Noriko taking off?"

Danny studied him out of the side of his eyes. "What do you mean?"

"I mean, do you think she's okay?"

Danny nodded. "Yeah. I mean, I kind of get the feeling Gerard likes her. I don't think he'd hurt her."

Rolly pulled Danny to a stop. "Look, I think Gerard will make sure no one hurts her. Heck, I think he'd probably rip someone to shreds if they even tried to. I'm not sure why he's so protective of her, but he is. But I also think Noriko is really naive and way too trusting. I'm just worried he'll hurt her, not physically, but emotionally."

Danny had seen Noriko looking at Gerard, then looking away when he turned toward her. He knew there was some sort of connection between them. Noriko had had some sort of vision involving Gerard that convinced her he could be trusted. "I don't know what to say to that."

Rolly sighed. "Yeah, me, either. Anyway, she's a big girl, I guess."

Danny hoped Rolly was right. Ahead, Zach and company reached the path that led to the apex. Rolly tugged on Danny's sleeve. "Come on. Let's catch up."

Danny jogged next to him, spying his all-black chow-shepherd mix Moxy dart out from the trees, her tongue hanging out her mouth. She ran over to Danny, who ran a hand through her fur before she darted away again. He grinned. She really loved being out here.

It was a pretty steep five-minute climb to the top, but as always, when Danny reached it, he knew it was well worth it.

The ground stretched out, undeveloped for acres in each direction. The walls of the preserve had been colored so they blended seamlessly into the background. Here and there, cats dotted the landscape, appearing and disappearing from view as they made their way through the trees. It truly was like they were completely out of contact with civilization.

Lou stepped next to him. "I love it up here."

"Me, too," Danny said.

Dov let out a laugh as Tiger nuzzled his cheek. Zach grabbed him, tossed him in the air, then caught him. Dov grabbed Zach tight, a giant grin on his face.

"What is that?" Rolly asked from behind him. Danny turned around, following Rolly's gaze. A small object flew over the fence.

Danny peered at it, dread coiling in his stomach. "That looks like a—"

The object landed and exploded. Danny stumbled back. Three more grenades flew over different spots on the wall, each one creating a crater and setting the trees nearby on fire.

Gunfire sounded from the front gate behind them, causing Danny to whirl around. More objects dropped over the main gate entrance and exploded.

"What's going on?" Sascha asked, her eyes wide.

Danny stared at the fire that was quickly spreading from tree to tree, growing in strength and size along with his horror. "We're under attack."

CHAPTER 25

GALETON, PENNSYLVANIA

Laney had dozed off during the chopper ride from Baltimore back to the cabin. The vibration of the chopper, the safety she felt knowing Yoni was at the stick, made for a perfect combination. She blinked at the bright sunlight as her eyes opened.

Yoni grinned over at her. "I thought you were going to sleep the whole way."

"Hey. Sorry. I didn't realize I was so tired." She rubbed her eyes.

"No problem. I even dozed off a little myself."

"Oh, that's—what?"

He winked. "Just kidding. But it was close."

Smiling, she shook her head. "How much longer?"

"Maybe five. I should probably give them a heads-up so they don't shoot us out of the air." He grabbed the mic, adjusting the channel. "Attention, Ground, this is Yoni. I'm bringing in Little Bo Peep."

"Little Bo Peep?"

"You know, because for a while you'd lost all your sheep."

"I didn't lose them. I was staying away intentionally."

He shrugged. "Tomayto, tomahto."

They waited, but the radio was silent. Yoni clicked the mic again. "Ground, this is Yoni. You guys asleep down there?"

Laney frowned, peering out the window. She saw a flash in the distance. Then another one. Her heart began to pound. The chopper was too loud to hear anything, but she knew a gunfight when she saw one. "Yoni, the cabin's under attack."

Yoni cursed, starting to turn the chopper. "We're out of here, Laney."

"What? What are you doing? We have to help."

"I am under strict orders to keep you alive."

"My uncle is down there, Yoni."

Yoni's eyes were full of pain. "I know, Laney."

"And—and there's a girl. She's not even two. Her name's Nyssa."

"Laney, I can't. I promised Henry, Jake, even Drake."

Laney narrowed her eyes. "Turn the chopper back, Yoni, or I will jump."

"Jump? Are you crazy, you'd probably"—he closed his eyes for a moment, shaking his head—"float down like a little angel." He turned the chopper back toward the cabin. "Friggin' superheroes."

"I don't suppose you brought any toys?"

"That hurts, Laney, it really does." He hooked his thumb over his shoulder. "Black duffel."

Laney undid her seatbelt and climbed into the back. She hauled the duffel from the floor onto one of the seats. Unzipping it, she smiled. "Yoni, I love you."

"That's what all the girls say. We're coming up fast."

Laney grabbed a shotgun, looping it over her shoulder and pocketing the shells. She also grabbed a Glock, making sure the safety was on. She leaned forward. "Fly over the cabin as low as you can."

"I thought I was doing this so you *wouldn't* jump?"

"Well, it's the fastest way down."

He groaned. "If I had any hair, I'd be pulling it out right now."

"Well, then I guess it's a good thing you don't." She moved to the edge of her seat, her hand on the door.

Yoni glanced back at her. "I'll set down and find you. Be careful."

"You, too."

She opened the door and stepped out onto the skids underneath the chopper. It never mattered how many times she did this, her stomach always flipped like it was the first time. Holding on to the door with one hand, she took one last look at the trees below and stepped off into nothing.

CHAPTER 26

BALTIMORE, MARYLAND

The fire spread quickly through the preserve. It had been so dry that most of the trees were practically kindling. No one's phones were working. Danny was pretty sure someone outside the fence had a jammer. They wanted to make sure no one could call for help.

Lou had taken charge, hustling everyone to a spot out of the wind, but the smoke was beginning to reach them.

The cats encircled them, almost like a protective shield, but Danny knew there was little they would be able to do against the fire.

"What do we do?" Zach asked, Dov clutched in his arms.

"Can you guys get over the fence?" Danny asked.

Lou looked over at the fence. It was thirty feet high. "Maybe, but we wouldn't be able to take anyone with us."

"And we are *not* leaving anyone behind," Rolly said.

"What about the creek? Should we head there?" Sascha asked, her eyes red from the smoke or maybe unshed tears.

Danny shook his head. "The water's not deep enough. The fire will evaporate it quickly."

"We need an exit big enough for all of us but that's also not in flames," Zach said.

"And we need to remember, someone set this. And that was gunfire at the main gate. Whoever did it is probably still outside," Lou said.

"We need to create an exit," Rolly said.

Everyone turned to look at Danny. He didn't meet their gazes, turning instead to study the walls of the preserve. They'd added the opaque walls when Laney had become the target of the media. But they had also made them incredibly strong, strong enough to withstand a Fallen attack. They were made of reinforced concrete poured over rebar thirty feet high and sunk another ten feet into the ground. They were not going to be able to punch through it, and they certainly didn't have any equipment in the preserve that would help them dig under it.

"What weapons do the guards have?" Sascha asked

"Just sidearms," Danny said.

Lou looked toward the house. "And tranq guns."

"Does that help us get out?" Sascha asked.

"No, but it might help up once we get out," Rolly said.

Danny's mind had been scrambling, trying to figure out any way they could get over the walls, under the walls, through the walls. But without equipment, it was impossible. "The only option is the front gate. We can't blow or power our way through these walls. Once we get there, we can open the main gate."

"That's where the gunfire was," Rolly pointed out.

Danny watched a tall oak erupt in flames by the base of the hill. Some limbs crashed to the ground, setting the bushes below them on fire. "I know. But there's no other way. This fire's moving too fast."

Rolly and Lou exchanged a look. "We'll go over the wall and

meet you there. Hopefully we can take out anyone who's still there."

Sascha gripped Lou's hand. "That's too dangerous."

Lou patted her hand. "Everything is too dangerous, but this is our best hope."

As a group, they made their way to the front gate. No one spoke. The smoke was too thick for that. By unspoken agreement, one enhanced individual stayed with each unenhanced individual. Rolly took Sascha's hand and helped her. Zach carried Dov, and Lou stayed with Danny. Moxy stayed glued to his side as well. The cats spread out around them. A few had singed fur, but so far, according to Danny's head count, they still had all of them. They stopped at the creek to soak their shirts, pulling them over their mouths. But even with that small aid, the smoke was making it tough to see and breathe. They crouched as low as they could while still moving forward, but it did little to help.

Finally they reached the road leading to the main gate. The road itself was clear of fire, although the smoke was extremely heavy. Lou and Rolly went over the wall without a word as soon as they got everyone on the road. Zach led everyone forward, Dov still carefully clutched in his arms.

Gunfire ripped through the air. Everyone stopped, gazes darting to the wall. Zach and Danny exchanged a look, but neither spoke. Sascha squeezed Danny's arm with a trembling hand. He gave her a nod, trying to look like he wasn't concerned while he silently prayed that Lou and Rolly were all right.

The gate came into view. It didn't look damaged. Danny stumbled to the small box on the left of the gate—the gate release controls. He flipped open the cover and punched the release button. Nothing happened. He hit it again. Nothing.

He stepped back, studying the gate. This part of the gate was only chain-link, held in place by a few metal binders. Then there was a twenty-foot space and the concrete wall. They needed to get past this gate. Hopefully Lou and Rolly would then be able to open the heavier gate from the other side.

Danny coughed, struggling to speak through the smoke. He waved Zach toward the gate. "Zach, can you—"

Zach didn't even need him to finish. He ripped through the bindings holding the chain-link in place, then yanked the fencing back. He held it there as everyone, human and animal, scurried through. They all hunched low to the ground.

Danny stared back into the preserve. The road was keeping the fire at bay from where they were, but it raged on either side. And none of them was going to last much longer in the smoke.

Come on, guys, Danny prayed.

All of them were lying flat on the ground, trying to keep out of the smoke as much as possible. Dov was crying. Tears tracked through the soot on his face. Sascha was trying to comfort him, but she was shaking so hard, he wasn't sure it would ever be possible. He met Zach's gaze. Danny nodded to Dov. "If it comes to it, can you jump with Dov?"

Zach looked back at him, his jaw tight, and gave an abrupt nod.

Danny didn't say anything else. After all, what was there to say?

"Guys?" Lou yelled through the gate.

Danny opened his mouth, but the wind blew smoke right at him. A coughing fit seized him. "We're here," Danny choked out.

"The gate controls are broken. We can't open the gate."

CHAPTER 27

GALETON, PENNSYLVANIA

Drake's eyelids felt heavy. He struggled to open them, knowing there was something he needed to be doing. His hand drifted up his side, coming in contact with a small metal object.

What is this?

He pulled it out, and his thoughts cleared. He bolted up, his eyes flying open. Cleo lay only a few feet away, two darts in her. He yanked them out. "Wake up, Cleo!"

Gunfire sounded to his right—from the cabin. In a blur, Drake was racing through the woods. He saw Nyssa scramble away as Cain fell to his side, blood soaking his shirt and pants. A gunman leaned from around a tree.

Drake vaulted across a ten-foot space, knocking the man's weapon up just as he pulled the trigger. Grabbing the man by the throat, he slammed him into a tree. With a roar, Cleo's jaw locked onto the arm of his friend ten feet away. Drake sprinted to her, and with a quick snap, broke the man's neck. He went still, glancing around but sensed no other dangers. The only sound was Nyssa's cries.

"Cleo?"

The fur on her back lay flat. But then her head snapped up, and she bolted away.

"I think it's okay, Patrick. We're—" He turned around and went still. Patrick lay on the ground, Nyssa trapped underneath him. Blood spread beneath him from a gunshot wound in his back.

∼

THE AIR WAS quiet as Laney used the wind to lower herself down. Then a gunshot shattered the air. Laney's control fumbled. She smacked into a branch, scratching her arm before reestablishing control. She landed next to the house, trying to sense where the danger was. Nyssa's cries cut through the air, followed by Cleo's call.

Laney. Uncle hurt. Cleo rounded the house. She stopped for only a moment to make sure Laney saw her before bolting back the way she'd come. Laney sprinted after her, Nyssa's screams growing louder.

Cleo ran past the entrance of the house and into the woods, traveling only a few dozen feet. Laney crashed to a stop as she took in the scene in front of her. Cain looked incredibly pale, lying on the ground on his side, trying to comfort a screaming Nyssa. Blood stained his arm and leg. Nyssa clung to him, her eyes wide, tears staining her red cheeks. Drake knelt over her uncle, a large pool of blood surrounding him.

Laney stepped forward on trembling legs. "Drake?"

His head whipped up, pain slashed across it. "It's bad, Laney."

Laney knelt down, everything seeming to slow down as she watched her uncle's blood seep into the ground. She placed her hands over Drake's, where they were pressing down on the wound on her uncle's back.

"Yoni's landing the chopper," she said. "Get the stretcher from it."

With a nod, Drake blurred away.

"I'm here, Uncle Patrick. I'm right here." The catch at the back of her throat made it difficult to get the words out. She looked across her uncle to Cain. "Is she all right?"

"She wasn't hurt. Thanks to your uncle."

"And to you as well, I'm sure. Are you all right?"

His eyes were full of pain as he looked at the ever-expanding pool of blood around Patrick. Guilt laced his words. "I'll live."

Laney nodded, turning back to her uncle. The pool of his blood now soaked her jeans from the knees down.

And you better live, too.

CHAPTER 28

BALTIMORE, MARYLAND

We can't open the gate.

Lou's words were a death knell. The fire had run roughshod through the preserve. There was no safe place inside these walls. But it wasn't the fire that was going to kill them. It was the smoke.

A hand touched Danny's shoulder. Lou knelt down next to him. She'd jumped back over the wall. Rolly was leaning down near Sascha and Dov. He pushed her away. "Go. You can get out. Go."

Lou wiped at tears in her eyes. "I am not leaving you."

"Get Dov, Princess, and Moxy out. You can carry them," Danny puffed out, his head pounding.

Zach bolted to his feet and ran to the gate.

Rolly stared after him. "What is he—"

Zach crouched down, slipping his hands under the gate. With a roar, he straightened. The gate lifted three inches.

Lou and Rolly sprinted for him, each of them grabbing the

gate and pulling it up. They managed to get it to the top of their thighs.

Voice tight with strain, arms trembling, Lou yelled. "Go, go!"

Danny reached over and yanked Dov from Sascha's arms while pulling her to her feet. "Come on, Sascha."

Sascha needed little prodding. She ran for the gate, rolling underneath it and reaching back for Dov. Danny handed him through and clambered through on his own. He ran twenty feet away, but he could still feel the heat. The cats all streamed through behind them, Moxy and Princess in the middle of the pack. As soon as the cats made it through, they scattered, but Danny didn't have time to worry about that. He kept count as each one crawled under. *Twenty-four, twenty-five.* "Guys, that's everybody. Get out!"

The gate slammed down. Danny took a step back. His foot crashed into something. He looked down at a guard, his neck at an unnatural angle. Danny reached down and pulled the man's sidearm free. The attackers were gone, but Danny felt too exposed and jittery to stand there defenseless. A coughing fit caused him to bend at the waist.

Sascha stood with Dov a few feet away, her eyes large, her mouth open as she stared at the flames that could been seen above the high walls. Down by the entrance, three figures leapt over the wall. Danny let out a breath.

Okay, that's everyone.

Lou, Rolly, and Zach blurred over to them. Lou and Rolly stopped in front of Danny. He grinned. "Good to see you guys."

"Good to see—" Lou's gaze whipped past Danny, and she shoved him to the ground. Danny hit the ground, Lou covering him, while Rolly landed next to him with a yell.

Sascha let out a scream as a dozen bullets rang through the air. Lou blurred away in the direction the bullets had come from.

"Stay down," Rolly yelled before following her. A second later, the bullets stopped. Everything went silent. Shaken, Danny lifted his trembling head.

Lou reappeared with a scowl. "We got him. He was human, hiding in wait."

"And he's . . .?"

"Dead," Lou said, no expression on her face.

Danny winced, knowing that Lou was still recovering emotionally from her violent interaction with the Priestess's followers. Today was not going to speed up that recovery.

"Zach, Sascha, you guys okay? Is Dov okay?" Rolly asked as he appeared, blood splashed across his upper arm. He made his way over to them as Danny slowly got to his feet.

Sascha lay on the ground, curled around Dov, Zach across the two of them. Rolly paused as he reached them. He leaned down slowly to peel Zach off of them. "Zach?"

Sascha sat up, tears in her voice. "Zach?"

But Zach didn't answer.

"Zach!" Sascha screamed, clutching at his arm. Her terror cut right through Danny, because even from his position, he could see Zach's blue eyes staring straight ahead, seeing absolutely nothing.

CHAPTER 29

GALETON, PENNSYLVANIA

Yoni called emergency services for three of the guards. They'd been hurt, but their injuries weren't nearly as dire as Patrick's. Two guards had died instantly. Patrick had been placed on the stretcher and put in the chopper. Yoni and Cain would take him to the nearest trauma unit. Cain's injuries were already healing, albeit slowly. He'd changed into clean clothes, then slipped on his dark glasses before climbing into the chopper. There wasn't room in the chopper for anyone else. Laney tended to the other wounded until the ambulances arrived. Then she packed Nyssa and Drake into the SUV and headed for the hospital.

Laney had called Henry but had been unable to get through. The phone at the gate also kept ringing out.

Neither Laney nor Drake spoke on the short drive. The Cole Memorial Health Center was only a few minutes away across Pine Creek. Laney felt numb for the whole ride. Her uncle had lost a lot of blood. And as tough as he was, he was still hitting sixty. His body was going to react like a sixty-year-old's. When he got through this, it was going to be a long recovery.

And how do I keep him safe so he can recover?

And he wasn't the only one who needed a safe place. She glanced in the back of the car to look at Nyssa. She didn't know what to do with her. She needed to leave her somewhere safe, but where exactly was that? They had thought the cabin was safe.

The hospital was a white building ten stories high. Lights shone through the windows. Traffic moved in and out of the U-shaped entryway. An ambulance roared toward the emergency room on the side of the building, sirens and lights screaming into the night. Laney pulled over to let it pass, saying a silent prayer for whomever was inside. Then she turned into the parking garage.

Drake frowned. "What are you doing?"

"Parking."

"Just park in front of the entrance."

"That's not how it works." It was one of the most disconcerting aspects of modern life as far as Laney was concerned. Rushing to a hospital for a loved one, sick with worry and having to wait for the machine at the garage to spit out a ticket. Then you had to wind through the garage looking for a spot.

But the worst had to be the paperwork. You wanted to stay by your loved one's side, but you had to provide your insurance information and explain how you planned on paying to heal them. Pulling into a spot, she glanced back at Nyssa, who'd fallen asleep.

"I'll get her." Drake squeezed her hand before he stepped out.

Laney pulled her phone from her pocket as she opened her door. She tried to reach Henry again, frowning when the phone just rang out. Why wasn't he answering?

Drake walked over with a drowsy Nyssa in his arms. "What is it?"

"I can't reach anyone at the estate. I don't know what's going on."

"Hm." Drake's gaze shifted away.

Laney grabbed his arm, turning him back to her. "What does 'hm' mean?"

"It's probably nothing."

"Drake, what are you thinking?"

He sighed, absentmindedly rubbing Nyssa's back. "I've watched Samyaza for centuries. And one of the tactics he/she's employed regularly is a multi-pronged attack."

Laney's mouth fell open. "You don't think—"

Drake spoke quickly. "That's why I didn't want to say anything. It's just a guess at this point."

But the growing pit of dread that appeared in her stomach knew it was more than a guess. She brought up her phone and pulled up a news service. "EXPLOSIONS AT THE CHANDLER ESTATE" was scrawled across the top of the page.

"Oh God."

Drake leaned in to read the screen. "Laney, we don't know anything for sure yet. And your people have proven to be incredibly resilient. So let's just focus on what's in front of us right now, okay? Let's go see about your uncle."

Laney nodded, but a vision of everyone at the estate raced through her mind.

"Come on." Drake tugged her toward the parking garage exit. Nyssa reached out a little hand. Laney forced a smile to her face as Nyssa wrapped her hand around her finger.

Laney looked toward the entrance. Yoni and Cain were waiting just inside the hospital entrance. Neither smiled as they caught sight of Laney, Drake, and Nyssa. In fact, their expressions grew more serious.

Laney's stomach clenched as she prepared herself for the news.

CHAPTER 30

BALTIMORE, MARYLAND

It had been two hours since the explosion. Jake had helped over two dozen people out of the wreckage. He'd seen the remains of at least another six people. Emergency services had arrived quickly and helped with the search and rescue, but there was just so much ground to cover.

Jake wiped the sweat from his brow. His hand came back dark with dirt. It was like a war zone—not a reminder Jake wanted. He took a swig of water. In the distance, he saw the triage tent that had been set up. All the people he could see were walking carefully through the debris, looking for survivors. He pulled out his radio.

"Fricano, switch to channel eight."

Rescue was using channel six, but he didn't want certain things broadcast.

"Roger. Switching."

Jake switched channels. "Mark?"

"Here."

"Any word on Henry or Jen?"

"No. No one's seen them."

"Okay, let me know."

"Will do."

Jake switched back to the group channel.

Damn it, Henry. Where are you?

Fallen SIA agent Hanz Olsen walked to the triage tent, carrying a man with a bloodied leg. He disappeared inside, then reappeared a few seconds later at the other side. He paused, looking around, but catching sight of Jake, quickly made his way toward him.

Jake had hired Hanz after the SIA facility had been closed. The tall agent didn't say much, but he did his job. Jake hadn't had any problems with him. But now he had to wonder...

Hanz stopped in front of him, but his gaze was on the debris a few feet away. "There's someone here."

"What do you mean?"

"I sense someone. There's someone under the rubble."

Henry. Carefully, he and Hanz started moving the debris. Jake called over some of the other movers in the area. Every once and a while, the removal of one piece would cause the others to shift.

Jake was about to call for a halt when he heard something. "Hold on. Everybody quiet."

Nobody moved.

"Here." The voice was weak, but Jake heard it.

Heart racing, he carefully picked his way over the debris. "I hear you!"

"Here," the voice came again.

In a blur, Hanz appeared at Jake's side and started to move the debris. "They're here."

"I need help over here!" Jake yelled into his radio.

Dylan and Mark hustled over. "What have you got?" Mark asked.

"Someone's under here. I think it might be Henry."

Dylan studied the pile. "We're going to need a crane."

"We can move some." Hanz picked up an incredibly large piece and tossed it toward open grass.

"Uh, I'll go grab some ropes and gear." Mark took off at a run.

Trying to get to the survivors underneath was a painstaking process. Jake wasn't even sure who it was they were trying to reach.

Forty-five minutes later, they had half the debris removed.

"I can see someone!" Dylan yelled.

Jake hurried over to him. Four feet down, he could just make out the back of someone's head. They were covered in dust, but he thought the person's hair was dark and from their size . . .

"Henry?"

"Yeah." His voice was weak.

"Move, people! Get him out!" Jake yelled. As everyone doubled their efforts, Jake realized that, from what he could see of Henry's position, he had been holding up the debris to keep it from crushing him.

Finally, piece by agonizing piece, they got the debris off of Henry. It looked like an entire floor had landed on him—parts of the floor were embedded in his back, which was now coated with blood.

Jake climbed down carefully and touched Henry's shoulder. "Henry, we're here. Let's get you out."

"Get her out first."

Jake's gaze whipped to the space that Henry was hunched over. He had been wrong. Henry hadn't been holding the debris up to keep it from crushing him. He'd been keeping it from crushing Jen, who lay unmoving beneath him.

CHAPTER 31

GALETON, PENNSYLVANIA

The automatic doors of the hospital opened up with a swoosh. Cain stepped forward, taking Nyssa from Drake with a hug. "Is she all right?"

"She's fine. She slept most of the way," Drake said.

Cain ran a hand over Nyssa, looking like he was trying to assure himself that she truly was all right. Satisfied, he turned to Laney. "How are you?"

"I'm, uh, I don't know. How's my uncle?"

Yoni and Cain exchanged a look that sent Laney's stomach plummeting. "What?"

Yoni's words seemed to be carefully chosen. "He was taken into surgery. He's holding his own."

She looked between the two of them. "That's good, right?"

Yoni was quiet for a moment before he spoke. "Laney, the doctors are working on controlling the bleeding, but they aren't sure how much damage has been done. With injuries like his, there's a good chance he may not regain control of his legs."

Laney stumbled. Drake reached out a hand, steadying her.

"We'll need to wait and see, but we thought you should know," Cain said.

Laney nodded, feeling light-headed. Her uncle might lose the use of his legs. While part of her knew that the fact that he was alive was a win, the cost of this attack was high.

"But he'll be all right?" Drake asked.

"The doctors are very hopeful," Cain said.

"Hopeful?" Laney asked.

"Stop," Drake ordered. "You will not lose yourself in possibilities. Now, Cain is going to show me the OR. I will stand guard against anyone who thinks to harm Patrick or to inspire any medical staff who think they are allowed to do any more than their very best. All right?"

Laney nodded. "I'll go with you."

Drake kissed her on the cheek. "No, I think you'll follow in a few minutes."

"What? Why?"

"Because I think Yoni has more to tell you."

Laney turned her gaze to Yoni.

He nodded. "It's not good, Laney."

"We'll be waiting for you." Drake followed Cain and Nyssa to the bank of elevators.

Taking a breath to try and calm her racing heart, Laney turned to Yoni. Yoni, who always seemed to have a smile no matter the circumstance, looked serious. No, not serious—devastated.

"I saw the news headline," she said. "Something about explosions at the estate."

Yoni nodded. "There were six—front gate, Sharecroppers Lane, and the main house. So far, over three dozen have been confirmed injured, another eight killed."

"Oh God." She swallowed, everyone at the estate flowing through her mind, but three people stood out.

Yoni nodded, reading her mind. "Jake's fine, but he couldn't find Henry and Jen for a while."

Laney found herself listening to Yoni's words but staring at the hospital tile. It looked exactly like the floor tiles in the last hospital she'd been in. Images of the Chandler estate in flames flashed through her mind. She shoved them away, focusing back on the tiles. And even as she did, she wondered if she was going into shock.

"Laney?" Yoni touched her arm, his big brown hound-dog eyes looking at her with concern.

She took a breath. "How bad?"

"Henry's arm was nearly torn off, and his back was full of shrapnel. It can't start healing until all the pieces have been removed. Jen . . . Henry covered her, but she received a serious blow to the head. She hasn't regained consciousness." Yoni paused. "Did you know she was pregnant?"

"What?"

"Some shrapnel embedded near the baby. There's a lot of bleeding. She's still being worked on."

Laney didn't even know what to think. Jen, pregnant? And the baby, good God. There was no guarantee the baby would develop abilities, but even if it did, they wouldn't manifest until his or her teenage years. Right now, that baby was as fragile as any other baby.

"They have good doctors working on her and Henry. It will be okay, Lanes. You have to believe that."

She nodded, even though optimism was the last thing she was feeling. "Okay. They're alive. That's good. As soon as we get an update on my uncle, I'll—"

"Laney." Yoni's voice was somber. "That wasn't the only attack. They went after the cats at the preserve."

"What? Are they okay?"

"They got out okay."

"Okay, that's good."

"Sascha and Dov were there, too."

"What? Why—" Laney stared at him. "Were the kids there, too?"

Yoni nodded. "Lou, Danny, Rolly, and Zach were with them."

Laney's eyes narrowed. "Are *they* okay?"

Yoni looked away for a moment. His chin trembled. "Zach. He saved Dov and Sascha. Offered himself as a shield for them." Yoni turned back to her, his eyes wet with tears. "He kept Dov and Sascha safe. They're okay. Zach protected them, but Zach . . . Zach's gone."

Laney felt her world tilt. Zach. He was the quietest out of the foursome, even quieter than Danny. He'd only been sixteen.

Tears sprang to her eyes, and she had to speak past the lump in her throat. "The other kids?"

Yoni wiped at his eyes. "They're okay, physically, at least. They're at Dom's. So are Sascha and Dov."

Laney nodded, not knowing what to focus on first—the grief of the teenagers, the worry about Jen's baby, her uncle upstairs, the others injured and killed at the estate. There was just so much.

Yoni wiped at his tears and nodded toward the elevator bank. "So that's Nyssa. She's cute. She looks a little like you."

Laney gave a small laugh, because otherwise she was going to cry. "Yeah. So I hear."

"What are you going to do with her?"

"I don't know. We were hiding her out at the cabin. Because she's, well, special."

"Henry and Jen kind of special or your kind of special?"

"Victoria kind of special."

Yoni's eyebrows rose. "Oooh-kay. So you need a place to keep her safe."

Laney nodded. "Yeah, but I can't think of anywhere."

"Oh, I can."

"Where?"

"Well, it just so happens I know a guy with his own bomb shelter."

CHAPTER 32

Laney stood on the hospital's helipad as Yoni strapped a car seat into the backseat of the chopper. Cleo hopped up next to him, watching him carefully. Matt had sent a group of SIA agents, who now covered the hospital, easing at least some of Laney's immediate worries, but getting Nyssa out was critical. When she'd reached Matt, he'd told her about the attack at Göbekli Tepe. Matt thought he might know what Elisabeta was after, but he said he'd brief her when he saw her.

She'd finally reached Jake a few minutes ago. He'd assured her the bomb shelter and all its defenses had not been damaged. Seven, not six, bombs had been exploded on the estate. Someone had *planted* them on the estate, which meant someone was on Elisabeta's payroll.

Yoni's annoyed voice cut through her thoughts. "Cleo, you need to back up."

Cleo inched her paw back, her gaze on Yoni.

Yoni glared at her. "You know staring at me like that is not going to make this happen any quicker."

Cleo lay down, not taking his eyes off of him, her nose inches from the seatbelt.

"Oh, that's much better."

Cain walked the edge of the roof, jostling Nyssa and speaking quietly to her.

"We'll get her there, and then I'll head right back here," Drake said.

"Okay." Laney smiled in spite of the pain in her heart.

Staring down at her, Drake paused. "I can't help but feel like I failed you. You left me in charge, and everything just—"

She put a finger on his lips. "Don't. You are not to blame for this any more than I am, or Cleo or my uncle or Cain. The only one to blame for this is Elisabeta."

"But I should have been better. They never should have been able to sneak up on us."

Laney opened her mouth, then shut it, not sure what to say. Because the truth was, she partly agreed with him. "Look, we all get distracted. They hit at the right time. That's all."

"Well, I promise, Nyssa will arrive safe and secure at this hermit's home."

Laney smiled. "His name's Dom, and he's a good man."

"Who lives in a bomb shelter." He raised an eyebrow. "You have some odd friends."

"I have the best friends."

He leaned forward to kiss her forehead. "That is true as well. I will be back before you know it."

"Okay." She held him tightly, part of her not wanting to let him go. But she needed Nyssa safe, and she needed to be here for her uncle. But she simply could not split her herself in two to make both of those things happen. She stepped back. "Be careful."

"You, too." He headed to the chopper, where Cain was carefully adjusting the straps on Nyssa. Drake gave Laney one last wave before climbing in. Cleo was already curled up next to Nyssa's car seat.

Cain made his way to Laney's side. The two of them took shelter in the overhang by the elevator, waiting while Yoni started the chopper up. Cain breathed in deeply. Laney placed her hand in his, but neither spoke as they watched the chopper lift off and fly out of view.

Laney called up the elevator, and the two of them stepped inside silently. They rode the three floors down, also without a word. Stepping out onto the eighth floor, they walked along the hall, maneuvering around machines, unattended stretchers in the hall, and the occasional patient or member of the medical staff. Finally they pushed through the doors leading to the surgical wing, leaving the hustle and bustle of the hospital behind. Now as they walked, their footsteps echoed off the halls.

"She'll be all right, won't she?" Cain asked.

"She'll get to Dom's. And Yoni's right—that's the safest place for her right now. Tiger and Snow will stay there as well as an added layer of protection." She glanced over at him. "You could have gone."

Cain nodded. "I could have, but Patrick was there when I was injured. I plan on being there for him."

Laney squeezed his arm. "How's your arm? Your leg?"

"They're fine."

"You were shot, Cain. I don't think they're fine."

"They're healing." Laney studied him. Cain healed faster than a human, although not Fallen fast. But he still looked a little pale from the blood loss.

He caught her concerned gaze. "I'm fine, Laney. It's Patrick we need to focus on."

"I can worry about you as well. Worrying about him does not preclude worrying about you."

Cain was quiet for a moment. "Your uncle, he wouldn't let me shield him. He could have. It would have kept him safe. But he wouldn't do it. Why didn't he let me?"

Cain's voice was full of pain and confusion, and Laney realized he truly didn't understand her uncle's motivations. He had spent so long on his own, he'd forgotten what people did for those they cared about.

"Why did you offer to be their shield?" she asked.

"To keep them from getting hurt. Why?"

"That's exactly what he was doing for you. You didn't want them to get hurt any more than my uncle wanted you to be hurt. He cares about you just as much as you do him. Maybe you'd heal quicker, but you'd still be in pain. And we're not sure you can't be killed. He wouldn't take that chance."

"I don't deserve that. Look at all your uncle has done. If anyone deserves to continue to breathe, it's him. Look at the pain and suffering I have caused."

Laney stopped, pulling Cain to a halt as well. "You need to stop that."

"What?"

"Thinking you don't deserve to be treated well. Yes, you've done some things. We've all done some things. But you've also paid for eons for those crimes. And that long life, I think it had been a burden, a further punishment. You're right about my uncle, though, he is a good man. And he sees good in you." Laney linked her arm through his. "And he's pretty good judge of character."

Cain patted her arm. "Selfish as it is, I'm glad you're here."

"Selfish as it is, I'm glad you're here, too." The two of them made their way to the waiting room, which was empty. The OR was right down the hall. They sat for an hour and a half, flipping through magazines, pacing the room. Laney was torn. She wanted to be in Baltimore. Drake had texted her thirty minutes ago that he and Cleo were on their way back.

The OR doors ahead of them cracked open. A doctor in blue scrubs stepped out. She walked over to the waiting room. "Are you the family of Father McPhearson?"

Laney nodded, holding tightly to Cain's arm. "Yes."

The doctor nodded, glancing between the two of them. "He

survived the surgery, which is a miracle. We had to replace five pints of blood—that's almost his full body's worth. He is still in critical condition."

"What are the next steps?" Cain asked.

"Well, we'll see if he makes it through the night and if his blood pressure and heart rate stabilize. If they do, well, that would be a great sign."

"And if they don't?" Laney asked.

The doctor sighed. "His body's been through a huge trauma, and although he appears to be in good shape, in these situations, your body reacts to your age. So at his age, it's tougher for the body to repair. I'm afraid I cannot give you much better than we'll need to wait and see."

"And his legs?" Cain asked. "Will he have use of them?"

The doctor shook her head. "I'm sorry, but the nerves were completely severed. He will not regain the use of them."

Laney took in a trembling breath.

"Look, he won't wake up tonight. Why don't you two go home, get some sleep—"

"We'll stay," Laney said quickly. "We'd like to stay."

"Okay. He'll be in recovery, and then they'll move him to the ICU. There's a waiting room there."

"Can we see him?" Cain asked.

"Once he's on the floor, yes. But it will be at least another thirty minutes."

"Okay. Thank you, doctor."

She nodded, heading back through the OR doors.

Laney collapsed in the chair nearest her. Cain sat down heavily next to her. Laney felt numb, her mind empty. Actually, not empty, but she couldn't seem to grab on to any of the thoughts racing through.

She wasn't sure how long she and Cain just sat there, but eventually he nudged her shoulder. "Come on. We should get some coffee. I think it's going to be a long night."

Laney nodded, heaving herself to her feet. God, everything felt tired. Two cops stepped off the elevator as Laney and Cain stepped out of the waiting room. Laney groaned, knowing they were looking for her. They probably needed her statement about the cabin attack. She knew she needed to come up with a cover story, but honestly, her brain was fried. She couldn't think of what the heck to tell them. Right now, she really missed her old SIA badge. It had managed to get her out of these types of conversations in the past.

The officers headed straight for them. "Delaney McPhearson?"

Laney nodded wearily. "That's me."

The taller officer glanced at Cain. "We need to speak with you privately."

Laney gave a tired wave in Cain's direction. "You can say anything in front of my uncle."

Both men stared at Cain, or more accurately, the sunglasses he was wearing. They probably thought he was hiding a drug problem.

"It's fine, really. What do you need?" Laney asked.

"Right, well, the Springfield police have been trying to track you down."

Laney frowned. "Springfield? Illinois?"

The officer nodded. "There's a double homicide that needs your attention."

"Look, it's been a really long night. So if this is a Fallen incident, you should contact the SIA. I haven't been officially reinstated with them anyway."

The shorter officer shook her head.

"This doesn't involve the Fallen, at least not to my knowledge."

Laney frowned. "I don't understand. Why then do you need me?"

"Because the surviving victim asked for you by name."

Laney darted a look at Cain before turning back to the officers. "I don't think I know anyone in Springfield. Who's the victim?"

The female officer spoke. "It's a child. His name is Max."

CHAPTER 33

Laney felt the world tilt. "Max?" She clutched onto Cain's arm as she swayed. "The woman, the man, who—"

The officer referred to his notes. "Um, both are late twenties, early thirties. Tentatively IDed as Maddox Finley and Kati Finley."

Oh God. Laney's vision began to shrink at the edges. *Kati. Maddox.* "What? How?"

From the corner of her eye, she saw Drake step off the elevator. He met Laney's gaze as he hurried toward her.

The officer plowed ahead. "Preliminary indications seem to suggest it was a home invasion. The child was found a few miles away."

Maddox, someone killed Maddox. It had to be a Fallen. "Where is he? Where's Max?"

"He's with social services—"

"He needs to be in protective custody immediately. I believe the Fallen may come for him. God, does Springfield have the capability of fighting them?"

"All police departments across the country have been brought up to speed on the abilities of enhanced humans. And yes, Springfield has a S.W.A.T. team."

"Get them to Max. He's in danger, and anyone he's with is in danger as well." Her gaze met Drake's down the hall, and she knew he'd heard enough to understand what was going on. She looked over at Cain.

He nodded at her. "Do what you have to do. We'll be fine."

"Tell the Springfield police I'm on my way," she said to the officers before striding down the hall. Drake changed directions, joining her as Laney bypassed the elevator, pushing open the door to the stairwell. "Laney, what do you need?"

Need? She needed to scream, cry, hit something. She needed to do something to protect those she cared about instead of just sitting back waiting to get more bad news.

"Cleo. Where is she?"

"In the car."

"Good." Laney hurried down the steps. "I need to get to Springfield, Illinois."

Drake pulled out his phone. "I need a plane to Springfield. I'll be at the airfield in twenty minutes. Have it ready to go." He disconnected the call without waiting for a reply. "You okay?"

She shook her head. Kati and Maddox were dead. She couldn't say the words. Not yet. Because if she said them out loud, she was going to lose it. And she couldn't do that until the plane was on the way to Illinois. "I need to go get Max."

Drake pulled her to a stop, looking into her eyes, then he nodded. "Okay. Then that's what we'll do."

"You should stay. My uncle, Cain, Nyssa. They all need to be protected. Cleo will go with me."

"They are all being looked after. You know as well as I do that your uncle and Cain are not top priorities. Samyaza's already hurt them. Besides, with the security Matt sent, they'll be fine. There are agents all over the place. And you need me by your side."

"I can handle any Fallen that appear."

"That's not why you need me."

She grasped his hand, and he kissed the back of it, making the tears she'd been forcing back press even harder against her eyelids.

"Where you go, I go, ring bearer," he whispered against her forehead.

She leaned into him for a just a moment, just enough time to regain her strength. "Thank you."

But even as she felt Drake's arms around her, she wasn't really there. She was back in her old house with Kati, pacing the floor with Max when he'd had colic, clasping Kati's hand in joy as he took his first steps, sitting with Kati on their back deck in the early morning light, enjoying their coffee together. Movie nights on the couch, birthday parties for Max, laughing so hard they could barely breathe.

A lifetime of memories flooded her brain. Pictures of a life before the Fallen, before their destinies changed everything. Back to a time when their family was smaller but no less loved.

She shuddered, tears rolling down her cheeks as she clung to Drake. Newer memories replaced the old with Maddox in the mix. He'd been the father Max had never known. Then they had left to keep Max safe and away from all of this.

But it hadn't worked. Kati and Maddox were dead. And Max was now a scared little boy on his own. Where had it all gone wrong?

CHAPTER 34

YESTERDAY

SPRINGFIELD, ILLINOIS

The Monopoly game was getting brutal.
"Ah-ha!" Maddox yelled as Kati landed on Maddox's Boardwalk with its two hotels. Maddox snatched his card from the rows of property he'd picked up. "Let's see. That will be $4,000."
Kati blanched, looking at the pitiful amount of play money in front of her. She pushed a stray lock of her brown hair to the back of her forehead. "I don't suppose you'd take an IOU?"
Maddox shook his head, his long dark ponytail swinging with the movement. "Nope, cash only."
With a sigh, Kati slid all of her money over to him. "I'm out."
"You can have my money," Max said, sliding his own money toward her.
Kati kissed him on the forehead. "You are the best son ever. But no, keep your money." Then she leaned closer to him, whispering in his ear. "And beat the pants off Maddox."

Maddox kept his attention on combining Kati's money with his own. "I can hear you."

Kati stood up, winking at Max. "You were supposed to." She headed to the kitchen, but Maddox reached out and snatched her before she could go more than two steps. He pulled her into his lap. Kati let out a shriek.

Maddox nuzzled her neck. "Mad?"

"Not mad, just not sure your cutthroat Monopoly playing is the best example for an impressionable boy."

"Nope, I think you're just a sore loser."

Kati laughed. "Maybe a little bit of that as well." She kissed Maddox, then pushed against his chest. "Now let me go. I need to figure something out for dinner."

Maddox released her. "I made lasagna earlier. It's in the back of the fridge."

"You are the best." Kati ruffled Max's hair as she passed him on the way to the kitchen.

Maddox looked at Max. "So what do you say? Do we keep going?"

Max nodded. "Yeah, for as long as we can."

"You got it." Maddox cracked his knuckles. "But be warned: I take no prisoners."

∽

THE GAME WENT on for another hour before Maddox conceded defeat. Max pulled his pile of money toward himself with a smile.

Maddox crossed his arms over his muscular chest. "You weren't using your abilities to win, were you?"

Even though Maddox looked about as tough as a guy could look, Max was never scared of him. "They don't work like that."

"Hmmm." Maddox watched him.

"Are you mad?"

Maddox's mouth fell open. "What? No, of course not. I'm kind of impressed how you turned it all around."

"Dinner," Kati called from the kitchen.

Maddox stood up, and Max had to strain to see his face. Maddox held out his hand. "You know you are my best bud. Nothing will ever change that."

Max nodded, feeling a knot in his throat. Maddox frowned, then knelt down. "Hey, what's that matter?"

Max stared at the tabletop. "Nothing."

"Hey, look at me."

Max turned, looking into Maddox's face. He wanted to tell him. He wanted to warn him. But it would do no good. And he wanted his mom and Maddox to be happy for as long as they could.

"What's going on?"

Max just flung himself at Maddox and hugged him tight.

Maddox wrapped his big strong arms around Max. "Hey, hey, it's all right. I'm here. Your mom is here. We'll never let anything happen to you."

For a moment Max let himself believe that Maddox's words were true. That Maddox, who'd protected him and his mom time and again, would once again succeed. But he knew fate had other plans. He just hugged Maddox tighter as a tear slipped down his cheek.

Maddox stood, still holding Max to him, and walked into the kitchen. Max felt his mom's hand on his back. "Max, honey, what's wrong?"

"The bad men are coming," Max said into Maddox's shirt. The words slipped out before he could stop them. But when they were out, he felt relief. Maybe this time would be like all the other times. Maybe they'd be able to get away.

Maddox's muscles tightened for a second before he pulled Max away, placing him on the counter. He looked into his eyes. "Did you see something?"

Max shook his head. He couldn't explain it, but he'd heard a clock ticking for the last few days. When he'd woken up this morning, it was louder and ticking faster. And he'd known time was running short.

Kati looked at Maddox. "Should we go?"

Maddox nodded. "Yeah. We'll leave as soon as possible. I'll need to get some things set up first."

His mom's hand was shaky when she cupped Max's face. "It'll be okay. The bad men won't get us."

But he didn't say anything, because he knew that no matter what they did, whether they stayed or left, the bad men would get them this time.

Kati hugged him tight as Maddox stepped away, pulling out his phone. "It's okay, Max. Everything will be okay."

Max shook his head, his voice shaking. "No, it's not."

The clock ticked all evening. All through Max's dinner, all through Maddox's plans and Kati's packing. Maddox carried Max to bed, tucking him in along with Lamby. Max clutched his old stuffed animal to him, and Maddox knelt next to the bed, pushing Max's hair out of his face.

"We'll leave in a few hours, but I want you to try and get some sleep, okay?"

Max nodded, keeping his gaze on Maddox.

"Hey, hey, I know you're scared, but it's going to be all right."

Max nodded, not because he believed it, but because he knew Maddox needed to think he did.

"All right, then, scoot down." Max did, and Maddox pulled the blankets over him, tucking them around him. He leaned down and kissed his cheek. "I love you, Max, always and forever."

"No matter what," Max said, finishing their nightly ritual.

Maddox smiled. "You got that right. Now try and sleep, okay?"

Max nodded. He watched Maddox leave the room, his head almost touching the top of the doorway. Maddox was so powerful, it was almost impossible to imagine that someone could defeat him. But Max knew no one was invulnerable, not yet. And now Maddox had two very large weaknesses—Max and his mom.

The clock ticked away in his brain, a constant metronome keeping time to the minutes that passed. Max thought the ticking, loud as it was, would keep him awake. But it didn't. Its consistent beat lulled him into sleep, even as he fought it, and finally his brain succumbed. He slipped into oblivion.

And he stayed there, in a dreamless sleep, right up until the moment the clock stopped.

∽

MAX JOLTED AWAKE. The silence was terrifying after a week of the clock ticking away. A scream sounded from downstairs.

"Mom." Max scrambled out of his covers, his feet getting caught in them. Maddox roared, and something crashed downstairs. Max shoved his feet into his rain boots, clutching Lamby to his chest, his whole body shaking.

Mom. But where he normally felt the comfort of her presence in his mind, there was now an empty space. He took a step toward the door when someone blurred into his room.

Max's scream was cut off by a hand over his mouth. Maddox crouched in front of him. "We need to go."

Even in the dim light, he could make out the blood stained across Maddox's shirt. Some of his hair had come loose from his ponytail. Without waiting for a reply, Maddox picked him up. Footsteps pounded up the stairs.

"Hold on, Max." Maddox pushed his head to his chest, covering it with his hand before he burst through the window.

Max's stomach dropped right along with their bodies, but he barely had time to register their descent before they hit the ground. Maddox rolled, keeping the ground from touching Max. And then they were running, blurring down streets.

Max's ears were filled with the rush of wind. He kept his eyes shut tight, clutching Maddox's shirt with one hand, his lamb to his chest with the other.

A sharp sound though cut through the roar of the wind. Maddox slowed. Another sound cut through. Maddox stumbled. Max tumbled out of his arms, hitting the ground hard.

Maddox grabbed him by the back of the shirt and yanked him behind a car. He pushed Max behind a tire, pulling his weapon as gunshots raked the car.

Maddox turned to Max. "They can sense me. That's how they're tracking us." He took a breath. "When I tell you to, you need to run. You run as long and as far and as fast as you can, okay?"

Max nodded, noting the two gunshot wounds in Maddox's arm and chest. He knew they were already healing, but Max knew there was at least one Fallen and three humans behind them. A car roared down the street toward them.

Maddox's voice was fierce. "I will not let them get to you."

Max nodded, tears welling in his eyes, his chin trembling.

Maddox leaned over the car and let off a volley of shots. Two screams sounded. He ducked back down. "Okay. Get ready."

Max flung himself at Maddox, sobs tearing at him. Maddox clutched him tight. "No matter what happens, remember you are loved. You have always been loved."

Max nodded.

Then Maddox pushed him away. "Run, Max, run!" Maddox leaped over the car, throwing himself on the Fallen blurring toward them.

Max got to his feet and ran in between the two houses near him. Gunshots tore up the earth next to him. Ahead, a fence loomed, but to the right was a small gap. With barely a pause, he slid through. Footsteps sounded behind him but then stopped at the fence with a curse. In the distance, Maddox roared. A man screamed.

But Max didn't stop. He flung himself at the chain-link fence at the back of the yard and vaulted over. He dashed through the next yard and turned, going through a house at an angle from the house he'd just burst out from—just like Maddox had taught him. *Never run in a straight line. It made you too easy to follow.*

He continued running, going through yard after yard, never stopping, veering away from a straight path, never looking back.

He ran until his breathing was all but gone and his legs had turned to jelly. He sprinted across a road and didn't see the dip in the ground.

He tripped. His arms windmilled as he landed face-first in the drainage ditch. He pulled himself out of the water, keeping a grip on Lamby and crawled into the bushes on the other side. He couldn't run anymore. He didn't have any strength left, even though he knew he needed to keep going.

But his whole body was shutting down. *Run, Max, run,* Maddox urged him on in his mind. Max stifled a sob. *I can't.*

His eyelids closed, even as he tried to force them open. He had no choice. He gave in to the dark.

∼

A HAND on his shoulder woke him. "Son? Son, are you all right?"

Max looked up at a man in a bright yellow vest with a construction helmet, who was crouched down next to him. Sunlight had chased away the night, confusing Max for a moment before everything came back. The clock. His mom's scream. Maddox. His run.

He scampered back, clutching Lamby to him, letting out a whimper.

The man stepped back, and a police officer took his place. She reached out a hand but didn't touch him. "Hi there. Can you tell me your name?"

She had blonde hair and tan skin. She looked a little like one of his teachers. "M-Max."

The officer smiled. "Max. I bet people are looking for you. Why don't we call your mom and dad?"

A deep well of grief surged up inside of him. "They're dead."

The police officer started for a moment before nodding. "Okay, Max. It's all right. We'll find out where—"

"Delaney," he whispered.

"What's that?"

He looked up into the officer's green eyes. She had kind eyes. "Delaney McPhearson. She's my family."

CHAPTER 35

Laney's footsteps echoed off the wall as she strode down the long, tiled hallway in the S.W.A.T. training building. The flight to Springfield had been uneventful. Laney had even slept, although it seemed less like sleep and more like her entire system had crashed. It was too much all at once. Too much pain, too much death. The human brain could only take so much.

Despite the rest, she felt only slightly better. She'd spoken with Jake before they'd deplaned. Henry was out of the woods, but Jen and his child were still in danger. Her uncle had been moved to a room. Henry was arranging his transport to Johns Hopkins. Jake was overseeing the estate. Yoni was wrangling the cats. And no one had any eyes on Elisabeta.

Anger pierced through Laney. The lights in the hallway flickered in response. Laney took a deep breath, yanking the anger back. Elisabeta would be dealt with, but right now, she needed to take care of Max. She wasn't going to let her anger at Elisabeta get in the way of that.

"He's in the rec room. The building's not really set up for kids, but it's got a TV and some video games," the officer escorting her and Drake said.

Laney just nodded, not able to talk beyond the lump in her throat.

"Has he been playing any games?" Drake asked.

The officer shook his head. "No. He's just sitting on the couch, hugging his stuffed lamb."

The image elicited a strangled breath from Laney. She'd given Max that lamb the day he'd been born. She picked up her pace.

The officer made no comment, just picked up his pace as well. "Second door on your right past the hallway."

Two officers stopped as they crossed the hallway, recognition flashing across their faces as they caught sight of Laney. She ignored them, her focus on the open doorway with the sound of a TV coming from it. She stopped when she reached it. The room was carpeted with a brown commercial carpet. A small kitchenette was along the left-hand side. In front of her was a large flat screen playing some overacted Disney show. The back of a plaid couch faced her. Two officers who sat flanking the couch on club chairs stood as Laney entered.

She ignored them, focusing on the couch and the small patch of brown hair she could see resting on the armrest on the right.

Rounding the couch, Max came into view. He lay curled up, Lamby clutched to his chest, his eyes closed. She knelt down by his side and gently brushed the hair from his forehead back.

Oh, Max. He looked so young.

"I can carry him," Drake said softly from behind her.

"No, I've got him." She reached down to pick him up.

Max's eyes fluttered open. "Laney?"

She stilled her hands, looking into his face. Seconds ago, he had looked so young. But now all she could see were the changes that made him look older. She'd missed him so much. "I'm here, Max."

Tears filled his eyes and sobs burst from his chest as he flung himself at her. Laney clutched him to her as tightly as he had been clutching Lamby. "I'm so sorry, Max."

Max only cried harder.

She dropped to the floor and pulled Max into her lap, letting him sob, and she sobbed right along with him.

CHAPTER 36

WASHINGTON, D.C.

Nervous tension ran along Nancy Harrigan's shoulders and down her arm. She had just finished reading the report on the attacks on McPhearson's people. They seemed to have been caught completely unaware. She pushed the file aside, staring off into the distance. It was a smart move on Elisabeta's part, pushing Laney back on her heels. And she'd have to be. Elisabeta had just robbed Laney of her sense of security, her safe havens, and all of that had been right when it seemed she was about to get her old life back.

Nancy leaned over to her desktop and brought up the satellite feeds from Baltimore. The fire at the animal preserve had been put out, but the land inside the walls had been scorched. Miraculously, no animals had been killed. But there had been one casualty.

The Chandler estate hadn't been completely destroyed, but the bombs had done damage. The main building was devastated, as were a few of the houses on Sharecropper's Lane. They'd found twelve bodies so far, another thirty individuals had been taken to the hospital, including Henry Chandler and Jennifer Witt.

And then there was the attack on Delaney's uncle, the priest. It wasn't looking good for him, either. The scale and timing of the attacks was impressive. They'd all been hit almost simultaneously. The resources needed to pull that off were significant. And the fact that they were able to get bombs into the Chandler estate with all of his security—that was beyond worrisome. However, the fact that there had been no hint of any of these attacks was the larger concern.

Nancy's phone buzzed. She reached over and punched the intercom. "What is it, Melanie?"

"The President is asking to see you in the Oval."

Nancy's hand hovered above the phone. This wasn't going to be good. The President was supposed to be in a cabinet meeting right now. "Did she say what it was in reference to?"

"She said you would know."

"Thank you." She sat back, trying to discern how the President would interpret this new information. And she had a sinking feeling she knew. Slipping her shoes back on, she strode from the office. Fifteen minutes later, she was at the door to the Oval, which was being held open for her by the President's executive assistant, Neil.

Nancy nodded her thanks as she stepped into the room, her heels sinking into the carpet. The President looked up from behind the Resolute desk and waved Nancy forward, pointing to a chair in front of the desk.

So it's going to be that kind of meeting. Nancy took a seat. When the President was trying to win people to her side, she had them sit on the couches, with no barriers in between, as a way to build a connection. When she placed the Presidential desk between you and her, she was reminding you of the power of her office before she told you what was *going* to happen.

The President made some final notes on the iPad she was

holding before she placed it on the desk. "I take it you are aware of the events in Baltimore and Pennsylvania?"

"And Illinois," Nancy said. She'd received the news on the short drive over.

The President frowned. "Illinois?"

"Apparently another two of McPhearson's associates were targeted. A man and a woman. The woman's six-year-old son escaped, and McPhearson just dropped everything to go to him."

"I see. Has there been any progress in tracking down Elisabeta?"

"Some, but nothing concrete. We believe she may have gotten weapons from an overlord in eastern Sudan, but that hasn't been confirmed. And there are rumblings she may be in one of the former Russian states, but again, nothing concrete."

"Do you believe this is the end of Elisabeta's focus on McPhearson?"

"No. I believe it is only the beginning."

"We cannot have these incidents on American soil. Innocent Americans will be caught in the crossfire."

Nancy had to bite her tongue to not correct her. Innocents had already been caught in the crossfire. None of those that had died or been injured had deserved what they had received.

"I have spoken with Patine at Homeland and my joint chiefs. They agree that the situation needs to be handled by the best of our forces, and that is not Delaney McPhearson."

Nancy frowned. "I don't think I'm following you."

"I was allowing McPhearson to handle this, but it has spilled beyond her sphere of influence. And obviously she is not up to the task. McPhearson will be sidelined, and I have put a special task force together, of military and Homeland people, to track Elisabeta down and bring her to heel, using whatever force they feel is necessary."

Nancy's mouth went dry. "And what is Delaney McPhearson's role in this?"

"To be determined. She may be an asset to the search, but if she gets in the way, she will be handled. She's a former college professor, Nancy. Don't make her out to be more than she is. And to be honest, I'm not entirely convinced yet that she is completely blameless in her previous incidents."

"With all due respect, Madam President, I believe this is a mistake. I realize the situation surrounding McPhearson is unusual, but we know these enhanced humans exist, and she is the one equipped to deal with them."

"Then she can tell *us* how to deal with them. McPhearson was not elected to office, she was not appointed by the government. She was not trained by us. She is a woman who has taken it upon herself to insert herself into situations that she is not qualified for."

Nancy knew the President was wrong. But she also knew that despite the public showings of the President attending mass, she was a decades-old atheist. And she had no doubt those beliefs were clouding her judgment of McPhearson at this moment.

"And what is my role?"

"I believe it is best if you step back as well. Let the task force handle it. You will, of course, be copied on any of their actions."

The dismissal in the President's tone was clear. Nancy stood. "Thank you, Madam President."

With a nod of her head, she strode for the door, her feet sinking once again into the carpet, matching the sinking feeling in her stomach, telling her that they were all making a huge mistake.

CHAPTER 37

SPRINGFIELD, ILLINOIS

Drake carried Max from the police building and onto the plane, and he'd fallen into an exhausted sleep almost immediately. Laney felt just as tired. Now, as the plane taxied down the runway, she sat with her feet curled up under her and Max's head in her lap. She adjusted the blanket over him, making sure he was covered before resting her hand on his arm. Cleo lay half on the ground, half on the seat, one paw and her head over Max's legs.

Kati was gone. Maddox, too. It was difficult to believe. But she'd seen the crime scene photos. Drake had tried to keep them from her, but Laney knew she needed to see. Kati's neck had been broken. It had at least been quick. But Maddox—that had not been quick. And Laney knew that Maddox had spent his last breath fighting to make sure that Max had time to get away.

She stifled a sob, pulling it back, not wanting to wake Max. The Fallen had somehow found Max. That meant his child status was no protection. In hindsight, she'd been a fool to think it would be. After all, they had been under the orders of a woman who had rounded up dozens of children barely more than infants to find Victoria. Max, with his developing precognitive abilities, was no doubt a prize that Elisabeta wanted in her arsenal.

Drake sat down across from her. "You should eat something."

"I'm not hungry."

"When is the last time you ate?"

She stared at him in annoyance. "I don't think my eating habits are a priority right now."

"I disagree. You need to keep up your strength. Samyaza is targeting the people you care about to weaken you. To pull your focus. You need to keep the goal in mind."

"The goal? She—" Laney glanced down at Max, who was in a deep sleep, and she shifted to a fierce whisper. "Zach is dead. She killed Kati and Maddox. She tried to kill Victoria. My uncle may be paralyzed. And the list goes on. How the hell am I supposed to stay focused?"

Drake met her gaze. "No matter what happens, no matter who gets killed or hurt, *you* must stay focused. Because *you* are the one who can defeat Samyaza. If you are not in the fight, then there will be more children who lose their parents. There will be more people who are damaged beyond repair. The rest of us can fight, but you need to lead."

Laney bit her lip, feeling the anger, the loss, the frustration. "I'm not ready for this."

"You are. You were born for this."

"*Helen* was born for this. Me? I'm a former college professor who's now supposed to lead what, the world's armies against Samyaza? What about my background suggests I'm ready for that?"

"What would you do to keep Max safe? To keep Victoria safe?"

"Anything. Everything."

"*That* is what makes you qualified. You will do whatever is necessary. You will face the devil herself to keep those you love safe, and even those you don't. You are a protector. And no one is outside that protection. It is not just your divinely provided skill that makes you the leader. It is your heart, Delaney McPhearson. A good leader never asks more of her people than she is willing to do. And you will do whatever it takes. That inspires people. That makes people want to follow you."

"But people will die."

Drake nodded. "Yes, they will. But more will die if Samyaza is not defeated. And you know that. Right now, you have been knocked back on your heels, but you need to get back up. You need to fight."

"I know. It's just—" She bit her lip, looking away as hopelessness threatened to overwhelm her.

Drake walked over to her and carefully slid her from underneath Max.

"What are you—"

He sat down, pulling her onto his lap. "You have to be strong, Laney, but right now, you grieve. You cry. You scream. You do whatever you need to do. And when the world sees you again, you show them your strength. But with me, I'll take your moments of weakness. I'll hold you up until you don't need me to."

She closed her eyes, letting herself sink into him. "How do you know what to say?"

"I know you. You're the other half of me. Loving you—it's the easiest thing I've ever done."

CHAPTER 38

CAIRO, EGYPT

The plane touched down around ten a.m. Egypt time, three a.m. Baltimore time. The flight from Baltimore to Cairo had taken sixteen hours, with a stopover in London for refueling.

Noriko stepped out, bracing herself for the heat. The airport in Cairo was surrounded by a vast brown desert. She was surprised to find that while hot, there was no humidity. It was almost pleasant.

"Not much like home, huh?" Gerard asked as he stepped next to her.

She gestured to the palm trees that dotted the landscape. "Actually, it is, in some ways. It's more brown, more barren. But there's a beauty here in its barrenness, in the history that's seeped into the sands."

Feeling Gerard's eyes on her, she felt flustered and warmer than she was a second ago. "What?"

"I don't think I've met anyone like you before."

She looked up into his face, and in it were the faces of two small children that she saw in her mind's eye.

Yes, you have. She opened her mouth to answer, but darkness rolled over her.

Noriko looked around, blinking up at the Great Pyramid and across at the Sphinx. Torches raced across the sands. People crested the hill, charging toward her. Noriko's eyes grew large as she turned to run. But there was nowhere to go.

Her eyes popped open. She looked up into Gerard's face. She was lying on the ground, her head in his lap.

"There you are," Gerard said.

A man with a dark beard hovered in the background. Gerard spoke to him in Arabic before turning back to Noriko. "Our driver Nadir is worried. He wanted to call for a doctor. I assured him you would be all right . . . I was telling the truth, wasn't I?"

Noriko nodded, then winced as her head began to pound. "How long?"

"Just a few heart-stopping minutes. I take it you had a vision?"

"Yes. It was of the Giza Plateau. I think that's where we need to go."

Gerard looked to the east. "There will be too many people now. That plateau is the most popular destination in all of Egypt."

Noriko started to nod but thought better of it as the pounding in her head increased.

"Well, there's no help for that, and since I think you could use a little rest, I'll get us a hotel, and we'll go visit the site after dark."

"Okay." Noriko pushed against Gerard to sit up, but Gerard slipped one hand under her knees. Cradling her to his chest, he headed to Nadir and the waiting Mercedes.

"I . . . I can walk."

"Ah, but then Nadir would think me ungallant. And I cannot have that. Besides, that vision seemed to take quite a bit out of you."

"I'm just tired."

"All the more reason to save your strength." He lowered his voice. "Did you see where exactly the Omni will be found?"

"No. I just know we're supposed to go to Giza."
"All right, then. Giza it is."

～

NORIKO FELL asleep in the car and barely woke up to walk into the hotel. Gerard got them a suite and steered her toward one of the bedrooms. She mumbled her thanks, then promptly fallen asleep again.

She didn't wake until well after dark. She stretched. A glance at the clock showed it was ten p.m. She'd slept for nearly ten hours. The suite was quiet, so she grabbed her pack and headed for the bathroom, hoping a shower would clear the last of the cobwebs from her mind.

As she stepped out of the bedroom fifteen minutes later, Gerard was signing the room service bill. The waiter took the leather case from Gerard and let himself out of the room.

Noriko's mouth watered at the sight of all the food, and her stomach rumbled.

Gerard nodded to the table laden with dishes. "I took the liberty. I thought you might be hungry."

"Starving." Noriko quickly took a seat, pulled a linen napkin across her lap, and dug in. She looked up at him, realizing she was the only one who was eating. "You're not hungry?"

"It's not that. There's something I need to tell you."

From the look on his face, she knew it wasn't good news.

She wiped the corners of her mouth with a napkin, then placed it next to her plate. "What is it?"

"There was an attack back in Baltimore."

Noriko gasped. "Why didn't I see anything? I could have warned them. I could have helped."

"It's not on you. It was Elisabeta."

"Is anyone hurt?"

"Yes. There were a lot of injuries and some casualties."

"Who? Who died?"

"I don't know the names of the people on the estate, but there are about twelve of them."

"And my friends? They're okay?"

Gerard shook his head.

Noriko's heart plunged. "Who?"

"It was Zach. There was an attack at the animal preserve. He died protecting Dov and Sascha."

Noriko pictured Zach, his hooded eyes, the pain she always felt around him. But it had lessened whenever he was around Dov. She wasn't surprised he had protected Dov, even to the death.

Gerard reached for her. "Noriko?"

She shook her head, the action drawing attention to the tears she had realized were on her cheeks. She wrapped her arms around herself and stood on wobbly legs. "I just . . . I need a minute."

Her chest felt heavy as she pictured Zach the last time she saw him. They'd been watching *Aladdin* with Dov. He'd looked so happy. *Oh God, he's gone.*

"There's more," Gerard said.

Noriko could barely see him through the tears in her eyes. More? Wasn't this bad enough? "What?"

"Jen, she's pregnant. But she was hurt, and the baby—they're not sure if the baby is going to make it."

Noriko and her biological sister had been trying to get to know one another. Noriko knew she and Jen had had vastly different upbringings, but even with Jen's difficult life, she had a heart that was impossible to miss. She'd known Jen was pregnant, even before Jen knew. And she would a great mother.

If she gets the chance . . . Her heart ached, and she couldn't seem to think straight. She began to shake. "I just . . . I don't know what to do." She looked at Gerard through a waterfall of tears. "What do I do?"

He pulled her into his arms. "Nothing. Right now, you do nothing. You grieve. Everything else can wait."

CHAPTER 39

BALTIMORE, MARYLAND

The engine of the plane droned on, acting like a white noise machine. Laney dozed on and off but got no real rest. Every time she would start to drift off into sleep, her unconscious would remind her of the horrors of the past day. Now she ran a hand through Max's hair, adjusting the blanket over him yet again, as if somehow by making sure that no chill reached him it would make things at least a little better.

But it wouldn't. Max had lost his mother and Maddox. They had practically been killed in front of him. How was he supposed to come back from that?

And her uncle had been taken back into surgery. The call had come in an hour ago. He was fine now, just some unexpected bleeding, but it had been terrifying. What if she had lost him? That thought had led to thoughts about all those they had lost—Zach, the guards at the preserve, and the staff at the estate, potentially Jen's baby. The list just seemed to keep going on.

Laney put her hand over her mouth, smothering the sob. It

was too much all at once. They had known Samyaza would strike, but not like this. Not on so many fronts.

Drake stepped in from the cockpit and gave her a look.

Now what? she thought with growing dread before looking at Cleo, who lay on the ground at her feet. *Cleo, stay with Max.*

Cleo lifted her head and rose gracefully to her feet. As Laney stood, Cleo hopped up on the seat. She tucked her tail underneath her as she curled around Max, laying her head gently on his chest.

Laney quickly made her way to Drake. "What's happened?"

"No one's hurt. It's nothing like that," he said quickly.

She blew out a breath and ran a shaking hand over her face. "Okay, so what, then?"

Drake nodded to the window. "We have an escort."

With a frown, Laney leaned down to look out the window. Beyond the wing of the plane, Laney could make out the outline of a jet.

Drake dropped into the chair next to her. "There's a matching one on the other side."

Laney's pulse raced. "Elisabeta?"

Drake squeezed her hand. "No, and we're in no danger. Our escorts are courtesy of the U.S. government."

"What? Why?"

"That is the question. The pilots were informed that they should continue on their heading and that agents would meet us on the ground."

"Agents? From where?"

"That was not specified." He paused. "Are you sure all charges against you have been dropped?"

"According to Brett, I'm in the clear."

"Well, the government apparently has a new interest in you."

Laney pulled out her cell phone to call Brett, but Drake just shook his head. "That won't work. I already tried. They seem to be jamming our calls."

"Is that legal?"

Drake shrugged. "Believe it or not, I am not well versed in the legality of government actions."

"And they didn't give any clue as to what they wanted?"

"Nope. Just said we would be met by agents."

Laney looked back at where Max had thrown an arm over Cleo, holding her tight. Now was not the time for some government agents to try to push them around. There was way too much going on. She needed to focus on that. The plane darkened as the sun dropped behind the clouds, and thunder rolled.

"Hey, hey." Drake turned her to face him. "Enough of that."

Laney jolted, not even realizing she'd called on her abilities. "Sorry."

He patted her hand. "Well, let's not toss a tornado at the nice government pilots. It might make whoever's meeting us on the ground a little testy."

"I know, I know. It's just with everything happening, I don't have time to sit down and chat with some government bureaucrats."

"Maybe, but unless you've decided to live outside the law, I think we have to." He raised an eyebrow. "However, I think you would make a very sexy fugitive. In fact, I think up until yesterday, that's exactly what you were."

She shook her head, but a smile crept its way onto her face. And that was why Drake was good for her. He made her smile even when what she really wanted to do was scream. "No, we wait. We'll talk to them and see what the hell's going on."

"And if you don't like the answers?"

"Then I guess it's back to fugitives."

CHAPTER 40

As the landing gear lowered, Max stirred. Laney hurried to his side, kneeling on the floor next to him so she could look into his eyes when he opened them. His eyelids flickered open.

"Hey, Max," she said softly.

"Laney?" Confusion crossed his face before he gasped. "Mom!"

"Shh, honey, shh." She ran her hand along his face as tears filled his eyes.

"They're gone." His voice sounded so young.

"I know. We picked you up from Springfield, and we're about to land back in Baltimore."

Max took a shuddering breath.

"It's okay now, Max. You're safe. I'm here, Drake, Cleo. We won't let you get hurt."

The tears disappeared from his eyes. Once again she saw the old soul that lived inside him. "You can't promise that. No one is safe, not even Mom and Maddox. Their time was up. There was nothing you could do. Things happen when they are supposed to."

She had to stifle a gasp. "You knew."

Max nodded, and Laney had to remind herself she was talking

to a child. He seemed so grown up. "It was their time. But I'll see them again. Samyaza is reaching for her power. No one will be safe until she is stopped." Max blinked and looked around. Laney had the feeling he didn't even realize what he had said, and she felt a chill crawl over her. She knew Max was right, but to hear him speak without emotion—it was disturbing. What was happening to him? It was as if the little boy was being replaced with the ancient soul.

The tears reappeared. He reached for her. Laney sat on his left side as Cleo pressed in from his right. "I've got you, Max."

But his words played through her mind. He was right. No one was safe while Samyaza was free. *No, not just free, alive.* For the rest of the world to be safe, Samyaza needed to no longer be in it.

A few minutes later, they touched down on the runway and taxied to a stop. Laney stood by the door, ready to open it as soon as the pilots gave the all clear.

Drake stood next to her, his arms crossed over his chest. "Absolutely not. You are not going out there alone."

Laney sighed. "Yes, I am. You need to get Max and Cleo to safety if this goes sideways."

"*You* get them to safety. I'll take care of these little agents." He cracked his knuckles.

"Yeah, that's exactly why you are *not* allowed to do the talking. Besides, I'm the one they want to talk to. And I don't want them boarding the plane and scaring the hell out of Max."

He puffed out his chest. "Lest you forget, I am an archangel."

She scoffed. "Yeah, I've met three of you guys. You're practically a dime a dozen. I, however, am the only ring bearer."

"You're insulting my archangel status?"

"No, merely suggesting you're not as unique as you think."

"Maybe, but I do heal quicker from bullet holes than you do."

"They won't shoot me."

"Really? Because yesterday they would have."

A small finger a fear crawled down her spine, but she refused to let Drake see it. "They won't. Now, help me open this door."

Drake grumbled as he pulled the lever releasing the door lock. The door cracked open. "If you get shot, I am going to be very mad at you."

"Noted." She grabbed the front of his shirt and pulled him in for a deep kiss. Releasing him, she smiled. "It'll be fine."

"It better be, or every last one of them out there is currently enjoying their very last breaths on this Earth."

"Go." She pushed him toward the back of the plane. He gave her a stern look before heading toward Max. Making sure he was out of the line of fire, she pushed open the door.

Three SUVS stood facing the plane. A ring of heavily armed soldiers in green uniforms rimmed the plane as well. She did a double take at the Hummer with what she thought might have a Gatling gun on top of it.

Well, that's not worrisome. Maybe I should have let Drake meet them first.

The doors to the SUVs opened. Six agents in suits stepped out, three of each gender.

Laney looked down. There were no steps. The drop was about six feet. She could have sworn there was a button or something that would release stairs, but she didn't see anything that might do the job.

Oh well. She called up a shot of air as she stepped from the plane and lowered herself down. Two of the agents jolted, glancing at their partners. Touching down, Laney walked forward. "What's the meaning of all this?"

One of the agents stepped forward. "Dr. Delaney McPhearson, you are hereby placed in the protective custody of the United States government."

CHAPTER 41

INVESS, CALEVITNIA

The small country of Calevitnia was a former Russian state that achieved independence after the fall of the Soviet Union in 1991. Calevitnia's main industry involved sheep and fishing, although tourists had been arriving more frequently at the remote country to take in some of the incredible castles left behind by the former Soviet officers who had often summered along Calevitnia's largest lake.

The door to the plane opened. Elisabeta pulled her fur coat closer around her. But it was not summer now. The air was cool. It felt as if snow was in the air. A quick look at the gray clouds covering them made that possibility seem even more likely.

"This way." Artem extended a hand to Elisabeta to help her down the steps. He led her to a waiting Rolls Royce. A uniformed driver held the door open for them. Climbing inside, Elisabeta initiated the privacy window. "How long?"

"A thirty-five-minute drive."

"Fine."

The landscape of Calevitnia was nothing to boast about. Flat lands, barely a hill or tree in sight. It looked like a barren wasteland. Which explained why, for a country the size of California, it had the GDP of Mississippi.

Luckily Elisabeta had some excellent reading material to keep her entertained during the incredibly dull ride: the reports from the multiple attacks in the United States. She read through the injury and death reports. She frowned, realizing none of Delaney's inner circle had been killed. She'd been hoping one of them would be, maybe the mortals, her uncle or that annoying Rogan. But the uncle was most likely paralyzed, her former roommate was dead, and her brother's child was in a very precarious position. All in all, not bad. It would be enough to make sure that whatever decision McPhearson made next was not well thought out.

By the time she'd finished her review, the stone walls of her estate had appeared. She had picked the place up years ago, right after the fall of the USSR. It had been renovated and stocked within the last few years, as she'd known it would be needed. The large reinforced metal gates opened as they approached. Elisabeta felt the familiar tingle roll over her. Three of her Fallen were here. The rest of her army, all three hundred, were in strategic positions across the globe, just waiting for her word. She was so close to victory she could taste it.

Artem's phone rang just as they pulled to a stop. He glanced at the message. "The scientists have completed each of their parts."

"And they're still here?"

"As per your instructions."

"Excellent. As soon as I conclude my business with Sergei, have them brought to my library."

"Yes, ma'am."

The driver opened the door as a second car pulled in behind them. She headed up the stairs as two guards opened the front doors for her. A blast of warmth greeted her. She sighed. Much better. She peeled off her coat and gloves, handing them to a uniformed servant. Without a word, she strode down the hall to the study.

The study was lined with bookshelves, and a deep brown leather couch with a coffee table covered with more books sat in front of one wall. A desk had been placed in front of the large window overlooking the courtyard. She made her way to the small bar in the corner and had just poured herself a scotch when Artem appeared with Sergei Yanovich.

Yanovich was not an attractive man. His nose had been broken one too many times, and his eyes were too small for his large beefy face. He was a solid man, with a deep chest and the ruddy complexion of a man who liked to drink. Years of fighting had given him a body of scars attesting to his tenacity and his ability to overcome. In the world of organized crime, he was known as the Raven. When he appeared, death followed.

Sergei bowed. "Samyaza, a pleasure as always."

Sergei was not a Fallen, nor a Nephilim. He had no abilities, but he had trained in war for decades, leading one of the most brutal crime syndicates in Russian history. But Elisabeta had lured him away with a more tantalizing offer—the control of an entire country.

"I take it everything is in order?"

"Your supplies arrived at long last. I assume the hiccup has been removed?"

"He has."

Sergei smiled. "It is nice to deal with someone who knows how to get things accomplished."

Elisabeta ignored the compliment. "How many men do you have?"

"Five hundred. The forces of Calevitnia are pitifully under resourced and underpaid. Most will run at the first sign of trouble."

"And if they don't?"

Sergei shrugged. "Then they die where they stand."

Elisabeta finally smiled. "I do like how you think, Sergei."

"Coming from you, that is indeed a great honor."

"How long will it take?"

"My people are all just awaiting your order."

"Consider it given, Tsar Yanovich."

CHAPTER 42

BALTIMORE, MARYLAND

Protective custody.
Laney wanted to laugh when the agent said the words. The U.S. government was going to protect her? The same government who had been trying to kill her for the last year? The same government who was woefully unequipped to deal with the Fallen? They thought they were going to protect her?

Laney glared at the agents. "Absolutely not."

The agents stepped forward as one, each of them placing a hand on their service weapon.

Laney gaped. They were going to try and shoot her. What the hell?

A fourth SUV sped across the runway, coming to a screeching halt next to the agents. An athletic blond man with bright blue eyes stepped from behind the wheel.

"Everybody back down. Right now." Mike Witt, Jen's brother and Jordan's twin, strode forward, placing himself between Laney and the agents.

Mike held his FBI badge up. "I have been given authority to

personally escort Delaney McPhearson to the office, where we will wait for instructions. Anyone who has an issue with that can take it up with the director of the FBI."

Laney watched the indecision on the agents' faces, then they stepped back. With a nod, Mike turned to Laney. "You okay?"

"What the hell is going on?"

"I'm not sure. When I heard about the protective custody order, I got here as fast as I could."

"What about Max, Cleo, and Drake?"

"They're being placed in protection as well."

"Why?"

"That is above my pay grade."

"Wait, then how did you hear about it?"

"Nancy Harrigan's office called me and warned me to be on the lookout for something like this."

"Harrigan? Is this from her office?"

"No. The order came from Homeland. Look, I don't know what's going on, but someone is supposed to be coming down to speak with you in an hour. That's where we'll get answers."

"Mike, I can't stay here for an hour. I've got Max with me, Cleo, my uncle's in the hospital. And Jen. How is she?"

"She's holding her own. They've been trying to place her in a medically induced coma to help the baby. But with her abilities . . ." He shrugged, but his eyes gave away how worried he was.

"I'm sorry, Mike. But that's all the more reason I need to get out of here."

Mike nodded, his gaze sympathetic. "I know. But I think you're going to need to stay anyway."

Laney scanned the area, noting all the soldiers and the weapons they carried. Another Hummer sat idling over near the hanger. "Tell me, Mike, are all these weapons part of the *protective* custody?"

"Yes."

"And if I decide to turn down the offer?"

"They have been okayed to use those weapons," he said quietly.

Laney studied the ring of government forces. She knew she could take them out with a few well-placed lightning strikes. But people would die. And these soldiers were just doing as they were ordered.

"Fine. The government has an hour. But *only* an hour."

CHAPTER 43

The government official showed up at the fifty-seven-minute mark. Laney was trying to stay calm for Max's sake, but she wanted to scream. Here she was, twiddling her damn thumbs, when destruction had just been rained down on her family and friends.

Drake moved closer to her, turning so he was not facing any of the agents. He dropped his voice so only Laney could hear him. "Easy, ring bearer. Getting angry will only make the wait more difficult. And your powers seem to be a little uncontrollable today when you are angry."

She blew out a breath.

"Try visualizing something that makes you happy. You've seen my show. Picture me in all my Vegas glory."

Laney slanted her gaze toward him.

He leaned toward her, his lips just grazing her ear. "Then picture me in all my natural glory. That should distract you."

Laney felt her cheeks color as that very image of him sprang into her mind. Then the door opened and Mike strode in, followed by two soldiers, one male, one female. Laney disregarded them immediately, her gaze directed at the third unknown guest:

a tall man with salt and pepper hair slicked back. He wore a dark gray suit, and his chest pushed against the buttons, suggesting he'd put on a little weight recently. The man's gaze raked over Laney before settling on Drake, who'd turned around.

"We need the room," he said.

Laney glanced over to where Max lay curled up on the couch with Cleo. "How about if we give them the room and we find another room to talk in?"

Slick Hair glared. "*You* don't call the shots here."

The man's aide, who'd slid quietly in the room behind him, leaned up and whispered in the man's ear while gesturing to Max. The man gave Max and Cleo a hard glare. "Fine. Follow me."

Without waiting for a response, he turned on his heel and stalked from the room.

Drake briefly touched her hand as he passed. "Remember: Patience, ring bearer."

The soldiers followed the man out. Mike waited for Laney just outside the door. She glared at him. "Who is this tool?"

"You have just had the honor of meeting Jessup Hankton Ianson the Third, Department of Homeland Security."

Ahead, Ianson disappeared into a room. "Call me crazy, but he doesn't seem to like me."

"Well, he was the mentor of Moses Seward."

Laney groaned. Moses had been the Homeland agent who'd taken over the SIA facility and tortured Cain, along with the other Fallen taken from the facility. After his activities in that incident became public, he'd been charged with multiple crimes ranging from unlawful imprisonment to torture. "Great."

"Yeah, so just watch yourself with him. He's looking for a reason to tie you up." Mike went silent as they approached the room. He gestured for Laney to go ahead of him.

Ianson glared at Mike as he stepped into the room. "You're not needed here, agent."

Mike smiled as he leaned back against a wall, crossing his feet at the ankles. "Well, according to my director, I am. So I'll be staying."

Ianson glared at him again before turning his attention to Laney. "You have been placed under the protective custody of the U.S. government. You will remain in our custody until such time as the U.S. government is convinced you are no longer in danger."

Laney stared at him, waiting for him to continue, but apparently he was done. "That's it? Until I'm no longer in danger? Do you have any idea what my life is like?"

Ianson scoffed. "I've been fully briefed on your *ring bearer* delusion."

"Delusion?" Laney took a breath. Drake's voice wafted through her mind. *Patience, ring bearer.* "Why am I being held in protective custody?"

"We believe that Elisabeta Roccorio has targeted you. And after the events of the last twenty-four hours, it is safer for everyone if you are taken off the playing field."

"Taken off the playing field? I am *never* off the playing field. Elisabeta targeted everyone around me to get to me. Taking me off the playing field will *not* keep that from happening. I need to be out there, going after her."

Ianson's gaze was lethal. "Please. You have been allowed to roam all over this world, leaving a trail of destruction in your wake. You are a public menace. Personally, protective custody was not what I argued for you, so you should just be happy you're not sitting in a jail cell, because that's where you belong. I'm not fooled by any of this biblical garbage. Ring bearers, fallen angels, Nephilim—save it for the gullible. If I had my way that cat of yours would been shot on sight and you'd be in cuffs, so don't test my patience." He smiled without warmth. "Or maybe that cat of yours won't be around for much longer."

Patience, ring bearer. Drake's voice again slipped through her mind, but she could barely hear him due to the blood pounding in her ears. "Are you threatening Cleo?"

He shrugged. "I don't threaten. I tell you what will happen."

Laney's control on her anger snapped. The lights in the room flickered. Gusts of wind battered the walls. The soldiers jolted, stepping back nervously.

Laney stepped forward. "You think you know what a ring bearer is? You think you know what a Fallen is? One Fallen could rip through every soldier you've brought with you in seconds. And all you would be able to do is call their next of kin. Protect me? You don't even know what you are up against."

Ianson paled as the windows rattled. "I am a representative of the United States government. You will—"

"You can follow me. You can accompany me, but I will not spend one more minute here while the people I care about need me. And I would strongly encourage you not to try to stop me."

"I have a warrant that allows me to—"

Mike pushed away from the wall, holding up his phone. "Actually the protective custody order has been rescinded. Dr. McPhearson and her friends are free to go."

Without a word, Laney spun on her heel. She was done with this bureaucrat. But apparently he wasn't quite done with her.

"McPhearson!"

She looked over her shoulder at him.

"You claim to be this powerful person. But where was that power when your friends were being attacked? What good did it do you then? You think the United States government can't protect you or the people around you? Well, you haven't done such a great job, either, have you?"

"You're out of line," Mike said, his voice ringing with anger.

But Laney just walked out of the room, saying nothing. Because as ugly as Ianson's words were, there was also an undercurrent of truth to them. Even with all her powers, she hadn't been able to protect the ones she loved. At the end of the day, they just weren't enough.

She wasn't enough.

CHAPTER 44

After the dustup with Ianson, Mike wasted no time escorting Laney, Drake, Max, and Cleo off the airport grounds. Laney wasn't sure whose anger he was more worried about, Ianson's or hers. She could not believe how she'd lost it back there. She'd basically threatened them with her powers. She sighed. But what was she supposed to do? The government was trying to push her into a hole. That was beyond unrealistic. And they simply had no idea what they were getting themselves into.

Mike drove them to Johns Hopkins in Baltimore. Patrick had been moved there, and Jen was a patient as well. In fact, an entire floor of the hospital was filled with people from the Chandler estate. And Henry had bought out the few empty rooms for family members to stay if needed.

Jen was holding her own, but there was shrapnel close to the baby's amniotic sack. The doctors were debating when to go in to remove it. Henry had already had all the shrapnel removed from his back. And he'd healed, not that you could tell from the paleness of his face. He was terrified for Jen and his child. But even with that terror, he'd arranged for a specialist to be flown in from

Switzerland to examine Patrick. She was supposed to be the best in the world. And if she said there was no hope . . .

We'll deal with it. She squeezed her uncle's hand. He was strong. He was a survivor. He'd adapt.

She sat down in one of the chairs next to her uncle's bed. Cain was in the chair next to her. Drake had gone in search of a decent cup of coffee. Max lay in the bed opposite her uncle, and Cleo lay curled up with him. Matt Clark had managed to pave the way for Cleo. When they arrived, a service-animal vest was waiting for her. It was probably the first time anyone had seen a giant leopard acting as a service animal, but no one had even questioned it.

Mike was down the hall visiting with Jen. He promised to grab Jordan and the two of them would personally deliver Max and Cleo to the bomb shelter. Until then, Laney wanted Max nearby.

Matt appeared in the hospital doorway. He gestured for Laney to come outside. Laney nodded, leaning over to Cain. "I'll be right back, okay?"

Cain spoke quietly. "Do what you need to do, Laney. I won't leave Patrick's side."

She stood, heading for the door before crossing back to Cain and kissing him on the forehead.

He looked up in surprise. "What was that for?"

"To thank you for being here."

Cain's chin trembled, and he gave her a nod. Clearing her head of her worries for her uncle, she met Matt in the hall. Matt hugged her. "I'm so sorry, Laney."

"Thanks. But I'm guessing you're not here for just moral support."

"I'm afraid not. Mustafa sends his thoughts as well."

Laney closed her eyes, more guilt piling on. With everything going on, she'd forgotten about the attack on Göbekli Tepe. She hadn't called Mustafa to see how his sister was holding up. She promised herself she'd call him as soon as she finished speaking with Matt.

Laney held up a hand. "Before you tell me your news, how are Mustafa and Fadil?"

"Shook up. Mustafa escorted her back home to Cairo. He's taking a few days off to stay with his family."

"That's good. Do you have any idea what they wanted?"

"It looks like they were interested in four carved skulls."

"Carved skulls? I didn't think there were any remains at Göbekli Tepe."

"To my knowledge, these were the first ones found. Fadil thinks they may have come from India."

Laney's head jolted up. "You mean Dwarka?"

Matt nodded. "I believe so." He led her to an empty room down the hall. Matt closed the door as Laney sank in a chair. "But that's not what you want to talk to me about, is it?"

"No. Ianson jumped the gun earlier. The government has decided to take the lead on the Elisabeta issue, but that was all Ianson's work getting you detained."

Laney frowned. "What do you mean the government is going to take the lead on the Elisabeta issue?"

Matt ran a hand through his hair, and Laney realized she'd never actually seen Matt look so disheveled before. "The simultaneous attacks—they changed the government's view of this issue. I think the government was happy to let you handle it. But now, everything's out in the open. Elisabeta is basically declaring war on you and yours. And the government will not let a war break out."

She sighed. "I think they're a little late for that. So what is their great plan?"

"A coalition has been formed, composed of twenty different countries. They are discussing how to handle Elisabeta and the Fallen problem. You have been forbidden from engaging in any aggressive action against Elisabeta, although you are allowed to defend yourself."

Laney couldn't keep the derision from her voice. "Oh, I'm allowed to defend myself. How nice."

"The coalition is looking at multiple ways to handle her and they want you to be a consultant."

"A consultant? Are you kidding?"

"No."

"Do they at least understand the threat she poses?"

"I don't think so. They still think she's a human with dangerous ties and inclinations. They do not seem to grasp the supernatural aspect of her abilities and those who are under her command. They're viewing her like a terrorist, but she is so much more than that." He paused. "Will you stay out of it? Will you consult with them?"

Laney looked away. "For now. I need to regroup, figure out how to attack her and where. They can provide me that information. But you know as well as I do they won't be able to defeat her. She'll run right through anyone they send to take her down, any plan they create. And even if they want me out of the game, Elisabeta won't let that happen. She wants to defeat me. That's what all this has been about—weakening me before she strikes."

"Did it work?"

Laney hesitated before answering. Had it worked? Was she weaker now that so many had been killed, so many had been hurt? She rolled the questions over in her mind before shaking her head.

"I won't deny how much this has hurt. But she overplayed her hand. She hurt me too much. She reinforced that there is no line she will not cross. Which means that I need to make sure there is no line I won't cross to defeat her."

"Even if people will get hurt?"

"Elisabeta made it clear that people will get hurt no matter what I do. Stopping her is the only way to keep that from happening. So even if people get hurt, that's what I need to do. Yesterday was one battle, and we lost. But the war, *that* we're going to win."

CHAPTER 45

Matt had gone to speak with his government contacts. Laney now sat next to Patrick's bed, his hand clasped in hers. He'd fallen asleep about an hour ago, so Laney moved and slept in the bed next to him while Cain sat next to him through the night. She managed to talk Cain into taking a nap in the room next door. He was healing well, but he was too pale for Laney's liking. She promised to wake him if anything changed. The doctor had said Patrick was in the clear. His life was no longer at risk.

Mike had taken Max and Cleo to the bomb shelter early in the night. Nyssa was also there, along with Sascha and the teenagers. From her phone call with Sascha, Laney knew they were all struggling with Zach's death. But Nyssa and Dov were at least a distraction for them.

Laney tried to push all of that away while she sat with her uncle, but her fears of what Elisabeta was up to wouldn't leave her. Fadil had some photos of the skulls from the site, but they didn't capture all of the carvings. And the carvings themselves would take time to translate. Time Laney did not think they had. Besides, in her gut, she knew it had to do with Elisabeta's quest for immortality. A wave of exhaustion rolled over her. She stifled a yawn, trying to keep her eyes open. Her sleep last night hadn't exactly been restful. Her mind had turned over every detail of the last day, trying to figure out how she could have prevented the attacks. A completely useless exercise that only served to make sure that after a night of lying down, she was still tired.

"You should get some more sleep, too," Drake said quietly from where he was stretched out on the other empty bed in the room.

She didn't take her eyes from her uncle. "In a little bit."

Drake sat up, swinging his legs over the side of the bed. "Laney, sleep when you can. These attacks, they are not the end of Samyaza's moves. You need to find rest where you can, because the war is coming."

All the damage Samyaza had caused flew through her mind. "No, the war is here."

Heavy footsteps pounded down the hall, causing Laney to turn toward the door with a frown. Drake stood up, crossing the room quickly to stand in the doorway.

"I believe we have company." He stepped back from the doorway and stood behind Laney's chair.

A man in a dark green uniform appeared in the doorway. Behind him were another four men who took position outside the room. "Dr. Delaney McPhearson?"

Dread rolled through Laney. Had they reissued the protective custody order? Because she was not going through that again. She stood, her voice taking on a hard edge. "Yes?"

"I am Captain Jerome Fielding with the United States Marine Corps."

Laney nodded. "What can I do for you, Captain?"

"The External Threats Task Force has been convened, and I have been sent to retrieve you."

Thanks for the heads-up, Matt. The External Threats Task Force had been Moses Seward's operation, which didn't exactly inspire trust in the government's motivation for resurrecting it. She raised an eyebrow, nodding to the other soldiers in the hall. "Is this a *voluntary* request from the task force for my presence?"

"As long as you agree, then yes."

Laney grit her teeth.

"Laney." Her uncle's voice was soft behind her.

Laney turned quickly. "Uncle, I'm sorry we woke you."

"It wasn't you. It was the sound of military boots."

Captain Fielding stepped to the side so he could view her uncle. He saluted. "Corporal Delaney. The Marine Corps wishes you a quick recovery."

Her uncle slowly raised his hand to his forehead, returning the salute. "Thank you, Captain. You should go, Laney."

"I don't want to leave you."

"There's nothing you can do for me. And I would feel better knowing that whatever the government is planning, you are a part of it."

"I don't think I'm going to truly be part of anything."

"Well, they'll change their minds about that pretty quick after they see what Samyaza can really do."

Laney searched his face. "Are you sure?"

He squeezed her hand. "I'm sure. Go on."

Laney turned back to the captain. "All right, Captain. I guess voluntary it is."

Drake stepped away from the bed. "And I will be going as well."

The captain shook his head. "No. My instructions are just for—"

Drake took a step forward. "I'm afraid *that's* not negotiable. I am Dr. McPhearson's personal bodyguard."

The captain frowned at Drake. "Wait, aren't you Drake? I saw your show in Las Vegas last year with my wife."

Drake smiled, showing all his teeth. "It's always nice to meet a fan."

The captain turned to Laney, skepticism etched into his face. "You have a magician for a bodyguard?"

"Illusionist, actually," Drake said.

Laney tried to bite back her smile at the disbelief on the captain's face. "Yes. Where I go, he goes. I'm afraid that *is* non-negotiable, *if*, that is, we wish to keep this voluntary."

The captain's gaze shifted between the two of them. "I'll need to call this in."

Drake waved him toward the door. "By all means. Take your time. I'm sure there's no pressing international incident we need to see about."

With a hard glare at Drake, Fielding stepped from the room.

Laney rolled her eyes. "Really?"

"What? You don't want me to come?"

"I'm just suggesting maybe you could be a little less—"

"Disrespectful," Patrick muttered.

"Snarky," Laney finished.

Drake grinned at her. "But where's the fun in that?"

"Not everything's fun, Drake."

He took her hand, bringing it to his lips. "But you see, that's my job, to bring more fun to your life."

Fielding stepped back into the room. "All right, the *illusionist* has been cleared to join you. But he will not be allowed in the briefing."

"Well, I suppose we will see about that when we arrive." Drake headed for the door. "Why don't we give these two a minute to say goodbye, hm?" He strode through the doorway, not waiting for Fielding's response.

Staring after Drake with a look of annoyance, Fielding turned back to Laney. "I'll be right outside." Once again he nodded at her uncle. "Corporal."

Patrick returned the acknowledgement. "Captain."

Laney waited until the captain had stepped outside before turning to Patrick. She had to admit, showing respect to her uncle did win him a few points . . . but only a few. "I'll be back as soon as I can."

"Laney, do not rush back on my account. You stay and do what you need to do. They need you at this moment more than I do."

Guilt flowed through her at his words.

He reached out for her hand. "Hey, hey none of that."

"I should have been there. I never should have left you guys."

He raised an eyebrow. "With only an archangel, a genetically altered leopard, and a dozen heavily armed guards to protect us? Yes, it was an absolute dereliction of duty on your part."

"Don't joke. You got hurt, and—"

"I am well aware of that. Laney, you take on too much. You are not responsible for everyone who gets hurt, for everyone who gets killed. You cannot protect the world. You are only one person. And you do more than any one person would be able to. You cannot be in multiple places at once. And we all signed up for this fight. We knew what we were getting into."

"Even Zach?"

Sorrow flashed across her uncle's face. "Zach maybe more than most."

"How can you say that?"

"He was a Fallen, Laney. At one point in his history, he chose to come to this planet, to live among mortals. And in each lifetime, he made a choice of what to do with the abilities he brought with him. This lifetime, he chose to save his friends and those he cared about. Don't take that away from him."

Laney nodded, her throat tight. "He was just so young."

"He was. And there will be more young people hurt, killed, if Samyaza gets her way. You cannot stop all the damage she is going to do, but you can limit it. And right now, the best way for you to do that is to work with the government. So go, help them. Make them see what she is capable of."

She knew he was right. She knew she needed to go. But she wanted more than anything to stay. She hated leaving her uncle when he was like this.

"I'll be with him." Cain stepped into the room. "I will not leave his side. And Henry has guards here as well. As soon as the doctors clear him, we'll move him to Dom's. Henry said it should be within the hour."

"Who knew having a friend with a bomb shelter was going to come in so handy?"

Cain squeezed her shoulder. "We have this, Laney. Now go do what you need to do."

Laney reached up and grasped his hand, giving it a squeeze. Then she reached down and kissed her uncle on the forehead. "If you need anything—"

"I will call Henry first."

Laney reared back. "Henry?"

"He's a billionaire, honey. I'm not sure you even know where your bank card is. Besides, you always call him right after I request something from you."

Laney laughed, realizing he was right. "Fine, make a girl feel useless."

Her uncle patted her hand. "Never useless, only poor."

Laney choked out a laugh. "Well, that makes me feel better."

Patrick smiled. "Good. Now go give them hell."

CHAPTER 46

WASHINGTON, D.C.

Captain Fielding led the way across a tiled foyer imprinted with the seal of the United States. Laney and Drake had been driven from John Hopkins to the outskirts of D.C. She had expected them to be in some underground bunker somewhere, but they were led into an office building that looked almost identical to the other dozen or so she had seen since they'd turned into the business park.

One of the soldiers who'd accompanied them punched the button for the elevator. Laney noted it was heading down. Drake leaned in. "Ah, so now we head to the dungeon lair."

Laney rolled her eyes. One of the soldiers glared at Drake. None of them had been happy when Drake had said he was coming along. Well, none except Laney.

They all stepped in.

"So, where are we all heading? Some secret alien base?" Drake asked.

Laney struggled not to groan.

Drake had been needling the soldiers ever since they'd gotten in the car back at the hospital. So far he'd asked them who'd really shot JFK, if they'd seen the *Twilight* movies, if they felt the military provided them enough medical coverage, their favorite color, their views on the healing power of crystals, and the list went on. Laney thought it showed amazing restraint on their part that they hadn't shot him.

In fact, they hadn't spoken to him at all. And apparently they saw no reason to change that approach now. The doors slid open twelve floors later, leading to a long hallway with uninspired brown tile. The seal of the United States was displayed on the wall directly in front of them. The words "honor, integrity, and respect" written below it.

"Subtle," Drake murmured in her ear.

"Mr. Drake, you will have to wait here." Fielding nodded to a conference room to their right.

"Lovely. Bureaucracy chic," Drake drawled. "And where will my lovely companion be?"

"Down the hall."

"It's fine, Drake," Laney said before he could argue.

"I know it is, because if anyone lifts a finger against you, you will break said finger." Drake smiled, meeting each of the men's gazes. "And then I will break their necks."

Laney rolled her eyes. "You will not."

All humor dropped from Drake's face. "Oh, but if they hurt you or try to restrain you, I will."

One of the soldiers took a step back.

Oh, for God's sake. "Right. Great. Well, see you in a little bit." Laney turned down the hall.

"Have a nice meeting, dear," Drake called after her.

Laney just shook her head, not turning around.

Fielding leaned toward her. "Is he serious?"

"Not usually."

Fielding straightened. "I thought so."

"But he *is* serious about protecting me. But I'm sure we won't have to test that resolve, right?"

Fielding glanced at her but said nothing, which did nothing to tamp down the nervousness racing through her.

Two metal doors stood at the end of the hall with a heavily armed guard on either side. The guards nodded at Fielding and pulled the doors open.

Here we go.

CHAPTER 47

BALTIMORE, MARYLAND

Henry had an entire medical suite set up for Patrick at the bomb shelter. Jen had been moved in down the hall as well. Patrick fell asleep as soon as they got him settled in, and now Cain was looking for something to do. He didn't feel like wandering around the bomb shelter with all the new faces and his decidedly usual eyes. Nyssa was taking a nap with Dov, which left Cain feeling out of sorts.

He looked at the stack of Patrick's mail that someone had brought in. It had piled up from when they were in Pennsylvania. Cain still had millions hidden in bank accounts across the globe. He figured he could at least take care of some of Patrick's bills while he recuperated. It would at least make him feel like he was helping. Patrick would object, of course, but by then the bills would be paid and there'd be little he could do about it.

Cain spent the next hour going through Patrick's correspondence, only opening obvious bills, throwing out a ton of junk mail, which he decided must account for fifty percent of all the landfills. He finally made it to the bottom of the pile and spotted a large yellow mailing envelope. He frowned, picking it up. It was heavy. The return address was Rome, Italy.

"What are you doing?" Patrick asked.

"Ah, you're awake. I was just going through some of your correspondence, throwing out junk mail and the like." He stood up, moving quickly to the bed before Patrick could ask about the bills. "This was in there as well. It's pretty heavy. Do you know anyone in Rome?"

"Just Sean."

It took Cain a moment to catch the reference. Father Sean Kirkpatrick, Patrick's priest friend, although Cain wasn't sure the title "friend" should still apply. "Did he mention that he'd be sending you something?"

Patrick shook his head with a wince. Cain leaned forward. "Are you all right? Should I get the nurse?"

Patrick waved his concern away. "I'm fine, just a little pain, and no, I'm not expecting anything from Sean. In fact, I think he's back in the States. Why don't you open it?"

"All right." Cain slid the envelope open and pulled out a large stack of paper bound together by two rubber bands. He flipped through it, frowning.

"What is it?"

Cain removed the rubber bands and handed the stack to Patrick. "It looks like copies of an old book."

Patrick flipped through. "I don't recognize any of this. Is there a note?"

Cain checked the envelope before shaking his head. "No. That's all there was." He flipped the envelope over before handing it to Patrick. "It was sent from this address in Rome."

"I don't recognize that either." Patrick flipped through the later pages with a gasp. "Look."

The sketch was a little blurry, but Cain had no trouble identifying the subject: Victoria as a mature woman.

Patrick slowly studied a half dozen pages, then he looked up at

Cain, his eyes wide. "I think this might be the Tome of the Great Mother. Look, there are images of Victoria all over these pages." Patrick flipped to another page and gave a sharp intake of breath.

Cain peered down. It was a sketch of a little girl, an exact replica of the little girl in the room down the hall. "It's Nyssa."

"Someone does have a copy of the Tome. I wonder if it's someone within Elisabeta's organization."

"I doubt it. But is it possible there's more than one copy out there?"

"Well, we know that the followers split off to go into hiding. One group came to the United States and hid the book in Salem. Elisabeta has that copy. But it stands to reason there would be another group that would hide it somewhere else." Patrick leaned back. "Imagine it, a group hiding one of the greatest treasure troves of knowledge known to man."

"Or woman."

Patrick smiled. "Or woman. I wonder . . ."

"Wonder what?"

"Do you think it's possible the Followers still exist? That they've been in hiding all this time?"

Cain raised his eyebrows. "I've never heard any inklings of them, not for centuries."

"But you didn't know of the group in Salem, either."

"True. Well, how about once all this is over, we go take Nyssa and Laney for a little trip to Rome?"

"I think that would be great." The smile dropped from Patrick's face. "Assuming we're all still here."

"We'll be here, Patrick. Laney will be here."

"I hope so." He flipped back to the first few pages. "I don't recognize this language." He handed the first few sheets to Cain.

Cain glanced at them and felt his heart still. *It can't be.*

"Cain?"

"It's . . . it's the first language."

"The what?"

"When the world was young, there was one language that united the world. I didn't think any of it still existed."

"First language? How long ago are we talking? Thousands of years?"

"*Tens* of thousands. This is the language of Mu, Atlantis." He paused, the grief surprising him. "This is the language of the Garden of Eden."

"Before the Tower of Babel?"

Cain nodded slowly. "Yes."

"Are you sure?"

"It has been some time, but yes, I'm sure."

"Do you think you could translate it?"

"It might take a little time, but I think I could. But I don't understand who sent this to you. Or why."

"I don't know, either. But I know Laney is worried about what Elisabeta is up to. What her plan is. And I wonder if maybe this might have something to do with it. Let me see that."

Cain handed him the envelope. Patrick pulled the bed table over him, placing the envelope flat, next to his tablet, which he quickly brought to life. He typed in the address. He frowned. "That's odd."

"What?"

"The address. It's an orphanage."

"An orphanage?"

"The School of the Holy Mother. It's run by the Church."

"Is your friend Sean affiliated with it?"

"I don't think he's ever mentioned it, although I suppose he could be." He brought up the website for the school. Pictures of children of various ages, nuns in white habits with them, dominated the edges of the screen. "It's a school and home for the children. They are taught by nuns from the Holy Order of Maternal Love."

"Two mother references," Cain said slowly.

Patrick nodded. "That can't be coincidence."

"No, it can't."

Patrick nodded to the sheets in Cain's hands. "I think you need to translate that as fast as you can."

Cain stared at the papers in his hands, recognizing one word that all but leapt off the pages at him: *immortal*.

"Yes," he said slowly, "I think you might be right."

CHAPTER 48

WASHINGTON, D.C.

Laney stepped into the room. It looked like something out of a movie set. Two dozen screens lined the wall on one side of the cavernous room. The screens depicted different scenes of conflict from around the world. A large conference table that looked like it could seat about two dozen stood about twenty feet from the wall of monitors. Beyond the table, dominating the other side of the room, was row after row of tiered desks and monitors, with uniformed and non-uniformed personnel at each spot. None of the analysts at the desks glanced up as Laney stepped into the room, but the crowd of ten men surrounding the table all stopped their conversation and looked her over.

Laney struggled not to squirm under their gaze, suddenly feeling self-conscious about her jeans, boots, and the sweatshirt with "Pennsylvania" emblazoned across it that Drake had picked up for her in the hospital gift shop. She was pretty sure they were all wondering who let the college kid in.

But you're not a college kid. You're the ring bearer, a voice reminded her from the recesses of her mind. Laney straightened her shoulders, meeting each of the men's probing gazes with one of her own.

"This way, Dr. McPhearson." Fielding headed toward the conference table.

Laney kept her gaze straight as she followed him.

A tall man in a gray suit separated himself from the group, meeting them halfway.

"Captain Fielding." He turned to Delaney. "I am Kurt Reyes, Department of Defense."

Laney shook his hand. "Kurt, I'm Delaney McPhearson."

"I'm afraid we don't have time for introductions. Some new intel has just come in, and we need to move on it."

Laney frowned, not sure what to make of that statement. "All right."

As Laney took the seat that Fielding indicated, she surreptitiously read the tag of the soldier across from her—Maldonado. She'd felt the telltale signal as she stepped into the room. She didn't meet Laney's gaze, but Laney felt the eyes of another on her, the man in front of Maldonado. If she'd seen him on the street, her gaze would have slipped right over him. He was balding with a rim of hair around his scalp, no chin to speak of and perfectly round glasses. He looked like the guy you would cast if you were looking for a mousy accountant. But Laney knew who he actually was: Bruce Heller, Deputy Director of the CIA.

Interesting.

Reyes stood at the front of the table, nodding as everyone sat down. "We just received a recording involving Elisabeta Roccorio."

"Where?" someone down the table demanded.

"Tokar, Sudan." The screens behind Reyes coalesced into one.

Laney tensed, knowing whatever she was about to see would no doubt be brutal. She studied the men around the table, wondering just how much they knew about who Elisabeta truly was. And whether what they were about to see would confirm for them their fears or increase them.

As the screen flickered to life, Laney felt a collective tension spread across the table.

Okay, Elisabeta. Let's see what new horror you've created.

∽

THE SUDAN VIDEO had been taken from a security camera inside General NaNomi Mansur's home. It had been brutal. And that had led to a long, drawn-out conversation on what Elisabeta was capable of. Sad to say, most still didn't believe what their eyes were showing them. Laney was more than glad when a thirty-minute recess was called. She headed down the hall to Drake, and a few minutes later they were stepping outside, along with their military escort.

Laney and Drake stepped away from the escort, who stayed by the entrance to the building.

"So how's it going in there?" Drake asked.

"It's painful. None of them want to believe what is right in front of their faces." She paused, thinking of the CIA deputy director. "Actually, I think one of them already understands very well what the Fallen are capable of."

Laney's phone rang. She pulled it out of her pocket. She really didn't want to speak with anyone. But she saw Cain was trying to Facetime her and quickly answered it. "Cain? Is my uncle all right?"

"Yes, yes, he's fine." Cain looked pale, his eyes almost haunted.

"What's going on? Are you all right?"

"I think I know what Elisabeta is up to."

"Hold on." Laney walked briskly away from the building. Drake stayed where he was to keep anyone from listening in. "What is it?"

Cain quickly explained about the package from the unknown sender.

"Wait, it's written in the first language?"

"Yes, but I can read it. I translated the first few pages." He took a breath, and Laney had the impression he was trying to steel himself. "It talks about your mother's early time on Earth, a time when she went by the name Gaia."

Gaia, the first Greek goddess from which all life was supposed to have sprung. The name was known within the academic world, but it was attached more to myth than history. Most people these days, if they were familiar with the name at all, knew it for its connection to a series of yoga videos.

According to legend, though, Gaia healed, nurtured, and supported all life on the planet, and all life and health ultimately depended on her. There were even some myths about her rebelling against the leader of the heavenly gods. Her children were the Titans, who were later imprisoned by Zeus. Some even maintained that it was Gaia who was behind the Oracle of Delphi, and in ancient Greece, oaths sworn in her name were considered the most binding of all. There was even one myth that she made a minor Greek god named Aristaeus immortal.

"I didn't realize that was her."

"It was. Before she became known as Lilith, she was the Earth Mother."

"What does this have to do with Elisabeta?"

"One of the topics touched upon in the pages is immortality."

"Victoria and I spoke about how early humans were essentially immortal. That she took that immortality from them."

"Yes. The pages go into that in quite a bit of detail. But that's not the immortality I'm talking about." He paused, and Laney braced herself, fearing she knew where he was going with this. "It also mentions how to reattain immortality."

"Reattain? You mean through Nyssa's blood?" Nyssa's blood, if ingested, could make someone immortal, but it required a full adult body's worth.

"No. There is another way. The writers call it mortus."

"Mortus?"

"Roughly translated, it means victory over death."

Laney closed her eyes. *Damn it.* "How?"

"An individual would need two things: the Omni and some of Nyssa's blood."

An image of the skulls from Göbekli Type flashed through her mind. The skulls had come from Dwarka. What if the priests had actually written down the instructions for how to make the Omni? That would explain why Elisabeta had attacked the site.

Cain's voice cut through her thoughts. "Laney? Is that why they attacked the cabin? Were they trying to get Nyssa's blood?"

"Maybe. How much blood do they need?"

"Not much. A few milliliters."

"Elisabeta may already have that."

"I thought you and Drake destroyed all the blood?"

"What we found in the lab, we did. But if Elisabeta knew about the blood link, she would have made sure to secure enough for that as a backup plan."

"But she didn't have the Omni."

"No, she didn't. But she is someone who plans. She would have made sure she had the blood available should her attempt at bleeding Nyssa have failed."

Cain winced. "To do that to a child . . ."

"I know. How is Nyssa?"

"She's all right. She seems quite taken with Dov."

Laney smiled, picturing the two little ones. "Well, if he's anything like his father, Nyssa will love him. Any ill effects from the attack?"

"I don't think so. She's snuggled up with Patrick for a few naps, and Cleo has been staying by her side, which I think makes her feel safe."

Laney knew that feeling well. She missed having Cleo by her side. But right now, she preferred having Cleo with Nyssa.

"What are you going to do about Elisabeta?" Cain asked, returning to the topic at hand.

Laney blew out a breath. "I don't know. This committee seems more interested in listening to themselves speak than listening to what anyone else has to say. And no one seems to believe what Elisabeta is capable of. But if this is true, I need to speak with them. And hope they believe me."

"You think they won't?"

"Yes, I think they won't. They have enough trouble accepting what *I* can do, even with everything that happened in Jerusalem, so getting them to accept that we need to stop Elisabeta before she becomes immortal? Not sure they are going to be able to get behind that."

"So what do we do?"

"Pray."

"There's one other thing." Cain's voice was hesitant.

Dread spooled through Laney. "What?"

"There's also something in here about the Omni and the ring bearer." Cain paused.

Her dread increased. "What does it say?"

"It says that if the ring bearer ingests the Omni, she will receive the greatest gift and the greatest punishment known to mankind."

Laney immediately knew what he was referring to. "I'd be immortal."

"That's how your uncle and I interpret it as well."

Laney blew out a breath. "Why would that—" She went quiet. "It's because I already have Nyssa's blood running through my veins."

"That's what we believe as well."

"Does it say if it is reversible?"

"No."

"So there's a chance if I take it, I won't be able to undo its effects."

"Yes. Or if you take it a second time, it might remove *all* your abilities."

"Oh." She had not considered that possibility.

"We don't know for sure. I may have interpreted this wrong. It's been so long—"

"Cain, it's all right."

"We thought you should know. But, Laney, I . . . I don't want you to have this burden. I hope you never have to make this choice."

"Me, too. But at least if I have to, I won't be alone."

"No, you will never be alone. I promise you that."

Laney nodded, but that was exactly how she felt—alone. She hung up with Cain and stared into space, trying to figure out how to convince the people downstairs that Elisabeta was now an even greater threat than they thought she was a few minutes ago. She knew there was no chance of that.

She pulled out her phone and dialed Mike. He answered on the first ring. "Laney? Everything all right?"

"Not exactly. I need you to put me in touch with the secretary of state."

CHAPTER 49

The meeting had been pushed back another half hour due to some situation that had developed that Laney was not privy to. Which was fine with Laney, because it gave her time to call the secretary of state from the conference room down the hall.

But the conversation with Nancy did not go well. Laney explained what she believed Elisabeta was up to. But as supportive as Nancy had been, Laney could hear the skepticism in the woman's voice.

And she couldn't blame her, because Laney could not tell her the whole story. She couldn't tell her about the Omni. Nothing good would come of letting the government know that there was a compound out there that could turn people into Fallen. Laney also couldn't tell her about Nyssa and what her blood could do. Which left her with vague explanations and a lot of conjecture. Laney hung up the phone, frustration rolling through her.

Drake sat down next to her, patting her knee. "So that went poorly."

"Yes, it did." She ran her fingers through her hair. "Why the hell can't they just take my word for it?"

Drake grinned. "You mean that Elisabeta is the reincarnation of the leader of the Fallen angels, hell-bent on world domination, and that she is now attempting to make herself immortal? Hm, yes, I see why you would be annoyed. It's such a rational argument."

Laney narrowed her eyes. "Are you trying to help?"

"Not at the moment, no."

"Well, then you're doing a great job." She started to stand.

Drake pulled her back down. "Hey, no storming off."

"I'm not storming. I was going to walk with purpose out of the room."

"My mistake. Now listen, the governments of the world will never believe you."

Laney narrowed her eyes. "Your pep talks need work."

"Will you let me finish?"

Laney crossed her arms over her chest. "Fine."

"Thank you. Now, as I was saying before I was so rudely interrupted, the governments of the world will not believe you. It is too fantastical, no matter how true it is. But that doesn't matter. It's never been about them. It's about you and her. It always has been."

"Great. No pressure."

He smiled. "Well, I happen to have faith in you. You always find a way. This time will be no different."

"Drake, she's trying to make herself immortal. There's no room for error. The amount of deaths that will result if she achieves that goal . . ."

"Lives will always be lost, Laney. You cannot prevent every death. But you can keep those numbers down."

"I'm not sure that's enough."

"I'm afraid it will have to be."

Laney leaned in to him with a sigh, knowing he was right. People were going to die. She wouldn't be able to stop that. But without her government at least loosening up the reins, she wasn't sure she was even going to be able to keep the final death toll down.

And Elisabeta/Samyaza had been playing this kind of game for much longer than Laney.

Laney knew she was outclassed. *The government is keeping me at arm's reach. Elisabeta has already targeted my people, leaving us weakened. How am I going to protect anyone else against her?*

Maldonado appeared in the doorway. "The council is reconvening."

Drake grinned down at her. "Time to get back in there, champ."

"I hate you."

He kissed her on the forehead. "Nope, you just wish you did."

CHAPTER 50

An hour into the resumption of the meeting, Laney was ready to start beating her head against the table. One of the men from the DIA was speaking.

"I think we should table this discussion until next week. Once we've done some research, we can have a clearer picture of what our next steps should be."

"Next week?" Laney said. "Do you know how much damage Elisabeta will do in that time? That Sudan tape is only a taste of what she is capable of."

The faces around the table all showed various shades of skepticism, if not outright derision. And Laney realized if she hadn't had the benefit of her extensive educational background, the knowledge of her uncle and mother, as well as all her experiences, she'd probably be just as skeptical. She really did not know how to get across to them just how quickly they needed to fall in line.

"Look, I realize this is a lot. But if you could just keep your minds open to the idea that humanity's history is a little more involved than you realize, it would save us a lot of time and lives."

Already one of the men down the table was shaking his head. He was the four-term senator from Oklahoma, Brad Cockburn. "I cannot listen to this nonsense any longer. It's blasphemy. Anyone who has read their Bible as I have knows God would never allow such a thing. As for everything else, it is very clear that the Earth is only ten thousand years old."

Laney stared at the man, wishing he was joking but knowing he was absolutely serious. His anti-science bias was well known, as was his strict interpretation of the Bible.

And Laney had no response for the man. After all, what did you say to a man who viewed science with the same reliability as horoscopes or tea leaves?

Reyes stood up at the head of the table. "I'm going to play the video again. Perhaps it will help address some of our issues."

The second viewing of the video was no less brutal than the first viewing, but honestly, Laney had seen worse. Elisabeta really did seem to love that hand through the chest thing. Reyes had it played four times, slowing it down for the last two so they could see exactly what Elisabeta was doing.

After the fourth viewing, Reyes had turned to the table. "Now the question is, what do we do about her?"

That had been an hour ago, and the only thing the people at the table had managed to accomplish was the formation of a dull headache behind her eyes.

"Look, I'm a lay-my-cards-on-the-table kind of guy," said Bart Shremp, senator from Minnesota and chairman of the Senate Foreign Relations Committee.

Laney tried not to roll her eyes. She found that when people said something along those lines, it was just an excuse to be rude as hell.

Shremp pushed the file in front of him toward the center of the table. The file had been given to every individual at the table. It contained a background on Samyaza, fallen angels, Nephilim, and the ring bearer. It had been a shock to see it all laid out in black and white like that. But Laney could also see how fantastical it would appear as well.

Shremp continued. "And I just don't buy any of this. I mean, fallen angels? A magical ring? Come on. This isn't some Hollywood movie. This is real life, and there needs to be a real explanation for what we're seeing. A new drug that enhances speed, strength, and other attributes. We know the Chinese have been working on something along those lines, and God knows the Russian are always trying to get a physical edge. Have we explored all those possibilities?"

"Explored and ruled out," Reyes said.

"Still, I don't think 'angels' is the answer we want to go public with."

This was a complete waste of time. If they didn't acknowledge the threat for what it was, they were never going to be able to combat it. She'd heard variations of Shremp's argument over the last hour. Obviously none of these people were going to accept what was happening. Laney had tried to offer her views, but she'd been talked over. Shremp was just the last straw amongst a group of really annoying straws.

She stood up. "Well, thanks for the invite, gentlemen, but I think I've heard enough."

"Where are you going?" Cliff Kinney from the NSA demanded.

"Back to Baltimore, where I can be of some use." She looked around the table. "You are letting your doubts interfere with what you have seen. In fact, one of you even has a Nephilim on your staff, and I'm guessing you are fully aware of their capabilities."

Laney was careful to look around the table at everyone, so as not to single out Maldonado. "You are sitting here arguing because you are scared. But we don't have time for that. You just saw Elisabeta put her first through a man's chest, and yet we are going back to the argument about whether or not people like her exist. News flash: They do. I do. So if you want to sit here and play 'are they or aren't they?' I'm out."

Shremp's face reddened as his eyes narrowed. "Who the hell do you think you are?"

"I'm the ring bearer. I am the one chosen to hold back the tide against the Fallen. So you guys can either fall in line or get out of my way."

"You have no authority to act—"

Laney laughed. "Do you realize what I have been doing for the last few years? You people are just learning about the Fallen, but you've known about them longer, haven't you? I'm betting there are files hidden away in government offices, aren't there?" She stared right at the director of the CIA, who met her gaze without blinking. "You have chosen to keep yourselves in the dark. Fine. But people are going to die while you debate."

She turned for the door.

"Dr. McPhearson," Reyes called.

She turned slowly back to the table.

"I am sure it took you some time to adjust to learning that these people existed. You didn't just accept—"

"I learned when they killed one of my best friends and then attacked me in my home. I didn't have the luxury of denying what was right in front of me." She looked around the room. "You think you are safe down here in your little war room. And perhaps you are, but the people in Israel weren't safe. The people in Australia weren't safe." Images of Kati, Maddox, and Zach wafted through her mind. "And there are countless others who weren't safe. And if you won't take the steps necessary, I will."

Laney headed for the door.

"And what if we tell you that you are not allowed? We can stop you, Dr. McPhearson," Shremp yelled.

Laney didn't stop walking as the lights in the room blinked, the monitors winking on and off. The double doors blew open with a huge gust of wind that curved around Laney and into the sides of the room. "You can try."

CHAPTER 51

Laney strode down the hallway toward the elevators. The two guards by the door stared at her and back into the room, not sure what they were supposed to do.

Drake was leaning against the wall outside the conference room, looking completely unconcerned, his feet crossed over one another. He raised an eyebrow as she approached. "So I take it we are no longer trying the diplomatic approach?"

"No, we are not."

Drake cracked his knuckles. "Think they'll let us out of the building?"

Laney stabbed the elevator button. "Not sure."

Running feet sounded behind them. Laney whirled around, her power on a short leash, ready to bowl down anyone who was going to try to stop them.

Fielding and Maldonado came to a sliding halt, their hands up.

"And what do you two want?" Drake asked, keeping his gaze on the Nephilim.

"The task force asked that you come back to the conference room," Maldonado said.

Drake snorted. "Tell them they can stuff their requests up their collective—"

Fielding cut in. "Elisabeta made her move."

Laney went still. "Where?"

"Calevitnia. She invaded the country. It is under her control now."

"She took over a *country?*" Drake asked. "That was fast."

Laney frowned, trying to place the name. "Calevitnia. It's a Russian satellite, right?"

Fielding nodded. "Yes. It achieved independence in 1991."

Drake frowned. "Why would she want some piddly little eastern European country?"

But Laney was afraid she already knew. "Loose nukes."

Fielding nodded.

Loose nukes, or unsecured Russian nuclear warheads, were a politically sensitive and world-concerning problem. Prior to 1991, there were 27,000 nuclear warheads in the former Soviet Union and enough plutonium and uranium to make three times that amount. After the fall, the security of those weapons and elements was a serious concern, in both Russia and the former Soviet states.

The Soviet states that broke away that had nuclear weapons within their borders returned their weapons, although they maintained their stockpiles of uranium and plutonium. There'd been over 100 reported cases of nuclear smuggling incidents since 1993. But there had always been suspicions that some of the governments had kept their nuclear weapons intact.

"Calevitnia has nuclear weapons, doesn't it?"

Fielding nodded. "According to our reports, they have twelve silos."

Laney closed her eyes. *Oh God.*

Drake put a hand on Laney's shoulder. "But that's not everything is it, Captain?"

He shook his head. "No. She sent a message."

"A message? To who?"

"The governments of the world." Fielding paused. "And it involves you."

Laney struggled not to groan. *Of course it does.*

CHAPTER 52

As Laney walked back into the control room, the first thing she saw was Elisabeta framed in the center of the screens. She sat on a red velvet chair between two ornate white columns. The chair contrasted nicely with her white suit; her dark hair was pulled back into a chignon. There was even a china cup and saucer on the antique table next to her. She looked the picture of cultured sophistication. A smile was on her face, and for once it reached her eyes.

Laney approached the conference table but did not sit. Drake stood at her side. "When and where was this posted?"

Shremp pointed a finger at Drake. "He is not permitted in here. Guards, get—"

"He stays." Laney's voice brokered no argument, and Shremp wisely shut up. Drake gave him a little wave.

"An hour ago, and on YouTube, believe it or not," Fielding said.

Laney believed it. There was no longer a need to gather a press corps together to release news. The Internet had a myriad of sites that were highly monitored. And Elisabeta and Delaney were hot topics right now. Laney was surprised it took an hour for it to go viral.

"Is it still on the site?"

"No, but it's been copied and posted on at least another two dozen sites we know of. The cat's out of the bag."

Laney sighed. "Right. Well, let's see what the cat has to say."

The captain gestured to an analyst. Elisabeta's image sprang to life.

Elisabeta inclined her head. "Most of you should know who I am. But for those of you who don't, my name in this lifetime is Elisabeta Roccorio. I am part of the Roccorio family of Italy, a long and illustrious line of financially beneficial positions and titles. I have been lauded for my philanthropic endeavors across the globe.

"But none of that is important, because you see, that person, Elisabeta, is merely one identity in a myriad of lifetimes. For my true name, my true role in this world, is Samyaza, the leader of the Fallen."

Laney's jaw fell open. She never expected Elisabeta to come out and own her identity like that. A chill fell over her, knowing that that reveal had nothing to do with feeding Elisabeta's ego. No, there was some larger strategy at play, and Laney had an inkling that she might know what it was. She prayed she was wrong.

"For those of you who have forgotten your history, you humans were once a bunch of sheep, walking around without a focus, without a goal. We Fallen provided you with that goal and the means to achieve it. We made you better."

Laney curled her fists. *You mean you tapped into our violent impulses and hate.*

Elisabeta spread her arms wide. "All you have now, all your great accomplishments, are due to the intervention of my people, the people I led to you at great personal cost. You have seen the clips of what my people can do. But that is just a taste of our abilities—speed, strength, healing almost instantaneously from what would be mortal wounds for a human. To my brothers and sisters that are hidden in the shadows, I call on you to join us and take your rightful place above the humans. To you humans, no longer will we pretend you are our equals. You are ants underneath our shoes."

She leaned forward slightly. "We are gods amongst you." She stared right into the camera, her tone cold. "And it is time for you to pay your tribute."

"I demand that the governments of the world turn over control of their treasuries, weapons, and armies to me. I have in my possession twelve nuclear weapons. If you do not acquiesce to my demands, I will annihilate one critical city every day until they are met. And I will let my troops run free, showing you exactly how powerless you are.

"You have twenty-four hours to comply."

Elisabeta paused with a smile. "Of course, the pain and devastation can be avoided. You simply have to hand over your resources to me. Oh, and there is one more thing I will require."

Drake took Laney's hand.

"I want Delaney McPhearson at my feet. Provide her to me, and I will grant you an additional twenty-four hours to get your affairs in order."

She smiled one more time, and the screen went black.

CHAPTER 53

Laney stared at the screen, stunned. She'd known Elisabeta would make a move, but not on this level. This . . . This was insane. The world would never hand over all of its control to her.

"She will do it," Drake said quietly next to her. "She will destroy as much as she can with the weapons at her disposal, and when the world is reeling from the devastation, she will step in and take it all anyway."

Laney looked at Fielding, who had stepped up next to her. "What is the task force's response?"

"The United States does not negotiate with terrorists."

Laney turned to look over the men at the table. "She *will* do what she says."

The chairman of the joint chiefs narrowed his eyes. "We have the might of United States military behind us as well as the might of all the worlds' governments. She will not be able to stand against all of us. We will strike her down before she has a chance to strike at us."

"And if that doesn't work?" Laney asked.

"She's enhanced, not indestructible," Reyes said. "We will bomb each of the nuclear sites. Bury the weapons under a mountain of earth. They will never be able to be used."

"She will count on you doing that. She will have planned for it," Laney said.

Shremp scoffed. "You give her too much credit."

"*You* don't give her enough. You need to think this through. She will—"

Reyes cut her off. "You were invited back as a courtesy. You know the threat against you. We are placing you under government protection."

"I decline."

"Fine," Shremp spit out. "It's your head you risk."

Laney turned and walked out, careful to keep her steps confident, because she knew the senator was wrong.

It wasn't just her head she risked.

It was everyone's.

∼

DRAKE STRODE next to her down the hall. He said nothing, and Laney didn't either. The entire elevator ride up to the surface was silent as well. Nor did either speak as they stepped outside into the bright sunlight. She blinked at the light as her mind turned over every possible option, looking for a way to prevent Samyaza from unleashing her plan of destruction. But she could not come up with one. All she could do was buy them more time.

She glanced over at Drake, who had stopped walking, his jaw set. "You're awfully quiet." He glared at her. She reared back. "What did I do?"

"It's not what you've done. It's what you're planning on doing."

"I haven't told you what I'm—"

"You are planning on sacrificing your life to buy the rest of the world more time to come up with a plan that *will not work*." He clamped his mouth shut, speaking through gritted teeth. "Tell me I'm wrong."

She opened her mouth, then looked away.

"God damn it. Why do you do this? Why do you always have to be the one who sacrifices everything?"

"Who else is there?" she yelled back. "Who else has a shot at giving the world even the slimmest of chances of surviving this? She will enslave them all, at least the ones who survive, the ones who don't die immediately or through the effects of the radiation."

"The government will bomb the missile silos. The weapons will be useless."

Laney laughed, but there was no joy in it. "Please. She is always ten steps ahead. Do you honestly think she hasn't thought of that? She hasn't planned for that? She knows exactly how they will respond to her threat."

"But that doesn't mean you have to throw yourself on the altar to be willingly sacrificed."

"People will die! Thousands of people!"

"People die every day! Volunteering to be one of them is not a plan. It is what she wants!"

"So what the hell am I supposed to do? Let people die so that I don't?"

"Yes," Drake said, his voice rising. "You are the *general*. You are the one leading the fight against her. Yes, you damn well should sacrifice other people in the battles so you can win the war. Because if you are not here, if you are not the last one standing when the final fight comes, humanity has no chance!"

Laney's chest heaved as she stared at him. She knew he was right. But she also knew she could not sit back while Elisabeta took out city after city. Millions would be killed. "I cannot sit back and let people die."

"And *I* cannot stand by and watch you die."

They stared at each other, the space between them only a few feet, but it felt like miles.

She looked into his eyes and felt his passion, his love. "I cannot do what you want."

Emotions played across his face before he shook his head. "Then I cannot stand by your side." He stared at her for a long moment before walking away, then he ran. Before she knew it, he had blurred out of sight.

Laney felt like the air had been ripped from her lungs. She had come to count on Drake as her one constant. No matter what had happened over the last few months, he'd been by her side.

I suppose everyone has a limit.

She closed her eyes, tears pressing against the back of them. She wanted to go after him, but it would change nothing. She knew what she had to do. She had to buy the world time.

Which meant she had to die. Ever since the vision of Yamini, she had known in her gut that it would come to this.

Now I just have to have the strength to do what needs to be done.

Laney looked around at the office buildings surrounding her and realized she didn't have a ride home. She laughed, if only to keep herself from crying.

The fate of the world rests in the hands of a woman currently stranded in an industrial park in D.C. God help us all.

"Dr. McPhearson?" Maldonado said from behind her.

She sighed, wiping her eyes without turning. "Yes?"

"I've been instructed to drive you home. If you'll follow me." She waited.

Laney stared at the spot where Drake had disappeared, feeling the gulf between them widening with each second that passed.

There was no sign of him. With a nod, she turned and followed the soldier, suddenly feeling so very, very tired.

CHAPTER 54

The drive back to the estate took double the time it normally did due to traffic. Maldonado turned on the radio to a news station. Panic had broken out across the nation. People were rushing to banks, to supermarkets, to gun shops. Elisabeta's recoding had terrified everyone. And Laney knew that that panic would only make things more dangerous for people. Panicked people tended to make poor decisions.

"Do you think we can turn that off?" Laney asked.

"Happy to." Maldonado clicked the radio off.

She eyed the tall Marine. "Does anyone know what you can do?"

Maldonado watched her in the rearview mirror. "I wasn't sure you could."

She shrugged. "One of the perks."

Maldonado nodded. "My mom knew. She said my dad was an angel."

"She's not wrong."

"Well, that *angel* ran off and left us when he found out my mom was pregnant."

Laney winced. "Sorry. What about the military? Do they know?"

"Not officially. I think some might wonder. And Heller in the CIA figured it out. It's how I ended up assigned to him."

"Just be careful. The government's interest in us, I'm not sure it's a good thing."

Maldonado nodded but didn't say anything. "You going to turn yourself in?"

"If I can't figure out another approach, I don't think I have much choice."

"Can you really do all those things that report mentioned?"

Laney nodded. "Yeah. Although they left out a few."

Maldonado raised an eyebrow at that. "I see why Elisabeta wants you out of the picture."

Laney looked out the window. "Yeah, me, too."

CHAPTER 55

CAIRO, EGYPT

Noriko didn't make it to the Giza Plateau their first night, and neither did Gerard. He sat by her side as she cried and called home to speak with everyone. But at his request, she didn't tell them where they were. But after another day in the hotel spent mainly sleeping, she was ready.

"You don't have to do this," he said. "I can find it on my own."

Noriko shook her head as she finished tying her boots and stood. "No. I'm supposed to be there. And we're already here. The sooner we finish, the sooner we can get back."

"Are you sure?"

She nodded, amazed that she could still feel tired with all the sleep she'd had. "Yeah. Let's go."

Ten minutes later, they were driving through the streets with Gerard at the wheel. Noriko watched the city in fascination as they drove. There was a lot she recognized—Western shops and restaurants like McDonald's. But there was so much she was seeing for the first time.

"What do you think?" Gerard asked quietly as they left the bustle of Cairo behind.

"It's all so much. So different and yet, under it all, we're the same, aren't we?"

"I suppose we are." He nodded ahead. "Look."

Noriko's mouth fell open as the Great Pyramid came into view. She'd read about it, of course, and she knew its dimensions. It was almost four hundred fifty feet tall, and each side was nearly seven hundred and fifty feet.

But seeing it in real life was something altogether different. It took over two million stones, each weighing over two and a half tons, to build. And still modern-day experts could not agree on how it had been possible. Most agreed that even with all our technological advances, it would prove impossible to replicate with the precision and care of the original builders.

But although she still wasn't sure where exactly they were supposed to head, the closer they drew to the plateau, the more confident she became that this was where they were supposed to be.

Gerard drove to a parking area near the Great Pyramid. Up close, it was an even more amazing sight. But as she stepped out, it wasn't the Great Pyramid that kept pulling her attention. No, it was another structure that lay silently guarding the Great Pyramid and the two lesser pyramids.

Gerard touched her on the shoulder. "What is it?"

"I think we need to head over there." She nudged her chin toward the Great Sphinx as a chill crawled over her skin.

Headlights flashed over them as a car pulled into the lot.

"Gerard?"

"Stay behind me." Gerard stepped in front of her.

The driver stepped out. "And just what are you two up to?"

CHAPTER 56

Noriko couldn't see the man, but she knew she'd heard that voice before.

Gerard peered ahead with a frown. "Mustafa?"

Mustafa stepped into the light, a shotgun in his arms.

Noriko's heart pounded at the sight of the weapon.

"You won't need that," Gerard said.

"Really? Because I'm not so sure about that."

"How did you know we were here?" Gerard asked, seeming completely unconcerned about the weapon in Mustafa's arms.

"You were flagged as soon as you stepped into the hotel. Matt contacted me to find out what you are doing in Egypt." Mustafa shifted his gaze to Noriko. "Are you all right?"

Noriko realized Mustafa thought she'd been kidnapped. "No, no. I mean, yes, I'm fine. I made him take me. I mean, I told him I had to come with him. That is—"

"Less is more sometimes Noriko," Gerard said.

Right. She took a breath. "I believe I need to be here. I had a vision. Gerard and I are both supposed to be here."

"Why?"

Noriko hesitated. She knew Laney trusted the SIA agent, but

she wasn't sure how Gerard would respond to her revealing the reason they were here. She wasn't sure what to do.

Gerard made the decision for her. "Because a few thousand years ago, I buried the Omni here, or at least the instructions on how to get it. And I think that could come in handy right about now."

Mustafa narrowed his eyes. "Handy for who?"

Gerard's tone hardened. "The good guys. I'm not on Elisabeta's side."

Noriko did not like the increase in tension she felt. "He's telling the truth. And, um, I think it's better if we get it back to Laney so she can decide what to do with it."

Mustafa kept his gaze on Gerard. "And that's your plan, too? To get the Omni back to Laney?"

"Of course," Gerard answered. Noriko wanted to hit him. He sounded so blasé.

"Why didn't you take her back home after the attacks?" Mustafa asked.

"I gave her the option. She chose to stay."

"You mean you wanted to make sure she stayed focus on your little mission."

Noriko stepped forward. "No. I chose. I can't change anything there. But Laney wants us to find whatever is here. And that I can do."

Mustafa studied her for a long moment before he nodded. "Well, then, I guess I'll be helping you. You know, to make sure it gets back to Laney."

Relief flowed through Noriko. "Great. "

"Yeah, great," Gerard muttered.

CHAPTER 57

Noriko looked out across the Giza Plateau. It was awe inspiring. The three pyramids were lined up in a row, matching the Orion constellation. But despite their impressiveness, it was the Great Sphinx that kept drawing her eye.

They walked around it. Well known across the globe, the Sphinx measured in at one hundred fifty feet long; the statue had the body of a lion and the face of a man. It had been a subject of fascination for thousands of years. No one was sure why it was created, or even when.

Noriko's musing came to a halt as they stopped between its front two paws, where the Dream Stele was located. The stele was a stone slab erected by Pharaoh Khufu. According to the stele, King Thutmose IV fell asleep at that very spot and dreamed of the Sphinx. The Sphinx told him to unbury his body, and if he did, he would one day rule a unified Egypt. So Thutmose excavated the Sphinx. And he did eventually rule a unified Egypt.

Mustafa nodded to the sign. "All that work, and by the time the modern era dawned, it was buried by the sands again."

"When was it uncovered?" Noriko asked.

"Fully in 1936," said Mustafa. "French Egyptologist, Emile

Baraize oversaw the dig when it began in 1925. It took eleven years to dig it out."

Noriko looked up at the face. "Is the head too small or is it just the angle?"

"It's too small," said Mustafa. "Archaeologists believe it was not originally a human head that adorned the Sphinx. Khufu is supposed to have been responsible for the reconstruction, not including the missing nose. Most people think that the vandalism was the result of Napoleon's troops, but there were sketches done prior to Napoleon's visit showing it was already damaged. Although there is still debate, the missing nose is attributed to a man named Muhammad Sa'im al-Dahr in the 14th century. Apparently peasants had been offering tributes to the Sphinx for aid in controlling the Nile's flooding. al-Dahr, incensed by the acts, took out his anger on the Sphinx. He was later executed for the act."

"If not a human face, what do they think it once was?" Noriko asked.

"Most argue it was a lion. The body seems to suggest that," Gerard said.

Noriko frowned, thinking that didn't seem right. It didn't feel right.

"What do you think, Noriko?" Gerard asked.

"I don't think that's right." On the plane, Noriko had read up on the Sphinx and the mystery that surrounded it. Mainstream archaeology dated the Sphinx to around 2500 BCE and the reign of Khufu.

But aspects of the Sphinx and the plateau suggested it was much older. One of the most compelling was the water damage to the Sphinx that could only have been caused by heavy rains. This part of the Nile had once been fertile with heavy rains. But that was long before 2500 BCE. The fertile period was around 10,550 BCE.

Edgar Cayce himself gave that date for when the Sphinx was

created. In fact, he maintained that the Sphinx was older than the pyramids and had been created by people who had come down from Mount Arat. The same mountain where the legendary Noah was supposed to have finally come aground after the floodwaters had receded.

But one of the other more intriguing questions about the Sphinx is the question of what its face had originally looked like. The hieroglyphs that adorn the ancient sites were surprisingly unhelpful—not a single depiction or reference to a sphinx with either the head of a man or a lion.

Almost without thought, she reached her hands out for the Sphinx. Everything around her disappeared, shifting to black before she pulled her hands from the Sphinx and stumbled back. She fell to the ground hard, but her hands touched only softness—grass.

She looked around in surprise. The desert was gone. Instead of sands dunes as far as the eye could see, she saw rolling hills covered in grass and trees. A path led to the Sphinx, and in the distance she could see the pyramids. They shone brightly in the moonlight, their sides covered not in a dull rock, but limestone worked until it was bright white. The light reflecting on it made the sides seem as if they were completely smooth, almost as if it were white glass rather than rock covering it.

Torches wavered next to her, making the shadows dance. She turned around and looked up at the face of the Sphinx. She gasped, recognizing it.

It's not a lion.

CHAPTER 58

It took Gerard a second to realize Noriko had slipped into a vision. She was tumbling for the ground when he caught her.

"Noriko!" he yelled. Her eyelids fluttered open. He let out a breath as relief flooded him.

"It's not a lion," she whispered.

Mustafa knelt down on her other side. "Are you all right?"

She nodded, struggling to sit up. Gerard helped her, moving behind her so she could lean against him.

Mustafa handed her a canteen. "What did you say?" he asked after she'd taken a drink.

Her voice was weak. "The Sphinx. It wasn't a lion. It was a jackal."

"Anubis," Mustafa breathed. Gerard knew that there had been speculation that the Sphinx had actually been a giant statue of Anubis. Anubis could be found all over ancient hieroglyphs. He was the god of the otherworld. The being who weighed an individual's soul to determine their worth. He would have been a fitting guardian for the ancient pyramids.

Whether the Sphinx once held a jackal's head was another mystery lost to the sands of time. But those mysteries hadn't counted on Noriko and her ability to pull back the veil of time. Anubis had a number of titles, such as the god of mummification or protector of graves. He was believed to be the person responsible for the resurrection of Osiris.

"That would explain his absence from the ancient hieroglyphs," Mustafa said. "But Anubis, he is everywhere in the ancient scripts. He is one of the most recognizable faces from ancient Egypt."

Noriko looked around. "This whole area, it was beautiful. Covered in grass, trees, I could even see the Nile in the distance from the reflection off the pyramids."

"You saw the pyramids before the covering had been removed?" Mustafa asked.

"I think the mainstream is about eight thousand years off in their time estimations." She looked up at Gerard. "I can get up now."

Gerard grasped her arm helping her to her feet. "Did you see anything about a hiding spot?"

"When I was here, it was well before Barnabus's time." Noriko dusted the sand from her pants.

Gerard started at her words. *When I was here.* There was no doubt in her voice that she had not just seen the ancient time but had visited it as flesh and blood. Gerard was familiar with the idea that time did not exist. According to physicists, time was an artificial construct depending on the person upon whom change was being measured. Everything happens in the now. There is no past there is no future. There is only this moment. But there were some who took the argument a step further and suggested that everything had already happened, allowing you to shoot between past future and present.

But until he'd met Noriko, he'd never put much stock in the argument. But now, as he watched Noriko, he wondered exactly how she managed to see the past and the future and how often a body could be split between two time periods before they were irreparable damaged.

And he did not like that line of thinking.

"Why do you think you saw the Sphinx? Was it just a random vision?" Mustafa asked.

"No. My visions always have a meaning, even if I don't understand it at first."

"Okay, so the Sphinx was actually created as a representation of Anubis, who was the protector of the sacred necropolis," Mustafa said.

Gerard went still, a memory unlocking at Mustafa's words. "And Anubis was responsible for the resurrection of Osiris, the god of the afterlife and resurrection."

Mustafa studied him closely. "You know where you hid the Omni."

Gerard nodded. "It's in the Osiris shaft."

CHAPTER 59

The Giza Plateau held more than just the three pyramids and the Sphinx. In fact, there was so much to be investigated that some finds were left practically unexplored after their discovery—like the Osiris shaft.

Technically discovered in 1934, the Temple of Osiris, or the Osiris shaft, as it was also called, had actually only been investigated a handful of times. The shaft itself sat flooded for decades and wasn't truly excavated until 1999. It contained three levels, the last one a hundred feet down. And in that final level was a nine-foot-long granite sarcophagus. The sarcophagus still lay where it had been found, thirty plus years after it had been discovered. Its removal was complicated by its size and weight, weighing in excess of one hundred tons, not to mention its location. Archaeologists had to drain the shaft of water to even consider being able to get to it.

Mustafa led the way to the Osiris shaft. "Are you sure this is where it was hidden?"

Gerard nodded, growing more certain as they approached. "Osiris was associated with immortality, albeit after he was resurrected. And he was guarded by the Sphinx, a being whose true face was hidden from the world."

Gerard looked at each of them but realized they did not get the reference.

"In our search for the Omni, Helen and I came across the minotaur on Crete. He appeared to have the head of a bull and the body of a man. But it was only a mask. His true face was also that of a man." Gerard looked back toward the Sphinx. "Just like the Sphinx's true face has been hidden. I would have liked the idea of the Sphinx guarding this hiding spot. It would have been a clue for Helen, or Laney, I guess."

Gerard yanked open the gate covering the entrance. The padlock crashed to the ground, and he hurried inside. The entryway was only about ten feet long, and then there was a ladder leading down. Mustafa pulled a light stick and cracked it on, dropping it down the hole. It illuminated the long passageway on its way down, the two offshoots and the metal ladder bolted into the rock wall.

Gerard grasped the ladder, swinging himself over. "I'll meet you guys at the bottom." And before they could reply, he leaped.

∼

GERARD GRABBED THE LADDER, slowing his fall as he approached the bottom. It would take Mustafa and Noriko a while to join him, but he was too impatient to wait. He touched down and only had a few feet before the water began. The sarcophagus lid was suspended above the water on heavy metal cables.

He slipped his pack off his shoulders and pulled out two light sticks. Snapping them to life, he tossed them into the water. As they sank to the bottom, they illuminated the sarcophagus resting six feet below the water.

He paused, closing his eyes. *Where are you?* He knew it was here, but he wouldn't have simply placed it in the sarcophagus, would he?

Closing his eyes, he slowed his breathing, emptying his mind of thoughts. It was silent. Then a picture of the shaft, completely dry with only the sarcophagus appeared in his mind. His eyes flew open. He looked around, spying a crowbar left amongst some other tools left behind. Grabbing the tool, he jumped into the water.

It was shockingly cold compared to the outside desert. But then with each foot below the surface he went, the temperature dropped. He bet it was probably only around forty degrees Fahrenheit. He swam his way to the bottom, wedging the crowbar underneath. Pushing down with all his might, he got little traction. The buoyancy of the water was nullifying his strength. This wasn't going to work.

He tried for another minute before growling and heading up. Breaking the surface, he took in a few deep breaths while he studied the underwater space. The sarcophagus sat under ten feet of water in a pit that was only about four feet wider on the ends and six feet on the longer sides. Hieroglyphs covered the walls surrounding it, Anubis prominently displayed.

Taking a breath, he dove back in, heading for the narrower end. Bracing his feet against the wall, he propped his shoulder against the sarcophagus and pushed. It gave an inch. Using his legs, he pushed harder. Slowly, inch by inch, it moved. He began to see spots and resurfaced, taking in large gulps of air before diving back under. Quickly getting back into position, he pushed again. Six inches, eight.

Come on. Come on. Spots began to swim before his eyes. He felt pressure in his head. But he continued to push until he'd moved the sarcophagus eighteen inches. Then he burst from the water, breathing heavily.

"Gerard? Are you all right?" Noriko called from up the ladder.

"I'm good. Almost there." He waited until the spots in his eyes and the ache in his chest disappeared before diving again. He grabbed the crowbar from where he'd discarded it on the bottom. Wiping the silt away, he saw the stone he had placed there eons ago. He hitched the crowbar into the small groove along the side of the stone and plunged the other end to the ground. The stone tablet popped up an inch. Discarding the crowbar, he worked his fingers under the edge and yanked. The stone gave way, revealing a small hole underneath. He smiled.

Found you.

CHAPTER 60

An hour after finding the Omni in the Temple of Osiris, Noriko was taxiing down the runway in Gerard's plane. This time, Mustafa was accompanying them as well.

Mustafa sat next to her, his gaze on Gerard, who was just entering the cockpit.

Noriko followed the SIA agent's gaze. "What's wrong?"

"I don't trust him."

"But you agreed with his reasoning when he said we shouldn't contact anyone about what we found. That Elisabeta would be monitoring our communications and anyone we called."

"Yeah, it's just convenient."

"Convenient?"

"We found a weapon that could help us in the fight, but we can't tell anyone about it."

"Not yet. But we found the Omni, and now we're returning to Laney with it, just like Gerard said we would."

"Why won't he let us see what's in the sack?"

"Well, he said that was for Laney, not us. I mean, she *is* the ring bearer."

Mustafa glanced at her. "That doesn't seem a little odd?"

"Odd?"

"You lead Gerard to Egypt, help him find something that's been buried for thousands of years, and he doesn't show it to you?"

Noriko shrugged, but Mustafa's skepticism was making her a little nervous. "Not really. I mean, I trust him."

"Why?"

Noriko opened her mouth, then closed it. She couldn't explain it, not in any way that would make Mustafa understand. She just knew that Gerard would never hurt her.

"He worked with Elisabeta for years. You really think he was willing to turn on her just like that?" Mustafa said forcefully, making Noriko jump. "Samyaza plays the long game. And what better long game than to get one of her people in with us, get us to trust them, and then have them betray us."

"He . . . he wouldn't."

"You sure?"

Noriko once again found herself without anything to say, so she just stared out the window. Neither she nor Mustafa spoke as the plane continued to ascend and then leveled off. But while outwardly she was silent as a mouse, inside, her mind was whirling. It wasn't possible, was it? Gerard wouldn't betray them, would he?

She knew he'd been with Elisabeta for years, since he was a teenager, in fact. But he hated her now, didn't he? Now that he knew who she really was? Now that she knew who he really was?

But wouldn't he have seen who she was at some point over the years? Noriko knew everyone thought she was incredibly naive. And she was the first to admit they were right. But even she realized Gerard had to have helped Elisabeta in some of the horrible things that she had done.

She jumped as the cockpit door opened. Gerard's gaze latched onto her. "You all right?"

"Yeah, just, I don't know. Everything okay?"

"Yes and no. I spoke with Laney to let her know we are heading back. But we are about to hit some bad weather, and the pilot says that our cells and TV reception is shot. So we won't be able to make any calls or get any service until we land."

Mustafa narrowed his eyes. "Is that so?"

"On the bright side, we should all be able to take a nice long sleep without any disruptions."

Mustafa crossed his arms over his chest. "I think I'll stay awake."

Gerard shrugged. "Suit yourself." He turned to Noriko. "The bedroom's yours if you want it."

"Uh . . ." Norio looked at Mustafa, who did not take his gaze from Gerard. "Actually, sleeping sounds good. I'm a little wiped out."

Concern immediately crossed Gerard's face. "Do you need anything? Juice or something to eat?"

"No, I just, uh, need some sleep."

"Okay. Pleasant dreams."

She nodded, scooting past Mustafa and heading to the bedroom. She turned to close the door and found Gerard watching her. Chills ran across her skin. She told herself they were the good kind of chills, the ones she normally felt when Gerard was around.

But even she wasn't naive enough to believe that one.

CHAPTER 61

BALTIMORE, MARYLAND

The bomb shelter was abuzz with activity. Patrick and Jen, who each had their own rooms in the full medical suite, weren't the only new additions. The furniture in the living area was being moved out to make room for bunk beds and hammocks. After watching Elisabeta's recording, they were going to stuff as many people into the shelter as possible.

Jake pulled out his phone to call Mary Jane, then put it away. He'd already spoken with her. She was fine. She didn't need him calling her every hour, although that's what he wanted to do.

"Coming through," a voice called behind him.

Jake stepped to the side as a staff member with a dolly full of dried milk headed past him toward one of Dom's storerooms. They were stocking Dom with as much as they could manage, in case one of the bombs went off somewhere around the shelter. Being they all had been a thorn in Elisabeta's side, Jake would not be surprised if they were the first target.

This section of the shelter would be off limits to everyone but their immediate unofficial family. Patrick, Cain, and Nyssa were given Dom's bedroom. As Jake passed, Snow looked up from where she was curled up with Nyssa on a rug on the floor. Patrick was sleeping, and Cain was reading. Jake passed by without disturbing them.

Dom would be bunking with Lou, Rolly, and Danny in Dom's office across the hall. Right now, the teenagers were all helping haul in supplies. It was good for them to have something useful to do. They were all still reeling from Zach's death.

Sascha was in the other guest room. Max was with her and Dov, although Patrick wanted Max with him. Once he was a little stronger, they'd make sure he was moved over. But right now, Max needed someone who could focus on him, and Sascha had volunteered to be that person.

Jen was in the last guest bedroom down the hall. Henry was just stepping out of the room as Jake approached. He closed the door softly behind him.

"How is she?" Jake asked quietly.

"She says she's fine, but she's not. She's worried about the baby."

Jake still found it unreal that the two of them had a little one on the way. And for there to be a chance that they might lose that child? It was just wrong on so many levels. "Have you decided on surgery?"

"The doctor wants to wait a few days, see if maybe the shrapnel shifts out on its own."

"Is that likely?"

"Possible, but they'll be monitoring it twice a day to make sure. Her mom's sitting with her now. Her brothers and dad are helping move supplies in."

"Yeah, I saw them." He paused. "You saw the recording?"

Henry's mouth tightened to a thin line. "Yes."

"She's going to hand herself over."

"I know."

"Any chance we can stop her?"

Henry gave a bitter laugh. "What do you think?"

"It can't have come to this. There has to be another angle we can try."

Henry leaned back against the wall. Jake had never seen him look so defeated. "If there is, I don't know what it is."

"She'll kill her."

Henry's eyes held a world of pain. "I know."

CHAPTER 62

As Maldonado pulled up to the gates, Laney got her first glimpse of the damage Elisabeta had done. She gasped at the gaping hole that had once been the front gates. Cars were lined along the front, waiting to get in.

"You want me to get in line?"

"No. I'll get out here." She placed her hand on the handle. "Dr. McPhearson."

Laney stopped.

"If Elisabeta attacks, do you have any advice?"

Laney looked back at the woman, thinking about all she'd done to hide who she was. But this was a new world they were about to enter. "Save as many as you can as fast as you can. Our time of hiding is over. If you need help, you can contact the SIA. And you can contact me here, at least for a little while longer."

Maldonado nodded. "Good luck."

"You too." Laney stepped from the car and began to walk toward the gate. People caught sight of her, whispering comments as she passed.

"It's her. She's here."

"She caused all of this. How dare she."

Laney kept her head high. She knew she was not responsible for Elisabeta's actions, but scared people weren't always rational.

People stepped out of her way. A cry went up from the front of the line. Laney smiled as Cleo raced toward her. Laney stopped, and Cleo leaped up, placing her paws on Laney's shoulders. Laney hugged her tight.

Cleo licked her cheek before dropping to all fours. She leaned against Laney, and Laney ran a hand through her fur.

It is good to see you, too, sweetheart.

Together they made their way to the front of the line.

Fricano glanced up from where he was checking people in. He grinned. "Hey, look what the cat dragged in."

Laney groaned. "Oh, that was bad."

"And yet accurate." Dylan Jenkins walked over from where the gatehouse used to be.

"I'm glad to see you guys are okay."

"It's been a little rough around here," Fricano said.

"Yeah, I know."

"Everybody's at the bunker," Jenkins said.

Laney nodded. "Let them know I'm coming?"

"Will do," Fricano said.

She paused. "Is Drake here?"

Jenkins shook his head. "We haven't seen him."

"Okay. Thanks." She patted Fricano's shoulder as she passed. She straightened her shoulders, pushing her thoughts of Drake aside.

Time to get to work.

And that's what she did. Henry, Jake, and Matt had already begun preparations, so Laney pitched in where she could. Cats were doled out to varying teams of SIA agents. The President had quietly broadened the agency's mandate. The agents and cats were being stationed across the globe to address any uprising. But it would not be enough. They all knew that. The governments of the world had gone on high alert. Military troops were moving into the streets across the globe to counter any threat. There were food runs, bank runs, huge lines at gas stations. The whole planet had collectively gone mad. Gun sales were going through the roof, as most states had just given up on the waiting period due to the demand.

Everyone was bracing for the worst. Laney arranged all the animal transports, coordinating with Matt. Through Matt, she learned that the United States was leading a coordinated strike against Elisabeta. While Laney prayed they were successful, she planned like they were going to fail.

Henry had stuffed as many people into the bomb shelter as possible. Now Laney sat outside with Cleo, watching the agents who were going to be outside the bunker when the deadline hit. They were saying goodbye to their families, who would be riding out the storm several stories below ground. Cleo stood up from where she had been lying with a deep stretch. Cleo had refused to leave her side for most of the afternoon. Laney knew she was afraid to let Laney out of her sight.

"Going for a run?"

Yes. Be back soon.

"Take your time."

Cleo stared at her. *Be back soon.*

"Okay, okay."

She slipped between the trees, disappearing from sight.

A man caught her attention from the corner of her eye. She whirled around. *Drake?* But he was a little too short, his shoulders not quite as broad. The hurt pierced through her again.

She looked at her watch. Time was getting tight. She stood and headed into the shelter. With the crowd of people, it took longer than usual to get down to the shelter itself.

She was actually happy for the delay. It let her put off the conversation that she needed to but absolutely did not want to have.

This might be tougher than facing Elisabeta, she thought as she stepped through the blast door and headed for Patrick's room.

CHAPTER 63

Laney stood outside the room Patrick was resting in. The bomb shelter was a hub of activity. Cots, hammocks, and sleeping bags littered almost every open space, reminding Laney of hurricane emergency shelters. Hopefully it would only be for a short while.

Unless, of course, the shelter ends up in the blast radius, and then everyone here will be here for life.

She pushed the thought aside, not wanting to think about that possibility. Taking a steeling breath, she knocked gently on the door.

"Come in," Cain called.

Laney opened the door, peeking her head in. Patrick looked up from the bed, a Sudoku book in his lap. "I was wondering when you'd stop by."

Laney winced before crossing the room and kissing his cheek. "Sorry, it's been a little crazy."

Cain sat by the bed, his own Sudoku book in his lap, his sunglasses perched on his nose.

"Back to the glasses?" Laney asked.

Cain shrugged. "Well, there are a lot of new faces, and more than one TV commentary is speaking about the end of days. I didn't think my eyes would help tamp down any of the rising hysteria."

"Probably a good call." She glanced beyond the bed, just noticing the playpen where Nyssa sat happily playing with blocks. "She looks good."

"She seems to like all the hubbub." Cain walked over and picked her up. "But I think I will take her for another stroll around the estate before they lock us in here." He headed out the door, closing it softly behind him.

Laney took a seat in the chair Cain had just vacated.

"You look tired," Patrick said.

"Well, thanks. Just what every girl loves to hear."

He smiled. "Beautiful, but tired."

Laney shrugged. "Just a lot to figure out."

"You mean how you are going to respond to Elisabeta's invitation?"

Laney winced. "I suppose it was too much to hope you might not have seen that part of the message."

He took a breath. "So, what exactly are you planning on doing?"

Laney shrugged, not meeting his eyes. "I haven't decided yet."

"Really?" She could feel his gaze on her. She nodded, still not meeting his eyes.

"Laney, look at me."

With a sigh, she looked into his face.

"I have known you for all of your life. I know you. I *know* what you have decided to do."

"How can I not?" she asked softly. "One life is a small price to pay for the chance to save millions."

"Do you honestly think that by letting Elisabeta kill you that you will be helping?"

"Yes, no, maybe." She ran a hand through her hair. "I know it's a long shot. But I can buy the rest of the world time. Maybe they can figure out a way that—"

"That what, Laney? The world of the Fallen is brand new to them. Elisabeta is brand new to them. Do you really think they will get up to speed in the twenty-four hours you will buy them?"

"I don't know. But how can I not, knowing their deaths could have been avoided?"

"You don't know that. Elisabeta is not exactly known for keeping her word. She could kill you and still set off a bomb."

She sighed, sinking lower into the chair. "I know, I know."

"Then why? Until we have a way to defeat her, you cannot risk yourself."

When Laney spoke, her voice was quiet, because somewhere down deep, she feared that by speaking too loudly her fears would be proven true. "Because what if there is no way to defeat her? What if millions die, and I still can't figure out how to defeat her?"

"Then it is *still* not on you. You are the ring bearer, yes, but you are not omnipotent. There is a limit to what even you can do. There is limit to what anyone can do."

"Except Elisabeta. She has no limits."

"Laney, give yourself time to figure something out. Give yourself time to come up with a plan. Promise me."

Laney stood. "I can't promise that."

This time Patrick was the one who looked away, a tremor in his voice. "I have said goodbye to you too many times now. I won't say it again."

She nodded, a catch in her own throat. "Then don't. But know that no matter what happens next, I love you. And that I thank you for raising me. Who I am is because of you."

He gave a small laugh even as tears crested in his eyes. "Don't blame that on me."

She kissed his cheek. "Oh, I do." She turned for the door, concentrating on keeping her breathing even.

"Laney," he called as her hand touched the doorknob.

She didn't turn around, knowing the tears would fall if she did. "Yeah?"

"I'll see you later, okay?"

"I'll see you later," she echoed before opening the door and closing it softly behind her. She bowed her head, leaning against the wall taking a moment to try and get her emotions under control. Then she straightened, running a trembling hand over the door.

Goodbye, Uncle.

CHAPTER 64

Drake pounded down the roads, cutting off a car that slammed on its brakes, but he didn't stop.

Stubborn, obstinate woman, he growled in his mind. She was handing herself over to Elisabeta on a platter, a gods damn platter.

And it wouldn't make a lick of difference. Elisabeta was still going to run roughshod over the governments of the world. She was going to destroy anyone who stood up against her. And without Laney, no one would stand for long.

Why didn't she see that? It was clear as day to Drake that the only reason Elisabeta demanded Laney's surrender was because she was the only threat. And how do you get Laney to do what you want? You threaten someone. Or a world of someones.

But Laney needed to realize she was not some nameless drone in a sea of people. She was the only one who could do what she could do. She needed to lead the fight, not martyr herself before it even began.

Drake's thoughts circled around and around, shifting from berating Laney for her foolishness to trying to figure out a way to talk her out of it. Before he knew it, he was standing on the water's edge, watching boats come in and out of Chesapeake Bay.

From here, the world looked peaceful. But he'd run through streets, seen the panic that Elisabeta had caused. More than one fist had been thrown in anger. People were losing their minds, and with good reason.

He breathed in deep, inhaling the air, knowing where he needed to be. With one last look at the water, he headed back to the estate, back to Laney's side. She might be about to do the stupidest thing she possibly could, but he'd be damned if he wouldn't be standing next to her when she did it.

He took his time getting back, wanting to give himself and Laney some time. More her than him, because, in all honesty, she was the one who needed to come to her senses. She needed to lead with her head and not her heart.

But he would stand by her side, no matter what she decided. He had lost her once trying to force his will on her. He would not do it again. But he sure as hell would rip Elisabeta's head from her shoulders the minute she or any of her people made a move toward Laney.

Feeling better, he jogged toward the estate with a wave at the guards as he bypassed the long line of cars and simply leapt over the fence. Cleo appeared from between the trees as he headed for Sharecropper's Lane.

"Where is she, girl?"

Cleo nudged him toward the bomb shelter. He nodded, changing directions. As he was about to step from the path, he saw her ahead, just exiting the shelter. Her shoulders were hunched, and she looked like she had the weight of the world on her shoulders. He was about to step out when she turned her head at someone calling her name. Jake waved her over to a golf cart. She climbed into the cart. Jake turned it around and headed for the main house.

Drake sighed, knowing he could have stopped them. But he was delaying the coming conversation.

"Drake."

He turned as Cain walked up the path toward him, Nyssa tottering behind him. Nyssa let out a squeal as she caught sight of Cleo. Cleo moved quickly in front of her. She grabbed onto Cleo with a giant grin, babbling something at the giant cat. Cleo gave her a giant lick in response.

"She looks no worse for wear," Drake said.

"Yes, she is doing well."

"And Patrick?"

"As well as can be expected." Cain nodded to where Laney had disappeared. "She is a strong woman."

"You mean a stubborn one," Drake muttered.

"That, too." He paused. "Patrick asked to speak with you."

"Me?"

Cain nodded.

"About what?"

"I think you know."

Drake paused. "Okay. Are you two heading down?"

"No. I think we'll spend some time outside with Cleo here."

Drake made his way down to the bomb shelter, carefully wending his way through the sea of humanity that milled around the place. Turning down the hall, he paused at Patrick's bedroom door, knocking softly.

"Come in," Patrick called.

Drake stepped inside. "You wanted to speak with me?"

"Yes. Close the door."

Drake did, then stepped to the bed, surprised by Patrick's sharp tone. "What can I do for you?"

Patrick glared at him. "You're an archangel, right?"

Drake nodded slowly. "Yes."

Patrick crossed his arms over his chest. "Just making sure. Because my niece is apparently planning on committing suicide, and I'd like to know just what you plan on doing to stop it."

CHAPTER 65

It was the first time Laney could remember that the path from the bomb shelter to the main house had people on it. She and Jake had to weave around kids, couples, and grandparents. It was surreal.

"How many extra people are on the estate right now?"

"Close to three hundred. We are going to put as many in Dom's as possible, but there are some reinforced tunnels underneath the estate as well that we'll make use of."

Laney nodded, trying not to imagine a direct hit on the estate or anywhere else. It would be a dystopian nightmare come to life. "What about Mary Jane?"

Jake shook his head. "She wouldn't leave Boston. Her family's huge, and we couldn't take them all. She's staying with them."

Laney's chest tightened. She didn't know what to say. That they'd be all right was guesswork at best, and anything else was probably too on the nose, so she switched the topic. "So what do I need to see?"

Jake glanced at her, then away. "Elisabeta put out another clip."

Laney's breath caught. "And?"

"And," he said, pausing, "just wait. You need to see it yourself."

Jake came around the last turn, and the main house came into view, or at least what was left of it. The two wings of the building were now just shattered remnants. But the central part of the house still stood. Jake pulled up to the veranda around the back.

"We're heading to the kitchen."

Laney nodded, heading to the right. Jake reached the door just ahead of her and held it open. Yoni and Henry looked up from the island. Neither of them smiled.

Laney stepped in. "Well, I'm guessing this isn't good news."

Yoni crossed his arms over his chest. "She doesn't need to see this."

"Yes, she does," Jake argued. "She'll see it eventually. Better here, surrounded by us, than being caught unaware."

Henry stood with his mouth in a tight line.

Yoni grumped, taking a seat. Henry pulled out the chair next to him for Laney. She took a seat slowly, eyeing the iPad on the table like it was a snake about to bite.

Oh, I so don't want to see this, she thought even as she found herself pulling the iPad toward her.

Henry put a hand on the iPad before she could straighten it. "You need to prepare yourself."

She nodded, but inside she felt the familiar lickings of dread. "Okay."

She propped the iPad up. Elisabeta's face was frozen on the screen, but the background this time was outdoors. She could see the sky, a dirt road or driveway, and just the edge of a building in the background.

Yoni stood. "I can't watch this again. I'm going to check on Sascha and Dov." He squeezed Laney's shoulder before disappearing out the back door. Jake took the seat he'd just vacated. Henry stood behind her, his hand on her shoulder.

Before she could talk herself out of it, she hit play.

Elisabeta sprang to life. "After my last broadcast, I began to think about my threats, and I realized perhaps some of you are under the illusion that the threat posed is not that great. That perhaps my people are not as strong as they appear. Or that I am not as committed as I appear.

"Let me put those fears to rest."

The camera panned to the right. A group of three dozen children in matching uniforms stood lined up. But then the camera operator pulled back, and Laney realized she had greatly underestimated the number. There were at least three hundred, all wearing matching uniforms—pale blue shirts and dark navy pants. About a dozen adults stood amongst the children, all of them looking terrified. They were in a courtyard, buildings surrounding them on all sides. Men with guns trained on the courtyard were positioned on all the rooftops Laney could see.

But those weren't the people Laney was worried about. No, the people she was worried about were the dozen or so unarmed men and women that stood on the edge of the group—the ones who did not look terrified.

"This," Elisabeta narrated, "is the St. Augustine Middle School, grades six through eight. Three hundred and twelve students and fifteen teachers. Now, as I mentioned, if you do not meet my demands, one of the repercussions is that I will let my Fallen run through your streets, destroying at will. I thought I would give you a little demonstration of what that would look like."

Laney gripped the table as the Fallen blurred, and the screaming began. But the screams were soon cut short. All she could see were objects flying across the screen. They were moving too fast for her to make out, but she knew what they were—bodies. But that wasn't the worst of it. The worst was how quickly all the action stopped, how silent the courtyard became, without a sniffle or a cry. Nothing. Not a single sound. None of the children or teachers were left standing. All now lay where they'd been felled, unmoving.

Laney put her hand to her mouth. Her mind struggled to accept the horror of what she was seeing. The camera operator panned across the bodies, most twisted at unusual angles. Others with gaping holes in their chest. One head was missing from its shoulders altogether. The camera operator stopped focusing on one girl, her neck bent unnaturally, her bright blue eyes staring at nothing, her mouth open in a silent scream.

The camera stayed on the girl for what felt like hours, but it was only seconds before Elisabeta's smug face reappeared.

"Now, for those of you who are a little too shell-shocked to pay strict attention, let me confirm: This little presentation took 4.7 seconds. Three hundred and twenty-seven lives in 4.7 seconds. Imagine what we can do with an hour? A day? A week? There will be nowhere safe from us.

"You will turn over control of your countries and Delaney McPhearson, or this small demonstration will be replayed in your countries over and over again." She smiled before the screen went black.

Laney sat back, feeling numb. All those children, gone. She *knew* who Elisabeta was, yet even she was shocked by the caliber of cruelty in the attack.

"She did this to make sure you would come to her," Jake said. "You can't let it work."

Laney said nothing.

"Laney?" Henry squeezed her shoulder.

But still she said nothing, her mind frozen on the little girl staring up at nothing.

"We never should have shown it to her," Henry said.

"It is everywhere now. Not showing her wasn't an option," Jake said. "Laney?"

She looked over at Jake, her mind feeling slow. "She killed all of them just to show the world she could."

"Yes, she did."

"She'll do anything to get to me."

"You cannot give in to her," Henry said.

"Even if I don't, what exactly is our plan? We have people

stationed all over the world. But we don't even know if they are in the right place."

"If you go up against her, you'll die," Henry said.

Laney nodded. Her inability to heal had always been her weakness. And never more than now. "I will fight her as long as I can. And when I'm gone, you need to figure out a way to stop her."

Henry shook his head. "Laney, you can't—"

"I can't stop her. But I can buy you time to stop her."

"Laney—"

She stood, shaking her head, cutting off Henry's argument. "She's won, at least this round. It's up to you to make sure she doesn't win the next one."

She kissed each of them on the cheek. "I love you both. And I pray that you will both survive this. And if you do, I want you to promise me you will live happy, fulfilled lives."

Henry's voice shook. "Don't you say—"

"There is no other decision to make. I'm going to pack a bag and leave for the airfield. This will be our goodbye. You two need to focus on the next step. But once you've taken care of everyone else, you need to take care of yourselves. Which means, Jake, you need to get to Boston and Mary Jane. It's where you should be. And Henry, you need to get to Dom's. If the unimaginable happens, you will be those people's best chance." She paused. "You will be your child's best chance."

"I should be out here. I should be with you," Henry said.

Laney opened her mouth to answer him, but Jake beat her to it, his voice heavy. "She's right. Once we've secured everyone, there's nothing more for us to do. You need to be with Jen. And I need to get to Mary Jane. Elisabeta's won this round." He turned to Laney. "You're not wrong, but I hate this."

The pain in his voice nearly dropped Laney's resolve. She hugged each of them, struggling to hold back the tears. "I've got this one. Whatever happens, it's okay. I accept it."

Henry held her close. "There must be another way. Something we can—"

Laney shook her head as she pulled back, taking a step away from them. "There isn't, and you know it. Good luck."

And before either of them could say another word, she walked out the back door.

CHAPTER 66

INVESS, CALEVITNIA

A sense of satisfaction rolled through Elisabeta as the camera zoomed in on Delaney McPhearson as she walked across the runway. She had to admit that there had been moments where she'd doubted that McPhearson would willingly turn herself in. That was the whole reason for the second video, just a little nudge to remind McPhearson of what she could help avoid, at least temporarily.

And it had worked. Elisabeta's lip curled in distaste at the woman walking confidently across the screen. All the trouble she had caused, and when push came to shove, she fell right over. She was not a worthy opponent. The woman was simply too soft for this battle. Elisabeta would never think to turn herself over to save a few pathetic humans. She would, however, sacrifice as many she needed to reach her objectives. Yet another example of how the strong would always overcome the weak.

A blur appeared from down the runway, coming to a halt in front of Delaney. Elisabeta leaned forward, wondering which one of McPhearson's merry band was trying to stop her. She frowned as the archangel materialized. He spoke with her, his shoulders tight, his body language angry.

Elisabeta glared at the screen. *Get on the plane.*

Finally, Laney reached up and placed a hand on his cheek. Drake leaned in to it, his shoulders drooping. Laney kissed him gently. Drake leaned back, wiping tears from her cheeks before taking her hand, walking up the stairs, and disappearing into the cabin.

Aw, how sweet. He wants to die, too.

A minute later, the pilot came hustling out, and the door closed. The plane taxied down the runway before taking off into the bright blue sky. Elisabeta immediately placed the call. It was answered on the first ring.

"Well?" she asked.

"They both got on the plane, and no one was seen leaving it besides the pilot."

"You're sure?"

"I'm sure. I have people positioned around the airfield. No one else got off."

"Good." She disconnected the call. She had her analysts pore over every piece of footage from the airport to make sure there were no mistakes, no chance that McPhearson had gotten off that plane. Luckily the media helped by covering the event like it was a Moon landing. Every news team in the world seemed to have a representative at the small airport, providing a slightly different camera angle on the plane.

Now she just had to wait for one last check. The hour passed incredibly slowly, with Elisabeta shifting between giddiness and concern. But giddiness edged out her concerns as she watched the news coverage again and again, confirming that both Delaney and the archangel remained on the plane.

Finally, she reached the hour mark. The plane should be a few miles off the coast of the United States. Her phone rang two minutes later.

"Yes?"

"I have two heat signatures on the plane."

"And there is no doubt?"

"None, ma'am. There are two people on the plane."

"Thank you." She disconnected the call with a smile. She had checked the heat signatures on the plane before Laney had boarded and there'd been only one: the pilot. So they had gotten on the plane and stayed there.

She smiled even more broadly. What a gullible fool. She smirked at the trust of McPhearson thinking she would let her anywhere near her.

As if I would take that chance when I am so close.

CHAPTER 67

BALTIMORE, MARYLAND

No one spoke in the bedroom as the news camera followed Delaney as she walked from the terminal toward the waiting plane, which was fine with Patrick because he didn't want to speak with any of them anyway. They had let Laney leave. They knew what she was going to do, and they still let her leave.

Cleo hopped up on the bed, lying alongside Patrick. If Cleo could talk, she would be the only one he wanted to hear from. She'd nearly torn the blast door down when she learned Laney had slipped off the estate, leaving large bloodied paw prints on the walls and floor. Yoni had had to tranq her. When she'd awoken, everyone gave her a wide berth. Cleo had headed straight for Patrick and not left his side. He liked to think they were offering each other comfort.

A hiccupped breath sounded from his left. Lou's eyes shone with tears as she stared at the camera. Rolly pulled her into his shoulder as tears rolled down her cheeks, his own chin trembling.

Around the room, the look of devastation on Rolly and Lou's faces was playing out on everyone else's faces. Cain, Danny, Dom,

Yoni, Sascha, Henry—they all stared in anguish at the screen. And he knew the emotion uppermost in each of them—powerlessness.

Because powerless was exactly how he felt.

But then a blur appeared on the screen. A kernel of hope grew in his chest. Drake materialized in front of Laney, glaring down at her as he argued with her. But then what little hope he had was dashed as Drake accompanied her onto the plane and disappeared inside after kicking out the pilot.

Onscreen, the plane began to taxi before taking off into the air. Patrick gripped Cleo tightly.

Don't do this, Laney. Please don't do this. But the plane kept flying until it disappeared from view.

Patrick sagged back against the pillows, closing his eyes. He'd been so sure Drake would be able to talk her out of it, or at least grab her and disappear before she could fight him.

"She's gone," Danny said, his voice full of disbelief.

"Hey, Laney's been through more than all of us combined," said Yoni. "She'll find a way. She always has."

"You really think so?" Lou asked.

Yoni nodded. "Absolutely." He kept his gaze on Lou until she nodded in return. But when she turned away, Patrick saw the doubt creep across Yoni's face.

Patrick kept the station on, listening to the newscasters talk about Laney, Elisabeta, what the world response was. He muted it after a while, but no one cared, and no one seemed ready to leave. And even though Patrick was mad at most of them, he didn't want them to leave either. He didn't want to be alone right now. They all spoke quietly, everyone needing the comfort of the group and not the stares of all those out in the rest of the shelter.

"Patrick, put the volume back on," Henry said, alarm in his voice.

BREAKING NEWS in bright red letters was emblazoned across the screen. Patrick fumbled for the remote. Hitting the volume button, the newscasters voice blasted out in mid-sentence.

"—news that there has been an attack on the plane carrying Delaney McPhearson to Calevitnia."

A gasp sounded across the room, but Patrick didn't turn his head to see who it was. If his life depended on it, he didn't think he'd be able to turn his attention from the screen.

"We go now live to our correspondent at Ocean City."

A woman's face appeared on screen. "An incredible development in the McPhearson incident. A family boating in the waters off Ocean City caught the scene with their camera. It shows . . . Well, I'll let the video speak for itself."

The screen shifted again, this time to a little girl only about six years old standing in the bow of a boat. "Is that her plane?" the girl asked.

"That's it, honey."

The camera operator zoomed in on the plane as it zoomed across the sky. An object appeared, heading toward the plane. Yoni and Henry leapt to their feet. Patrick just stared in growing horror.

And then the plane exploded, pieces flying off in all directions. It felt like years as Patrick watched small pieces of the plane drop into the ocean below, piece by piece.

The female newscaster returned to the screen. "The plane carrying Delaney McPhearson has exploded en route. The Coast Guard was on scene almost immediately as they were carrying out a routine patrol nearby. They have not, as of yet, found any survivors."

Cleo let out a strangled cry. Patrick's jaw fell open, his mind failing to work. The newscaster in the studio reappeared along with a close-up of the plane on the screen. They slowed it down enough that the impact of the missile right into the fuselage was clear.

Patrick gulped for air. The room started to close in on him.

Vaguely, he could hear the cries surrounding him, the gasps of shock as the reality of what had just happened settled in on them.

Cain appeared at his side, his eyes wet with tears. "Patrick?"

Patrick gasped, his chest feeling tight, with no air getting through.

"Patrick!" Cain yelled.

Then Yoni was there, lowering the bed and yelling for oxygen.

Dom placed a mask over Patrick's face, even as tears streamed down Dom's face.

"Just breathe, Patrick. Just breathe," Cain said, keeping his gaze on Patrick, not letting him look away.

Patrick felt the air finally reach his lungs, and he breathed more easily. But his eyes welled with tears. Patrick pushed the mask aside. "Laney?" he gasped out.

Cain knew the question he was asking. He shook his head, his voice shaking. "It's real, Patrick. She's gone."

CHAPTER 68

INVESS, CALEVITNIA

Ordering the missile to launch on Delaney McPhearson's plane might have been one of the highlights of Elisabeta's life. She had watched it on the two screens her technician had set up in the room—one radar screen, one satellite feed. The plane was the only object on either screen until a small dot had appeared, heading straight for the plane.

Excitement had coursed through Elisabeta as she watched the dot grow closer and closer. She shifted her gaze between the satellite image and the radar image until she could just make out the movement on the satellite image. Then in one big beautiful explosion, the plane blew into thousands of parts, raining down into the Atlantic Ocean.

Elisabeta laughed out loud again at the memory. Finally. It was done. All of the obstacles were now out of her way. And all of Delaney McPhearson was scattered across the Atlantic Ocean.

She watched the footage again. She'd sent a drone up to make sure she had conformation. It never got old. Each time she watched it, the wider her smile became. The missile had struck the fuselage, ripping it to shreds. There'd been no sign of the ring bearer using any of her abilities to save herself or Drake.

She'd watched it carefully, slowing it down, inspecting each piece of the plane as it rained down. But they were not there. She was dead.

Elisabeta leaned back, feeling contentment drift through her. Finally. The woman had been a thorn in her side. Killing her—it was never an easy proposition. But with this approach, she had caught all of them unaware. Did they really think she was going to let the ring bearer within shooting distance of her? That she was going to let an archangel within reach?

Fools.

A knock at her door caused her to look up. Artem stood in the open doorway. She waved him in. "What is the status?"

"The governments of the world have been mobilizing. Their armies and law enforcement have all been put on high alert. And the big eight are in constant contact."

"No doubt discussing how to take me out. Have the packages all arrived?"

"Almost. The first six are in place, and the second six will be in place within the hour."

"Good. Let me know when the first government folds."

"Yes, ma'am." Artem bowed before backing out of the room.

Elisabeta pushed back from the desk and walked over to the large world map on the wall. Twelve blue pushpins had been placed on the map on twelve different countries. These twelve had been chosen for a variety of factors: population size, recognizability, economic impact. Some would no doubt be predicted, but she'd added a few that no one would guess.

But which one to begin with? It was important to set the right tone. The right level of fear. Not blind panic, because panicked people made horrible decisions. A calculated strike that would make all others fold.

She smiled, removing one of the blue pins and replacing it with a red one.

You will be perfect.

CHAPTER 69

WASHINGTON, D.C.

The Oval Office was tense. Nancy shifted on the gold-striped couch, trying to find a more comfortable position. But she'd been sitting in meetings all day. Her body was dying to stand and stretch.

Elisabeta's second little video had sent shockwaves through the halls of the White House. The pure brutality was sickening and clarifying. They knew who they were dealing with now, what type of person she was. For those who'd at one point argued that Elisabeta could be reasoned with, the video had at least given them pause. The assassination of Delaney McPhearson had made them choke on their words. Elisabeta was not a woman who would be reasoned with, that was now agreed upon by all individuals in the room and across similar rooms situated in every country on the planet.

But that did not mean that everyone agreed with how to handle her demands.

"We cannot hand over control of the United States. That is not open for debate," stated Senator Franklin Bash, head of the Senate Homeland Security Committee.

"But if we did, and if we did so first, perhaps it would allow us a chance to work with Elisabeta," the DIA analyst argued.

"*Work* with her? She's a psychopath. There is no working with her," Senator Shremp argued.

"All right." The President stood up. "Thank you for your counsel. I will let you know what I decide."

Each person stood up, walking past the President with a nod and a "Madam President." Nancy was the last to leave.

"Nancy, stay a minute."

"Of course, Madam President."

The President waited until the door to the Oval was shut and it was just the two of them. Then she walked over to the windows and let out a breath.

Nancy waited.

Finally, the President turned. "Do you think Elisabeta will follow through on her threats?"

Nancy didn't hesitate. "Yes."

"And if we don't agree to hand over control? If we take the hits and fight back?"

"The Fallen—they are more powerful than any human. We can fight them, but the cost—it will be huge. In lives, resources, money. And I'm pretty sure Elisabeta is a dirty fighter. She will go for the big hits. Not just our people. Our infrastructure, our economic hubs. She will cripple us if we cross her."

"And if we agree? If we hand over control?"

"I don't know. A woman willing to kill children to make a point—I can't see how her as a leader would benefit us. And we know from history that leaders with too much power are rarely kind to those they control."

"I've been thinking a lot about history lately. The twentieth century saw the rise of some of the cruelest leaders imaginable.

People tend to think of Hitler as the worst of the modern-day dictators, but he wasn't even close."

"Mao Zedong," Nancy said quietly.

"Yes. Over forty-seven million victims. But I have a feeling that those numbers will pale in comparison to Elisabeta's numbers."

Nancy nodded. Her thoughts, too, had strayed down through history. Removal of all rights, censorship, physical attacks, slavery—all seemed possible in Elisabeta's future.

The President turned back to Nancy, her eyes hooded. "Did we make a mistake?"

"Madam President?"

"In not letting Delaney McPhearson take the lead. In not backing her."

"I don't know. I think killing McPhearson, who Elisabeta sees as a roadblock to her goals, was always Elisabeta's goal. But as to whether or not we could have changed her fate and then ours as well, I don't think anyone can know that."

"She knew she was going to die as soon as she agreed to get on that plane."

Nancy nodded. "Yes."

"I'm not sure if that makes her brave or stupid."

"I like to think it made her optimistic. Optimistic that her death could buy the rest of us some time."

"The joint chiefs have a plan of attack. They want to take out all the missile silos. They should be finalizing the details."

"I figured that was in the works."

"Hundreds of innocents could be killed. Some of the silos are in the middle of towns. But millions might be saved if it works. It would be a joint effort—a coalition of all the world's nations working together. But will our efforts help or only make things worse?"

"Ma'am, with all due respect, America was not built on the backs of people afraid to fight. It was built on the backs of people who embraced freedom, people willing to die for freedom. As much as the country has changed since the time of our founding fathers, I don't think we as a people have changed. And I think even if we hand over control, people will fight."

"I don't disagree." The President sighed, looking back out the window. "When I decided to run for President, I knew that the decisions ahead of me would be difficult. That they could involve war and the deaths of thousands. But I never imagined the stakes would be this high."

"Can I ask what the other world leaders think?"

The President shrugged. "The same as we do. But they all are waiting for someone to make the hard decision."

"They're waiting on you."

The President nodded. Then she picked up the phone. "Get me Admiral Tully." Then she surprised Nancy by putting the call on speaker.

"Admiral, tell me you have something."

"We have the location of all the missile silos."

"How accurate are they?"

"We believe they are accurate."

"That was not my question," the President said.

"We do know where all the silos were at the fall of the Soviet Union. We do not know if any of the missiles have been moved. But they are not easy objects to move. To build another platform to launch the rocket is no easy feat either. And there has been no indication of that kind of movement."

"I see."

"There is one other piece of intel we have picked up."

"And what's that?"

"We know where Roccorio is."

"What? Where?"

"We had a report that she was sighted at an estate outside the capital of Calevitnia. Satellite images confirm it's her. We have eyes on her. We could take her out in the same strike that takes out the silos."

"How would you take her out?

"Drone strike. Smaller yield to reduce collateral damage."

"What would the collateral damage be?"

"The estate is relatively isolated, so it should be low."

"Very well." The President stood.

Nancy tensed, waiting for the President's next words.

"Admiral, the attack is a go."

CHAPTER 70

BALTIMORE, MARYLAND

Patrick had closed his eyes after Cain confirmed what he'd seen was real. Cain had then chased everyone from the room, knowing Patrick needed to be alone. Needed to think for just a moment. To wrap his head around the horror that had just played out on the TV screen for all the world to see.

But how could he do that? How could wrap his head around Laney being gone? And she hadn't died staring down Elisabeta but in the air. It was a coward's move on Elisabeta's part. She was too afraid to meet Laney.

But it was also the smart move. After seeing that video, he knew the countries of the world would fold. If not immediately, then after the first city was bombed. He had no doubt about that.

Even though Patrick had closed his eyes, he hadn't intended to sleep. He just wanted the world to go away. But his body had shut down. When he opened them again, Cain was sitting in the chair next to him, the TV muted across from him. Patrick didn't say anything to let him know he was awake.

His body had needed the sleep, but it hadn't been peaceful. It had been full of images of bombed-out landscapes, people scavenging for food, children dying in the streets. At least, he hoped they were dreams. They had *felt* real. And with all the abilities of the people he had surrounding him, he prayed that he wasn't tapping into some latent ability and seeing what the future held.

It felt like Armageddon or the end of days, he thought. *Is that what this is? It feels like it.*

Cain looked over at him, his face drawn, but he forced a smile. "You're awake. Can I get you anything? Tea? Something to eat?"

"No. Thank you." Patrick tried to push himself up and winced at the pain in his back as he forgot about the uselessness of his legs.

Cain stood quickly, grabbing the remote for the bed and pushing a button. "Let me."

Patrick nodded his thanks as the back of the bed began to rise. His gaze shifted to the muted TV, where a newscaster was speaking, Laney's plane flying in a box in the corner. He winced as he lost her once again. "Have they found anything?"

"No, Patrick, I'm sorry. The Coast Guard has been all over the area, along with quite a few boats that had been nearby. There's been no sign of her."

Patrick took a shaky breath, a tremor working its way through his hands. He didn't know why he'd asked. He'd seen it for himself. He kept seeing it, even when he closed his eyes. Laney had been through so much. But surviving that blast—it wasn't possible.

He frowned as a breaking news report cut across the screen. A different newscaster appeared, his face pale. If Patrick didn't know any better, he'd think the man was in the beginning stages of shock. He unmuted the set. "We have just received word that the U.S. has led a counter strike against the hideout of Elisabeta Roccorio. A hacker managed to access the government feed of the attack and broadcast it online. I will warn you: What you are about to see is graphic."

The screen shifted to a grainy black-and-white video. Three people were walking in a courtyard. He recognized Elisabeta in the middle. The three looked up as a missile slammed into the courtyard. Patrick held his breath.

They got her. That was a direct hit. There's no way she could have survived. He closed his eyes. *Thank God.*

At the same, he was filled with anger. If they had attacked Elisabeta before Laney got on that plane, she'd still be alive.

Cain sucked in a breath. And Patrick's eyes flew open. On the screen, the smoke was clearing, and movement could be seen. Patrick leaned forward, straining to see through the haze. What was that?

But then the smoke cleared, and Patrick got a clear view. Elisabeta stood up, one arm hanging by a thread, deep gashes in her torso, neck, legs, everywhere. But even with the poor quality of the video, he could see the wounds slowly healing.

Horror, disbelief, and shock rolled through Patrick. He looked at Cain. "She did it. She figured out how to do it without Nyssa. She's immortal."

CHAPTER 71

BOSTON, MASSACHUSETTS

Mary Jane McAdams put her phone down with a shaky breath. Jake was about to land at Logan. *Thank God.*

Originally, he'd planned on staying in Baltimore, and Mary Jane felt she had no right to ask him to stay with them. He had important work to do, and holding her hand wasn't it. Besides, he'd already done so much for their family by bringing back Susie. And according to Jake, Delaney McPhearson was the one who'd actually found her. Mary Jane took a breath, the image of that poor woman's plane exploding wafting through her mind. She knew Jake and Laney had been close, and she could hear the pain in his voice that he was trying to hide.

All of Jake's people seemed to be targeted right now, even Jen, who'd been so helpful with Molly. She and Molly had been speaking on the phone almost every day, ever since they'd learned she was a Nephilim.

Mary Jane was still having trouble accepting it. Her sweet little girl was as strong as Superman. And if Mary Jane was having trouble accepting it, she couldn't imagine how anyone whose first exposure was Elisabeta's broadcast was handling it.

Mary Jane had been trying to hold it together ever since that first horrible broadcast. She could not understand how someone could be so evil.

And then that second one. She put a hand to her mouth, the loss of those children cutting too close to home. She had almost lost Susie not that long ago, when that same madwoman had arranged for her kidnapping. She slumped onto the bed, the reality of how easily the woman who'd taken her daughter could have taken her life. Footsteps approached her bedroom. She quickly composed her face, standing up as the door opened.

Molly peeked her head in, her long curly red hair still damp from the shower. "I got my stuff."

"That's great, honey. Um, why don't you put the clothes and stuff in my closet?"

"Okay. Um, I can't reach Jen. Do you think I should try again?"

Mary Jane had chosen to keep Jen's injuries from Molly. It would do nothing but worry her, and right now, there was enough to think about.

She shook her head. "No. I'm sure with everything happening she's just busy. But that was Jake. He's flying in. He'll be here in an hour or so."

Molly smiled. "Good. I like him."

"Me, too."

Molly placed her bag in the closet. "Uncle Jimmy is looking for you. He said they've started a countdown."

She tried to pretend that Molly's words did not terrify her. "Okay."

After Elisabeta's first broadcast, their large extended family had decided to all bunk down together until whatever this was had passed. Two of her brothers and their families were now staying at Mary Jane's. Their parents were down in Florida with her sister and their family. They would be flying back in three days. They hadn't been able to change the flight.

They'll be fine. We'll be fine. Maybe she's bluffing. But while Mary Jane didn't believe that last part, she was also really hoping that first part was true. She had seen the video of the attack on that crazy woman. Had seen her rise up from the ashes. So she had no hope that the woman would not rain down hell when the deadline arrived. And she was struggling to keep the terror that was crawling around her mind from shooting out of her mouth. Feeling Molly's gaze, she forced a smile to her face. "Is Aunt Su'Ona getting the twins set up okay?"

Molly grimaced. "Yeah, she's trying to get them down for a nap. It's not going well."

Mary Jane smiled. Her brother Charlie's kids were beautiful, intelligent, and a complete handful, especially the four-year-old twin boys. She said a small prayer of thanks that Susie was so easygoing, even with what she had been through.

Molly looked around. "Where should I put my sleeping bag?"

"No sleeping bag for you, my dear. You take the other half of the bed. We'll let your brothers have the floor."

"It's okay. I can do it. I mean, I'm . . ." She cut off her sentence at Mary Jane's look.

Mary Jane sat back on the bed, patting the space next to her. "Sit."

Molly dropped the sleeping bag and sat, not meeting Mary Jane's gaze. Mary Jane tipped her daughter's face up to look into her blue eyes. "You do not owe anything to anyone because of your abilities. It does not mean you are less than or deserve less than anyone else. Your brothers are older. They can sleep on the floor."

"It's just . . . I feel like I should be doing something. I mean, maybe I could help."

Mary Jane's heart clenched at the thought. "Abilities or no abilities, you are way too young to be thinking along those lines. And besides, what did Jen tell you?"

Molly scuffed the carpet with her toe. "That I need to train. That I will only get myself hurt."

"That's right. And these abilities do not mean you have to use them. Your father never did."

Molly leaned against Mary Jane's shoulder. "I miss him."

"I do, too," Mary Jane said lightly, although her feelings toward Billy were a little more complicated lately. She loved him. She had since she was a little older than Molly. But right now she was so mad at him for not warning her that one of their kids could have these abilities. And for it to be Molly, her quiet one, was a dagger through the heart. The boys were disappointed they didn't have the superhero abilities of their little sister. They thought of it as cool. But even at her young age, Molly had a sense of duty that came along with her abilities.

And that scared the hell out of Mary Jane. She'd seen the videos of what these people could do. She did *not* want her innocent little girl anywhere near them. She hugged Molly tight. When she was little, she'd promised Molly that there were no monsters in this world. And that if there ever were, she would protect her from them.

But how was she supposed to protect any of her children from the monsters poised to attack them now?

CHAPTER 72

INVESS, CALEVITNIA

Elisabeta threw her shredded shirt into the roaring fireplace of her room with a growl. The rest of her clothes quickly followed before she stormed to the shower. She had driven from the wreck of her estate to the safe house Sergei had set up for her. Stepping in only once the steam rolled from the water, Elisabeta let the water wash over her. Her skin was once again unblemished. In the thirty-minute drive, her wounds had completely healed.

She stayed in the water until the cold that had seeped into her bones had disappeared. She had miscalculated. She'd known they would strike the silos. Their locations had been known for decades. They'd have to be absolute idiots not to take them out. But she had not counted on them finding her home.

She wiped the last bits of moisture from her skin, slipping into her robe and tying the belt securely. *But on the bright side, they now know who I am.*

She smiled. She would never admit it to anyone, but she had had her doubts. After all, the carvings on the Göbekli Tepe skulls were thousands of years old, and she was relying on the translations of a modern-day scholar. One small misinterpretation would have rendered the entire formula useless.

She poured herself a glass of wine from the decanter on the table by the window. *Dr. Chen, apparently you were as good as you thought yourself to be. Well done.*

She tipped her glass to the heavens in silent salute before taking a sip. A knock sounded at the door. "Enter."

Two men in dark fur-lined jackets walked in, a trunk between them.

"By the fireplace."

Without a word, the men carried it over. After lowering it down, they straightened and looked at Elisabeta.

She waved them from the room. "You're dismissed."

They bowed and retreated, closing the door behind them. Elisabeta walked over, cradling her glass of wine to her chest, studying the trunk. It was an old green steamer trunk, with thick leather straps around it. It looked as if it had been kicked around quite a bit in the decades since it had been created.

Placing her glass on the mantel, she opened the trunk. The four skulls from Göbekli Tepe grinned back at her. She picked one up, feeling a bit like Hamlet. *Ah, Yorick, what a tale you could tell.*

But unlike Hamlet's departed friend, this skull could still talk. Elisabeta ran a hand over the etchings, a simple technique that contained knowledge that would change the course of humanity forever.

Placing a hand on either side of the skull, she crushed it, then dropped the pieces into the fire. Each of the other skulls experienced the same treatment. The pieces smoldered, some of the smaller bits catching fire. She knew they wouldn't be completely destroyed. The act was more symbolic. The pulverizing of the bones insured that no one would ever learn the secrets of the priests. Even the world's foremost puzzle solver would be unable to put these particular pieces back together. She grabbed the poker, shifting the pieces around.

Now they truly have taken their knowledge to their graves.

Only one more object remained in the trunk. Carefully nestled in reams of cotton, Elisabeta pulled out the Tome of the Great Mother and uncovered it.

She prepared to heave it into the fire as well but caught herself. *Perhaps not.*

Walking over to the bed, she placed the book down and flipped through it. As much as she despised the woman captured on the pages, she had to admit the women who had created the pages were true artisans. It would be a shame to destroy such a piece of beauty. Besides, there might be more knowledge that she'd need to glean from its pages. She had learned the hard way that Victoria was not someone who gave up her secrets easily. No doubt her followers were the same.

Nonetheless, she ripped the first six pages from the tome.

Certain knowledge will die with me. She smiled. *If I could die, that is.*

She walked back to the fireplace and tossed the pages in. The edges of the pages curled as they blackened. Smoke wafted out into the room. Elisabeta had memorized the instructions, should she ever need them. But she never planned on creating the mortus again. *After all, one immortal in this world is all it needs. And I am more than happy to fill that position.*

Elisabeta reclined in her chair, sipping her wine and watching the fire burn away the last chances anyone had of stopping her, or of even competing with her. Finally, she stood as the papers were reduced to ash. She changed into thick wool slacks and a heavy sweater, shivering in the cold. Why anyone would choose to live in this armpit of the world was beyond her. Lacing up her heavy boots, she strode from her room and down to the living room.

Artem looked up from where he stood at the computer desk. Luckily, he had not been with her in the courtyard. That would have truly been a loss. He had been overseeing the movement of her control room to this safe house at the time. Radar arrays lined the walls, and a long control panel ran underneath it and three other monitors.

"Are we ready?" Elisabeta asked. Elisabeta had originally planned on giving the world governments an extra twenty-four hours if McPhearson had been turned over. But then they'd tried to kill her.

"We are only your word."

"Then you have it."

CHAPTER 73

BOSTON, MASSACHUSETTS

"Five minutes!" her brother Charlie yelled from downstairs.

Mary Jane put down the book she'd been pretending to read for the last thirty minutes. She and Molly had curled up on the bed together, each with a book. She wasn't sure Molly was truly reading, either, but the reading at this moment wasn't important so much as just stealing a moment together for just the two of them.

Mary Jane sighed. "Let's go before he starts yelling a countdown every ten seconds."

"Why does Uncle Charlie yell everything?"

Mary Jane stood up. "He's a middle child, honey. He grew up thinking if he didn't yell, he wouldn't be heard." *And apparently he never grew out of it.*

They made their way down the stairs, following the noise to the family room. Jimmy stood against the back wall, a mug of coffee in his hands. Charlie turned at her arrival. Like everyone else in her family, Charlie and Jimmy had the red hair and blue eyes that were their family trademark.

"About time," he said.

Mary Jane just gave him a grimace. She really did not want to see which target that madwoman chose. But she also knew sticking her head in the sand wasn't going to help either.

Three of her nieces, Jimmy's girls, sat cross-legged on the ground in front of the TV, ages eight, nine, and ten. Susie was curled up in little Jackie's lap. Their mother, Shelly, was in the kitchen putting together some food. Shelly was always cooking.

Her nephews, Jason and Griff, Charlie's boys, were sitting at the back table with Mary Jane's two boys, Joe and Shaun, a card game in front of them.

"Where's Su'Ona?" she asked.

"Putting the twins down," Charlie said. "She's going to stay with them."

Mary Jane wended her way through the girls on the floor while Molly plopped down with them. Susie immediately crawled into Molly's lap. Mary Jane glanced out the window at the unusually quiet street. No kids raced by on skateboards. No one was taking their dog for an afternoon stroll. There wasn't even traffic.

It's like a bomb already went off.

Mary Jane took a seat on the couch, looking at the nine children in the room. They had debated whether or not to let the kids see the news coverage, but the story was everywhere. And there was no way to shield them from it.

Charlie sat down next to her, and Shelly, Jimmy's wife, walked in, leaning up against Jimmy as the countdown clock on the TV reached twenty seconds. Charlie put the sound on and grabbed Mary Jane's hand. Mary Jane grasped it back tightly. *Oh God, please help us.*

All the talk in the family room died away. There wasn't a sound in the family room, not even on the TV. The anchors had even gone mute. It was as if the whole world was collectively holding its breath as the clock counted down. Mary Jane tensed as the clock ran out.

And then . . . nothing. No sounds, no big ball of fire taking them all to the next life. A nervous laugh sounded from the boys' table before nervous smiles were shared.

Thank you. Mary Jane closed her eyes. It had been a bluff. She hadn't been able to destroy any—

"We are receiving reports of an explosion in Denver."

Mary Jane's eyes flew open.

"We go now live to a reporter on scene."

The image onscreen shifted to a nervous-looking man in a tan suit. Behind him, a large cloud of smoke could be seen. "A bomb has exploded in downtown Denver along the 16th Street Mall. We have received word of mass casualties. First responders are on the scene. And—" The man paused, his hand to his ear. His mouth opened. He swallowed hard then stared back into the camera. "We have received word that radioactive material has been detected. People need to stay away from the Denver area. If you are heading here, you need to immediately turn around."

"How far out should people be?" the anchor asked.

"At least fifty miles."

"Jack—"

Smoke wafted across the screen as Jack nodded. "Yes. I'm in the infected zone. I will keep providing coverage as long as I can. But, uh, I need a minute."

The image switched back to the anchor, who looked shaken, his face pale. He cleared his throat, but a tremor remained in his voice. "According to public records, Denver has more than half a million residents. Those not killed in the initial blast will be exposed to high levels of radiation that will take days to run their course. The death toll will be beyond anything this country, this world, has seen before. You know, um, let's just take a quick commercial break."

Charlie muted the screen as an ad for paper towels came on. But then two commercials later, the newscaster was back. The news was not any better. In fact, it was much, much worse.

"We are now receiving reports of attacks occurring at major cities across the country. The attackers appear to have enhanced speed and strength. We do not have numbers yet, but the casualties and injured are going to be high. Law enforcement asks that everyone stay indoors and if you are not, to find cover immediately."

The family room was silent. *All those people.*

"Dad?" her niece Meghan asked.

"Hey, come here, baby." Jimmy opened his arms, and his girls ran to him.

Molly looked toward the windows, then at her mother, tears in her eyes. "Can you take Susie?"

Numb, Mary Jane could only nod. She clutched Susie to herself, wondering what kind of world her children would now face. Everything had just changed, and Mary Jane didn't know how to prepare them for that. She watched numbly as the anchor returned. Images of violence flashed across the screen. People lying in the streets, cars crashed through store windows.

"It looks like a war zone," Charlie whispered.

But Mary Jane couldn't muster up a response, too horrified at what she was seeing. If this had been a movie, she would have turned it off, not wanting these images in her head or her children's. But how did you turn off real life?

Time passed, although Mary Jane couldn't say how much.

A commercial appeared, and Charlie once again muted the set. Slowly, he stood up, looking toward the window with a frown. "What is that?"

Pulled from her fog, Mary Jane stood as well. In the background, car horns blared, metal on metal crunched, followed by screams, some cut short.

Jimmy pushed off the wall, grabbing the hands of two of his girls. "Everyone in the basement."

Charlie vaulted up the stairs to get Su'Ona and the twins. Mary Jane shoved Susie at Shaun. "Get her downstairs."

Mary Jane hustled up the stairs, sprinting down the hall to her room. She ripped open the door to the closet and pulled out the shotgun Jake had left her. She grabbed the shells, dumping them in a shoulder bag before looping it over her shoulders. She ran out of the room, heading down the stairs after her brother and his family. His eyes grew large at the sight of the shotgun in her arms, but he just gave her a nod.

They hustled down the hall to the basement stairs, but before they could head down, Joe was heading back up. Mary Jane pulled him out of the way so Charlie and Su'Ona could get down with their boys. "What are you doing? Get downstairs."

Joe shook his head. "Molly's not down there."

"What? Molly!" Mary Jane yelled turning back for the stairs.

Joe raced past her. "I'll check upstairs."

"Molly!" Mary Jane yelled as she ran through the rooms on the first floor.

Jimmy appeared in the family room as Joe raced down the stairs. "What's going on?"

"Molly. We can't find her. Joe?"

"She's not upstairs."

"Where would she go?" Jimmy cried.

"I don't—" A car alarm sounded outside, followed by a scream. Chills ran over her skin.

Oh God. "She's out there."

CHAPTER 74

BALTIMORE, MARYLAND

Patrick wanted to turn off the set. He wanted to pretend that none of it was real. But he could not look away, not with the deadline having hit. He was waiting to see what new hell Elisabeta unleashed. He knew about the attack in Denver, but he knew more would be coming.

The newscaster returned, having just replayed the video of the drone strike on Elisabeta, his face ashen. "As you can see, somehow Elisabeta Roccorio survived the attack and seemed to heal. I . . . I don't know how to explain any of what we have just seen. But I know analysts will be poring over—"

The newscaster went silent as he pulled over a sheet of paper. He looked up, his jaw dropping. "Um . . ." He pulled at the collar of his shirt. "I have just received word that the explosion in Denver was not, I repeat, not the only explosion. We have reports that bombs have been detonated in Paris and Beijing as well. There is no word on casualties yet, but they are believed to be in the thousands, if not higher. Early reports indicate that the bombs were not delivered by missiles but were already on site. I have been told that radiological alarms have gone off."

Another piece of paper was slipped to him. "We, um, we have some video, I am told, from another situation breaking in the country's capitol."

The image shifted to a shaky video that looked like someone had recorded off their phone. People screamed. A fire was burning at a building down the street at the edge of the screen. A woman appeared on camera, blood splashed across her face. She kept glancing around her as she spoke.

"I'm in Alexandria, where it appears a group of Fallen have begun to attack the area surrounding the city of D.C. I, uh, I believe there are four of them. And they have killed at least twelve people that I have seen and set fires and destroyed property along the way. The police and National Guard have been mobilized but do not seem to be having any effect."

The video froze. The anchorman reappeared. "We have lost contact with Suzanne Wu. And we have been informed that military and law enforcement troops are engaged in conflict with the Fallen across the country. If you are in a safe place, police are asking that you stay where you are while they get a handle on the situation."

Cain flipped to another channel, then another. It was always a different city, but always the same violence being perpetrated. Patrick realized that his whole body felt numb now, not just his legs.

"It's starting," Cain said softly.

Patrick stared at the screen. People ran, but he focused on a little child standing still, clutching his mother lying in the street, tears streaming down his cheeks. No one stopped to help.

"No," he said, "it's ending."

CHAPTER 75

BOSTON, MASSACHUSETTS

The SUV swerved as Jake avoided a hatchback that had crashed into a telephone pole. The ride from the airport had been heartrending. All hell had broken loose. From what Jake could tell, the same was happening across the country. Elisabeta had made good on her threat. She was terrifying the world.

Jake slammed on the brakes as a man and woman sprinted in front of the hood of his Jeep. "Shit."

Zane, the large yellow spotted Javan leopard in the back of the car, let out a roar.

"I know, I know." Jake wanted to get out and help, but he wasn't sure where to start. Besides, he needed to make sure Mary Jane and her family were okay.

Get to Mary Jane. Laney's voice wafted through his mind. His grip tightened on the steering wheel. How could she be gone? After all they had been through, for it to end like that. For her to just be snuffed out of existence. Anger boiled in him. He wanted to smash everything Elisabeta held dear to pieces. But he knew there wasn't much that woman held dear. Power was all she truly craved. And with Laney out of the way, and the bombs, it was only a matter of time before she had everything she wanted.

Laney had been right. Elisabeta had been prepared for the missile attacks on the silos. Jake guessed Elisabeta had moved the radioactive material out of the missiles well before the attack had been initiated. Then she'd smuggled them in to various countries. Which meant at least nine other radioactive bombs were no doubt already in place around the world. That is, if she hadn't split the material, in which case there could be double that.

His cell rang. He answered it quickly. "Yeah?"

Mary Jane's voice was rushed. "Molly's gone. I think she went outside to help."

"I'm almost at your place."

"I'm heading out to look for her."

"No! Stay inside. It's not safe out here."

"And my daughter is out there somewhere." She disconnected the call. Jake stared at the phone in disbelief. One would think at this point he'd be used to women completely ignoring his statements, yet somehow it surprised him every time.

He drove forward slowly, not liking anything about the situation. Zane prowled between the windows in the back, his fur standing on end. Then he stopped and let out a roar. Even without Laney and Noriko's abilities, he knew what it meant. He slammed on the brakes, a telephone pole crashing to the ground, missing the Jeep by inches.

Jake's hand had barely grazed the gearshift to throw the Jeep into reverse when his window shattered.

A split second later, he was being pulled through it.

CHAPTER 76

Jake was nearby. That was good. Mary Jane loaded the shotgun, chambering a shell, glad Jake had taken her through the steps when he'd given her the gun—and also glad he hadn't let her turn it down the way she had wanted to.

"What are you doing?" Jimmy asked, his eyes large.

"I am going after Molly."

"Mary Jane, it's crazy out there. I'll go after her."

"You can come with me, Jimmy, but I am not sitting back and waiting." She headed for the door.

"I'm coming, too," Joe said.

Mary Jane didn't even turn around. "No, you're not. Get downstairs."

"I'm going with you. She's my sister. And I'll just go without you if you say no."

Mary Jane whirled around, ready to give him hell. He stood with his arms crossed, staring down at her. Down, because he was now a few inches taller than her. She recognized the stubborn crook of his jaw—Billy had had the same stubborn look.

"He's not a kid anymore," Jimmy said quietly.

"He's *my* kid," Mary Jane lashed out.

Jimmy put his hand on her shoulder. "Janie."

She took a breath. "Fine. But you stay with us."

"Great. Um, hold on." Joe sprinted down the hallway and was back seconds later. He handed Jimmy a wooden bat. He had another one in his hand.

Mary Jane swallowed hard seeing it there but just nodded. "Okay. Let's go get your sister."

CHAPTER 77

WASHINGTON, D.C.

The Oval Office was silent. Not a single person of the two dozen inside made a sound as the images of violence played out across the screen in horrific detail. Nancy's gaze was focused on a screen tuned to a local channel, showing a Fallen wreaking havoc just a few blocks from the White House.

"Madam President, we must get you to a secure location," the Secret Service agent Darrel Saunders insisted again.

The President shook her head, not taking her gaze from the screens. "My husband and son?"

"They've been secured, ma'am."

"Good."

"Madam President," Nancy said quietly, "the country needs you. We have been dealt a horrible blow, but we are going to need you to lead us through this. We need to get you to safety."

The President looked into Nancy's eyes for a long moment before nodding. "The secretary of state stays with me."

"Yes, ma'am," Saunders replied. He placed a hand on the President's shoulder, pushing her toward the door while speaking into his mic. "The Phoenix is on the move."

President Rigley had been named the Phoenix because she grew up in the Arizona city. But now, as the scenes of fire and blood played out across the world, Nancy had to wonder if there hadn't been a bit of prophetic wisdom in her call name.

Secret Service agents fell into formation around them as they hustled the President down the hall. A window shattered as a wooden flagpole slammed through it, and Nancy was shoved forward. The flagpole missed her but impaled the Secret Service agent who'd saved her.

"Move, move, move!" Saunders yelled. Gunfire sounded from right outside the White House.

As they sprinted past the windows, Nancy caught sight of a blur shifting into a man as a hail of bullets raked his chest.

Someone grabbed her shoulder and shoved her around a corner and into a waiting elevator. Half the agents piled in with Nancy and the President, and the other half took up position outside. More gunfire sounded in the distance as the elevator doors closed.

"Did he get in?" the President demanded.

"No, Madam President. He was shot. He did not make it into the building."

Nancy grabbed the agent's arm.

"Remind them to shoot them multiple times in the heart. It is the only way to kill them." The Secret Service agent nodded at Nancy, relaying her message into the radio.

The doors slid open. Concrete walls and a floor greeted them. They were fifteen stories beneath the White House, in what the public considered the emergency bunker. But it was much more than a bomb shelter. The entirety of the United States government could be run from the four rooms that made up the control room. Missile control, electrical grids, water security—they were all headquartered here.

There was even rumor of an Internet kill switch that could be activated if it became necessary, although even Nancy didn't know if that was true. The original underground bunker had been created in the 1950s under Truman, but it had been added on to over the years. Now there were rumors that an entire tunnel system had been created under the White House leading to Camp David, the Pentagon, the Capitol, and the VP's residence. She'd never been in a position to care more about it than idle curiosity. But with everything happening, she had a feeling she might soon learn a great deal about the incredibly secret tunnel system.

Ahead, two Marines stood on guard on either side of two metal doors. They started to swing them open as the President approached.

The President shook her head. "I'm going to the apartment."

Saunders relayed the instructions over his mic as they strode past the doors and down the hall. Another set of double doors guarded by another two Marines was at the end of the hall.

"Are we secure?" the President asked.

"Yes, ma'am."

"Good. It will just be myself and the secretary."

"Yes, ma'am." Saunders nodded to the Marines at the door, who swung them open.

The President strode through. Nancy followed, looking around. She'd never been in the apartment. It had been set up in case there was an attack that required the President to remain in the bunker for weeks or even months. Down the hall, on the other side of the elevator, was another larger apartment that could hold up to fifty people.

But Nancy was sure it was not as comfortable as this apartment, with its plush carpet, small kitchen, three bedrooms, two bathrooms, and a study.

"You've never been down here?"

"No. Luckily there's never been any reason until now."

The President nodded, slowly looking around. "What have I done, Nancy?"

"This isn't your fault."

"You say that, but I think the history books will have a different interpretation. What was the last count?"

"Three thousand in Denver from the initial blast, and the analysts only have estimates for the Fallen attacks."

"What is the estimate?"

Nancy hesitated. "A million."

"My God."

"What would you like me to do, Madam President?"

"What can we do? She has us. We've already lost a million people to this madness. How many more will Elisabeta demand?"

"All of them. Until she gets what she wants, she will demand all of them."

"I'm afraid you're right." The President stopped pacing, looking at a bust of George Washington. "You know, when Washington crossed the Delaware, he was faced with impossible odds. They planned three crossings, and only one made it. The Hessians knew they were coming thanks to a British spy and two American deserters. Even Mother Nature fought against them with an ice storm."

Nancy was familiar with the story. "Yet they continued on, and they won."

"They did. Because the morale of the army was fading. Washington knew they needed a victory, something to rally the troops and get more men to join, so he did the impossible. I've thought about him more than any other president since this all began. I've found myself wondering more than once: What would he do in this situation?"

Nancy had no answer for that. Their odds made the crossing of the Delaware look like child's play.

But the President continued, apparently not having expected an answer. "Historians say if he hadn't managed the crossing, the

United States never would have been. He also stepped down after two terms, saying that no one should have the power of the Presidency at his fingertips for longer than that. He was a most reluctant President, according to many, with no ambitions of power beyond being able to serve the public trust."

"Elisabeta does not seem to share his view of the restraint of power."

"No, she certainly doesn't." The President turned to face Nancy. "Is there anything else we can try?"

Nancy wanted to give the President something. She wanted to say that the United States of America would never bow to terrorists. But at what further cost? Would they have to sacrifice millions more, only to come right back to the same decision? "I do not believe so, Madam President."

"No, I don't believe so, either." The President blew out a breath. "All right. I think I need a little time alone. If you can, set up the call in the control room in five minutes."

Nancy bowed. "Yes, Madam President." She knocked on the door, and the Marine outside opened it for her.

Nancy headed down the hall, feeling the weight of what they were about to do. After two hundred years of being a beacon of freedom to the world, the United States was going to hand over their control to an autocrat with unlimited power. The fact that this was the only option that would save millions of lives was cold solace.

CHAPTER 78

BOSTON, MASSACHUSETTS

When they were kids, every time Mary Jane and her cousins got together, they played the same game—Bloody Murder. They'd wait until dark, and then one person would go hide in the yard. The other fifteen cousins would count to twenty on base. Then they would spread out across the yard, looking for them. The person who was "it" would leap from their hiding spot and try to tag as many people as possible before they made it back to base. Then all the people tagged would be "it," too. It got to a point where there were fourteen people hiding and only two slowly walking through the yard looking for them.

Mary Jane hated that game. The dark, the shadows, the cousins waiting to jump out at them—it had been terrifying. Her heart would pound, her head would swivel back and forth at every sound, every shifting shadow.

But right now, Mary Jane would take a hundred games of Bloody Murder with her cousins over this real-life version. Even though it was daylight, Mary Jane's heart still pounded. She tried not to jump at every shift of the wind, but it was so hard.

They were only two blocks from home, and already they had seen two houses on fire. The neighbors had gotten out, and other people were trying to contain the blaze with garden hoses until the fire department arrived. But from the amount of sirens she'd heard in the distance, Mary Jane was sure that was a long way in coming.

She honestly felt like she was in one of those zombie shows her boys watched. The normally bustling neighborhood was absent of pedestrian traffic. And any people they did see were running.

"I don't like this," Jimmy whispered from next to her.

Mary Jane didn't answer, just nodded her head.

Joe was a few feet in front of them and didn't hear the comment. He put his hand in the air, which Mary Jane thought meant stop. But being Mary Jane wasn't a soldier and Joe had learned all his hand signals from TV, she couldn't be sure. She stopped anyway.

Joe turned around, his eyes wide. "Hide."

Jimmy grabbed her arm and dragged her behind a car. Joe dove in behind them, his finger to his lips.

Mary Jane struggled to keep her breathing quiet, which made it sound like a freight train in the silence. She strained, trying to hear anything over it. But then she heard the sound of footfalls on gravel. Her breath no longer became a problem, because she was pretty sure she had stopped breathing.

She leaned down to look under the car and could just make out a pair of sneakers about twenty feet away on the other side. A car engine sounded. The sneakers disappeared from view in a blur.

An awful crash sounded down the street. Joe ducked his head out to see. Jimmy yanked him back. "What are you doing?" he whispered furiously.

"It's the Ilahis' minivan. It's on its side."

Mary Jane edged past Joe to peer out. The blue car was on its side, but she couldn't see any sign of the man who'd done the damage. "I—I think he might be gone."

"We don't know that," Jimmy said.

Mary Jane turned to Joe. "How did you know he was a Fallen?"

Joe wiped at the sweat that dotted his forehead. "When I reached the intersection, he blurred into shape a block away, his back to us."

Mary Jane's heart lurched. If the man hadn't been facing the other direction . . . She gripped Joe's hand. He squeezed hers back just as tightly.

A baby's cry sounded from inside the van, but no one moved.

"That's Gurriya," Joe said.

Mary Jane looked between Jimmy and her son. And it was like Bloody Murder all over again. Although now, that horrific name took on an even greater meaning. "Okay. We help them, but if we see any sign of that man, we hide, okay?"

"Mom—"

"Joe, we can't help anyone if we're dead, okay?"

He nodded, and Mary Jane knew it was tough for him. He was a teenager and still thought he was invulnerable.

After a quick glance back out, she scurried from their hiding spot, crossing the street to hide behind an old green Ford F110. No one yelled. No blur appeared. She peered around. The minivan was just around the corner. Gurriya had gone silent, which made Mary Jane nervous. The windshield was cracked. Someone was slumped over the steering wheel. It had to be Obeid. His wife Ayesha was a police officer who was on duty today. Obeid didn't move. Joe and Jimmy sprinted across the street, ducking down low next to her.

"It looks clear," Joe said.

Gurriya cried again.

"Let's go." She raced toward the van. Joe outpaced her and got there first.

Heart in her throat, she watched in terror as her son hoisted himself onto the side of the van and through the driver's open window. He wiggled past Obeid.

"How is he?"

"Alive," Joe said.

"Check the kids."

Joe disappeared inside, then reappeared only seconds later. "Ehsan and Gurriya are here. Both are awake but just kind of staring."

"They're in shock." Mary Jane looked around the windshield. "Joe, get in the passenger seat and kick out the windshield."

Joe scrambled into the seat.

"Shouldn't we break it from out here?" Jimmy asked.

"No. This way will be safer."

Joe slammed his feet into the windshield, one, two, three times. The edge of the windshield lifted up. Mary Jane and Jimmy helped peel it back, jumping back as the whole thing came loose and crashed onto the street. Mary Jane quickly climbed through, checking Obeid's injuries. She really would prefer if they had a backboard to put him on, but they didn't have time to wait. "Jimmy, I need your help."

Jimmy stood in front of Obeid outside the windshield frame. "How do you want to handle this?"

"I'm going to see if I can release his seat belt. Can you brace him and then pull him out?"

"What about me?" Joe asked.

"Help guide his feet out when he's free."

Jimmy moved closer. Crouching under Obeid, Jimmy pinned him to the seat. "Go."

She hit the release and said a quiet thank-you when it let go of the seat belt without any fight. Obeid tumbled forward, but Jimmy caught him. Carefully, he slipped his hands under Obeid's arms and stepped through the windshield frame. As Jimmy pulled him through, Joe helped guide his feet out. Mary Jane slipped into the back of the van.

Ehsan was only two years old, just a little older than Susie. They played together a lot. "Hey, Ehsan."

Ehsan's bottom lip trembled.

"Hey, hey, it's okay." Mary Jane quickly felt around Ehsan's car seat, but felt no injuries, and Ehsan didn't cry out.

"I'm just going to check on your sister real quick, okay?"

Gurriya stared up at Mary Jane with her big brown eyes. "Hey, sweet girl. It's okay. I'm going to get you out of there."

Joe appeared right behind her. "What do you need, Mom?"

"I'm going to see if we can keep Gurriya in her car seat. It's probably the safest way to transport her right now. Can you stand underneath and brace it like your uncle did with Obeid while I release it?"

"Sure." Joe slid past her, crouching low under the seat. With a quick prayer to the gods who made infant car seats a nightmare for parents everywhere, she pulled on the release while tugging the car seat toward her. It came free.

Oh, thank you, Jesus.

Joe helped her right the car seat. Then he stepped through the two front seats, and she handed the car seat to him. "Get her outside to your uncle. Then come back and help me with Ehsan."

"Okay." Joe disappeared.

Mary Jane made quick work of Ehsan's straps and huddled him close to her. He gripped her tightly. "It's okay, little man. I've got you."

Joe reappeared. It took her a minute to get Ehsan to release her, but she finally managed to hand him through the seats. Quickly following them, she climbed out of the car.

Jimmy had Obeid lying on the side of the road. Gurriya was in the car seat next to him. Mary Jane hurried over, leaning down to Obeid. "How is he?"

"Breathing, but I think he took a pretty good hit to the head from the steering wheel," Jimmy said.

"He probably hurt his ribs too, then." Mary Jane pulled back one of Obeid's eyelids. The pupil was rolled back. "I don't think he's waking up anytime soon."

Joe stood behind her, holding Ehsan while rubbing his back. "What do we do?"

Mary Jane looked around. There was no sign of that man, but she didn't think waiting out in the open for an ambulance was the best idea. "Okay, we need to get them back to our house. Su'Ona can look them over. Jimmy, can you manage Obeid?"

"No problem."

"Joe, can you get Gurriya and Ehsan?"

He frowned. "Yeah, but what about you?"

"We came out here to find Molly. You two are going back. I'm going to keep looking."

Joe shook his head. "What? No."

Mary Jane put up her hand. "I'm not debating this, and I'm not asking for anyone's permission. I am telling you what is going to happen."

"I don't like this," Jimmy muttered.

"You don't get a vote. Now go."

With one last look, Jimmy swung Obeid's body over his shoulder and headed back toward their house. Joe slipped the car seat handle over one arm, cradling Ehsan with the other. He turned toward her, his worry clear. "Mom?"

She forced a smile to her face. "I'll only go a little farther, and then I'll be right behind you, okay?"

"Promise?"

She nodded. "Promise. Now get going."

Mary Jane only watched their progress for a little while before turning and starting back down the street. She'd lied to her kids before. All parents did. The lightning can't get you. Yes, Santa is watching, even in February.

But this lie, it felt heavier, because she knew in her heart she wasn't going back without her daughter. Last time, she had been powerless to help Susie. This time, she was getting her daughter back.

No matter what.

CHAPTER 79

BOSTON, MASSACHUSETTS

Jake had his hand on his Glock as soon as the driver's window broke, and he pulled it free as he was yanked from the car. Without looking at his assailant, he pressed the Glock up against the man's ribs and pulled the trigger four times.

With a yell, the grip on the back of his shirt lessened. Jake slammed to the hard asphalt as Zane burst through the window behind him. His large jaw closed around the back of the man's throat. Blood poured onto Jake's neck as he yanked himself from the Fallen's grasp.

"Release," he ordered Zane, who'd dragged the man to the ground. Jake placed the muzzle of his gun against the man's chest right over the heart and fired three times.

The light in the man's eyes dimmed, then went out. Zane let out a roar.

"Thanks, buddy."

Reaching in through the shattered window, Jake turned the engine off. Pulling out the keys, he scanned the neighborhood. Two houses were on fire. Cars were smashed, although it looked like they had been parked when the destruction happened. His car was still drivable, but with the telephone pole blocking the road, he had a feeling it would be quicker to get to Mary Jane's on foot. He looked down at the large leopard who stood next to him, doing his own scan of the area.

"Now go see who you can help."

Zane hesitated.

"I'll be okay. You know where I'm heading."

With one last look, Zane bounded through a yard and over a fence.

Checking to make sure the man who had attacked him was truly dead, Jake ejected the magazine and loaded a full one. Holstering it, he went to the back of the Jeep and pulled out his M60. Slamming the door shut, he paused, getting his bearings. A blur flashed across the street. The front door of a house obliterated. Screams sounded from inside. Jake took off at a run.

~

TWENTY MINUTES LATER, Jake was still moving. He'd killed one additional Fallen, wounded another, saved maybe a dozen people, and seen at least twice that many dead. He'd tried Mary Jane again, but either the cell towers were down or overwhelmed with calls. He'd spotted Zane a few times in between houses, and in one case, he was dragging a child from a burning house.

But he still hadn't seen any sign of Molly or Mary Jane. A shadow shifted behind a car. Jake whirled around, his finger on the trigger, and Zane stepped out.

"Jesus, Zane. I almost shot you."

Zane bumped him.

"No, I wouldn't have really shot you. You okay?"

Zane just looked at him. His face and fur had spots of blood, but it didn't look like he had any injuries.

"Okay, good."

At the end of the street, an SUV came around a corner too fast. Jake stepped toward the street. "What the hell are they doing?"

A blur bolted out from between two houses and slammed into the side of the car. It flipped twice before coming to a stop on its roof. The engine caught fire.

A second blur bolted from the opposite side of the road. The driver's door went flying. Jake could just make out red hair as the driver stumbled into view. Jake started to run.

Molly disappeared again, then reappeared. She pushed a baby toward the driver and told him to run. She turned just as the Fallen slammed into her. Molly flew across the road, crashing into a car across the street. The windows shattered with the impact.

"No!" Jake yelled. Zane was already outpacing him.

But neither of them was fast enough. Molly crumpled to the street, and the Fallen was on her. He grabbed her by the neck, pulling her up, then he turned, placing Molly so Jake had no shot.

The Fallen smiled. And Jake knew that no matter how fast he ran, he wasn't going to get to her in time.

CHAPTER 80

Jake had never run so fast in his life, but a second Fallen swooped in and dove for him. By what could only have been divine intervention, Jake caught sight of the movement from the corner of his eye and threw himself to the side, firing as soon as he landed. The shot caught the Fallen in the shoulder and turned it from a blur into a woman. Jake fired again and again, catching the woman in the chest.

He didn't check to see if the woman was dead, just unloaded three more shots in her chest. He scrambled to his feet in time to see Zane launch himself at the back of the Fallen holding Molly. The man screamed. Molly kicked herself free as Zane took a chunk from the man's back.

Molly hit the ground hard and scrambled back. The Fallen reached over and grabbed Zane to throw him.

"No!" Jake's heart was in his throat as Molly tackled him at the waist, hitting him right at the hip. He buckled, losing his grip on Zane as he fell back. Molly rolled to the side, crashing into the wheels of a panel truck. The Fallen got to his feet a little wobbly, but he still advanced on Molly.

"You little—"

A shotgun blast caught him in the upper back. He whirled around, and another one caught him in the stomach.

"Get away from my daughter!" Mary Jane yelled.

Jake pulled his M60, finally having a shot, and caught the Fallen in the back of the head. He toppled forward. Mary Jane ran around him, sprinting for Molly. She yanked her up into her arms as Jake advanced on the Fallen. He unloaded three more shots into the man's heart before turning to Mary Jane.

Mary Jane ran a hand through Molly's red curls. "What were you thinking? You could have been killed!"

Molly was shaking. "I was helping people. People need help, Mom."

"But *you* don't have to be the one to help them."

"If not me, then who? God gave me these powers, and you always tell us God has a plan. I think He'd want me to use them for good."

Mary Jane ran a hand through her hair before pulling Molly back toward her. "Stop sounding so smart. I'm supposed to be the parent."

Molly wrapped her arms around her mom.

"Are you both okay?" Jake asked as he approached.

Mary Jane nodded. "Yes. Thank you again."

"I'm not sure you needed me."

Mary Jane's eyes grew large as Zane sat down next to Jake.

Jake scratched the giant cat behind the ears. "This is Zane. He's a friend of mine."

Molly reached out a hand. Zane licked it. She smiled before looking up at her mom. "There are still people who need help."

"You're not trained to fight—"

"I'm not fighting," she said quickly. "I've helped people get to safety, get out of houses, things like that. I'm not fighting, I swear."

An explosion sounded a block away, causing all of them to jump.

Molly turned back to her mom, her voice pleading. "People need help, Mom. And I can help."

"I hate this," Mary Jane said, her chin trembling. She kissed her daughter on the forehead. "Be careful."

Molly smiled. "I will."

"Zane, stay with Molly," said Jake.

Molly looked at Jake in surprise, then grinned down at Zane. "Come on, Zane." She took off down the street.

"I'll take you home," Jake said.

"No. My daughter's out here helping people. I should be, too." She put up a hand before Jake could say anything. "I'm a nurse, Jake. I'm pretty sure there are more than a few people nearby who could use my help."

He took in the set of her jaw and knew she was going to help no matter what he said. He nodded. "Okay. But you stay with me, all right?"

"All right." She paused. "And Jake?"

"Yeah?"

"I'm glad you're here."

He smiled. "Me, too."

CHAPTER 81

INVESS, CALEVITNIA

The numbers were beginning to be broadcast across the news outlets. Two million dead in the United States, half a million in England, twenty thousand in Japan, and so on. The death tolls rolled from the news anchors' mouths like music to Elisabeta's ears. Such beautiful deaths, all done to make sure Elisabeta achieved glory. She smiled. Her people would be well rewarded for their efforts. Each would be given a little piece of the world to rule. Within limits, of course. Elisabeta would be the final rule of law, but she would give them free rein so long as they followed her dictates and didn't get too out of hand.

She frowned at the screen as the news anchor switched from reciting deaths to narratives from the violence.

"There have been some reports that some enhanced humans have been fighting back against the attackers. We have confirmed at least a dozen cases of such incidents, suggesting that not all enhanced beings are on the side of Elisabeta Roccorio. What this means in the days going forward is anyone's guess."

Well, that just won't do. As soon as the countries of the world bowed down to her, she would have to root out those traitors and make an example of them. The world needed to know what she did to traitors.

Artem knocked on her door, a smile on his face. "The President of the United States is on the phone."

"Well, by all means, let's not keep her waiting." She reached for her phone as it buzzed. "Margaret, how lovely to hear from you."

"Ms. Roccorio."

"I assume you are calling about my offer?"

The President hesitated before speaking, her voice stiff. "On behalf of the United States government, I bequeath the control of our country to you."

Elisabeta smiled. "Well, that's just wonderful." She waved to Artem.

"I have just instructed my associates to discontinue any attacks in the United States." She waited. "Do you not have anything to say to that?"

"Thank you."

"You are very welcome. Now, I am going to need you to contact the other members of the Big 20 and tell them of your decision."

"All right."

"And I'd like you to make an announcement to the press. *You* will make the announcement, not one of your lackeys. My people have a statement prepared for you to read. There are a few details we will need to work out, but as soon as the statement is finalized, you will release it immediately."

"Very well."

"And I will need your help with one of those details."

"And *what* is that?"

Elisabeta narrowed her eyes. "Careful with the tone, Margaret. I can easily begin the attacks again."

The President released a breath. "How can I help you?"

"That is more like it. And don't worry. No one will be hurt. In fact, what I need from you is a quintessential American tradition."

CHAPTER 82

LYNCHBURG, VIRGINIA

The plane carrying Noriko, Mustafa, and Gerard landed at a small airport in Virginia, south of Baltimore. Noriko had slept for most of the trip, but when she'd awoken, the tension in the cabin had not eased. They'd had no communication from anyone back home, which was making her nervous, even though it was part of the plan. Mustafa looked like he wanted to kill Gerard. Gerard was ignoring him, but there was a tautness to his movements that he usually didn't have. The plane touched down with a little bump, then they were taxiing off the runway.

As soon as the plane stopped moving, Mustafa stood up and stretched. "Finally. Now let's get back to Baltimore."

"Actually, we are heading to North Carolina."

"Why?" Mustafa demanded.

"I don't suppose if I asked you to trust me, you would?"

Mustafa snorted. "No chance."

"Look, there's stuff going on you don't know about. No one can know we're back yet."

"Why?" Mustafa asked again.

"Laney's orders."

Mustafa eyed Gerard. "Convenient that I haven't been able to reach her."

"No, not really convenient," Gerard muttered.

Mustafa pulled out his phone. "Finally a signal. I'm going to touch base with Matt. You can do whatever you—"

Gerard moved so fast it was almost like he materialized right behind Mustafa. He hit him on the back of the head. Mustafa pitched forward, and Noriko screamed. Gerard caught him before he could hit the ground. He hoisted him over his shoulder with very little effort, grabbing Mustafa's phone, which had fallen to the ground, and sliding it into his back pocket.

Noriko backed away from him. "Wh-what are you doing?"

"Mustafa can't call in. Not yet."

"But why?"

"It's complicated, Noriko, but I need you to trust me."

She did trust him, even though every action since they'd gotten back on the plane suggested she shouldn't. But she couldn't figure out which side to listen to—the side that told her to trust him or the rational side that told her she was crazy if she did. "And if I don't want to trust you? If I want to leave?"

He shook his head, pain in his eyes. "I can't let you do that."

"Oh."

He extended his hand to her, but she skirted around it, wondering just how stupid she had been this whole time.

CHAPTER 83

NAGS HEAD, NORTH CAROLINA

Gerard had driven her and Mustafa to the edge of some large body of water. Noriko wasn't sure what it was. He had a boat waiting, which had taken them to a small island with a well-laid-out cottage. Then he'd just left after sedating Mustafa with something. That had been four hours ago.

Mustafa had only come to about an hour ago. He'd searched the small island, but without a boat, there was no way off. They couldn't see the mainland in the dark, so swimming was out. For now, they just had to wait.

Noriko had scrubbed down the surfaces she could reach to pass the time, but now she had nothing to do but pace. "Where did he go?"

"I don't know." Mustafa fiddled with the rabbit ears on the old TV. Noriko didn't think there were TVs anymore that used antennas, but Mustafa mentioned something about a digital converter box that allowed analog TVs to receive digital signals or something like that.

It was the only piece of electronics on the island besides the toaster. There wasn't even a coffee machine, just a French press. Gerard had left Mustafa's phone, but there was no signal. Mustafa had been quiet since he'd come back from searching the island, but Noriko could feel his anger. She couldn't blame him.

"I don't understand any of this," she said. "Why aren't we going back to the estate? Laney needs to know what we've found before she makes any decisions."

"Ah! Yes!" Mustafa stepped back from the TV. "Success."

Noriko tried to smile, but she was worried. What was Gerard up to? He wasn't working with Elisabeta again, was he?

She glanced over to the table at the sack they'd uncovered from the Osiris Temple. He'd left it behind, just asking Noriko not to open it, saying that that honor belonged to Laney.

He wouldn't have done that if he was betraying us, right?

Plus he'd left Mustafa his gun and an additional shotgun that Mustafa had found in a closet. It could have been an oversight on Gerard's part, but he was pretty thorough. Of course, if he wasn't planning on coming back, whether or not Mustafa was armed was irrelevant.

Lights and sounds from the TV interrupted her thoughts as Mustafa tried to find a channel without too much static. Mustafa muttered to himself as he switched the channels. Noriko vaguely listened to him and the sounds of the TV as she walked to the front window to look and see if Gerard was returning. But yet again there was no sign of him.

"—Delaney McPhearson's plane."

Noriko whirled around at the familiar name coming out of the anchor's mouth. "What ha—"

But Mustafa put up a hand, turning up the volume. "The Coast Guard reached the crash site and found no survivors. For those just joining us, we are recapping the events of the last few hours. The plane carrying Delaney McPhearson to Calevitnia, at the demand of Elisabeta Roccorio, was shot out of the sky. McPhearson and the man accompanying her, Drake, a Las Vegas entertainer, are both presumed dead. Their deaths have rattled—" Mustafa lowered the volume, his jaw hanging open.

Noriko sunk on the couch. She felt numb as all of Gerard's actions came into clearer focus. Her hand flew to her mouth.

What have I done?

Gerard had asked her not to say anything about her vision of Elisabeta, but maybe if Laney had known, maybe she would have done something different. And now she was dead.

"That's why we didn't go back to the estate," said Noriko. "Gerard knew. Somehow he knew."

"There's more." Mustafa turned the volume back up. The anchors described the last hour in excruciating detail. The radiological bombs, the Fallen attacking across the country. Noriko sat with her hand to her mouth, horror growing with each new violent act discussed. They'd been in the air when all this had happened. In the air and kept off any media that would give them news. The betrayal cut her quick and deep.

How could you, Gerard? She couldn't deny what was in front of her. Gerard had kept them from learning about any of this. He'd used her to help find the Omni, and then . . .

Her head turned to the table where the leather sack lay. But why leave it with them? Why not take it with him?

"That bastard." Mustafa muted the TV before he strode across the room. He grabbed the shotgun he'd placed on the kitchen table. Loading it, he thrust it toward Noriko.

She backed away, her hands up. "What? What are you doing?"

"You need to take this. And if you see Gerard, you need to shoot him."

"What? Why?"

"He played us, Noriko. We should have gone straight back to the estate when we arrived. But we didn't. We came here so Gerard could do what, exactly? Get the lay of the land?"

"But he wouldn't—"

"Laney is dead." Mustafa stumbled over the word, then

straightened his shoulders, his eyes burning. "It's not a coincidence that she dies and he disappears. He's probably been feeding information to Elisabeta this whole time."

"But why? I mean, why bring us along?"

"For cover. To ensure he could get his hands on the Omni."

"But why not kill us once he had it?"

"I don't know. But I know if we had gone straight to the estate or even just called her, Laney might still be alive. She could have used the Omni. Given herself powers that could have protected her. But he kept that from her."

Noriko knew what Mustafa was saying was plausible, but it didn't feel right. "No, Gerard wouldn't do that. He wouldn't."

"He did, Noriko. And now you need to protect yourself." Mustafa took a breath. "We need to go. We need to find a boat, a canoe, a log, and get the hell out of here."

"But Gerard—"

"Is not coming back, and if he does, we need to shoot first and ask questions later."

Noriko's gaze flashed back to the TV, where an exploding plane took up the screen. She flinched, imagining Laney in that plane. Was it true? Had Gerard been deceiving them this whole time?

Mustafa slung his pack over his shoulder. "Let's go."

Noriko nodded slowly, moving with not nearly as much energy. How had she been so wrong? She pictured him, the look in his eyes.

Did you betray us? Betray Laney?

Mustafa opened the door and found Gerard reaching for the handle from the other side.

Mustafa had his gun clear of the holster in a split second and pulled the trigger. Noriko screamed as Gerard pushed the gun to the left, just avoiding getting shot. Gerard grabbed Mustafa's wrists, holding them against the open door.

"What the hell are you doing?" he yelled.

"You betrayed us! You sold us out to *her*." Mustafa sneered the last word. "And Laney's dead because of it."

"Not exactly," a voice said from behind Gerard.

Noriko stumbled back as two people appeared from the shadows.

"How?" Mustafa breathed out.

"Well, if you promise not to try and shoot Gerard again, I will be happy to tell you the whole story." Laney shivered, and Noriko noticed her damp clothes and hair for the first time. "*After* a shower and some warm clothes."

CHAPTER 84

The fire in the fireplace had been built up when Laney stepped back into the main room of the cabin. Mustafa stepped away from the window and embraced her. "Thank Allah you're all right."

"Well, this time I think it's Gerard we have to thank for that."

Mustafa's face tightened. Laney squeezed his hand. "He's been helping me."

"How?" Noriko asked from the kitchen table. Laney opened her mouth, then closed it as the scent of fresh brewed coffee hit her. "I will tell you everything for a cup of that coffee."

A few minutes later, they were all sitting at the kitchen table. Laney took another sip of the coffee, savoring its warmth. It was filling in the few cold spots the shower had left behind. She still couldn't believe she and Drake were here—alive. And from the looks on Mustafa and Noriko's faces, she was not the only one.

"Okay, I think we've been patient enough," Mustafa said. "How on earth are you two alive? And what does this have to do with Gerard?"

Drake draped his arm along the back of Laney's chair. "We are here because Delaney McPhearson is a brilliant woman."

"I don't know about that," she said. "I think luck played a big role, too."

"Nope. I stand by brilliant."

Laney smiled.

Mustafa rolled his eyes. "Right, brilliant, lucky. I'll agree to both. Just how did you get out of the plane before the missile hit?"

Laney took a sip. "We didn't. We were in the plane when the missile hit."

∼

Drake sat at the controls as the plane taxied down the runway, then took off. Laney's knee bounced up and down continuously in the copilot's seat.

"I realize our first plane ride together was a little stressful, but I think I've demonstrated I can fly. And out of our entire trip, this part is going to be the least nerve-wracking."

She just gave him a distracted smile.

He frowned. But then the plane began to level out as Drake set the plane on auto-pilot. "I cannot believe I let you talk me into this."

Laney clipped off her seat belt, vaulting to her feet.

"What are you—"

But Laney didn't answer, as she'd already disappeared out the cockpit's door.

Unbuckling himself, he followed her. "Laney, what's—" He stopped.

Laney had a knife in her hand, and she had started cutting the cushions off the seats.

Drake stared at her, dumbfounded, wondering if she had finally lost it. It would be understandable, he supposed, with everything she'd been through. "Uh, what are you doing?"

"Help me." *She handed him the knife.* "Cut off the ones on the other side."

"Um, why am I—"

But Laney had already hurried down the aisle, disappearing into the plane's galley. He looked around the cabin as if somehow answers to Laney's behavior were going to appear. But nothing jumped out at him. With a sigh, he ripped through the seat, yanking off the padding.

Great. She's lost it. She's probably scrounging around for tinfoil to make us matching hats.

Laney hustled back down the aisle, two small oxygen tanks in her hand and two helmets. He frowned. "What are those?"

"Specially designed helmets that double as oxygen masks."

"And Gerard has them on his plane because . . . ?"

"Because he is well prepared." *She thrust one of the helmets toward him.* "Put this on."

She pulled on the other helmet, clipping the tank to her belt before grabbing the padding she'd cut off and heading back toward the galley. "Come on."

Grabbing the padding and cradling the helmet under his arm, he frowned as he followed her. "Have you lost it? Should I be binding you up in straps or something? Because the plane already has oxygen."

She glared at him. "I have not lost it. And I am trying not to lose it, so do what I say for once without argument. Please?"

It was the please that caught him as she swung two cabinets away from the wall. He shoved the helmet on his head, clipping the tank to his belt as well. She reached behind another cabinet and pushed a button. The metal siding slid back, revealing a space in the wall.

"What is that?"

"A smuggler's box. It's in the wing. Grab that iPad." *She nudged her chin toward the counter as she threw all the padding into the space, lining it up around the edges.* "And hurry."

He grabbed the iPad, handing it to her as she crawled in. Drake crawled in after her, wondering what the hell was going on. Laney hit a button on the inside of the space. The metal door slid shut. It was a really tight fit.

"Laney, what's—" *But he cut himself off as he saw the image on the iPad. The picture was broken up into four quadrants, all shots of empty sky.* "Is that around the plane?"

Laney nodded. "Elisabeta's never going to let us get to Calevitnia. I figure she'll do something when we are over the water."

"What's that?" Drake pointed to the bottom-left screen.

Laney sucked in a breath, enlarging the image. "Hold this." Laney shoved the tablet into his chest.

Drake grasped it. "What are doing?"

"Praying I don't miscalculate," Laney said.

∼

MUSTAFA LOOKED between Drake and Laney. "I don't get it. How did you survive?"

"I managed to turn the plane enough that the missile hit the fuselage as far from the wing we were in as I could manage, and just as it hit, I released the wing."

"Released it?" Noriko asked.

"It was designed to come off and act as a dump for any contraband," Gerard said.

Noriko frowned. "But the plane would crash, wouldn't it?"

"Yeah, well, it was only meant for extreme situations," Gerard said.

"Which this definitely qualified as," Laney said.

"Once we hit the water, I swam us out of there as fast as I could manage," Drake said.

"And I picked them up," said Gerard.

"That's the part I don't get. How is Gerard part of this? How did he find you?" Mustafa asked.

"A tracer. He gave it to me before you guys left," Laney said.

"I had to head a little farther north so we would come into the coast well away from the crash site," Gerard said.

Laney took another sip of coffee, keeping her hands around the mug as she spoke. "Gerard came to the cabin in Pennsylvania. He told me about your vision. We agreed to keep it to ourselves until we figured out what to do. Once it became clear that Elisabeta was not going to allow me to interfere with her plans, we decided I needed to die."

"Did anyone else know?" Mustafa asked.

"Just Gerard."

Drake grunted.

Laney took his hand. "I wasn't sure it would work. I didn't want to get anyone's hopes up. And it was safer for everyone to think I died. There was no guarantee it would work."

Noriko looked at Drake. "You got on that plane thinking you were going to die."

Drake shrugged. "Temporary insanity."

Laney looked over at him. "No, you were running to my rescue."

He picked up her hand and kissed it. "And I always will."

Noriko sighed across from them.

When Laney had been walking across that runway, she had been terrified. She knew Elisabeta would try to take her out en route. She had her escape plan, but it relied on perfect timing. And she'd also have to convince the pilot to go along with her.

So many things could have gone wrong. But then Drake had appeared, first yelling at her that she was playing right into Elisabeta's hands, then promising to stand with her until the end.

Her heart filled again thinking of his words. *If you are resolved to do this, then I guess I am as well. Because without you, it is not a life I wish to live.*

Noriko looked at Gerard. "So you didn't betray us?"

"No," he said softly, and Noriko smiled.

Drake cleared his throat. "Well, touching as this little moment is, perhaps we should focus on the issue at hand." Laney elbowed him in the ribs.

"What was that for?"

"For being thick. Ignore him, but maybe you guys could catch me up."

Mustafa's mouth fell open. "You knew we were looking for

the Omni?"

"She sent me to get it," Gerard said.

"So all of this, it was a sham?" Mustafa asked.

Laney nodded. "I wasn't sure how it could help us at first. I thought giving me the powers of the Fallen would give me an edge in a face-to-face battle with Elisabeta. But now I think it might do even more."

"Elisabeta set things up to work in her favor," said Laney. "Threatening all the governments, inciting them to act. She knew it would tie my hands, which it did. I need to be able to get to her without going through a committee *and* without it being on every news station. The only way for that to happen was to take me out of the picture. And I knew Elisabeta would not risk a face-to-face. She couldn't chance that I might win. She would take the first opportunity to take me out and to demonstrate to the world her power. And she did exactly that."

"So what is the plan now?" Mustafa asked.

Laney held out her hand. With a nod, Gerard crossed the room to his pack and pulled out the box with the Omni. He handed it to Laney.

The box felt heavy in Laney's hands as she stood. "Have you looked inside?"

"Only to verify that the box was in there," Gerard said.

Mustafa brought over a lamp. Turning it on, he placed it on the table. Laney nodded her thanks. Her heart rate ticked up. She took a breath, trying to calm her breathing, but it was difficult. The moment she had seen the bag, the moment she'd known the box was in there, she had these flickers of memory rolling through her mind, flickers from her life as Helen.

The people she had known came through like a tidal wave, especially her siblings Castor, Pollux, and Clytemnestra.

Clytemnestra, her sister. That memory was the most difficult, because as soon as Clytemnestra appeared in her mind, she knew her relationship with Clytemnestra wasn't relegated to only the past. It had made it through to today with Max's mom, Kati. And the grief from that loss hit her incredibly hard. Kati-Clytemnestra had never been gifted or cursed with abilities, but she had been part of Laney's life both now and in the past. Laney took a deep breath, pushing past the grief, promising herself that if Kati had been in her life before, she would be there again. Laney *would* see her again. In her soul, she knew that was true.

But Kati wasn't the only old soul that Laney recognized. All the pieces fell into place: Castor-Henry, Pollux-Dom, Menelaus-Jake. They all had a bond that transcended breakups and heartaches and even death. Proteus, her mother Leda's faithful guardian, was also her mother Victorians' faithful guardian, Ralph. And Barnabus, who once again stood across from her, helping her on her quest like he had all those eons ago.

Clytemnestra's daughter was here too—Noriko. That recognition had been a painful blow as she relived Iphigenia's death all over again. Even Mustafa—Achilles's second-in-command, Dugal.

"Laney?"

She looked up into Drake's concerned eyes. *And my Achilles*. Images from their former life flashed through her mind—the love, the passion, the friendship. The connection neither of them had been able to sever. She reached out her hand, and he clasped it.

She looked around at the people with her now—all of them had been with her before, the last time the ring bearer had been called. Each of them wore a different face, but the soul . . . the soul remained the same. It was overwhelming and terrifying and somehow comforting at the same time. She had never been alone. These souls had journeyed with her across lifetimes. And here they stood, ready to face danger with her again.

"Are you all right?"

"Yes." There was no hesitation in her answer. Because these people, these souls, had traveled with her across lifetimes. And it was not so that Elisabeta could win. No, Elisabeta, no matter her abilities, her resources—she was the weak one. She was alone.

Laney took a breath, pulling her hand from Drake's to open the bag. "Okay. Let's see what we've got." She opened it slowly, staring at the box inside.

With a tremble in her hands, Laney gently pulled the box from its covering. Even though it had been buried for thousands of years, hidden in a forgotten grave, it had surprisingly little damage.

It was an ivory box about eighteen inches long and ten inches wide. The lid had two intertwined triangles carved into its center, with ornate drawings rimming its outer edge: someone falling from the sky, a group standing on a mountaintop, other signs of nature—wind, rain, animals. All aspects the ring bearer could control.

"It's beautiful," Noriko said softly.

"That it is," Laney said.

"Who crafted it?" Mustafa asked.

Laney paused. "Actually, I don't know." She looked at Drake, who shook his head. "I don't know, either."

Laney opened it.

Mustafa frowned. "It's empty."

"No. Its contents are just hidden." She ran a hand over the inside lid, and words appeared.

Noriko gasped. "It's in English."

Laney had been worried about that herself. She wasn't sure what language the instructions for the Omni would appear in. But apparently it appeared in the language of the ring bearer. She supposed she shouldn't be surprised. Saving the world probably shouldn't be held up by translation issues.

"So, now that we have this, what do we do?" Mustafa asked.

"Now we craft the Omni."

Drake raised an eyebrow. "Um, not to rain on your parade, but this looks a little complicated. Do you have a hidden talent for chemistry that I don't know about?"

Laney shuddered. "God, no. I once nearly set myself on fire

during a high school chem lab. But luckily I know someone who knows his way around a lab."

She copied down the instructions, then looked at Mustafa, Gerard, and Noriko. "I need you three to head to the estate. Get these instructions to Dom. Gerard will bring the Omni back when it's ready."

Mustafa took the paper. "What about you?"

"I have to stay here. For now, I remain dead."

"We can't tell any of them?" Noriko asked.

"No. We know Elisabeta has spies somewhere on the estate. We can't take the chance of her finding out. Okay?"

They nodded, and a few minutes later, they took their leave. Laney stood looking out the window as their boat's lights disappeared from view.

It would take at least two hours, depending on how long it took Dom to create the Omni. And even then she wasn't sure how useful her having the powers of the Fallen would be now that Elisabeta had achieved immortality.

She turned away from the window, stretching her back. God, she was tense.

Drake's hand slid up her back, coming to rest at the base of her neck, kneading the muscles there.

She groaned. That felt good.

Drake stepped closer, his chest almost touching her back. She could feel the heat of him through her shirt. "I know some better ways to make you groan."

She turned slowly to face him. All that he had done for her raced through her mind. And in that moment, she knew it was useless to fight this feeling between them. More importantly, she didn't want to fight it. She wanted to revel in it. She grabbed the front of his shirt, pulling him closer. "Prove it."

He gave her that slow, sexy smile of his that made her toes curl. "Your wish is my command."

CHAPTER 85

Laney lay on the bed, her hand drawing lazy circles on Drake's chest. The man didn't have an ounce of fat on him. He was like Michelangelo's David brought to life.

Drake trailed his fingers down her back. "I know I may be opening a can of worms here, but what exactly are you thinking?"

She leaned her chin on his chest with a smile. "Nothing, actually. I'm just enjoying." And she realized she was. Even with everything stirring around them, for this moment in time, she wasn't worrying about the future or the past. She was firmly living only in this moment.

"Gerard should be back soon."

She dropped her head. "Way to kill the mood."

He laughed, his stomach muscles moving under her cheek. "I just thought you might want to put on some clothes. I know in this lifetime, you are not quite as into nudity."

"I was before?"

"Not as much as I would have liked, but it was a freer time than this modern era."

She ran a hand along his side. She couldn't seem to stop touching him. "Was I very different then?"

"Yes and no. You looked different, of course." He kissed her on the forehead. "But the heart of who you are, it remains the same."

She leaned up to look at him. From time to time, he'd drop little facts about her from her Helen incarnation. She never failed to be fascinated by them. She snuggled closer to him, amazed that she was here. But she felt at home with Drake in a way she had never felt before. He knew her in a way no one else did. He could make her smile when she wanted to cry. He had given her this moment of peace in a time of hell. How could she not love him?

She jolted at the thought but recognized the truth of it. She'd known ever since she'd woken up with him next to her bed in Alaska. And she had fought it from almost that same moment. But how could she deny what was truly in front of her? The man would go through hell for her. And he had. And she would do the same for him.

Drake ran a lazy hand along her spine, sending delicious tingles through her. "So, when Gerard returns, you will take the Omni, right?"

She looked up at him with a frown. "Of course. It's the only way for us to have a shot at defeating Elisabeta."

"And you will take it again after all this is done?"

If Cain and her uncle were right, the Omni would give her immortality, but taking a second dose would remove that same immortality or even all her powers. But to walk around with that much ability, it wasn't right. No one should have that. Not even her.

"Yes."

He nodded, looking away from her probing gaze. "Are you really going to do that? Become immortal and then mortal again?"

She shifted to get a better view of his face. "Yes."

He pushed her hair behind her ear. "Why? Would that really be so bad? After all, I'm immortal. You could stay immortal."

Laney met his gaze. "Immortality is not a gift. It's a curse. Cain has shown us that. History has shown us that. Victoria was right—

the threat of things ending is what makes us appreciate them. So no, when this is over, I will take the Omni again and become mortal."

"Even if it means losing your other abilities?"

She hesitated. When she'd first learned of her destiny, she'd been terrified. But now the idea of not having her abilities terrified her.

As if sensing her waffling, Drake pressed his case. "It doesn't have to be like that. You and I, we could be together. See the world like no one else has."

She watched him, knowing how much he wanted her to agree with him but also knowing she couldn't. "I can't do that. I can't watch everyone I love die and just continue on."

"They're dying anyway, Laney."

Laney flinched.

Drake's mouth dropped open as he reached for her. "I didn't mean—"

She pulled away. "Gerard will be back soon."

Drake nodded but made no move to get up. He just kept his gaze on her.

She was the one who broke the contact, reaching for her shirt on the floor next to the bed. "We need to go."

"Of course, ring bearer." Drake's voice was stiff.

Laney cringed, sensing a wall appear between them. She reached out a hand for him. "Drake."

But he rolled away from her, pulling on his pants. "I think I need some air."

Laney watched him stride across the room and close the door behind him with a slam. She closed her eyes. *Damn it.*

She knew what the right thing to do was. With a shock, she realized the two of them were in the same place they were eons ago. He wanted her to turn her back on what she knew to be right.

And when I didn't, I lost him. The pain of that possibility reoccurring had her sinking onto the bed. *You survived losing him once. You can do it again.*

And she had. But life with him, it had more color. She wanted that color.

She pulled on her clothes and headed after him. She hadn't gone after him last time, but she wasn't letting him walk away this time without a fight.

CHAPTER 86

Drake stormed from the cabin, but he only made it to the edge of the water. He stood, his hands in his pockets, staring at the water. He'd known. Deep down he'd known that she would choose mortality. But he had hoped that finally, she would choose him. *A fool's hope.*

The hair on the back of his neck rose as he heard her footsteps approach. "Are you all right?"

He sighed. "I don't know. I'm feeling a little . . . rejected."

She reached out a hand and touched his shoulder. He closed his eyes, feeling her warmth through his shirt. "I'm not rejecting you."

"Aren't you? We could have what everyone wants—unlimited time together. I would never have to worry about you getting sick, hurt, or killed. We would have forever."

She moved to stand next to him. "Yes. We could have forever. But would we appreciate forever? Would we look at each day with excitement or apathy as the years, centuries, dragged on? And as all the other people in my life disappeared, would I add new people to my life or be content to stay apart, so as to never get hurt? And then who would we be? These people with unlimited power? How long would we be content to just exist? When would we start to crave more? When would we demand our due from this world we helped, that we are so much better than?"

"That wouldn't happen."

"Are you sure? From my understanding, that's exactly what happened with the Fallen."

Drake stared up at the sky. "It could be different. You don't know for sure."

Laney smiled, but there was no happiness in it. "True, but I am human, and so are you, at least in your nature. Are you going to tell me you never take advantage of the power you wield?"

Drake looked away.

"And I can't say I wouldn't, either. The people I love keep me grounded, even now with the power I have at my fingertips. But what about when they are gone? When the people that know me best are no longer with me, will I still keep those restraints on my behavior? I honestly can't say I will. What if the government decides to track me down again? Who's to say I won't turn into an avenging god? I won't chance that."

"I'm not asking you to choose to become a god. I'm asking you to choose me. To be with me."

She placed a hand on his cheek. "And I choose to be with you. Until my last breath."

"But I want longer."

"That longing is what makes our time together all the sweeter."

He pulled her close. "I love you, Delaney McPhearson. And I want to spend lifetimes with you, not just one."

"But one is all I can give you. Will you accept that?"

He sighed, wishing he could talk her into it. But he also knew that his inability to see what she needed, to support who she truly was, was how he had lost her before. And he had promised himself if he ever had the chance with her again, he would not make the same mistake. "I will take every minute you give me."

"Good." She leaned toward him, and he met her halfway,

sealing their pledge with a kiss, knowing he would cherish her for as long or as short as he had.

A tingle ran over Drake's skin, and he pulled away. "Gerard's here."

"Again, ruining the mood."

Drake chuckled, taking her hand. "Come on. Let's go see what your mad scientist came up with."

CHAPTER 87

Laney took a shower before joining Gerard and Drake. She needed an extra few minutes to sort through her thoughts. As committed as she was to doing what it took to defeat Elisabeta, this next step was a big one. They weren't entirely sure how the Omni would affect her. And she wasn't even sure it was reversible. She'd told Drake the truth—she had no interest in being immortal, watching the people she loved, dying one by one—but she'd be lying if she didn't think there was a little appeal in the idea.

They're dying anyway. Drake's words crashed through her mind. She sat down heavily on the bed. Zach, Kati, Maddox—all gone. In one fell swoop, Elisabeta had torn three people from her life and left the others ravaged. The need for revenge burned through her. But more than that, she wanted to somehow turn back the clock. She wanted to save them or at least make sure they knew how much she loved them. How grateful she was to have each of them in her life.

She pictured Zach. For some reason, his death was even more poignant than the others. Maybe it was because he was so young. Or because he had already been through so much at the hands of his father. Or because he had died protecting another innocent life. It was just such a waste. A precious life gone because Elisabeta needed more.

Laney took a deep breath, pulling back her grief. She hadn't had time to grieve yet. This wasn't the time either. Grief was a luxury of the safe. And no one would be safe until Elisabeta was taken care of.

Pulling her damp hair back into a ponytail, she stood and crossed the room, opened the door, and stepped out. Drake and Gerard both looked up. "Any problems?"

"No." Gerard held up a small test tube. "He only had time to make the one dose. He said he would make the other one when you needed it."

"And the instructions were destroyed?"

"Burnt to a crisp."

"Good." She hesitated for only a second before holding out her hand. "Then let's see if this works."

∽

THE OMNI WAS a soft blue color and almost seemed to glow in the glass container. Laney held it up, inspecting it. Such a small, innocuous-looking substance, and yet the power it held was awe inspiring.

"The power of the gods," Gerard said softly.

Laney nodded. "And not a power to be taken lightly." She thought about the government task force and knew they would give anything to have the abilities she currently held the key to. "The Omni must be hidden again as soon as we are done. And no one can ever know that Dom created it."

Laney had not wanted to draw Dom into this, but she could not create it on her own. With his memory, though, Dom would be able to recreate it even without the instructions before him.

She knew he wouldn't. But if anyone learned that he knew how . . .

She straightened her spine in resolve. No. No one would learn, and he would remain safe.

"Well, I guess there's no time like the present." She started to unstop the tube.

Drake's hand snaked out, grabbing hers. "Wait."

She looked up at him in confusion.

"We don't know what it will do to you. It's meant for a normal, non-enhanced person. Or to nullify the effects on a Fallen. It's never been tried on a ring bearer before."

He was right. They were choosing to believe that the Omni, if taken by the ring bearer, would make that person immortal. But the Tome didn't specifically say that. It said it would grant the ring bearer the greatest punishment and burden. That's how Laney thought of immortality. But there was always a chance she was wrong.

She had to believe that it was not intended to hurt her. It was a leap, but the benefits far outweighed the risks. With Elisabeta immortal, they had no hope of defeating her. They needed to take this chance.

"There could be another way," Drake said as if he could read her mind.

"The world doesn't have time to figure it out." She tipped the tube to her lips and drank.

CHAPTER 88

WASHINGTON, D.C.

The drive from the airport to Matt's home took longer than normal. The area outside D.C. had sustained significant damage. Telephone poles and electric wires seemed to be down on almost every block once he'd left the highway. Jake had had to backtrack four times to find another route.

With each mile he drove, he questioned his decision to return even more. Mary Jane and her family were safe. Elisabeta had stopped the attacks when the U.S. President had conceded to her demands. And with Molly and Zane there, they should be fine. But he wanted to be there with them as well.

But Mustafa had contacted him, insisting he return. Jake turned to Hanz, who sat in the passenger seat. Mustafa had sent Hanz to track him down and give him the message in person. He said Mustafa did not want to discuss anything over the phone. "Are you sure you don't know what this is all about?"

"No. Only that Mustafa insists it is critically important."

Jake wasn't sure how that was possible. Elisabeta had won. The President had capitulated, and with Laney dead . . .

The wave of grief flowed over him. He had been moving ever since Laney had died. First preparing everything in Baltimore, then rushing to Boston, then helping Mary Jane and her family. But on the plane ride here, he'd had time to think. He gripped the steering wheel. Dead. It didn't seem possible. Part of him didn't believe it yet. But then he knew, even if he had seen her die with his own eyes, he would have not believed it. Laney had literally become a force of nature. It was difficult to believe she could be snuffed out by such a cowardly act.

Elisabeta's act had confirmed one thing for Jake: They had missed something. If Elisabeta had been afraid to face Laney, that meant Laney somehow had the power to end her or at least stop her.

But now we'll never know.

"Turn here," Hanz said.

Jake nodded, making the left. Three more turns and he was pulling to a stop in front of a small two-story house set on five acres of land. Two other cars were already parked in front of the garage. Jake pulled in right behind a Land Rover.

He sat behind the wheel for a minute without saying anything.

"Are you coming?" Hanz asked.

"Yeah, in a minute."

Hanz nodded, stepping out and disappearing into the house.

Jake just sat there, wondering what the hell he was doing there. He pictured Laney the first day he'd met her. She'd been scared and fearless at the same time. And in the intervening years, she'd just grown into that fearlessness. When they'd met, he'd taken care of her. Somewhere along the way, that had changed. They'd become equals, and then she'd stepped ahead. The ring bearer had been who she was. She'd embraced that role, sacrificing time and time again for the greater good.

And I let her make the ultimate sacrifice. Guilt pulled him down as tears rolled down his cheeks. *I'm sorry, Laney. I never should have let you get on that plane.* A car pulled in behind him.

Glancing in the rearview, he caught sight of Henry in the driver's seat and Cain in the passenger seat. Before he stepped out, he wiped at his eyes and cheeks. Stepping from the car, he waited for them to extricate themselves. "So, you were summoned as well?"

Henry nodded, dark circles under his eyes. "Yeah. Apparently turning down the summons was not an option."

Jake extended his hand to Cain. "Good to see you."

Surprise flashed across Cain's face before he returned the handshake. "You as well."

"How's Patrick?" Jake asked.

Cain shook his head. "Not well. I-I don't know how to help him. When I realized Henry was heading out, I made sure he took me. I need to do something."

Jake recognized the need. The same one burned deep inside him. "I understand."

"Well, let's see what is so top secret. I need to get back soon." Henry headed toward the front door.

Jake fell in step with Cain behind him and nearly walked into Henry when he stopped dead. "Henry, what are you—" His mouth fell open, and for a moment he thought he must be imagining things.

Cain grabbed his arm. "Do you see her?"

Jake nodded slowly. Then Henry sprinted forward, yanking Laney off the ground and into his arms.

∼

LANEY HAD BEEN RECOUNTING everything that had happened over the last few days since she had learned about Noriko's vision, confirming the details of her own vision. Matt, Mustafa, Henry, Jake, Drake, Gerard, and Cain had stayed silent for most of the retelling.

"And then I took the mortus." Laney went quiet, waiting.
"Did it work?"
She nodded. "Yes. We did a trial run of sorts. I can heal. I have speed. And I still have my abilities."
"That's why she needed you out of the way," Jake said. "She was afraid you would be able to go toe to toe with her."
"I think so."
Henry crossed his arms over the chest. "Why didn't you tell us any of this? Warn us? My God, Laney, we thought you were dead."
Drake's voice whipped out. "Watch the tone, Henry."
Laney put a restraining arm on Drake's hand. "No, no. It's okay. He's allowed to be angry." She turned to Henry. "I couldn't risk it. Everyone needed to believe I was dead. Elisabeta has spies everywhere, and we've all been tracked by law enforcement and the media. If even one person looked less than upset after my death, Elisabeta would know. And any chance of surprising her would be gone. Besides, there was no guarantee it *would* work. So now we just need to figure out a way to get me close to her. She thinks I'm dead. And she can't sense me."
"But you can't kill her," Jake said.
Laney looked at Cain. "Actually, I think I can."
"How?"
"I can command her to not fight. Then we use the Omni on her. It should remove her powers."
"Should?" Henry asked, incredulous.
"If not, I beat her into a pulp and we keep her drugged up forever. Either way, she needs to be eliminated."
"Whenever this last fight is, I will go with you," Cain said quietly.
Laney shook her head. "No, absolutely not. You're not a fighter."
"Perhaps, but even without landing blows themselves, I can offer you protection. And I cannot be sensed."

"No. It's too big a risk."

Laney looked around the room, but no one nodded their head in agreement.

"You are going to need help," Henry said. "And none of us with abilities can be nearby. Cain needs to go. And I'll be there, too, far enough away that I can't be sensed but close enough that I can get to you if you need me."

"What? No. You need to stay with Jen. And we still don't know who planted those bombs."

Henry's voice was grave. "Actually, we do. There was a gas company that was let in the day before the explosions. The two men who came in and the guard who showed them around were all found dead earlier this morning. I'm not letting you do this on your own."

"And Mustafa and I will be by your side as well," Matt said.

Cleo let out a roar. *I will be there, too.*

"No. I can't hide you."

You can. I will stay hidden until I am needed.

"She wants to go?" Jake asked.

Laney nodded.

"Good."

Laney whirled on him. "Good? I'm not risking everyone's—"

"We are at war, Laney. This is the last battle. If you do not succeed, none of us will survive this. We need to make sure you get a chance to fight Elisabeta. Which means we need to put everyone that we can into play."

"But—"

"It's not just your fight, Laney. It's not just your life. It's all of ours. And none of us is going to sit back and let you fight it alone. So let that go and let's come up with a way to beat this bitch."

Laney looked into Jake's eyes, reading the commitment there. Then she looked around the room at everyone else. Jake was right. It wasn't just her life at stake. If she failed and Elisabeta succeeded, all their lives would change, along with the lives of all those they cared for, and not for the better. She didn't have the right to tell them to stay out of it. She nodded.

"Okay. Let's figure this out."

CHAPTER 89

They strategized for the better part of an hour, but they kept running into the same stumbling block: How would they get everyone into place in Calevitnia? Elisabeta was undeniably taking careful note of everyone moving in and out of the country. There was no chance she wouldn't notice a couple dozen heavily armed people moving around the country. They needed to take her by surprise. Until they figured out how to do that, any plan they had was doomed to failure.

Matt's phone beeped. He stepped back from the table to read the text. He made his way quickly to the TV in the corner of the room. "You guys need to watch this. The President is about to make a statement."

On the TV, President Rigley stepped to the podium, her face pale. But she looked straight into the camera. Her voice did not waver. "As you know, yesterday I bequeathed control of the United States government to Elisabeta Roccorio. She will rule the United States with strength and intelligence. We are lucky to be the beneficiaries of her generosity."

The President cleared her throat and took a sip of water.

Laney thought she might be trying to swallow down the bile that was no doubt trying to choke her.

"The countries of the world have joined me in embracing Ms. Roccorio's role as liberator to mankind. To celebrate this magnanimous occasion, we will hold a coronation of Ms. Roccorio as the ruler of all humanity in two days' time in Washington, D.C. She is to be celebrated. Those who embrace her will be rewarded. Those who do not will be punished. This is a glorious day for all mankind." The President stepped back from the podium and strode from the room, ignoring the questions called out from reporters.

The news anchor reappeared, but Matt muted the TV. The room was silent, everyone with the same expression on the face—disgust. But Laney smiled at the screen.

"Why on earth are you smiling?" Jake asked.

"Because Elisabeta just gave us our way in."

CHAPTER 90

INVESS, CALEVITNIA

Elisabeta hung up the phone. The calls had been coming in over the last two hours. Once word spread that the United States had capitulated, everyone else fell like dominoes. Everyone wanted to make sure she knew they had given up. Of course, there were a few holdouts, but they would fall in line after the next deadline. She planned on detonating bombs in each of the countries that still refused to hand over control. And where she did not have bombs, she'd send her army.

Currently, she had representatives stationed at each of the critical countries in the world, overseeing the exchange of power. But she had not initiated anything. For once, she basked in the anticipation, waiting for the single moment when it all gloriously became hers.

She looked at Artem, who sat patiently waiting for her. "Where were we?"

"We were discussing the security protocols."

For the last hour prior to the phone call, she had been dictating her expectations to Artem to give to the United States in preparation for her coronation. It would take place in two days' time. Enough time to clean up the streets in D.C. and get everything ready, as well as have the holdouts fall in line. She wanted this to be a truly victorious celebration.

"Right. And make sure there are no Fallen anywhere near the celebration except for our people. If I sense even one Fallen or Nephilim, I will send my Fallen through the streets of their capital and right to the heart of their city to rip out its beating heart."

Artem nodded. "Yes, ma'am."

She smiled. "Make sure there are balls set up for afterward. I like how the American President flits from ball to ball; I'd like to do the same. And a representative from each world government must be in attendance, and not some little nobody from the accounting office. The first- or second-in-command must be in attendance. That is *not* negotiable."

"Yes, ma'am."

"Am I forgetting anything?"

"I do not believe so."

"Neither do I." She smiled. "Get that out right away, and send me the designer sketches that arrived earlier."

He bowed. "Yes, ma'am."

Elisabeta smiled. *Time to celebrate.*

CHAPTER 91

WASHINGTON, D.C.

The last two days had been an absolute flurry of movement. D.C. had been left in shambles after the Fallen had whirled through it. Electric lines were down. Water lines had burst. Fire had consumed about ten percent of the city. And everything along the parade route needed to be clean and in working order. On top of that, they had to set up for a coronation.

As Nancy strode through the halls of the West Wing, people hurried past, all with bags under their eyes. Each one seemed to be in one of two emotional states: panic or denial. Personally, she preferred the people in denial. They were continuing to get their work done, ignoring the stirrings of fear that had to be bubbling up in them.

The same bubbles stirred within herself. After the first call between the President and Elisabeta, the attacks had stopped. Slowly, the same happened across the globe as each country folded. But a private acknowledgement of her power hadn't been enough. No, Elisabeta wanted a public spectacle for all the world to see. And she had chosen for it to happen here, in the United

States. Her world coronation attended by representatives of each country in the world.

A shudder ran through Nancy. It could not come to that.

Nancy took a breath as she strode into the outer office of the Oval. She nodded at Neil. "Is she in?"

"Um, yes, but she asked not to be—"

"It's important. I need in."

Neil met her gaze, shaking his head. "I can't."

"Neil, you need to open the door."

Neil held her gaze for a long moment before gesturing to the Secret Service agent by the door. "Let her in."

He opened it with a nod.

Nancy stepped in, spying the President behind her desk. She didn't turn when the door opened or when it closed.

"I asked to not be disturbed." The President's voice was resigned.

"I ignored that." Nancy strode across the room.

The President finally stirred herself. She swung her chair around with a frown. "Nancy? What are you doing here?"

"We need to discuss your plan."

The President laughed. "My plan? My plan is to hand over the reins of the country to a madwoman in the hopes that she will spare some of our people. Beyond that . . ." The President shrugged.

"Defeat does not suit you."

The President narrowed her eyes. "In the more than two hundred years since this country has existed, we have stood up to every threat we have faced. And now I am the President when that threat is more than we can bear."

"You had no choice. This was the only avenue left open to you."

"So what did you want to discuss? What bow color to use for the keys to the country?"

"No, I thought we could discuss how to save the country. Along with the rest of the planet."

The President frowned. "Elisabeta can't be killed. We tried that, and the world saw that attempt fail in gloriously brutal detail."

"There is one last attempt that we need to support. And I will need your help with that."

"What kind of help?"

"Help that involves trust and more than a little faith."

"Elisabeta will unleash hell if we attempt anything. The amount of lives . . ." The President shook her head. "We can't risk it."

"What if I told you we have an ace in the hole?"

"An ace? What is it?"

"Not a 'what' but a 'who.' Doesn't this country deserve one last chance?"

The President studied her. "And what are the odds of this plan of yours working?"

"I give them a forty-percent chance of succeeding."

"Forty percent is not very high."

"No, it's not. But weren't you the one who brought up Washington crossing the Delaware? What were his chances?"

"Your plan has a George Washington?"

Nancy smiled. "Oh, my plan most definitely has a George Washington."

CHAPTER 92

The last two days had been a rush of activity as Laney and company tried to get everything in place for the coronation. The U.S. government, meanwhile, was clearing the streets and setting up like it was a Presidential inauguration. They were doing everything in their power to make sure that the coronation went off without a hitch.

Laney and her team were doing everything in their power to make sure they not only stopped it but took down Elisabeta as well. They had pored over plans, figuring out angles and approaches. One of Elisabeta's demands was that no one with abilities be within two miles of the coronation site, so they worked out the boundaries where anyone with powers would have to be beyond to make sure they were not sensed, as well as the quickest way from those points to the Mall once Laney made her move. Matt was their link to the government. He'd arranged for Laney, Jake, Mustafa, and Cain to be on the dais with Elisabeta. Cleo would be hidden underneath it.

Now they were as ready as they were going to be. They'd leave for D.C. in an hour. Laney was putting the final touches on her disguise. The reflection in the mirror was disturbing. She ran a hand through her now black hair. Her eyebrows had been darkened to match. Her skin had been spray-tanned to a color so dark she could pass as mixed race. Being she could normally pass for a ghost, it was unsettling. They were leaving her eyes alone, because if someone got close enough to recognize her from them, well, the gig was up anyway.

Drake leaned against the doorway behind her. "Personally I prefer pale redheads, but I'm game to spice things up a bit."

Laney rolled her eyes. "This is not for your enjoyment."

"Who says it can't be both?"

She shook her head, pulling on the black suit jacket and buttoning it. "Well? Do I look like a Secret Service agent?"

"Can't say I've seen any Secret Service agents quite as beautiful, but yes, I suppose you will pass." He stepped in and wrapped his arms around her.

Laney leaned back against him. Neither of them spoke as they just breathed together. Finally, Laney met his gaze in the mirror. "I'm nervous."

"I'd be surprised if you weren't. But you've got this. You were born for this."

"You need to stay beyond the perimeter until the signal."

"We'll see."

Laney turned to face him. "Drake, I mean it. You need to stay back. If she gets a hint of any of you, it will all be over."

"She can't sense me."

"We don't know that. With the mortus, she could. We cannot take the chance."

He glared down at her. "I do *not* like that part of the plan."

"I'm not crazy about it, either. But Cain and Cleo will be by my side, Jake and Mustafa as well."

Drake snorted. "Cleo will be hidden, not by your side, and Cain will be taken out by the first punch."

"I think you underestimate him. Besides, as soon as I reveal myself, I am counting on you to come running."

"*That* you can count on."

"I know I can. But do me a favor, and if you can, protect my friends."

"*You* are my priority."

"I know that. But I am asking you to make them one as well."

Drake blew out a breath, staring up at the ceiling. "You know, I never realized how high maintenance you are."

Laney smiled. "It's part of my charm."

He ran his hand along her cheek. "That it is. But if anyone hurts so much as a single hair on your badly dyed head, I will snap their neck."

"You say the sweetest things."

"And that is part of *my* charm."

He lowered his head, and she met him halfway. Her head cleared of doubts and fear. For this perfect moment in time, there was only her and Drake.

Her watch beeped. With a sigh, Laney pulled away from him. "Time to go."

"Then let's go finish this."

CHAPTER 93

The National Mall was filled with about half the crowd of a normal presidential inauguration. With her dark hair pulled back and sunglasses covering half her face, Laney surveyed it from her position on the dais located on the western side of the U.S. Capitol Building. She tried not to cringe each time a camera pointed her way. She knew she was unrecognizable. At the last minute, she'd even added some rubber to change the shape of her cheeks. Probably unnecessary, but she did not want to tip anyone off.

So far, no one had even blinked at her. Matt had added them to the security detail. The IDs he'd provided to her, Mustafa, Cain, and Jake had gotten them right through. The guests had begun to arrive and make their way down the long red carpet that covered the steps leading to the podium. The senators and congresspeople had been slowly filtering in and taking their spots. None looked happy. A few looked downright ill. But their attendance, like the President's and other world leaders, was non-negotiable.

The wind whipped the flag above her, sounding like a rifle shot. The senator from Michigan nearly jumped out of his skin at the noise. She couldn't blame the poor man. No one's safety could be guaranteed today.

A laugh sounded from the crowd milling below, drawing her attention. A man who couldn't be more than twenty jostled his friend next to him with a grin. The laughter was an oddity. Most people looked terrified. But Elisabeta had demanded a crowd, so some brave souls had come out today. Most were military or law enforcement in plain clothes, but Laney knew some citizens had arrived as well. Some to watch, some to protest. The protestors had been corralled to a far-off point. She prayed the protestors didn't draw too much attention to themselves. Laney wasn't sure what Elisabeta's reaction to them was going to be. She hoped she simply didn't care, too focused on the bigger picture, but she had not demonstrated an ability to ignore slights, no matter how minor.

Cain stood next to her, his dark eyes covered by sunglasses. He had cut his long hair for their mission to make sure no one recognized him. Keeping his gaze on the crowd, he spoke quietly. "You all right?"

"I'm good. You?"

Cain smiled. "Right as rain."

She looked up at him, realizing how far they'd come. When she'd first learned of his existence, they'd been enemies. But since that time, he'd grown into one of her closest confidants. "Thank you for doing this."

"Thank you for letting me." His hand brushed hers gently for a moment before he turned his gaze back to the crowd.

Cleo, you all right? Laney asked.

Small. Hot.

I know, but it shouldn't be for much longer.

Cleo grumped, and Laney tried not to smile. It was odd being able to sense her grumpiness.

"The motorcade is ten minutes out," Matt's voice said through her earpiece. She and Cain were not tapped in to the Secret Service channel. Matt would relay any information they needed.

Laney kept her voice low. "Is everyone staying beyond the barrier?"

Matt's response was delayed for a few seconds. "So far."

Laney tried not to groan. She was pretty sure Drake was giving Matt fits. "Roger."

She turned her gaze back to the crowd before them. Ten minutes, and then the show would begin.

CHAPTER 94

Crowds lined the streets as Elisabeta's motorcade drove toward the National Mall. Unlike during Presidential motorcades, the crowds lining these streets did not cheer. Nor did they jeer. They simply stood in silent witness to her passing.

But that was all right. They would cheer for her soon enough. The limo slammed to a stop. Elisabeta's head jerked up as a fire burst across the street in front of them. The fire was small, nothing that could do much damage. A Molotov cocktail, no doubt.

"Who?" she asked through gritted teeth.

Artem sat across from her, holding one finger to his earpiece before speaking. "They have the man who threw it."

"Where?"

"They're bringing him to the car."

Grasping the door handle, she opened it and stepped out. The street was silent except for the sounds of a struggle in the distance. Two of her men pushed past the barricades, dragging a man with them. No, not a man, a boy. He couldn't be more than sixteen or seventeen. When the crowd caught sight of him, they started to yell.

Elisabeta ignored them as the boy was dragged to her. Her men held him tightly between them.

He had short blond hair, dark glasses, some sort of trendy T-shirt, and a flannel thrown carelessly over it, although Elisabeta was sure he'd spent time making sure he had the right look. His clothes were too clean, professionally faded, not faded through wear.

For a moment, she imagined ripping through his chest. But no harm was done, and she was in a good mood. Besides, mercy was often as effective a tool for controlling people as strength.

Elisabeta smiled in response to his glare. "You are a child, so you don't understand. You should be honored that you are alive at a time to witness greatness. This will be a day you will tell your grandchildren about. And you will tell them of my mercy." She waved her hands at her men. "It is my coronation day. He is free to go."

The men released their grip on him. The young man stood hunched there between them, like he was waiting for the trick.

"It's all right. You may go." She waved him toward the crowd.

The boy lunged for her, swinging wildly and managing to connect with the edge of her chin. Anger roared through her. She grabbed him by the shirt and hauled him toward her. "I showed you mercy and you strike me?"

He spit in her face.

With a roar, she slipped her hands around his neck and twisted. His eyes bulged, and his lips parted before he dropped to the ground like a stone. "Apparently you don't deserve mercy."

The crowd went silent. Then with a roar, everyone was in motion. In a wave, they pushed against the barricades, rushing toward Elisabeta. The police tried to stop them but got trampled in the effort.

Artem grabbed Elisabeta's arm and hustled her back to the car. Elisabeta dove in, not in fear for her life, but in fear her outfit might be damaged.

"Ingrates," she muttered, grabbing a wipe and cleaning her hands.

Artem nodded toward the windows. "Um, the men are killing the spectators."

Elisabeta nodded. "Good."

CHAPTER 95

There was a collective gasp in the command room as everyone took in the scenes of violence on the street in response to Elisabeta's latest stunt—the public murder of an American citizen. Drake gripped the back of the chair in front of him, breaking the plastic.

"Nobody moves," Matt barked into his mic, his gaze raking the members assembled in the room in front of him. Everyone in the room was either a Nephilim or a Fallen, and everyone looked as if they were going to bolt for the door.

Dozens more were scattered at the very outskirts of city, half moving into place to close up the net around Elisabeta.

"More will be hurt if we move now." Matt gestured to the screen. "Horrible as that is, it will be acted out all over the city if we move before Laney gives the signal, so everyone *stays put*. Clear?"

Everyone in the room nodded, albeit reluctantly. Drake could hear the replies over the earpiece coming in as well. But Matt didn't relax, no one did. Instead, he contacted Laney.

"Laney, there was an incident on the road. Elisabeta killed a young man, and the crowd in that section is now rioting. Elisabeta's men are fighting back."

Drake saw her close her eyes on the monitor, and he knew that she was piling on the guilt for these deaths as well.

It's not your fault, Laney. None of this is.

But even if she could hear him, he knew his words would have no effect. He'd never met someone who embraced responsibility the way Laney did. Even as Helen, she'd put duty well above her personal wants.

Drake lived by a slightly different creed. He was more of a "there's no time like the present" kind of person when it came to his personal desires. And Delaney was what he desired more than anyone or anything, which meant the rest of his wants were placed on the back burner. The funny thing was, the more he placed them there, the less important they actually became.

Drake took a deep breath, releasing the chair. This was why he never got himself involved with humans beyond shallow interactions. Everything they felt and did was intense. And once you spent time around them and began to care for them, everything you did became just as intense.

He stepped closer to the screen that showed Laney on the inauguration dais. Cain was right next to her. Mustafa and Jake were somewhere nearby, although Drake couldn't see them in the sea of bodies.

"I've got the police trying to cordon off that area to keep the violence contained, but there's a chance it could spill over to here when word gets out," Matt said.

"Take out the network," Laney ordered. "We can't let word spread until we have Elisabeta handled."

"The President is arriving, and Elisabeta is just three minutes behind."

Drake didn't take his eyes from the screen. Just a few more minutes and it would begin. By the end of the day, he would either begin to plan for his future with the woman he had loved for thousands of years, or he would lose her.

And losing her was not an option.

CHAPTER 96

A ripple of excitement tinged with fear wafted through the crowd. "The President has arrived," Matt said in Laney's earpiece.

"Here we go," Cain said quietly next to her.

Laney scanned the crowd. She still couldn't believe people had shown up. She could pick out the law enforcement and military members in the crowd. They kept glancing around, unsmiling. But there were hundreds of others who were less stoic. They smiled, laughed, or cried. The criers tended to have signs announcing the end of days were upon them.

Laney wasn't sure they were entirely wrong, although one of the characteristics of the end of days was absent: country fighting country. Through Elisabeta's actions, the countries of the world had come together, joined in their fear of this one threat. There were still pockets of resistance in every country proclaiming that they would fight back if Elisabeta attempted to take them over. Laney knew that if today went poorly, those people would be the first to die tomorrow. They didn't understand what Elisabeta was capable of. She would sacrifice anyone and anything to get what she wanted.

And what she wanted was complete power.

The President's Secret Service detail appeared at the top of the stairs. They scanned the area as they began to descend the steps. Then the President appeared. Unlike the last time Laney had seen her on those steps, she wasn't smiling or waving. Her face was solemn, as was her gray coat. The President also examined the area, her gaze skipping right over Laney.

The President hadn't been briefed on Laney's resurrection. That was information on a strictly need-to-know basis, and they were not taking any chances. She had been needed to get Nancy access to the security protocol, but that was all she was told. If they couldn't trust the people at the estate, they certainly couldn't trust the people they didn't know in the government.

Catching sight of the President, the crowd burst into cheers and jeers. More signs appeared above people's heads. Some cheered on the President. Others accused her of treason and worse.

The President straightened her shoulders, giving the people a wave as she headed down the stairs. Laney noted the President's son was not with her, although her husband offered his arm as they headed down the steps.

Dr. Ben Rigley was a former surgeon who'd given up his position when his wife had been elected. He usually stayed in the background, so Laney had to give him credit for being here today.

Together, they walked arm in arm down the stairs. Nancy Harrigan followed, escorted by a Marine, her son. Harrigan scanned the dais, her gaze holding for only a second longer than necessary on Laney before moving on. Nancy had recognized her.

Smart woman. Nancy knew a plan was afoot, but she had not been given the details either. She had, however, given Matt whatever he asked for to make this happen.

The Vice President would not be joining them. Being there was a good chance the President would not survive this, the VP had been whisked away to a secure location.

Matt's voice rang through her earpiece. "Elisabeta's motorcade just pulled up."

Cain tensed next to her. Laney calmed her breathing, scanning the crowd. The President and Nancy glanced up toward the stairs. Tingles ran over Laney's skin. "She's got seven Fallen with her," Laney said softly into her mic.

"Roger," Matt said.

She glanced up as Elisabeta's security appeared at the top of the stairs. Laney did not recognize any of them. And from their gazes, she knew they had not recognized her. They swept the area with arrogant smirks, knowing no humans here could hurt them.

Four of them started down the steps, then Elisabeta stepped out. The crowd roared—anger, cheers, all of it together made the cries indistinguishable. A small smile played across Elisabeta's face. She waved a hand at the crowd, the light catching a thick diamond bracelet on her wrist. For some reason, the sight of that bracelet sent Laney's anger spiking.

This woman, even without her abilities, had been blessed from birth. Wealth, schools, prestige—she had had it all. And it wasn't enough. Her greed, her need for power; it was insatiable. But Laney knew that as soon as she had all the world's governments cowering at her feet, she would demand even more. Nothing was going to satisfy her.

"Easy, ring bearer."

Laney jolted as Drake's voice came through the earpiece.

"I recognize that look," he continued. "Just breathe for me. Your anger will only make this harder. Stay calm."

Laney took in some breaths, trying to tamp down her anger. Drake was right. "I'm all right."

"Of course you are. Now, I'm going to hand this mic back to Matt before he turns a darker shade of purple. You have this, ring bearer. Now go kick some ass." He paused. "And who knows, maybe she'll trip down the stairs, break her neck, and we can all go get a beer."

Laney smiled.

Next to her, Cain shook his head. "Is that man ever serious?"

But Laney didn't answer, because Elisabeta's men were now only a few feet away. She focused on keeping her expression calm, unthreatening, and hopefully unfamiliar. The men's gazes glanced over her, focusing more attention on Cain than her, but then they turned away, watching Elisabeta descend the stairs. Sadly, she did not trip.

Nor did she even glance at Laney as she reached the bottom of the stairs and took her place in the front row. The President stepped up to the microphone.

Laney tensed. "We good?"

"We don't have the shots lined up yet. You need to hold until Elisabeta is at the podium," Matt replied.

There were snipers in place for each of Elisabeta's guards. Then Mustafa and Jake would move in to neutralize each of them once they were down, hopefully before they could fully heal. But Laney needed the okay to begin. Because just one of the Fallen could do irreparable damage to the people on the dais.

The President stepped up to the podium. "Ladies and gentlemen, this is a historic day."

CHAPTER 97

BALTIMORE, MARYLAND

The bomb shelter was quiet, but Patrick could hear murmuring in the large room beyond. He knew that the coronation of Elisabeta would be playing. Patrick had no interest in watching it. He had little interest in anything these days, ever since learning about Laney.

Grief choked him as it crawled up his throat. He slammed his eyes shut, willing the pain of her loss to go away. But it didn't. It rolled through him and over him, battering him with images of her plunging to her death in a fiery explosion.

"Patrick?" Charles, the nurse who'd helped out at the Pennsylvania cabin when Cain had been injured, hurried over to the bed. He started to place the oxygen mask over Patrick's face, but Patrick batted him away.

"Go away."

"Patrick, I know you're hurting. But you need to calm down. You are still recuperating. Let me help you."

Patrick turned his head. "No."

Charles hesitated. "I know how much Laney meant to you."

Her name sent fresh waves of grief through Patrick.

"But there's another little girl here who is relying on you. She needs you to get better. And Max, he needs you, too. He's been asking for you."

His grief for Laney was compounded by his grief for Kati. But then he remembered the first time he'd taken Max out for ice cream. The smile on the boy's face. And now that little boy was all alone, in a bomb shelter full of people he barely knew. He was no doubt hurting as much as Patrick. Patrick clawed his way through the pain, turning his head to nod at Charles, who lowered the mask over Patrick's face. "There we go. Just breathe normally."

Patrick closed his eyes, letting the oxygen fill his lungs. He felt his heart rate slow.

Charles patted his shoulder. "That's good. You're doing great." Charles stayed with him for another ten minutes before removing the mask. "You want me to turn on the TV? The coronation should be—"

"I don't want to see it, but thank you."

Charles nodded, stepping back outside. Patrick looked around the room. With Cain gone, it was quiet. He hoped Cain was all right. He said he wanted to help out where he could, but Patrick was pretty out of it when he'd explained what exactly he'd be doing. But without him, Patrick found himself a little restless. There was a wheelchair over by the wall, but he hadn't quite worked up the nerve to try it out. Besides, he really didn't feel like facing a bunch of strangers. Most people had elected to stay until after the coronation. No one felt like taking Elisabeta at her word that the violence was over.

The remote lay quietly next to him. He stared at it and finally swiped it up. He hit the button to raise the back of his bed until he was in a more comfortable position and then turned on the TV. He didn't want to watch the coronation. He hated that woman, but at the same time, he knew he needed to watch it. This was history in the making. With dread, he turned to a twenty-four-hour news station. Tuning in to the news channel was a habit, but he could have chosen any channel. Everyone was covering this event.

It had already begun. The President was walking down the stairs toward her spot on the dais. He frowned as the President walked in front of a Secret Service agent that looked familiar. The man looked like Cain but with short hair.

Then Patrick's gaze shifted to the female agent next to him. His breath caught. She had dark hair, darker skin, and her cheekbones were different, fuller. But he knew her. He gripped the remote, not sure if he was going crazy or if in his grief he was seeing only what he wanted to see.

The camera panned up to the top of the stairs, stealing his view of the woman as Elisabeta and her security appeared. She walked down the stairs, but Patrick kept glancing at the bottom right of the screen, willing the camera operator to go back to the female agent. Then when Elisabeta reached the bottom of the stairs, Patrick could see the agent again. She was only a few feet from Elisabeta.

He gripped the remote hard, staring at her while praying with everything in his being.

Help her. Whatever she has planned, help her.

CHAPTER 98

WASHINGTON, D.C.

The President was wrapping up her remarks. She called for calm, for understanding, as the United States entered a new phase. Laney thought she handled the whole thing with remarkable grace. Now Laney just needed her to get the hell out of the way so she could get to Elisabeta.

Laney was tempted to spring across the space and grab Elisabeta while commanding all of the men with her not to fight back. But there were too many things that could go wrong with that. Elisabeta could see her coming and slip away. Her men could intercept her before she reached Elisabeta. No, she needed to wait so her guards were neutralized and Elisabeta was closer. It was the only way this whole plan had a shot.

"And now, Elisabeta Roccorio." The President backed away from the podium, not waiting to shake Elisabeta's hand. If Elisabeta noticed the snub, she gave no sign of it. She stepped up to the podium.

Movement in the crowd pulled Laney's attention.

Oh no. About two dozen people unfurled banners they'd

hidden amongst their clothes. Collectively, they read: *Resist. Tyranny will never defeat us.*

"This is a glorious day for mankind. No longer will you be shackled with decisions. You will be freed from all of that." She glared down at the group holding up the banner. "You will fall in line or you will simply fall." She looked into one of the TV cameras. "People of the world, you have a chance to live in peace. Those who go along with my rule will live. Those who do not will be eliminated."

"Matt?" Laney whispered, not liking Elisabeta's gaze continually straying to the group of protestors.

"One guy is out of range."

"Which one?"

"Farthest east of your location, red tie."

Laney nodded, sending a mental image to Cleo. She was located right under the man. *You got him?*

Yes.

"Cleo will take him," she whispered just as Elisabeta held up her hand. Gunfire burst out. The group with the handmade signs screamed as bullets tore through them.

"She brought snipers! Open fire!" Matt yelled, but Laney didn't respond. Lightning crashed down to Elisabeta's sniper's location as Matt's snipers opened fire. Laney tore across the stage, tackling Elisabeta as she whirled around, her mouth hanging open in a surprised O.

Laney slammed Elisabeta to the ground. "Do not move."

Elisabeta smiled and rammed her fist into Laney's jaw. Pain radiated through her skull as she flew across the stage, crashing into a row of people, taking them down with her. And the reality of what had just happened slammed into her harder than Elisabeta's punch. The Omni had given her abilities, but it had also taken one away.

I can't command her.

CHAPTER 99

They had talked about the effects of the Omni. Laney had never tried the commands once she'd been certain her other abilities remained intact. She extricated herself from the people she'd landed on, her jaw already healing. Vaguely, she heard Matt give the command for everyone to move in. But all her attention was on Elisabeta.

Elisabeta rolled to her feet, her eyes staring daggers into Laney. "You're supposed to be dead," Elisabeta snarled.

"Not yet." Laney leapt toward her, her fist crashing into Elisabeta's face before tackling her at the waist and sending the two of them crashing through the stage.

Laney and Elisabeta hit the ground under the stage with a thump. Elisabeta managed to fling Laney off before leaping back through the hole they'd created. Laney quickly followed her.

Up top, all hell had broken loose. The attendees on the stage were madly scrambling for the exits. People dove off the stage. Others rushed up the stairs. Some tripped and were trampled. Screams and yells punctuated by gunfire pounded all around. But with their panic, the dais was almost empty. The Secret Service was picking up and moving the last few dozen people as quickly as possible.

Elisabeta made it clear she wasn't going anywhere. She stood waiting, two of her men behind her. Before Laney had a chance to do more than realize they held guns in their hands, they pulled the triggers.

"Laney!" Cain dove for her, tackling her to the ground, bullets slamming into his back. The barrage cut off as the men collapsed to the ground.

With grunt, Cain rolled to the side.

"Cain."

He grimaced but waved her away. "Got the vest. Go, go."

Laney stood, keeping Cain behind her. Elisabeta's men were now out of the fight. Any injury that resulted from trying to harm Cain would heal at a human rate, but being they'd each shot Cain twice, they probably wouldn't survive their injuries.

Elisabeta spared her men only a quick glance before she smiled at Laney. "This is how it should be, don't you think? Just you and me? Of course, I have a bit of an advantage being I can't be killed. But then you seem to have been juicing a little as well."

Laney smiled. "Guess we're evenly matched."

"Oh, child, we are not equals. You still have all that pesky baggage weighing you down. Like all those people safe in your little bomb shelter."

Laney's heart stopped. *She couldn't have.*

"And that's not your only weakness is it?" Elisabeta waved to the crowd. The Fallen were rippling through them. A familiar tingle ran through her. Drake appeared at the edge of the dais.

"The people. Help the people!" she yelled, pulling her gaze from Elisabeta for only a second.

But that was all the time she needed. Elisabeta thrust her fist toward Laney's chest.

Laney managed to fling herself to the side. If she hadn't, rather than crushing her ribs, Elisabeta's fist would have plunged through her chest.

With a roar, Drake dove across the stage, but Elisabeta danced away. "Tut, tut, tut. You were not invited to this dance."

Crap. Laney curled around her ribs, flames of pain roaring through her side. She got to her knees, then pushed to her feet. "Drake, go."

"I'm not leaving you." Drake didn't take his gaze from Elisabeta, who just smiled at him.

"Drake, you promised me. The people, help them."

Drake glared at her. "Same rule applies as earlier, ring bearer, you get yourself killed and I'm going to be really mad at you."

"Noted." She squeezed his hand. "Go."

With one last hard look at Laney, he dashed into the crowd.

Elisabeta shook her head. "What is wrong with you? You have an archangel on your side, and you send him to what, help a bunch of strangers? If I were you, I would have ordered all my people to attack me. Remove the biggest threat. And sacrificing a few people to attain that goal? Just the cost of getting it done."

Laney rolled her hands into fists, her side thankfully healing but still burning. "It's an unacceptable cost." Laney grabbed the folding chair to her left and heaved it at Elisabeta. Elisabeta ducked, but Laney was right behind the metal chair, her knee slamming into Elisabeta's face. Blood burst from Elisabeta's nose. Laney threw a hook that caught Elisabeta in the jaw and sent her sprawling.

With a growl, Elisabeta rolled to her feet. Her nose healed in front of Laney's eyes, and her jaw realigned. She sneered at Laney. "You thought you'd walk in here with your fake abilities and what, take me down? That you would become this ultimate weapon?"

Laney shook her head with a smile. "No, I'm not the ultimate weapon. I'm the distraction."

The ricochet of the bullet was deafening. Elisabeta's back arched as the bullet filled with the Omni buried itself in her skin.

CHAPTER 100

The backup plan. If Laney couldn't get to Elisabeta, Jake was supposed to fire the Omni into her system and destroy her. Laney stumbled to her feet as Jake stalked toward Elisabeta, holstering the gun with the Omni and pulling a separate Glock from the other holster. He fired at Elisabeta again and again. He stopped next to Laney but kept his eyes on Elisabeta.

"You okay?" he asked.

"I'll live. What do you—" Elisabeta rolled to her feet, grabbing the podium and chucking it at Jake.

"Jake!" Laney lunged, barely yanking him out of the way in time. The podium splintered into shards next to them.

Laney was already moving for Elisabeta, but her mind was practically frozen in fear. *It didn't work. The Omni didn't remove any of her powers or her immortality. What the hell are we going to do now?*

But while her mind was splintering almost as much as the podium, her body was on automatic pilot. She slammed her foot into Elisabeta's chest, followed by a round kick to the knee and spinning back kick to the chest. With a yell, Elisabeta went flying into a row of chairs.

From the corner of her eye, she saw Cain crawl over to Cleo

and grab on to her fur. He stared intensely at the cat, his mouth moving furiously. Laney lunged toward Elisabeta, who managed to get to her feet and roll out of the way.

Cleo? What's going on?

Cain says you are the counterweight.

For a moment, she didn't understand what he meant. Then it hit her. It wasn't just the Omni that would remove Elisabeta's immortality. *My blood.*

Cain nodded across the distance at her as if he had heard her. Elisabeta stumbled to her feet.

Laney tackled Elisabeta at the waist, slamming her onto her back. Elisabeta elbowed Laney in the chin, but Laney managed to yank her head back enough that it didn't knock her out. Instead, Laney held on, dragging Elisabeta to her feet. She wrapped her arms around her, turning her back to Jake. "The Omni, Jake! Shoot me! Now!"

The bullet tore through Laney's chest, punching out the other side and into Elisabeta. Laney let her go as she stumbled back. She struggled to breathe as one of her lungs filled with blood.

"Laney!" Jake yelled, scrambling over to her, his face pale.

Laney struggled to get her words out. "Mortal. Shoot her."

Kneeling on one leg, Jake dropped the gun with the Omni bullets and pulled out his sidearm. In quick succession, he hit Elisabeta three more times, center mass.

"You fool. I can't—" Elisabeta's words choked off as blood bubbled from her mouth. She crashed to her knees, a look of disbelief on her face. Jake aimed for her head and pulled the trigger. A perfect circle appeared in the middle of her forehead as her mouth fell open, her eyes going wide.

Laney dropped to her knees as Jake kept firing until the magazine was spent. He ejected the cartridge as he stalked toward Elisabeta and loaded another. He placed the muzzle against her chest and pulled the trigger over and over again, emptying the magazine yet again.

Jake's shoulders heaved as he stared down at Elisabeta. A gaping hole took up the majority of her chest. Her face was splashed with blood, her look of surprise frozen in death.

He turned to Laney. She tried to smile at him, but blood bubbled up her throat, spilling out her mouth. Jake's mouth fell open. He sprinted toward her, catching her as she toppled back. "Laney!"

Jake loomed above her, his hand pressed to her wound. Laney blinked hard. *Weird. I don't feel anything.*

Jake's eyes were large. "There's too much blood, Laney. I can't stop it."

Laney nodded. She'd known when she told Jake to shoot her what would happen. The Omni combined with Laney's blood would take Elisabeta's powers, but there was a good chance they'd take hers as well.

"What do I do?"

Laney grabbed Jake's arm, feeling her strength fading quickly. *I don't know.*

CHAPTER 101

Laney knew she was dying. But if she died and so did Elisabeta, she could live with that.

Ha. Or die with it.

Jake was fading from her view. Cold was seeping over her hands, working its way down her arms. She closed her eyes. She sensed rather than saw someone approach. *Cleo.*

Get up, Cleo ordered as she nudged her cheek.

Sorry, girl. Laney tried to reach up a hand to scratch her chin, but she didn't have the strength.

Stay, Cleo ordered.

Trying.

Vaguely, she sensed a new pain entering her leg, but she didn't really feel it. It was as if her mind couldn't quite register it.

But then the pain grew more and more intense. Her eyes opened. Slowly, the three people kneeling above her came into focus.

"She's coming around," Drake said.

Pain lanced through her leg and her side. She sucked in a breath.

"It's okay, Laney. Breathe. It will pass in a minute," Drake said.

But the pain was already subsiding even as Drake spoke.

"I'm okay," Laney said, surprised to find she was. She tried to sit up, and Jake was there, propping her up. Laney spied Elisabeta's body sprawled only a few feet to her left. "Is she . . .?"

Jake nodded. "Dead. It's over, Laney. Elisabeta's people are retreating. We're giving chase to remove any immediate threats."

"Good."

Cleo licked her cheek. *Live.*

It looks like. Cain?

Hurt. I stay with. Cleo gave Laney another lick before crossing toward the immortal, who was sitting, leaning heavily to one side.

"I need to check in." Jake looked at Drake, who nodded, taking his place holding up Laney. She was almost fully healed, but right now she was happy to have the human contact, especially his.

"Are you all right?" Drake asked.

"Almost as good as new."

Drake nodded across the stage to where Cain sat, a grimace on his face as Cleo helped him to his feet. "I think your immortal may have bruised or broken a few ribs."

"Saving me. If I had gotten shot, it would have taken me time to heal. And by then . . ." She shrugged.

"Perhaps I underestimated him." Drake paused.

"Do you know what just happened?"

"Someone shot me in the leg with the Omni."

Drake winced. "Yeah, that was me. Sorry about that."

Laney waved his words away. "Ah, it's all right. Jake did, too. Jake's shot killed Elisabeta, and yours saved me, so thank you."

He raised an eyebrow. "You realize you're thanking me for shooting you?"

She smiled, then immediately regretted it as her chest ached. "It must be the blood loss."

Drake gently pulled her back against him. "We have a very unusual relationship."

Jake disconnected his call and walked over to them. "Elisabeta's people are being apprehended. The net Matt put in place ensnared them. He thinks we'll have them all."

"Good."

"Emergency services have moved in across the city to help the wounded."

"How many wounded?"

"A lot. But if you hadn't taken out Elisabeta—"

"If *we* hadn't taken out Elisabeta."

Jake nodded. "If we hadn't taken out Elisabeta, it would have been a lot worse. I can't believe it's over."

"Me, either. After everything she did, for it all to end, it just seems so—" Elisabeta's words wafted through her mind. *Like all those people safe in your little bomb shelter.*

"Laney?" Drake asked, his brow furrowed in concern.

She gripped his hand. "The bomb shelter. We need to call the bomb shelter."

Jake was already dialing.

"What is it?" Drake asked.

"Elisabeta. I don't think she's done yet."

CHAPTER 102

BALTIMORE, MARYLAND

The camera operator had stayed zoomed in on the fight scene between Laney and Elisabeta, leaving Patrick glued to the screen. Lou, Rolly, and Danny had come into the room to watch it with him. Charles had walked in as well, staying right next to Patrick, monitoring his vitals, but even though what was occurring onscreen was wreaking havoc on his blood pressure, Charles did not mention turning the TV off.

On screen, Laney grabbed Elisabeta and yelled at Jake. Patrick frowned, trying to figure out what she was trying to say a split second before Jake shot her.

Rolly jumped to his feet. "What the hell was that?"

Patrick gripped the blankets, his knuckles turning white. *The Omni. Jake must have the Omni, but it won't work without Laney's blood. Oh God.*

"He *shot* Laney," Lou cried.

Patrick clutched the bed railings, not sure he could handle watching much more of this. "It's the only way. Watch."

Laney and Elisabeta crashed to the ground. Jake ran up to her as she rolled off, firing at Elisabeta over and over again.

But Laney only lay on the ground next to her. Patrick leaned forward, remembering what Cain had translated from the Tome. *She's no longer immortal. Oh my God.*

Drake blurred into sight and rushed to Laney's side. He pulled a gun from the holster at Jake's side and shot Laney in the leg.

"What the hell?" Lou yelled.

But Patrick didn't say anything. He couldn't as Drake knelt down next to Laney.

Work, damn it. Work.

On screen, Laney sat up, and Patrick fell back on the pillows, wiping at the tears in the corner of his eyes. "She's okay."

"I don't understand how. Drake shot her. Jake shot her." Rolly ran a hand through his hair. "Why the hell is everybody shooting her?"

Patrick opened his mouth to explain about the Omni and its effect when mixed with Laney's blood, but then he thought better of it. The less the world knew about a potion for immortality, the better.

Charles patted his shoulder. "Okay, Patrick, I think we need to clear everybody out so you can get a little rest."

Patrick nodded, suddenly feeling tired. "Okay. Thanks for—"

A sharp crack cut through the air. Patrick's head whipped to the side as blood spurted from Charles's shoulder.

"Patrick!" Rolly dove across the room, landing on Patrick. Crashing over the bed railing, Rolly rolled him off the bed. Lou shoved Danny to the ground just as quickly, then tackled a man in the doorway.

Pain lanced through Patrick's back and his head as it cracked onto the ground. But he forced the dizziness aside as more gunshots rang out from the hall.

"Lou?" Rolly yelled.

"He's out," she said. But more gunfire and additional screams answered as well.

Charles grimaced next to them but he nodded at Patrick. "I'm okay."

Patrick grabbed Rolly's shirt. "Nyssa. Max."

Rolly looked at him, his eyes deadly serious. "I'll find them." In a blur, he disappeared, and Patrick wondered if he'd done the right thing. Rolly was still just a teenager.

Patrick glanced under the bed in time to see Lou blur out the door as well, and his heart nearly stopped as Danny raced after them.

"Danny, no!"

CHAPTER 103

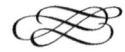

Danny ran after Lou and Rolly. Neither of them paused as they bolted into the giant living space. Rolly tackled a man over by the living room who'd opened fire. Lou blurred for a man by the kitchen island.

Danny stopped at the edge of the hall, not stepping into the big room. The gunmen weren't Fallen or Nephilim. If they were, Lou and Rolly would have sensed them. This was Elisabeta's backup plan. Danny was sure of it.

Lou and Rolly disappeared down the other hallway, where the kids had been playing. Dom had taken them into his lab. Danny frowned, watching the big room. He didn't recognize the two men Lou and Rolly had taken out.

He glanced back down the hall. The place was secure, so how did they get in? There was no chance they made it through all the locks. There were two other entrances, but both were supposed to be guarded. But they would be easier to move through or to station people at. People lay in pools of blood, but others were already moving to help them. And he knew that security was already on the way. They didn't need him here, but he had a feeling he was going to be needed somewhere else.

He turned back down the hall. Elisabeta wouldn't just attack the shelter. She'd give them specific targets. Patrick, yes. Nyssa and Max, of course. But there was one other target that would definitely be on that list.

The door to the supply room slowly slid open. Danny ducked into Dom's office, peering through the door. A man stepped out, pausing for just a moment before he headed to the right and the one other room that was occupied.

The room where Jen lay sleeping.

CHAPTER 104

There were no guns in Dom's office, not even a knife, but he did have a fire extinguisher. Danny hefted it up.

This will have to do. He cracked open the door and slipped silently into the hall.

He tried to run-walk while not making any noise. Jen's parents had been in the living room, which meant Jen was now unguarded. She was on a drip that was keeping her sedated. She probably wouldn't even realize anything was happening until it was too late. Danny picked up the pace, the unusual thought of Jen being helpless terrifying him. He stopped at the end of the hall. The entrance to her room was only six feet to his right around the corner.

Holding his breath, he glanced out. The gunman had his back to Danny, but his weapon was pointed into the room.

"Hey!" Danny yelled as he sprinted around the corner. The man's neck snapped around. Danny aimed the foam right at the guy's face. He thrust the extinguisher into the guy's chest, shoving him back. The man rolled onto his back. But Danny couldn't slow his momentum. The man upkicked, sending Danny flying over him.

The landing was not soft. Danny hit the wall and slid down to the ground in a heap, but he managed to roll to his feet just as the guy got to his. But Danny had lost his only weapon.

The guy had not lost his. He smirked as he raised his gun hand. "Nice try, kid."

Two hands appeared on either side of his head, then there was an audible snap as his head whipped to the side. The man dropped, revealing Jen in pajamas.

Her face pale, dark circles under her eyes, she held on to the wall for support. "You okay?" she asked, her voice strained.

Danny got to his feet. "Yeah, I'm—"

Jen's eyes rolled back in her head. She pitched forward. Danny lunged, grabbing her before she could hit the ground.

"Jen? Jen!" But then his heart nearly stopped as he saw the blood staining her pajama bottoms.

The baby. Tears sprang to his eyes as he clutched Jen to him. "Help!"

CHAPTER 105

WASHINGTON, D.C.

Laney stared at Jake, knowing Elisabeta had not ended things here at the Mall. She had backup plans upon backup plans.

Jake hung up his phone. "There was an attack."

Laney slowly got to her feet. "What happened?"

"It was handled. But Jen... it's not good. We should—"

"Drop your weapons!"

Laney, Jake, and Drake went still. In disbelief, Laney studied the ring of Secret Service agents that had encircled them and were moving in. All looked angry, and she tried not to be angry at the fact that they had waited until after the threat was gone to act.

Terror tore through her though when she saw more agents approaching Cleo and Cain. *Cleo, don't move, and don't fight them.*

Want to hurt me.

I know. Stay still, and you'll be all right. Cleo lay down on the ground. Cain knelt down over her, offering her any protection he could.

"Is this a joke?" Drake asked.

Jake slowly started to raise his hands. "I don't think so."

Laney started to raise hers as well, taking a step closer to Jake. She nodded to the weapon with the Omni cartridge that Drake had left on the ground only a few feet away, right at the edge of the ring of agents. Two more steps and one would be on top of it. "How many doses of Omni are left in that magazine?" she asked quietly.

"Two," Jake said.

"Stop talking, and kick your weapons away," an agent ordered.

"Not quite yet," Laney murmured. A wind slammed into the agents, blowing them ten feet back.

"Oh boy." Drake yanked Jake back as two bolts of lightning tore into the weapon holding the Omni rounds.

Laney turned her head but still felt the heat from the strikes. When the she turned back, there were scorch marks on the stage. But more importantly, the gun and the rounds inside were now just molten pieces of metal. Her gaze shifted to where Elisabeta lay.

Your turn.

Four additional strikes tore into Elisabeta's body, setting it on fire.

"Get a fire extinguisher," one of the agents yelled from the ground.

"No." Laney held them down with more wind. She created a vortex around Elisabeta's body, sending in more strikes.

"What are you doing?" Jake whispered.

Laney kept her attention on the vortex and on keeping the agents back. "Destroying any evidence of the Omni."

"Is that really necessary?" Drake asked.

"Not sure, but I think it's probably best if the United States government does not have the means to create an army of super soldiers."

It took fifteen minutes to destroy Elisabeta's body. As soon as it was reduced to bone, she released the agents and the vortex.

The agents struggled to their feet. One surged forward. "On your knees! On your knees!"

Jake dropped to his knees with a sigh.

"Get Cain and Cleo out of here," Laney murmured to Drake out of the corner of her mouth.

"I'm not leaving you."

"Drake, please. If the government gets their hands on them..."

"Oh, fine," Drake muttered.

"You, on the ground," an agent yelled at Drake.

"I think not." Drake blurred. The agents around Cain and Cleo crashed to the ground just before they disappeared, leaving the agents looking dumbfounded.

Laney dropped to the ground next to Jake. "You know, you'd think they'd be a little nicer to the people who just rid the world of Elisabeta."

"Well, they might be nicer if you hadn't just made them all look like idiots."

"They were telling us to get down before I did that."

"True."

The agents moved in and shoved Laney and Jake to the ground. Laney grimaced as her cheek slammed into the rough dais. Jake wasn't being treated any kinder.

"Maybe they don't realize we're the good guys," he said.

"Not sure they agree with that title," Laney muttered as cuffs were slapped on her wrists. They yanked her to her feet.

"You are under arrest for the attempted assassination of the President of the United States and assault on"—the agent looked around—"two dozen federal agents."

Another agent stepped up to Laney. Laney frowned. She was already in cuffs and not resisting. What was he—

He plunged a needle into her arm.

"No!" Jake yelled, surging against the agents holding him. He was shoved back down to the ground, and that was the last thing Laney saw as the world turned black.

CHAPTER 106

Concrete walls, a concrete shelf to sleep on, and a toilet in the corner were all the amenities of the cell Laney woke up in. With a groan, she looked at the ceiling through slits in her eyelids. She wasn't sure how long she had been out, but her head was pounding.

She took an inventory, starting at her toes and making her way up. Nothing seemed to be damaged or even bruised.

Guess I still have my abilities. The lights winked in the room. *Yup, still there.* Whatever they had given her must have been some sort of sedative. She had a feeling it was supposed to have her knocked out for longer or they'd have given her another dose, because right now, she could rip through the door with her strength or a good strong blast of wind.

But being she did not want to be a fugitive for the rest of her life, she figured she'd wait and see what the plan was. Matt and Nancy were no doubt working to get them freed. She just needed to wait.

Thirty minutes later, her patience was running thin. She needed to be back in Baltimore. Jake had said Jen was in trouble. She didn't know if Drake had gotten away with Cain and Cleo.

There was so much she needed to be doing. People she needed to check on. She rolled her hands into fists.

Come on, Matt. Get me out of here.

Thirty minutes turned into an hour, and then two. No one came to check on her. No one walked by. In fact, she hadn't seen a single sign of life since she'd woken up.

Laney gave up her pacing and finally lay down on the uncomfortable bench. The toll of the last few hours and days was catching up with her. Flinging her arm over her eyes to block out the fluorescent lighting, she closed her eyes. *Just a few minutes.*

A buzz rang through her cell, jarring her from sleep. She opened her eyes, wiping them and the side of her mouth.

"Only guilty people sleep in a jail cell."

Laney turned toward the clear cell wall. Jessup Hankton Ianson III from Homeland Security stood there glaring at her.

Great. She sat up. "So do people who just fought off an immortal woman after surviving a missile attack on the plane she was flying in."

"You always have an answer, don't you?"

Laney sighed. "What do you want, Ianson?"

He nodded at the guard next to him, who slid open a drawer in the wall. Curious, Laney walked over. A small vial lay there.

"Drink that," Ianson ordered.

Laney laughed. "No."

Ianson's face turned red, the veins prominent on his forehead. "I am speaking on behalf of the United States government. You have been ordered to drink that."

"Yeah," Laney drawled, "that's a firm no on that order."

"You will not be let out of this cell until you—"

"Look, I have stayed in your cell, waiting for someone to come along and ask me some questions. I have been playing nice. So either ask me some questions, or I'm out of here."

Ianson crossed his arms over his chest. "You're not getting out until you take that sedative."

The lights flickered in the hall. "I think we've already covered the fact that I don't take orders from you. Ask your questions."

"I won't let—"

A tingle ran over Laney's skin.

"Ianson."

Laney turned as Bruce Heller from the CIA strode down the hall toward her cell, Maldonado and Matt following him.

Ianson turned his glare from Laney to Heller. "This doesn't concern you, Bruce."

Heller held up a piece of paper. "According to the President, it does. The CIA has been given the authority to conduct this interrogation."

Laney tried to swallow down her smile at Ianson's expression. *And that's the first time in history that hearing the CIA was now in charge of their interrogation was actually a relief to anyone.*

Matt stepped to the wall. "You all right?"

"I'm fine. How's Jake?"

"He was released a few minutes ago with the thanks of a grateful nation."

"The bomb shelter?"

Matt grimaced. "Thirteen people were shot, none life threatening. But Jen . . . Jen lost the baby."

Laney closed her eyes. *Oh no. God damn you, Elisabeta.* Laney wanted to kill her all over again. She opened her eyes to see Heller and Ianson arguing a little away from her cell. Finally, Ianson stormed off.

Heller stepped up to the wall, ignoring Ianson's histrionics. "Dr. McPhearson, I was hoping you could answer a few questions before you leave."

Laney studied the CIA director. She didn't trust him. She wanted nothing more than to get out of here. But she figured she owed the government some sort of explanation. "I am willing to answer *some* questions."

Heller smiled. "Wonderful."

CHAPTER 107

BALTIMORE, MARYLAND

It took Laney another two hours of questions from Heller before she'd been able to get out of D.C. She'd just gotten back to the estate an hour ago. She'd gone straight to the bunker to visit her uncle and Max and hug about three dozen people. Then she'd gone for a quick shower and change of clothes before heading to Henry's house.

Drake walked with her, his hand clasped in hers. "You haven't taken the mortus again."

"Not yet," Laney said.

"Why not?"

Laney hesitated. She had planned on taking it immediately after Elisabeta was neutralized, but the government's response to the events in D.C. had rattled her. And Heller had been a little too interested in the formula. He'd even asked for a blood sample, a request Laney had declined. He had been polite, but behind his eyes, she knew he was interested, very interested. And the idea of making herself weaker right now made her nervous. Plus she did not want any vials of Omni around, just in case.

"It's just not the right time."

He wrapped his arm around her shoulders. "Whatever the government is planning, we'll handle it."

"I know."

Her skin tingled as Henry stepped out of the house. His face was drawn with dark circles under red-rimmed eyes. Laney slipped from under Drake's arm and hurried forward. She wrapped her arms around him.

"I'm so sorry."

CHAPTER 108

WASHINGTON, D.C.

The White House was still on high alert hours after the coronation. It would be on high alert for the next few days, or even weeks, until they could be sure the threat had been neutralized. Armed guards lined the way leading to the Oval Office. The President had refused to go back into the bunker. She wanted to show that America's leadership was in charge.

But they all knew that was not true. American leadership had not saved them. Delaney McPhearson had. Bruce Heller had watched the incident with rapt attention from his office. McPhearson's powers were extraordinary. All the strength, healing, and speed of a Fallen but with the ability to control the weather. Those lightning strikes had been things of beauty.

What I wouldn't pay to have a few people with her abilities on my payroll.

The President's aide hurried from his chair as Bruce stepped into the outer office. "She's expecting you." He opened the door to the Oval.

The President whirled around from where she had been pacing. "Finally."

Heller inclined his head. "Madam President."

The President waved him toward the couches. "Tell me about McPhearson."

Heller gave her a rundown of the questioning as he took a seat.

"Do you believe her?" the President asked when he was done speaking.

Heller paused. "She didn't lie, but she did not admit everything. She's hiding something. I'm guessing quite a lot of somethings."

The President nodded. "I think I may know what that is. This was sent to us after Elisabeta's death. We have to assume it went out to other governments as well."

She picked up a remote and pressed play. The TV above the fireplace came to life.

Elisabeta smiled on screen. "Well, it seems the unimaginable has happened and I am dead. Or perhaps someone has merely managed to hack into my system."

She sighed. "If it is the former, then what I am about to say will be of great interest to you. If it is the latter, I will track you and your family down and make you my pets." She was silent for a moment. "Anyway, if I am gone, the only way that is possible is if Delaney McPhearson made herself immortal. The only way for her to have done that is through a substance known as the Omni, mixed with a little extra something special.

"The Omni also bestows strength, speed, and healing upon the recipient. I took the last known dose. But Delaney McPhearson must have done the same. Imagine that, an individual who could grant the powers of the Fallen upon anyone she chose. Wouldn't that be something?" The recording ended.

The President turned to Heller. "What do you think? Is she telling the truth?"

"I believe she is. McPhearson is unique, even amongst the Fallen. Her abilities are greater than any of the others."

"Did McPhearson mention this Omni?"

"No."

"Can McPhearson be trusted?"

Heller studied the President. She looked haggard but also intense. She knew that the last few days had made her look weak in the eyes of the country. She was looking for any and all threats to her position. Heller chose his words carefully. "I do not believe she has any aspirations to rule. She seems to act based upon what her conscience tells her is the right thing to do."

"Will she hand over the information we need on the Omni?"

Heller shook his head. "No. I believe she knows about it and intentionally kept that information to herself. I would say she does not trust the U.S. government with that information." On one level, he thought that was wise, but on another, it could place the United States in a very vulnerable position should another country discover the Omni.

"I will not allow the United States to be under the thumb of a foreign power."

"Yes, Madam President. I believe we may have some people who can help us with this dilemma."

CHAPTER 109

BALTIMORE, MARYLAND

Laney stopped outside Jen's room, partly to try and steel herself. She didn't want Jen to see how worried she was about her. She also didn't want Jen to feel as if she needed to comfort her. She stopped when she heard voices and peeked her head in. Danny had pulled a chair up to the bed.

He sat there, his back to the doorway, his voice shaking. "I'm sorry, Jen. I should have done—"

Jen gripped Danny's hand. "Hey, you saved me. The baby . . . that just wasn't meant to be. Not this time."

Danny's head hung low as he nodded, wiping at his eyes.

Jen's heartbroken gaze caught sight of Laney, who wiped her own heartbreak from her face and stepped inside. "Hey."

Danny hastily wiped at his eyes. "Hey. Didn't see you there."

"Just got here. I saw Lou and Rolly outside. They were looking for you."

Danny glanced at Jen, who nodded. "Go ahead."

Danny walked over and hugged Laney before sliding past her for the door, fresh tears in his eyes.

Laney watched him go, her heart heavy. She turned back to Jen, who was still watching the empty doorway. "He blames himself for the baby. I told him not to, but . . ." Jen shrugged.

Laney moved to the bed, sitting down gingerly, facing Jen. "I'm so sorry."

Jen nodded, not meeting her gaze. "I never pictured myself as a mom. I mean, I didn't exactly have the best childhood, you know?"

Laney nodded, but she knew Jen wasn't looking for a verbal response.

"When I first found out I was pregnant, I was shocked." She gave a small laugh as tears appeared in her eyes. Laney took her hand. Jen gripped it tightly. "I took five pregnancy tests. They all said positive, but I still didn't believe it. I mean, Henry and I were always so careful."

She took a shuddering breath. "Then the doctor confirmed it. I walked out of that office in a daze. I practically walked into traffic. Then I sat in my car in the parking garage. I must have sat there for forty-five minutes. I just kept thinking it wasn't possible.

"But then, then I began to picture this little kid with these violet eyes and dark hair. And I prayed he or she would have Henry's brain and my guts." Jen wiped at the tears that traced down her cheeks but then gave up as the tears kept coming.

Jen took a long stuttering breath. "I never wanted kids, Laney . . . but I *really* wanted this one."

Laney pulled Jen to her as Jen's shoulders shook and sobs wracked her frame. Tears trailed down Laney's cheeks at her friend's pain. Elisabeta had done this. And as angry as Laney was, right now all she felt was the horrible loss.

Laney struggled, trying to come up with something to say but then just gave up that attempt. After all, sometimes when a pain was this deep, there was nothing you could say to make it better. All you could do was be there to share it.

EPILOGUE

WASHINGTON, D.C.

David Okafor stepped off the elevator and strode down the concrete hallway. He was fifteen stories below the White House. The bunker was only to be used in emergencies. The fact that the President had chosen this location for the meeting only highlighted the top-secret nature of it.

His job usually did not involve invitations to meet with the President. In fact, before he was sent on most of his missions, he was given the same warning: If you are caught, the U.S. government will disavow any knowledge of you or your actions. He didn't even think the President was aware of his team's existence. So the fact that he was here, without any sort of indication as to what this meeting was about, had piqued his interest.

Of course, given the events of the last few days, he had a pretty good idea what the overall topic was going to be. He just wasn't sure what direction the response was going to head.

Two Marines snapped to attention as he approached. David gave them a nod and strode through the doors as the soldiers pulled them open. Fourteen people looked up from the table, including the President, who sat at its head. Okafor knew all of them at least by sight, but one he knew well—his mentor, Bruce Heller from the CIA. He did not acknowledge him, and Heller kept his face blank. From her seat at the head of the table, the President nodded.

"Mr. Okafor."

"Madam President." David pulled out a chair and took a seat. "My apologies for being late."

"It's all right. Continue, doctor."

The woman displayed on the large screen to the left of the table nodded. "As I was saying, we were able to retrieve the formula from the Ruggio lab in New Mexico that created the cats. We believe we will be able to replicate the process in as little as two months."

Surprise filtered through him. He didn't realize the President had already gone down that road. He'd seen some of those cats in action. They were formidable: strength, speed, and intelligence. That intelligence, if it could be trained . . .

"How long will it take the cats to reach maturity?"

"We believe two years. The process could be sped up, but we believe that is inadvisable until we fully understand everything about the cats' nature."

"Do you believe the cats will be able to be trained?" the President asked.

"We have one of the cats in custody. So far, it has been unresponsive to our efforts. But we believe if we are able to raise one from birth, we will have much more positive results. Nevertheless, we will continue our efforts with the captured leopard."

"Good. Keep me updated."

"Yes, Madam President." The screen went black.

The President turned back to the table. "Now that we are all here, let's begin the more critical aspect of this meeting."

Elaine Vaughn from the Department of the Interior frowned. "Secretary Harrigan is not joining us?"

"No. And the secretary is not to be included in the task force moving forward. The only people cleared for this conversation are in this room."

David frowned. Harrigan was out? What had happened?

The President pushed back from the table. "I don't need to tell you how the events of the last few weeks have shaken this country, this world, to its core."

David glanced around the table, seeing the same concern on everyone else's face that he knew was on his. Enhanced human beings who were almost impossible to stop. And there were possibly thousands of them.

The President continued, her voice grave. "The threat they pose to our nation's security is beyond any other threat facing the United States government. The threat they pose to the *world* is beyond any other threat. I have no doubt my counterparts across the globe are having this same conversation with their government leaders. And they will also be looking for ways to protect against the abilities of the Fallen or take advantage of these enhanced humans for their own gain."

David nodded. He had been thinking along the same lines. If they could figure out how to enhance the abilities of their own troops, it would change every conflict they were in. If they didn't, and other countries managed to, it would also change those conflicts—to the detriment of the United States.

"So now we need to figure out where we go from here." The President fell silent.

David glanced around the room before speaking. "Madam President, I'm not sure I understand exactly what you are asking for."

The President glanced around the table before her gaze fell back on David. "I'm asking for a risk assessment on the threat these so called Fallen pose. I'm also asking for suggestions as to how their abilities can be incorporated into our defenses." She paused. "But most importantly, I am looking for a way to control the Fallen population, both through policy means and more permanent approaches. Is that clear enough for you, Mr. Okafor?"

"Yes, ma'am." In his mind, he translated her political speak. *Find me a way to keep them under my thumb, and if that doesn't work, find me a way to kill them.*

"And Delaney McPhearson? She did save us," Heller said.

The President's gaze swept across the table. "Delaney McPhearson is an American hero. That cannot be denied. But the power held within her grasp is too much for one individual."

Shremp cut in. "I was under the impression she is no longer immortal. That she voluntarily gave up the ability."

The President shook her head. "We have no confirmation of that. But the potential for her to become immortal again is still at her fingertips, and hers alone. Who's to say one day she doesn't change her mind? And even without that ability, she is a force. Can you imagine someone who could call down a lightning strike, a tornado, or hurricane-level winds against a target of her choice? And with her ability to control the Fallen without immortality, she still poses a significant threat, not just to this country, but to the world. She may be an even graver threat than Elisabeta was."

Uneasy glances were shared across the table.

The President put up a hand. "I realize this is not an easy conversation to have. But we are the leaders of this country. We are required to make the hard decisions. And regardless of Delaney McPhearson's past actions, she is a threat to this government. We cannot rely on her better nature. We can hope for it, but we cannot rely on it."

"So are we looking for the same options regarding McPhearson?" Heller asked.

"Yes. How to control and contain her."

David once again translated the carefully worded statement. *Find Delaney McPhearson's weakness—the people and things that can be used to pressure her into behaving.*

And simultaneously figure out the easiest way to kill her.

FACT OR FICTION?

Thank you for reading. I hope you enjoyed yourself. *The Belial War* has been a long time coming. This is the twelfth book in the series. And I'm actually excited about where we go from here! Yes, the series will be ending soon but I am happy with how the story will come to a close. Now enough about that and on to the facts!

Temple of Osiris. The Temple of Osiris or Osiris shaft is real. It can be found on the Giza Plateau. As mentioned in *The Belial War*, the shaft extends one hundred feet down into the earth where a nine-ton granite sarcophagus can be found. The sarcophagus still lies there. The shaft was flooded at some point after its creation. It was found in the early twentieth century but due to the water in the shaft it was not excavated until 1999. Even with the removal of the water, the shaft has received scant attention compared to other sites nearby. The sarcophagus still lies submerged in a pool of water, with the lid suspended above the water, held in place by metal wires.

Cole Memorial Hospital. Real hospital but the description is completely fictional.

Seven Wonders of the Ancient World. The seven wonders of the Ancient World were the hanging gardens of Babylon, the statue of

Zeus at Olympus, the temple of Artemis at Ephesus, the Mausoleum at Halicarnassus, the Colossus of Rhodes, the Lighthouse at Pharos, and the Great Pyramid of Giza. Of those seven, only the Great Pyramid remains, although remnants of the rest have been found.

The Oval Office. When writing *The Belial War*, I did quite a bit of research on the White House. I did not realize that the Oval Office was a relatively modern creation. The office as we now know it, was first used by William Taft and was remodeled after a fire destroyed it in 1929. FDR moved it closer to the residence and it remains largely the same since he occupied it.

Gobekli Tepe and Skulls. Skulls *were* found at the ancient site of Gobekli Tepe. The skulls demonstrate evidence of post mortem manipulation, i.e., they had lines painstakingly carved into the skulls. No one knows why. They also however had holes drilled into the skulls, in a manner similar to that of the Naga people of India. The Naga drilled the holes the place the skull on a string or rope. Archaeologists theorize that the skulls may have similarly be hung around the different henges in Gobekli Tepe.

Lighthouse at Pharos. Evidence has been found that at one point there was a giant lighthouse on the island of Pharos off the northern coast of Africa. As described in *The Belial War* and according to historians, the three hundred and fifty feet tall lighthouse had been covered in mirrors that allegedly had been used to set ships that entered Alexandria Bay illegally on fire. It was reported to have been visible from as far away as thirty-five miles. At the time, the only taller structure in the world was the Great Pyramid at Giza.

The Great Pyramid at Giza. The information on the Great Pyramid is accurate. Along with being the last remaining seventh wonder of the world, it was once covered in a white limestone. People began removing the limestone in the eighteenth and nineteenth centuries until none remained. In its heyday however, the Pyramid would have shown brightly when the sun or moon struck it. The dimensions of the pyramid as well as the fact that scholars still are not sure how it was built are also accurate.

Calevitnia. Calevitnia is not a real Russian country. (I'm guessing most of you already knew that.) In 1991, when the USSR dissolved, the former soviet republic broke up into fifteen countries; Russia and the fourteen satellite countries of Armenia, Azerbaijan, Belarus, Estonia, Georgia, Kazakhstan, Kyrgyzstan, Latvia, Lithuania, Moldova, Tajikistan, Turkmenistan, Ukraine, and Uzbekistan. I did not want to cast any of those satellites in *The Belial War* so I simply made up a country.

Loose Nukes. The information on the problem with nuclear warheads within the former Soviet Union is accurate. Nuclear weapons as well as stockpiles of uranium and plutonium were left completely unsecured. Some were only protected by a padlocked door. The result had been over 100 reported cases of nuclear smuggling incidents since 1993. If you're looking for more information, check here.

George Washington. The information on George Washington and the crossing of the Delaware is true. Three separate parties set out across the river but only one managed to cross. There was an ice storm and the Hessian knew they were coming due to a turncoat and spies. Washington pushed on though because he believed the continental army would be destroyed if they did not win this battle. They needed new recruits to replenish their ranks. So the crossing of the Delaware was a critical and necessary battle if the United States was ever going to exist.

Great Sphinx. Traditional archaeology dates the Great Sphinx to about 2,500 BC. Wear and tear on the Sphinx, however, point to it having existed at a time when heavy rains were commonplace in Giza which would place its creation closer to 10,500 BC. The human face of the Sphinx is disproportionately small for the body. Most people therefore believe it was remodeled at some point. Most argue that the body resembles that of a lion and therefore the head must have at one point also been that of a lion.

However, as mentioned, there are no pictures of the Sphinx with either the face of a human or a lion. Anubis, the jackal headed god, who was also the guardian of the afterworld, can however be found represented all over ancient hieroglyphs.

The Dream Stela. The Dream Stela is real and is located between the front paws of the Sphinx. Thumtose allegedly had a dream that if he excavated the Sphinx, which once again had been buried up to its neck, he would one day be the ruler of a united Egypt. He had the Sphinx excavated and was the ruler of a united Egypt.

Underground Bunkers at the White House. The first underground tunnels were created under the White House during Truman's renovation. A tunnel was connected from the east and west wings and as well as a bomb shelter. In 1987, another tunnel was built. There are also rumors of tunnels connecting the White House to the Capitol, Blair House, VP Residence, Camp David and the Pentagon, but these are unsubstantiated at this time. What technological capabilities exist in the bunks is a matter of speculation although most believe that the country would be able to be essentially run from there.

Thank you again for reading. If you'd like to be notified about upcoming releases, please sign up for my mailing list.

ABOUT THE AUTHOR

R.D. Brady is an American writer who grew up on Long Island, NY but has made her home in both the South and Midwest before settling in upstate New York. On her way to becoming a full-time writer, R.D. received a Ph.D. in Criminology and taught for ten years at a small liberal arts college.

R.D. left the glamorous life of grading papers behind in 2013 with the publication of her first novel, the supernatural action adventure, *The Belial Stone*. Over a dozen novels later and hundreds of thousands of books sold, and she hasn't looked back. Her novels tap into her criminological background, her years spent studying martial arts, and the unexplained aspects of our history.

If you would like to be notified about her upcoming publications, you can sign up for her mailing list. Those who sign up will receive a free e-book copy of *B.E.G.I.N.* and other freebies over time. Email addresses are never provided to any other sources.

For more information:
https://rdbradybooks.com
rdbradywriter@gmail.com

ACKNOWLEDGMENTS

First, I want to thank all of you reading this. I know there was a long break between the last book in the Belial series and this one. After writing thirteen novels, two novellas and two short stories, I needed a little break. Happily, the break also helped spur some creative juices and therefore there is quite a bit coming out in the next two years. So thank you for the patience!

Thank you to Crystal Watanabe and her editorial team at Pikko's House. I am thrilled to have found you and always look forward to receiving your comments. Thank you for all your hard work!

Thank you to my three little ones. As I get close to the end, I slowly disappear into my office until I am a mere specter around the house. Thank you for your support and for always checking in on how mommy's books are going and understanding when I say I need just five more minutes I am completely underestimating the time I'm going to need. :).

Thank you to my writing group who is always supportive and always there to keep me company through the process.

Thank you to The Cover Collection for their great work on *The Belial War*.

THE CHARACTERS OF THE BELIAL WAR*

The Triad
Delaney McPhearson: Ring bearer with the power to control the weather, the Fallen, and animals
Jake Rogan: Former Navy SEAL, Laney's former love, Henry's best friend
Henry Chandler: Nephilim, Laney's brother

Laney's Allies
Yoni Benjamin: former Navy SEAL, Israeli born, married to Sascha Benjamin with whom he has a young son named Dov
Cain: the biblical Cain, who has been alive for thousands of years, anyone who harms him receives an injury seven times their intent.
Patrick Delaney: Laney's uncle, Roman Catholic priest, raised her since she was eight, born in Scotland
Drake: Las Vegas's Entertainer of the Year ten years running also archangel on sabbatical; was Achilles in the one life he lived as a human and he loved Helen of Troy (Laney) passionately
Rolly Escabi: teenage nephilim

THE CHARACTERS OF THE BELIAL WAR*

Zach Grayston: teenage Fallen

Fadil Massari: sister of Mustafa, archaeologist

Mustafa Massari: head SIA agent

Noriko: Jen's recently discovered biological half sister, has visions and can communicate with animals, direct descendants of Lemurians

Lou Thomas: teenage Fallen

Gerard Thompson: formerly Elisabeta's right hand man until Victoria opened his eyes to his past lives. She helped him recall the time after the Fall when he had a family that Samyaza killed; formerly, Barnabus, close friend of Achilles and Helen of Troy

Danny Wartowski: teenage genius, started working at Chandler at age ten, head analyst, unofficial adopted son of Henry Chandler

Matt Walsh: Director of the Special Investigative Agency (SIA), under the auspices of the Department of Defense tasked with tracking and containing Fallen, Fallen

Jennifer Witt: Love of Henry Chandler, best friend of Delaney McPhearson, sister of Noriko, nephilim

Jordan Witt: Jen's brother, served with Jake in SEALS, operative with Chandler, Mike's twin

Mike Witt: brother of Jen, twin of Jordan, FBI agent

The Bad Guys

Elisabeta Roccorio: reincarnation of Samyaza

Na Nomi Mansur: General: Sudanese overlord

Artem Danvers: Elisabeta's right hand man

Hilda: Elisabeta's former assistant who was arrested by the FBI

US Government

Nancy Harrigan: United States Secretary of State

Margaret Rigley: President of U.S.

Bruce Heller: Deputy Director of CIA

Moses Seward: former head of the Homeland Security's External Task Force, tortured Cain

The McAdam's Family
    Mary Jane: widowed mother, nurse
    Joe:16
    Shaun:15
    Molly, 13, nephilim
    Susie-2, kidnapped in *The Belial Plan*
    Billy- deceased father and Fallen

* This list is not a complete list but contains a number of characters that readers will have seen in previous books.

BOOKS BY R.D. BRADY

The Belial Series (in order)
The Belial Stone

The Belial Library

The Belial Ring

Recruit: A Belial Series Novella

The Belial Children

The Belial Origins

The Belial Search

The Belial Guard

The Belial Warrior

The Belial Plan

The Belial Witches

Stand-Alone Books
Runs Deep

Hominid

The A.L.I.V.E. Series
B.E.G.I.N.

A.L.I.V.E.

D.E.A.D.

Be sure to sign up for R.D.'s mailing list to be the first to hear when she has a new release and receive a free short story!

Copyright © 2017 by R.D. Brady

The Belial War

Published by Scottish Seoul Publishing, LLC, Dewitt, NY

All Rights Reserved. No part of this book may be reproduced or transmitted in any form or by any means, electronic or mechanical, including photocopying, recording, or by any information storage and retrieval system without the written permission of the author, except where permitted by law.

Printed in the United States of America.